W9-APW-090

SPEAKEASY

Also by Nathaniel Benchley:

Novels

SIDE STREET
ONE TO GROW ON
SAIL A CROOKED SHIP
THE OFF-ISLANDERS
CATCH A FALLING SPY
A WINTER'S TALE
THE VISITORS
A FIRM WORD OR TWO
THE MONUMENT
WELCOME TO XANADU
THE WAKE OF THE ICARUS
LASSITER'S FOLLY
THE HUNTER'S MOON
PORTRAIT OF A SCOUNDREL
SWEET ANARCHY
ALL OVER AGAIN

Biographies

ROBERT BENCHLEY
HUMPHREY BOGART

Play

THE FROGS OF SPRING

Editor

THE BENCHLEY ROUNDUP

Junior Books

GONE AND BACK
ONLY EARTH AND SKY LAST FOREVER
FELDMAN FIELDMOUSE
BRIGHT CANDLES
BEYOND THE MISTS
A NECESSARY END
KILROY AND THE GULL
SNIP
DEMO AND THE DOLPHIN

Motion Picture

THE GREAT AMERICAN PASTIME

Speakeasy

A Novel by

NATHANIEL BENCHLEY

Doubleday & Company, Inc.
Garden City, New York
1982

Quote from "Blazing Publicity" by Walter Lippmann courtesy *Vanity Fair,* copyright © 1927 (renewed 1955) by the Condé Nast Publications Inc.

Lines from "Birches" are from *The Poetry of Robert Frost* edited by Edward Connery Lathem. Copyright 1916, © 1969 by Holt, Rinehart and Winston. Copyright 1944 by Robert Frost. Reprinted by permission of Holt, Rinehart and Winston, Publishers.

ISBN: 0-385-17385-7
Library of Congress Catalog Card Number 81-43406

Printed in the United States of America
FIRST EDITION

For KATE
with love–if Forde doesn't mind

NOTE:

This is a work of fiction, and with obvious exceptions the characters are fictitious. The exceptions speak for themselves, and need no further explanation.

N. B.

Dunroamin
Dannemora, N.Y.
June 1981

SPEAKEASY

1

It was late afternoon, and the speakeasy was almost deserted. Behind the bar Charlie, the barman, peeled oranges and lemons for the old-fashioneds, whisky sours, and Tom Collinses that, with Manhattans, martinis, sidecars, and Bronxes, made up fifty per cent of the orders. The rest of the customers preferred highballs—either Scotch or Canadian, depending on what was most recently off the boats. It was a point of pride with Charlie always to serve the real stuff; no doctored alcohol or needled beer had ever crossed his bar, and the house was able to charge accordingly. Nick, the owner, maintained that people would pay almost anything provided they got what they were paying for, and the loyalty between him and his customers was unshakable.

The speakeasy occupied the ground floor of an old high-stoop brownstone house, on the east side of midtown Manhattan. The door, with its peephole, was behind an iron grille alongside the front steps. It had once been the delivery entrance, and now, for all practical purposes, was the only means of ingress to the establishment. A back door, beyond the kitchen, was for emergency only, and was always kept locked. The entire place consisted of three rooms: the entrance hall, with two coat racks and an old-fashioned umbrella stand; the bar, which ran the length of one wall and served not only the stand-up customers but also those who chose to sit at the red-check-covered tables; and the kitchen, where Nick's wife, Marie, ruled with the authority of Boadicea. There was a male chef, and two overworked busboy-waiters, but the kitchen was Marie's, and nothing went through its doors without her approval.

In the bar Charlie continued his preparations, trying not to notice the small, dark-haired woman who sat alone at a table at the dimly lighted end of the room, alternately talking to herself and dabbing at her eyes with a crumpled handkerchief, while the watery remains of a Scotch highball stood on the table in front of her. She had been there since lunch, but Charlie had been too busy to notice her until the crowd thinned out. All he knew was that she seemed to be coming quietly unglued, talking–and apparently apologizing–to the empty chair across from her, and then wiping her eyes and blowing her nose. The only words he could hear were "I'm sorry," repeated over and over, with other indistinguishable phrases every now and then. She was causing no trouble and he saw no reason to interfere, assuming she would eventually leave of her own volition. He'd had some experience with weeping women, and he knew they were better left alone. Then suddenly, without looking at him, she spoke.

"Charlie, may I have another Scotch, please?" she said in a clogged voice. "This one seems to have passed its prime."

"Yes, ma'm," Charlie replied. "Coming right up." He reached behind to the back-bar, poured Scotch in a glass, then filled it with chopped ice and water. He took it around to her and removed the other glass, trying not to look at her as he did.

"Charlie, you're a gentleman," she said, "and when I come into my inheritance, I shall build you a city."

"Think nothing of it, Mrs. Peters," he said. "Any time."

"Any time." She thought for a moment, then said, "There's a splendid phrase for you. There's a real jim-dandy. Any time what? Any time I have is yours? Any time you want a good laugh–" She stopped abruptly, and shook her head. "I'm sorry, Charlie," she said. "Forgive me."

"That's all right, Mrs. Peters," he said. "I understand."

"If you do, you're the first man this side of Pasadena who does. Men, as a breed, have about as much understanding as three-toed sloths–although who am I to knock a three-toed sloth? God must have had something in mind when He created the three-toed sloth, and I'm certainly going to be the last one to cast aspersions at God's handiwork. I apologize, God. I apologize, sloth. I apologize, every man, woman, and child in the United States . . ." She started to say more, but then her voice broke and she resumed weeping. Charlie went quietly back to the bar and rinsed out the glass he'd been holding in his hand.

There was silence for about five minutes, and then Nick, the owner, came in from the kitchen. He was in his early thirties, dark-haired and lean, but his chest and shoulders were those of a much heavier man. It was as though the thorax of a wrestler had been grafted onto the frame of a sprinter, and his double-breasted suits were specially tailored to fit his unusual proportions. He never carried anything in his pockets that might cause a wrinkle. He glanced briefly at the woman, then went to the bar and spoke in a low voice to Charlie.

"Raid tonight," he said.

"What time?" Charlie replied, polishing a glass.

"Twelve-thirty."

Charlie nodded. "I'll be ready."

"But be ready to pull the plug. These are Feds."

Charlie digested this. "Oh," he said. "Who told you?"

"McGinty."

"He isn't making the raid?"

"He'll be along. But there'll be Feds, too. From Washington."

"All right," said Charlie. "I'll be ready."

Without looking at her, Nick indicated the woman. "Any trouble there?"

"Not so far as I'm concerned," Charlie replied. "*She* seems to have a mess of it, though."

"That's nothing new. Who'd she lunch with?"

"McClain. Who else?"

"You needn't worry, Nick," the woman said, having either heard or guessed what they were talking about. "I'll be out of here shortly. I just have to get up the guts to face the world. Gird up my loins, I believe the expression is."

"I wasn't worried, Mrs. Peters," Nick said, going toward her. "Is there anything I can do for you?"

"Yes—you could make me a queen. Or better yet, an empress. How are you at changing dowdy little women into Catherine the Great?"

Nick smiled. "I've never tried," he said, "but in your case it shouldn't be too hard."

"Five'll get you three I blow it."

"I won't bet, but I'll be glad to buy you a drink."

She glanced at the half-finished highball in front of her. "Do you think I'm a good risk? Aren't you afraid I'll become a public charge?"

"Nonsense." Nick signaled to Charlie, and Mrs. Peters finished her drink.

"Those are the nicest words I've heard today," she said. "Will you join me? No—on second thought, don't. I'm rotten company." She paused, then added, "Or so I've been told."

"As you wish." Nick had started to pull out a chair, and stopped.

"I'm sorry," she said quickly. "I didn't mean to sound ungrateful. Please sit down. Forgive me—my God, all I seem to be doing today is apologize. I've apologized to God, to three-toed sloths, to you, to—" Charlie brought her new drink, and she said, "Thank you, Charlie. Thank you, Nick. That sounds a lot better. Now, please. Sit down, and I promise to be witty and scintillating and wise. Mme. de Staël won't hold a candle to me. Bards will sing of my—" She stopped in midsentence and said, "Oh, really, now. Whom do I think I'm kidding?" She took a long swallow of her new drink.

"I don't mind," Nick said, sitting down. "If you've got something you want to get off your chest, go right ahead. At the moment, I have nothing to do but listen."

"I'd tell you, but it would bore you so rigid you'd probably topple right out of your chair. The oldest story in the world is interesting only to the person to whom it happens—to everyone else it is a royal pain in the ass."

Nick spread his hands. "Try me out and see."

"No. You're too much of a gentleman to have that happen to you." She finished the drink and set the glass down. "And if I have one more of those I *will* tell you, and we'll all be sorry. I'm going to get out of here before your more refined customers begin to arrive, so that I don't make a spectacle of myself in front of them."

"I don't know what customers you're talking about."

"Do I have to name them for you? Calvin Coolidge, Herbert Bayard Swope, that new Mayor—what's his name? Walker?—"

"He was in here last week, as a matter of fact," Nick said. "Unofficially, of course."

"I'll bet. My point is, you have a very classy clientele, and at the moment I'm feeling very unclassy."

"I won't press the point. But it's still early; what you call the classy set won't be here for a matter of hours."

"I wouldn't be so sure. Young Barrymore blew in from the Coast this morning."

"Oh, swell. That's just what I need."

She stared at her empty glass, as though trying to find something in it. "I don't suppose a small one would hurt, do you?" she said.

"You're the judge of that," Nick replied.

"All right, then. Just one, and then I'll be gone." Nick signaled to Charlie, and Mrs. Peters went on, "Is it dark out yet?"

Nick looked at his watch. "It shouldn't be. The days are getting longer."

"I can't go out till it's dark. All the makeup in hell couldn't put this face together again."

"It's not that bad. Your eyes are a little red, is all."

"A little red, he says. A little red like the gutters in an abattoir."

"No. Really. I can lend you some dark glasses, if you'd like."

She took her new drink and raised it in salute. "Mud in your eye," she said, and drank.

"Do you know why Barrymore's in town?" Nick asked. "I understood he was working in California."

"He was, but they had some production problems. I think they fired the whale."

"Is that the one about Moby Dick?"

"Yes. They don't like the real name, so they're calling it *The Sea Beast*. That should show Melville who has talent and who doesn't."

"People won't care about the title. They'll go to see Barrymore."

For the moment diverted from her problems, Mrs. Peters said, "Remember that book he wrote about the San Francisco quake?"

"I can't say I do," said Nick.

"He wrote what was supposed to have been an eyewitness account of the quake and fire. Very gory, very graphic. It now turns out he went to a friend's house and stayed drunk the entire time, and dreamed the book up as an afterthought. Talk about publicity—that boy could give lessons to P. T. Barnum."

Nick laughed. "I guess there's tricks to every trade," he said.

"I wish someone would teach me a few."

"You'll be all right."

"Sure, and Edith Cavell is all right too."

"Who's she?"

"That British nurse, shot by the Germans. And Joan of Arc and Mata Hari—they're all right because they can't feel pain any longer. That's quite a knack, if you can work it out."

"All you need is a firing squad, or a stake and some fagots."

"Find me a willing firing squad and we'll talk business. But you can forget about the stake. I don't burn, I just tan."

Nick laughed. "You'll be all right," he said.

"You said that once before. You haven't convinced me yet."

"That's not up to me—that's up to you."

"A fine friend you turn out to be. Here I come to rest my teary head on your shoulder, and you tell me to do it myself. Very well, then, if that's the way you feel I'll *have* another drink, just for spite. And when I tear off my clothes and run screaming among your customers, you can tell them it's my way of convincing myself I'm all right. It's going to make for a gamy little evening, don't you think?"

"I'll take my chances," Nick said. "There'll be other entertainment."

"Such as what, pray?"

"We're going to have a visit from the authorities."

"You mean one of those charades where you take away the drinks and put popcorn on the table, and Charlie and the busboys play the ocarina?"

"In a sense, but I'm told the Feds are coming up from Washington. They can be much tougher."

"Well, well. I was thinking of killing myself tonight, but this may be more interesting." She looked around at Charlie. "Just one more, Charlie," she said. "And this is definitely the last." Then she turned back to Nick, and her eyes didn't quite focus on him; she seemed to be looking at something just behind his left ear. "You were in the war, weren't you, Nick?" she said.

"Yes, ma'm," he replied. "I was with the First Division."

"May I ask you a question?"

"Of course."

"Did it take you long to settle down afterward?"

"In what way?"

"In any way. Did you keep looking around after you got home?"

"You mean for girls?"

"Girls—women—whatever."

"Well, I met Marie over there, so I didn't have any further to look."

She considered this a moment, then said, "Perhaps I'm not being clear. The war's been over six years now—seven years this fall. Right?"

"That's right."

"Well, what would you think of someone who in all that time—all that almost seven years—says he can't settle down yet because the war made him restless, and he's got to look around? Would you think he was indecisive, or just handing you a line?"

"Well—seven years is a long time, I'll grant you that."

"I was married to a soldier, you know—a lieutenant. And it didn't take me any seven years to find out what looks good in a uniform doesn't have to look good in salesmen's clothes. That must have taken all of a day and a half to sink in, and I don't have the world's quickest reflexes. A horse can step on my foot, and I don't know it until I try to move away."

"I just don't know what to tell you. But seven years is a long time, no getting around it."

"I haven't known him all those seven years, mind you. I came along about the time he should have been deciding to settle down. In fact, that's what he told me. 'Let's settle down,' he told me. 'Come live with me and be my love, and we will all the—' Ah, the hell with it." She tasted her new drink. "Will you tell me one more thing? And then I'll shut up and go home."

"I'll tell you if I can."

"Do you think the whole thing was worth it?"

"What whole thing?"

"The war. Making the world safe for democracy."

"No."

"So what's the point? What's the point in anything? A lot of nice young men get killed, and the others come back to a country where they're not allowed to drink—"

"Legally," Nick interrupted, smiling.

"You know what I mean. And the country's being run by a bunch of crooks like Honest Al Fall and Straight Eddy Doheny and all the rest of that Teapot Dome gang, and two little Italians get sentenced to death just because they're anarchists, and—my God, Nick, you're Italian; aren't you afraid? Aren't you afraid the Ku Kluxers are going to come after you some night and nail you to a cross?"

"I'm not afraid," Nick replied. He could tell she was about to start crying again, and he tried to think of a way to change the subject. "Some of my best friends are policemen," he said. "They–"

"Don't talk to me about policemen; talk to Sacco and Vanzetti about policemen. *They're* the ones who can give you the lowdown on policemen. Vanzetti, selling his little eels from his little pushcart, and suddenly these big bulls–" Her voice choked, and she bit her knuckles.

"It wasn't the police, it was the judge," Nick said. "If you're looking for the villain, it's Webster Thayer."

"They're all the same," she said, sobbing. "And to think of all those nice young men who went to war to make it safe for– Do you know what I heard the other day? About Joyce Kilmer?"

"What?"

"He was killed, and–"

"I know. In the counterattack at Soissons."

"And they tried to find a tree to bury him under–because of his poem and all, they thought it'd be nice–and *there wasn't one tree left standing!* They had to bury him beside a stump."

"They were lucky to find a stump. I was there."

"But *think of it!* Not one tree! That's the saddest thing I ever heard." She began to weep again. "A poet writes a lousy little poem about a tree, and then they can't find a single goddam tree to bury him under! Not one! They have to scoop out a hole beside a goddam stump!" She took out a handkerchief, wiped her eyes and blew her nose, then looked around at Charlie. "Charlie, I'll just have one for the road, if you don't mind," she said. "This is definitely the last."

"Are you sure that's a good idea?" Nick asked. "Don't you think a nap might make you feel better?"

She looked at him through puddled eyes and drew herself up. "Is that a reflection on my capacity?" she asked, not getting the words quite right.

"Not in the least. I just thought–"

"I know what you thought, and you're wrong. I can have one for the road *and* a nap, and then I'll feel all that much the better." She rose with careful dignity, said, "Put it on my tab," and made her way to the vestibule. Nick followed her. When they reached the door he said to Max, the doorman, "Get Mrs. Peters a cab, will you?" Max nodded, and went out.

"This is very gracious of you," she said, "considering the fact that I'm being ejected from your joint."

"You're being no such thing. You said you–"

"I can tell a bum's rush when I feel it. It takes a bum to know a real bum's rush, and don't let anyone tell you different."

"Whatever you say."

"Now you're being honest." She patted his arm. "I like an honest man–it's such a refreshing change."

"In my business, you have to be honest," Nick said, and laughed.

2

A Checker cab drew up in front, and Max put Mrs. Peters in it, then came back inside. He bolted the door, closed the peephole, and looked at his watch. "I think I'll grab a bite," he said. "I like to eat sitting down if I can."

"I'll mind the door for you," Nick told him. "There won't be much business for an hour or so."

"Do you want Mrs. Peters' drink?" Charlie asked, as he wiped off the table. "I got it all made before I saw she was leaving."

"Everything considered, I better hold off," Nick replied. "Take it yourself, and put it on my tab."

"I'm not much of a Scotch man. Maybe Max'd like it with his supper."

Charlie took the drink to the kitchen, and Nick opened the cash register and examined the tape. It had been a busy lunch hour, and he was deep in the figures when the buzzer at the front door sounded sharply, three times. He closed the register, went to the door, and opened the peephole. It was getting dark, and he couldn't recognize the two men who stood outside the door.

"Frank sent me," the nearest one said. Frank was Nick's partner, who handled the ordering and dealt with the bootleggers, while Nick stayed home and, so to speak, minded the store.

"Did he give you a card?" Nick asked.

"Here." The man held up a card, and Nick reached through the peephole and took it. It was one of the new ones, stating in tasteful Roman and italic type that Frank DiMotto was General Manager of the Club Circe Restaurant & Lounge, and in the lower left-hand corner, under Frank's name, was penciled the number 86. This was code that the bearer be brushed off as quickly as possible and under no conditions be served anything.

"I'm sorry," Nick said, handing the card back. "We're closed right now."

"What do you mean, closed?" the man said. "Frank gave me this a half an hour ago."

"We had an emergency in the kitchen," Nick replied. "Water main backed up, and the place is full of sewage. Sorry–some other time." He closed the peephole and went back to the bar, wondering what had caused Frank to give the man an 86. This usually meant that someone was a bad drunk and likely to cause trouble, but it could also mean that Frank suspected him of being a Fed. Next to Max, Frank had the best nose for sniffing out disguised Feds; he seemed to feel their presence in the air around him and became as restless as an animal before an earthquake. The periodic, perfunctory raids were usually made by New York police, and by gentlemen's agreement enough advance notice was given so that all incriminating evidence could be removed, but when the Feds became involved it was another matter. And if they had been sent by orders from Washington, as was rumored to be the case this time, it meant that someone high up had directed that the bust be made, and be made to stick. I guess Frank was taking no chances, Nick thought, and went back to examining the cash register tape.

Max came out of the kitchen, and resumed his post by the door. He had rigged up a small desk with a shielded reading light, where he could examine people's credentials, and in his spare time he used the light to study law. From two or three lawyer customers he had compiled a list of the basic books, such as the Horn Book series and McKinney's book on statutes, and he had already worked his way through the penal code and was deep into procedure and the code of civil practice. He was a long way from taking his bar exams, but he was slowly acquiring a grasp of the fundamentals.

Around five o'clock, when the homebound traffic rush began, the club's regular customers started to arrive, first singly and then in a trickle that became a flood. By six-thirty the standees were two deep at the bar, and some had taken their drinks out to the vestibule, where they could raise glasses to their lips without being joggled by other lifted elbows. This first, or cocktail, phase lasted until perhaps a quarter to eight; some people then went home or to other engagements for dinner, others drifted loudly into the night in search of further entertainment, and a third group took tables and ordered hurried suppers before heading for the theatre. These last negated any good the food might have done by ordering double drinks while they waited, and as curtain time approached it was clear that the professional actors were in for some raucous competition.

In the kitchen, Marie was making salad while Louis, the chef, tried simultaneously to cook five steaks—three rare, one medium rare, and one medium well—and at the same time brown a scallopini of veal without burning it. One of the busboy-waiters was splitting the tops of baked potatoes, while the other hurried in and out with loaded trays. Nick came in, patted his wife gently on the behind, and said, "How's it going, keed?"

Marie shrugged, tossing salad in a large wooden bowl as though she were cocking hay. Her face was round and full-lipped, the curve echoing in the contours of her breasts and upper arms, and at the moment her face was flushed, and curls of hair clung damply to the back of her neck. When at ease, and dressed for the evening, she had a quality that made the loudest man turn suddenly thoughtful.

Nick put his hand in the salad bowl and, barely avoiding the blow she aimed at his knuckles, popped a piece of lettuce and a garlic crouton into his mouth. "Aha!" he said. "This time I think you've got it!"

"C'est pas mal," she replied. "But it still isn't it." By "it" they were referring to the salad she'd made the first night the club was open for meals. No early customers came, and Marie eased her nervousness by mixing salad dressing, more or less at random, and at the same time drinking red wine from a tumbler. By the time the first dinner was served, and the salad declared a triumph, she had no idea what had gone into it, nor was she ever able to do it again. She even tried drinking wine while mixing the ingredients, hoping to recreate whatever had sparked her imagination, and although the wine induced a certain cavalier approach it never unlocked the secret of that first, glorious salad. "What I need is a larger kitchen," she told her husband. "If I had that I'd be able to relax, and then perhaps the

recipe might come to me. This kitchen is a *cage aux folles* most of the time."

"And how should we enlarge it?" Nick asked. "Out into the street?"

"In a sense. Move to another location. You could double the size of the bar, and it would still be crowded."

He shook his head. "People like the atmosphere as it is," he said. "If we got any bigger, we'd spoil it."

"Then don't expect miracles from the kitchen. Louis and I are bruised purple from bumping into each other."

Nick glanced at the chef. "I don't see any bruises," he said.

"You wouldn't. They're not out in the open."

"Then how–" Nick began, and stopped, realizing he'd stepped into a trap she'd set for him. "We're going to need emergency rations," he said, changing the subject. "We're being raided at twelve-thirty, and the customers'll need sandwiches and whatnot when their drinks are taken away."

"Those *salauds,*" Marie said. "Why did they have to pick tonight?"

"They pick the most inconvenient times they can. We're just lucky we know it in advance."

"If we had a larger place they wouldn't dare raid us. They're only picking on us because we're small."

Nick laughed. "That's a beauty. Even for French logic, that's bizarre."

"What's the matter with French logic? What's the matter with Descartes? With Pascal? With Voltaire? With–" She stopped, as Max came into the kitchen bearing a card, which he held out to Nick.

"This guy says you told him the kitchen was flooded," Max said. "He says you told him to come back later."

Nick took the card and saw the 86 that Frank had written on it. "Tell him we're closed," he said.

"He says we can't be," Max replied. "He says he can hear the customers, so we must have got the kitchen fixed."

"Then tell him we're full. Tell him anything you like, but don't let him in." Max started away, and Nick added, "What did you think of him?"

"I think he's a Fed," Max replied. "I only asked you because he said he'd talked to you."

Max left, and Nick looked back at Marie. "Don't get me wrong," he said. "I love French logic. I think it's the greatest logic in the world. I only wish it applied over here."

"You'll see where it applies and where it doesn't. Won't he, Louis?"

Louis, who knew when to keep his mouth shut, said nothing, and Nick smiled, gave Marie's behind a parting pat, and went through the swinging door into the bar.

Two newcomers were there, and they greeted him cheerfully. One of them was tall and thin, with a bow tie and an embryonic moustache, while the other, somewhat shorter, had dark curly hair, slightly pointed ears, and the face of a faun. "Good evening, gentlemen!" Nick said. "I haven't seen you about recently."

"We've been busy," replied the faun-like one, whose name was George MacDougall. "We've been trying to stay out of jail."

His companion, Roland Butterworth, laughed. "We picked a peach of a way to do it," he said, reaching for the drink that Charlie had automatically slid in front of him.

"No real trouble, I hope?" Nick said. "If you need a lawyer, I–"

"No real trouble now," Butterworth replied.

"You know what we ought to do," MacDougall put in. "We ought to get football pennants made, with 'The Bastille' on them. That would show people where we stand."

"How's your play coming?" Nick asked him.

"I'm letting it write itself," MacDougall replied. "That way, I figure the dialogue will be more natural."

"Do you know John Barrymore's in town? You might get him to play it for you."

"Do I know Barrymore's in town?" MacDougall looked at Butterworth, and they both laughed. "We just left Tony's, where he was imitating King Lear playing Hamlet. He wanted Roly, here, to be Laertes."

"I pleaded a sick headache," Butterworth said. "I don't think he believed it."

"That's the worst excuse in the world," MacDougall said. "You ought to know that–you're a married man."

"It usually works," Butterworth said quietly.

"I don't see where any of this had to do with your going to jail," Nick said.

"Oh, that," said MacDougall. "We were just trying to get the

Mayor of Cambridge to exhume the body of Henry Wadsworth Longfellow."

"In God's name, why?"

"It seemed like a good idea at the time."

"I mean, who knows if it's really Longfellow?" Butterworth said. "You can't be too careful about these things."

"And then just now," MacDougall went on, "we're on Fifth Avenue, and Roly spots Charles Evans Hughes coming down the street, so we tag along behind him, shouting 'Beaver,' and things like that. The only way he could shake us was to grab a cab."

"I think we had a legitimate point," Butterworth said. "What business does the Secretary of State have walking down Fifth Avenue in New York? He damn well ought to be in Washington, and he knew it as well as we did. *That's* why he jumped in the cab."

"He was probably here on an assignation. Has a love nest in the Village."

"With whiskers like that? You're mad, MacDougall. Mad as a March hen."

"For your information, it's March hare."

"I prefer hen."

MacDougall sipped his drink, and looked at the door. "Oh-oh," he said. "Here comes trouble."

The other two turned and saw John Barrymore, complete in evening dress and opera cape, entering the room. His eyes had a slightly maniacal look as he went to the bar, pointed one finger skyward, and said, "A draught, landlord, to salve these parchéd lips."

"Yes, sir," said Charlie, getting out a glass. "What'll it be?"

Barrymore pretended to think a moment, then said, "The bawdy hand of the dial is now upon the prick of noon–fetch me a flagon of your best Scotch whisky." Then he rolled his eyes toward the startled customer on his right and said, "Lest you think I was speaking gutter talk, cousin, I was but quoting the immortal Bard. *Romeo and Juliet,* Act Two, Scene Four."

"That's all right," the man said calmly. "It takes a lot more than that to shock me."

Barrymore studied him a moment. "You like to be shocked?" he asked.

"I didn't mean that," the man said. "I just meant–well, what's a little prick between friends?"

Barrymore took the drink that Charlie handed him, and continued to study the man. "I like you," he said at last. "I think there's more to you than meets the eye—although I grant you that would not be hard. I think perchance—" He stopped, as his eyes lit on Butterworth, MacDougall, and Nick. "Soft you now, the fair Ophelia!" he said, heading toward Butterworth. "Nymph, in thy orisons be all my sins remembered!"

"Hello, Jack," Butterworth said. "How's tricks?"

"Who is yon burgher with whom I just had converse?" Barrymore asked in a lower voice.

"I don't know," Butterworth replied. "I've seen him around, but I don't know his name."

"It's Hopkins," Nick said. "He's a stockbroker."

Barrymore considered this. "There's more to him than that," he said. "And you can mark my words." Then, to Butterworth, he said, "As for you, my rump-fed runagate, are you still pounding the drums for Wily Willy Brady?"

"I left Brady last year," Butterworth replied. "I'm on my own."

"I'm trying to get him to do some acting," MacDougall said. "I think he'd be a better actor than press agent."

"It's all the same thing," Barrymore said. "A press agent has to be an actor as well. Speak the speech, I pray you, as I pronounc'd it to you, trippingly on the tongue . . ." His attention was caught by a couple who had just entered the room, the man short and stocky, and the woman comparatively tall, willowy, and beautiful. "Good God!" he said. "My leading lady, out with that snaggle-toothed whoremonger! I'll put an end to this!" He left them, and made his way to where the couple had taken seats.

"Who's his leading lady?" Nick asked nervously.

"This one happens to be Dolores Costello," Butterworth replied.

"Is he going to make trouble?"

"God knows. The way he's feeling, anything could happen."

Nick left them and whispered something to Charlie, then circulated through the crowd in such a way as to keep within jumping distance of Barrymore. Individual voices were lost in the general babble of conversation, but every now and then a sentence or a phrase would emerge, like a fish flashing clear of the water, then vanish again.

"Floyd Collins need never have died in that cave," a man said loudly. "All they had to do was block up the other end and smoke him out."

"Did you hear about Coolidge?" someone else put in. "He opened his mouth to speak, and a moth flew out."

Above the din Barrymore's voice soared like an eagle, and then a woman was heard to say, "I came all the way from Larchmont for a glass of gin. I think that has elements of high tragedy."

"If it's gin you're after, they have gin in Larchmont," a man replied. "My bootlegger lives there."

"Give me his number. Fred makes our gin in the bathtub, and always at the wrong time."

"This is my first time in a speakeasy," another woman said, "and I must say I'm disappointed. I thought it would be exciting."

"We can always go to my place and listen to the radio," her escort replied. "I managed to get Toledo last night."

"Is that exciting?"

"If you go about it right, it is."

Max made his way in from the front, frantically looking for Nick. He found him and drew him to one side. "The Feds are outside!" he said.

Nick looked at his watch, which showed eleven twenty-five. "They can't be!" he said. "They're not due for an hour!"

"They're here," said Max, "and they're about to bust down the door!"

"Stall them for a minute, if you can." Nick clapped his hands, and shouted, "Ladies and gentlemen, quiet, please! We're being raided, and I'll ask you all to put your drinks in the buckets at either end of the bar. Hurry, please!" There was a scramble and a crashing of glass as people complied, and Nick said, "Charlie, pull the plug!" From the front door came the sound of pounding, as Charlie reached beneath the bar and pulled a lever, and the entire back-bar, on which the bottles were stacked, collapsed and emptied its contents down a chute. There followed an explosion and clatter and crash as the bottles smashed against an iron grillwork below, and then Nick and Charlie grabbed the buckets with the remains of the customers' drinks, and headed through the kitchen to the back door. "Raid!" Nick shouted to Marie as he unlocked the door. "Get food on the tables!" He opened the back door and was confronted by three Federal agents, who lunged at him as he threw the contents of the bucket into the alley. Charlie, behind him, turned back and emptied his bucket into the chute behind the back-bar, then pulled the lever that restored the back-bar shelves to their horizontal positions.

Two of the Federal agents grabbed Nick, while the third tried to salvage any possible legal evidence, but the watery remains of the drinks had been absorbed in the gutter, and broken glass was worth nothing in court. The agents marched Nick back into the building, where other agents were searching the premises for any signs of alcohol. The customers, stunned into silence, either sat at their tables or stood along the walls, as far from the bar as they could. Marie and the two busboy-waiters hustled plates of sandwiches out of the kitchen and scattered them on the tables.

Nick spotted George McGinty, the precinct captain who'd warned him about the raid, and McGinty's shoulders gave an almost imperceptible shrug. Clearly the Federal men had changed the timing to negate any warning that might have been given, and just as clearly there'd been nothing he could do about it. The senior Federal officer came toward Nick and gestured for the other two to release his arms. "All right," he said. "You the owner?"

"I'm not talking till I see your badge," Nick replied. "Who gave you the right to break in here, anyway? This is a private club."

The officer brought out a badge wallet, flipped it open, then put it away. "You know goddam well who gave us the right," he said. "Where do you keep your stock?"

"I'll remind you there are ladies present," Nick replied, "and any further profane language will be reported to your superiors. Do you have a search warrant?"

The officer produced a piece of paper. Nick read it carefully, then handed it back. "All right," he said. "Go ahead and search, but I'm warning you—I'll hold you personally responsible for any damage."

"You're some wise guy, aren't you?"

"Not particularly. Just wise enough to know my rights."

"Sez you. We'll see who's wise and who isn't." Turning to the other agents, the officer said, "O.K., boys, search the joint. I don't care how long it takes, just find out where he keeps his hooch."

"I'll make it easier for you," Nick said. He reached in his pocket, withdrew a bunch of keys, and tossed them to the officer. "That'll save your breaking down the doors."

The officer's jaw tightened, and he handed the keys to one of his deputies. "O.K.," he said. "Get going."

"I might as well tell you this now," Nick said, as the men started to leave the room, "you're in for a long evening, because I have no stock. This is a musical club, and the strongest thing we serve is sandwiches."

"That's why you were throwing all that broken glass in the alley," the officer said.

"Precisely. We had a singer earlier, whose voice shattered every glass in the room."

As though on cue, the door to the kitchen opened, and Marie and the two busboys entered. One of the boys was playing a violin, while the other made reedy noises on a clarinet. They and Marie lined themselves in front of the bar, and Marie started in on a spirited rendition of *Auprès de Ma Blonde.* There was a certain amount of laughter, and applause when she finished, and Nick went up to her and assumed the role of master of ceremonies.

"Thank you, ladies and gentlemen," he said. "I apologize for the—ah—ill-mannered interruption of our program, but I feel sure that the quality of our music will rise above such sordid nuisances. As the second number in her repertory, Marie Dubois, the Songbird of the Somme, will now sing *Mademoiselle d'Armentières.*"

"Ta gueule, salautier," Marie hissed at him, and he laughed.

"Excuse me," he said. "She seems to have forgotten the words. Very well, then, it will be that stirring song, known to every *poilu* from Verdun to Amiens, *Madelon de la Victoire.*"

Marie sang the song, and those of the customers who knew it joined in, and that led to *La Marseillaise,* and everybody stood. At the conclusion, when people were sitting down, the voice of John Barrymore sounded like a peal of thunder. "Who is yonder varlet," he intoned, "who keeps his grubby hat upon his head?" People turned and saw him stalking toward the Federal officer, who was leaning against the doorjamb with a thinly veiled expression of contempt. "Answer me, varlet!" Barrymore went on. "When you were an infant, mewling and puking in your nurse's arms, did they teach you to wear your hat during the singing of a sacred anthem? Did they teach you to spit on the flag of a sister country, at the same time as you were desecrating that of your own? Were you intentionally brought up with the manners of a whoreson, or did it just turn out that way by chance?"

"Pipe down," the officer said. "You'll live longer."

"Is that a threat?" Barrymore's eyes popped wide, and he pointed a finger at the ceiling. "If it is, then by the gods I'll—" He stopped, as Nick came through the crowd and got between him and the officer.

"It's all right, Mr. Barrymore," Nick said. "He's just acting under orders."

"That's what I want to know. Was he ordered to be a swine, or is it something that just comes naturally?"

"Forget it," Nick said. "It isn't that important."

"It's a matter of honor," Barrymore said. "Rightly to be great / Is not to stir without great argument / But greatly to find quarrel in a straw / When honor's at the stake."

"Is this guy crazy, or something?" the officer said to Nick.

"No," Nick replied. "He's an actor."

"*An* actor?" Barrymore exclaimed. "What do you mean, *an* actor?"

Before Nick could reply, one of the Federal men appeared, said something in a low voice to the officer, and handed him the bunch of keys. The officer looked at Nick, who returned the look without expression. "He says these keys just lead to empty rooms," the officer said.

"That's what I told you," Nick replied. "There's nothing here."

"Except those broken bottles he found in the cellar."

"We collect old glass. There are just so many places to keep it."

"Preferably over a drain, where the booze will run off?"

Nick shrugged. "Look at it any way you want. There's no legal evidence of liquor on these premises."

The Federal officer continued to look at him. "O.K.," he said, at last. "You win. But we'll be back."

"Any time you like," said Nick. "Just remember to bring a new warrant each time."

"Don't worry about that."

Nick saw the other Federals appearing behind the officer, and said, "Would any of you gentlemen care for a sandwich? We have plenty in the kitchen." The officer grunted and turned away, and Nick said, "This is probably a stupid question, but may I ask you something?"

The officer paused. "What?"

"Who ordered this raid?"

"Like you said, that's a stupid question," the officer replied, and herded his men out of the room. The last to go was the precinct captain, George McGinty. He spread his hands in embarrassed apology, then clasped them together and grinned as he went out.

There was total silence until the click of the outside gate was heard. Then Nick went to Marie, kissed her, and, turning to the customers, said, "Let's give them a little time to leave, and then we can carry on. In the meantime, if anyone cares to sing, he can feel free to do so."

Nobody sang, but the babble of voices reached a decibel count equal to that of the Mormon Tabernacle Choir. A well-dressed woman, who looked as though she should have been at the opera, said, "Can you i*ma*gine–I've been in a *raid!* I feel just like Al Capone!"

"You don't look like him," said someone else, and then another woman's voice cut through the din saying, "If he'd made one move at me I was going to give him the old heel in the groin!" As Marie and the boys went back to the kitchen several people applauded, and Barrymore's voice was heard to proclaim, "Once more unto the breach, dear friends, once more–" and then his words were lost in the overall noise. "How did you like the theatre?" a man asked a woman standing near him, and she replied, "To be frank, I don't remember much about the first act." "Yes," the man said. "I've always found it's better to sit facing the stage."

Nick went into the kitchen with Charlie behind him and reached in a small closet in which the employees' coats were hung. He took a carving knife and laid the blade across two metal coat hangers; there was a click, and the back of the closet swung open to reveal a flight of stairs going down into darkness. He and Charlie descended, then he switched on an overhead light, produced a long, skewer-like piece of wire, and ran it into a crack between two bricks in an apparently seamless wall. The wall pivoted, and opened into a room that was piled high with bags and cases and bottles. Nick stepped to a small intercom mouthpiece and pressed a button. Max's voice, garbled and metallic, said, "Yeah?"

"All clear?" Nick asked.

"All clear," Max replied, and Nick and Charlie began to load a dumbwaiter with bottles.

Up in the bar, Butterworth and MacDougall shared a sandwich while they waited for the liquor to arrive. MacDougall nibbled at the crust, put it down, and said, "I've got an idea for a business."

"What kind of business?" Butterworth replied.

"This is only in case the play fails–we can rent rowboats in Central Park. The beauty of it is you need no overhead; just one rowboat and one sneaker, and the customer does the rest."

"Why only one sneaker?"

"The man who pushes the boat off needs only one sneaker, because his other foot is in the water."

Butterworth smiled. "You may have something there," he said. "Should we try it first, to make sure it'll work?"

"Probably."

"O.K. What are we waiting for?"

"Let's have a nightcap here, and then try it. It may be cold in the park."

"You're right. Where'd Charlie go?"

"I guess he's getting out more hooch."

A latecomer made his way to the bar, and said to Butterworth, "Was Dottie Peters here tonight?"

"Not that I know of," Butterworth replied. "Why?"

"She just tried to kill herself."

"Where? When?"

"In her apartment. She took some pills and got in the tub, then left the water running and it overflowed into the apartment below."

"Where is she now?"

"In the hospital, I presume. McClain was the one told me."

"I told her she'd never make it with pills," MacDougall said. "I told her to use a gun, or take a running jump off the top of a building."

"I don't think she was trying to make it," Butterworth said. "I think she may have come closer than she intended."

MacDougall finished the crust and licked the tips of his fingers. "Well, she ought to make up her mind," he said. "If she keeps on like this, she's going to become an old bore before her time."

3

Out of habit, Roland Butterworth awoke at quarter to nine the next morning. He had a dull pain behind his eyes and his mouth was dry, and he lay for a few minutes among the twisted bedclothes, trying to reconstruct the previous evening. He remembered having dinner at the Algonquin with George MacDougall, and MacDougall's promising him a part in a still-unwritten play; he and MacDougall then went over to Broadway to check on two shows for which he was press agent, and after that they went to Tony's, where John Barrymore was in full cry; the memory of Barrymore led him to Nick's, and the raid; and then, with an almost audible jolt, came the memory of Dottie Peters' attempted suicide. Butterworth swung his feet over the side of the bed, stood up, and thought for a moment he was going to pass out, then went into the bathroom, drained off what seemed like thirty gallons of Scotch, and brushed his teeth. By the time he had started making coffee it was nine o'clock, and he picked up the telephone to make his daily call to his wife in Crestwood.

Sarah Butterworth answered on the first ring, glancing at the clock as she did, and she felt, as always, a small glow of satisfaction at his promptness. His work might keep him in the city, but he was still the same small-town boy she'd always known, and this was more important to her than anything else. "Hello, dear," she said, before he'd had a chance to speak. "Did you sleep well?"

"Fine," he said. "First rate. How are the kids?" This was the standard opening for their conversations; over the more than two years he'd been making the calls the preamble had not changed by so much as a word. What came after that depended on the circumstances.

"They're fine," Sarah said. "Nancy may be starting a cold so I'm keeping her inside today, and Puddin skinned his knee yesterday, but he didn't even whimper when I put peroxide on it. He was very brave." Puddin was the nickname of their three-year-old son, who for some arcane reason had been christened Lionel.

"That's nice," Butterworth said. "I mean, it's nice he was brave." The palms of his hands were beginning to perspire, and he wished he'd waited until the coffee was ready before placing the call.

"What did you do last night?" Sarah asked.

"Oh, Mac and I had dinner at the Gonk," he replied. "He had some business he wanted to talk over."

"I suppose he plied you with liquor. That's the only business that interests him."

"He did no such thing. In the first place, the Gonk doesn't serve liquor."

"Then what did he want?"

"Oh"–Butterworth tried to dismiss the whole subject–"it was some crazy idea he's had. Nothing's going to come of it."

"It must be pretty important, if you're keeping it this deep a secret."

"There's no secret to it! He's writing this play, and he thinks I'd be good in one of the parts."

"I hope you told him no."

"I– As a matter of fact, it was so silly I didn't even bother to say no. I just changed the subject and went on to something else."

"I'd certainly like to know what he had in mind."

"I just told you! That's absolutely all there is to it!"

"He almost got you arrested with that Longfellow idea of his."

"This is completely different! That was a–well, a–"

"A drunken prank."

"If you will. But he wasn't all that drunk. He was just–"

"A man is either drunk or he isn't, and you know that as well as I do. You've said the same thing yourself."

"All right. But this has nothing to do with drink. He just thought of me when he was writing this particular character, and he said he'd like to see me play it."

"What kind of character is it?"

"I have no idea. I told you, I simply changed the subject." He heard the coffee begin to percolate, and wondered how he could bring the conversation to an end. The matter of Dottie Peters could wait until another time, and since there was very little else he could report he said, "It was really a pretty dull evening. I'll give you a call later–"

"Wait a minute," she said. "Don't hang up yet. What train are you taking on Sunday?" It was his custom to have Sunday midday dinner in Crestwood, an operation that required a forty minutes' train ride each way, and for some reason the Sunday afternoon sunlight brought upon him a mood of depression that developed into a cracking headache. He looked forward to his Sunday trips to suburbia the way he looked forward to having a foot amputated.

"The usual one, I guess," he said. "Why?"

"It would be nice if you could get the ten-fifteen. The Thatchers are having a family reunion, and their children have written a little play they want to perform."

"What does that have to do with us?"

"I told Violet we'd come, just to fill out the audience. The children want to pretend it's a real play, in a real theatre."

"Is it going to *be* in a real theatre?" Butterworth was horrified at the thought.

"Of course not, silly! It's going to be on the sun porch, but they want as big an audience as possible."

"Well, I'll let you know." Butterworth could smell the coffee by now, and his hands were trembling. "I was hoping I could get you all to come in town, and we could have lunch at the Gonk. Don't you think that would be a nice change of pace?"

"Some other time it would be lovely. But I've promised Violet we'll be there."

"Well, we'll see."

"It can't be that much trouble to get the train an hour earlier. After all, it isn't as though you were a late sleeper."

"I know. There are just– Well, we'll talk about it later. Right now I've got to–"

"Wait a minute. The children want to speak to you. Nancy, come say hello to Daddy."

There was a pause, and a clunk, and then Nancy's voice came on, high and excited. "Hello, Daddy," she said.

"Hello, honey," Butterworth replied. "What's this I hear about you getting a cold?"

"I don't really have a cold but Mummy thinks I might get one if I go out so she won't let me out of the house and that's dumb," said Nancy, all in one breath.

"You may not think you have a cold, but you do as your mother tells you," Butterworth said gently. "She knows what's best for you."

"Here's Puddin," Nancy said, as though her father hadn't spoken.

This time there was a muffled crash, as the telephone was apparently dropped, and then a small voice, suggesting that of a mouse, said, "Hello?"

"Hi there, sport," Butterworth said. "How's the knee?"

"Yes," said Puddin.

"How'd you hurt it?"

"It broke."

By now beginning to wonder if he was losing his mind, Butterworth said, "Well, I'll see you Sunday," and was about to hang up when Puddin said, "Here's Mom," and Sarah's voice came on.

"I do hope you'll get that early train," she said. "It will mean a great deal to Violet."

"I'll do what I can," said Butterworth.

"It will also mean a great deal to me."

"I said, I'll do what I can. I can't promise anything more than that."

"I just wish you didn't sound so evasive. It sounds as though you're already trying to think up an excuse."

"I'm doing no such thing! Suppose I promise you I'll be there, and then get hit by a truck? Nobody knows what's going to happen on Sunday—there might be a blizzard, and all the trains'll be snowed in—I might come down with bubonic plague—any number of things could happen—I simply said I'd do what I can, and beyond that I can't promise anything. Can't you see that?"

There was silence at the other end of the line, and he knew she was crying. "Look—I'm sorry," he said. "I didn't mean to sound testy. I'll get the goddamned ten-fifteen, provided it's running and provided I don't break an ankle on the way to the station. How does that sound?"

The silence continued, and then there was a click, and the line went dead. Butterworth sighed, hung up, then went and, with fluttering hands, poured himself a cup of coffee.

He felt somewhat better after the second cup, and, putting on a bathrobe, he went to the door and picked up the morning papers. He usually read the *Times,* the *Herald Tribune,* the *Daily News,* and the *Daily Mirror* before going to his office, but this morning there seemed to be a flannel blanket around his brain, and the only news he could find was of Coolidge's inauguration, the day before. The only quotable thing Coolidge had ever said had been six weeks earlier, when he stated that "the business of America is business," and Butterworth didn't feel he was up to another dose of such profound thinking. He skimmed the entertainment pages, hoping to find a story he'd sent out about Jane Cowl, but the only paper that had even printed it was the *Mirror,* which had boiled it down to two paragraphs. Butterworth started to clip the item, then crumpled the paper and jammed it in the wastebasket.

His mind drifted back to Dottie Peters, and his emotion was one of irritation only faintly tempered by pity. He felt sure that her taking the pills had been done in a transient moment of black depression, or perhaps even consciously to arouse pity, but the effect was spoiled by the fact that she'd tried it before and had always survived, and now nobody could take her seriously. Her suicidal moods usually came at the end of a love affair, one in which she had been the jilted party, and he couldn't escape the conclusion that she was simply thumbing her nose at the vanished lover. If, as occasionally happened, she was the one who broke off the affair, she immediately became so desperately sorry for her ex-lover that she went back to him, thereby giving him the chance to be the one to walk out. Her problem, and it seemed an insoluble one, was that she was nine-tenths emotion and one-tenth common sense. Butterworth thought briefly of going to see her in the hospital but decided that the scene would be more than he could handle. She would be a puddle of remorse, begging forgiveness for having put everyone to so much trouble, and her contrition would last until she had her first drink, when she would turn either vengeful, maudlin, or glum. In any event, she was better left alone. He poured a third cup of coffee and, for purely medicinal reasons, put in a splash of brandy. By the time he finished the cup, his recovery was complete. He considered calling his wife to apologize for his earlier brusqueness but, on second thought, felt it would be better to wait until she'd had a chance to get control of herself, and the conversation could be on a more rational level.

On his desk, behind the telephone, was his diary, a red-bound book with the year 1925 embossed in gold, and he picked it up and leafed idly through it, noticing how many blank pages there were. It had been a habit, as regular as brushing his teeth, to write in his diary the last thing before going to bed, but for one reason or another this no longer held true. Sometimes he wrote it the next morning, but by then the details of the day before were blurred and usually seemed not worth putting down. Then there was one day, he noticed, where the only entry was: "It is harder to get a pig under a fence," and that was all. He could remember neither what it meant, nor what he'd had in mind when he wrote it. He stared at the page for a long time, then riffled through the diary until he came to Wednesday, March 4, yesterday's date. Taking a deep breath and a firm grip on his pen, he wrote:

> Up at the usual time, and after Crestwood call went through the papers. No news, except that if something isn't done about it Coolidge will be inaugurated at noon today. Who knows? Already he's been better than Harding, which is saying less than nothing. Spent the afternoon doing a feature piece on Jane Cowl for general release. The *Times* probably won't touch it—they like all their stories to be exclusives—but the *Trib* ought to give it good space. (He thought of crossing out the last sentence then decided to let it stand, just for the irony.) To the Gonk for dinner with Mac, who is all hot on having me in his new play, whenever he gets it written. Says he has a part in it that's hand-tailored for me. Might be fun to give it a try. Checked the two theatres, no problems. Then to Tony's, where J. Barrymore was being a horse's ass, and thence to Nick's, where of all things we ran into a real raid. Somebody must have double-crossed someone. Found out later that D.P. had taken another shot at suicide, with about the usual success. Bed around ???

There, he thought, shaking his hand to ease the writer's cramp. It may not be literature, but at least it filled the page. And it's honest: I really believed yesterday that the *Trib* would use the Cowl piece. Reid must still be sore. Well, the hell with him. In fact, the hell with them all. There are other things in the world than being a press agent.

In a reminiscent mood, he reached in the desk drawer and pulled out his diary for 1922, the year when he'd first gone to the Club Circe. He was, at that time, a dedicated Prohibitionist, firm in his belief that Demon Rum was at the root of all evil, and he was loud in his scorn for anyone who would deliver himself into its clutches. It took MacDougall who, with him, was a fledgling reporter on the *Tribune,* nearly a week to persuade him even to put foot inside an establishment that sold liquor. Finally one evening, when they'd both got their good-nights at nine o'clock and were waiting for the elevator, MacDougall said, "Where are you going from here?"

"Home," Butterworth replied. "Twelfth Street."

"Had your supper?"

"No. I'll stop at the Automat on the way."

"What can you get at the Automat?"

Butterworth shrugged. "You name it. Chicken pie—club sandwich—cream cheese and olive—"

"That's no meal for a growing boy. How'd you like a steak sandwich?"

"I can't afford a steak sandwich." The thought of steak made Butterworth salivate slightly.

"For fifty cents?"

"Where can you get a steak sandwich for fifty cents?"

"I know a place. Come with me, and you'll eat like a king."

"Do they sell liquor?"

"What difference if they sell liquor? You don't have to have any."

"I know, but—"

"Oh, for Christ's sakes, stop being so prissy. They're not going to spray it on you. If you don't like it you don't have to come back. I just thought you might like a change from the Automat."

"Very well, then." Butterworth was startled by MacDougall's burst of profanity, which he'd thought was used only if a man was about to fight, and he didn't want to do anything to irritate his friend. He knew MacDougall had been in the Army, and reasoned he'd had a momentary lapse into barracks language. The elevator arrived, and as they got in Butterworth said, "What's the name of this place?"

"Officially it's called the Club Circe; otherwise, it's known as Nick's. Nick Baldino is the owner."

Butterworth thought a moment, then smiled. "He must have a sense of humor."

"Why?"

"Circe was that woman who turned men into swine."

MacDougall's eyes widened. "I'm damned," he said. "I never thought of that. I'll have to find out who named it."

"Whoever it was, I like him."

They took the subway to Forty-second Street, then walked the rest of the way. The block was dimly lighted, and lined on both sides with high-stoop brownstone houses, and Butterworth marveled that MacDougall knew where to stop. He followed behind as MacDougall went down two steps, stopped at an iron gate, and rang a bell. There was a click as the peephole opened. MacDougall said, "Evening, Max," and then the door swung open and the gate was unlocked.

"Evening, Mr. MacDougall," Max said.

"This is Mr. Butterworth," MacDougall said, as they went in. "Mr. Butterworth is here to sample one of your famous steak sandwiches."

Butterworth was aware that Max was scrutinizing him carefully, apparently to be able to remember his face, and then Max said, "Good evening, Mr. Butterworth. I hope you enjoy yourself."

"Thank you," Butterworth replied, feeling as though he were entering some dragon's lair, from which he might never return.

Instead of going to a table MacDougall went directly to the bar and ordered a drink, so Butterworth held back and waited, unsure of what to do. There were four or five other people at the bar, among them a small, dark-haired woman with large eyes that peered out from beneath a fringe of bangs, and MacDougall began to talk to her, although Butterworth could not make out the conversation. Then MacDougall beckoned to him, and as he approached the bar MacDougall said, "Mrs. Peters, may I present Mr. Butterworth. Mr. Butterworth is a co-slave with me in the vineyards of the Reids."

"How do you do?" Mrs. Peters said. "I feel as though I should curtsey."

"Please not on my account," Butterworth said. "I'm trying to travel incognito." He had no idea what made him say it; the words were out of his mouth almost before he'd thought of them, and he could only conclude they'd been said out of nervousness. Mrs. Peters smiled a slow, appreciative smile, and looked at MacDougall.

"Why haven't you told me about *him?*" she said.

Before MacDougall could answer, Butterworth said, "There was some talk about a steak sandwich, and I wondered—"

"It's already ordered," MacDougall replied. "They'll bring it to a table when it's ready. In the meantime, what would you like for your thirst?"

"I don't care. Ginger ale . . . soda . . . could I get a cup of coffee?" Butterworth was aware that Mrs. Peters was staring at him, and he smiled at her and said nothing.

"Charlie," MacDougall said to the bartender, "a ginger ale for my friend here, and a cup of coffee when his steak comes."

"Right," said Charlie, shoveling cracked ice into a glass. "Is that ginger ale straight?"

"Straight as an arrow." To Mrs. Peters, MacDougall said, "I hear Old Ralph became a public charge the other night."

"You didn't hear the half of it." She glanced down the bar, to where a large, brawny man was in earnest albeit incoherent conversation with a smaller one, whom he had pinned against the end of the bar as he might a butterfly. "Old Ralph doesn't know it, but his time is running out. Just once more he's going to show me how he won the Eastern Intercollegiate Wrestling Championship, and then he and his toothbrush and his letter sweater are out in the street. A girl can take just so much, and then she blows the whistle."

"At least I never tried wrestling holds on you," MacDougall said.

"I wish you had," she replied.

Nick came out of the kitchen, and MacDougall said, "Nick, I have a question for you. First, I'd like you to meet my friend, Roly Butterworth. Nick Baldino." Nick and Butterworth shook hands, and for a moment Butterworth thought all the small bones in his hand had been crushed. "Second," MacDougall went on, "who was it that thought up the name Club Circe?"

"Marie," Nick replied. "Why?"

"Roly, here, has pointed out that Circe was the enchantress in the *Odyssey,* who changed men into swine."

Nick grinned. "Marie thought that was her little joke," he said. "She didn't think anyone would catch on." To Butterworth, he said, "I'll have to tell her we have at least one literate customer. My congratulations."

Butterworth was about to protest that he wasn't really a customer, then decided against it. He couldn't show his real feelings without being offensive, and at the moment he felt surprisingly cheerful and at ease. So he simply said, "Thank you. I think it's a splendid name," and let it go at that.

His steak arrived, and MacDougall ordered one more drink and brought it to the table. "Aren't you eating?" Butterworth asked, as he started to cut his meat.

"I don't have to be home," MacDougall replied. "I may make a little whoopee first."

This time, Butterworth couldn't resist. "Why do you do that?" he asked. "Don't you realize liquor makes you into a different person?"

MacDougall laughed. "And probably just as well. It also got me the Silver Star."

"What do you mean?"

"On the way to Blanc Mont we came on a cellar full of cognac, and by the time we got in the line I was so cockeyed I couldn't spit straight. But they tell me I wiped out two machine-gun nests, and took a dozen prisoners before I passed out. If I'd been sober, I'd have been scared as a rabbit. And if I'd been a Regular, I'd have got the Congressional Medal of Honor."

"I suppose it was different in the war," Butterworth said.

"Cognac is cognac, no matter where you drink it. Right now, all I can afford is Scotch."

"This is really a swell steak. You don't know what you're missing."

"I'll have one later. I just don't feel like it now."

Butterworth saw that MacDougall was watching Mrs. Peters, who had moved down the bar and was talking to the large man who was apparently Old Ralph, and he said, "What does Mrs. Peters do?"

"For a living? Believe it or not, she's a fashion writer. She likes to refer to herself as the foundation editor at *Vogue*."

Butterworth ate his steak in silence. "I gather you know her pretty well," he said at last.

"Reasonably."

There was a slight commotion at the bar: a man said, "Shut up!" and then a glass broke, and Mrs. Peters headed quickly for the door. MacDougall stood up.

"Excuse me," he said, and followed her out into the vestibule. After a few moments the click of the front door was heard, and then silence. A waiter brought Butterworth's coffee and the check, and for a moment Butterworth had the panicky feeling he was going to owe for everything. It was only Wednesday, and he wouldn't be paid until Friday. He brought out his wallet, but before he could find any money Charlie saw him, and called to the waiter. "Joe, that's Mr. MacDougall's tab," he said. "He said the whole thing was to be on him."

"Sorry." The waiter retrieved the check, and gave it to Charlie.

As Butterworth put his wallet away he found himself thinking that a thing like that would never happen in the Automat.

When he got home, Sarah was mending the baby's clothes. "Did you have a night assignment?" she asked, as he kissed her.

"No. I had supper with Mac."

"In a restaurant?" It was tacit that all restaurants were too expensive.

"No." He gave a short, dry laugh. "In a speakeasy."

Sarah put down her mending and stared at him. Her blond hair, which was drawn back in a bun at the base of her neck, was in slight disarray, and stray wisps shone like a halo around her head. "In a *what?*" she said.

"Well, technically it's a speakeasy, but they also have very good food," he said. "And very cheap. A steak sandwich cost me fifty cents—or, rather, it cost Mac fifty cents. He paid for the whole thing."

"I should hope he would. I just don't understand why you went there in the first place."

"He told me about the food, and pointed out I didn't have to drink if I didn't want to. I had a ginger ale to begin with, and coffee after. I can't see there's any harm in that."

"But the people you must have run in to. Wasn't it full of drunks?"

"There was one man I saw who'd had too much. Otherwise, I might as well have been at an Alice Foote McDougal's."

"There is no comparison between a tearoom and a gin mill."

"I simply meant that nobody was drunk."

Sarah picked up her mending, took two stitches, then threw it all on the floor. "My God, if you knew how I hate this city!" she said. "I hate it, I hate it, I hate it!"

He went to her, and kneeled down and took her hands in his. "I hate it too," he said, "but this is where I work. I'm lucky to have a job, and we just can't afford to live anywhere else. Some day we'll be able to afford—who knows?—maybe we can even live in the country—but for now there's nothing else I can do. Believe me, if there were any way to make things easier for you I'd do it, no matter what it was, but I just can't see any alternative. Can you?"

"I'll tell you how much I hate this city," she said, ignoring his question. "I hate it so much that every morning I think of going out on the fire escape and throwing myself into the street, and if it weren't for the children I might do just that. But the strain of *not* doing it, of holding myself in and trying to behave normally, is so terrible that I have a constant headache. From morning to night I live with one long, pounding headache, until I think I'm going to scream. And to think that the children are going to be brought up here is more than I can stand. If I didn't think there was some way out for them, I'd close all the windows and turn on the gas. That, in a nutshell, is how I feel about New York."

Butterworth was quiet for a few moments, then said, "Do you think it might help if you saw a doctor? For the headaches, I mean?"

"Nothing will help, except getting out of here."

His legs were beginning to cramp, and he stood up and kissed her on the forehead. Her skin was hot, and small beads of perspiration glistened above her eyebrows. "I'll do what I can," he said. "I can't promise any more than that, but believe me, I'll do what I can."

4

When, on Good Friday, April 6, 1917, Congress declared war on the German Empire, Nick Baldino was one of the first to enlist. Twenty-four years old, he was aching to escape from the noisome streets of the Lower East Side, where his father ran a grocery stand and his mother made pasta for a nearby restaurant, and to him the Army seemed the perfect way out. His parents had wanted him to go to college and become a lawyer, but by the time he was through high school the matter of bringing in money became more important than anything else, and his further education had to be shelved. He became a delivery boy, a waiter, a butcher's assistant, and a sometime street fighter, and loathed every minute of it. His father's stories of the exploits of Giuseppe Garibaldi had led him to admire the dedication of the true patriot, and he now had a chance to demonstrate his own patriotism, all the stronger because it was for his native country, as opposed to his parents' adopted one.

Slightly over two months later, on June 28, Nick found himself among the fourteen thousand American troops disembarking at Saint-Nazaire, troops that with few exceptions were totally innocent of the art of warfare. With no more training than learning to distinguish one end of a Springfield 1903 rifle from the other, they were rushed pell-mell to France to act as props for the sagging French morale, and, as symbols of what was still to come, they were greeted with hysteria wherever they went. On July 4 a battalion of the 16th U. S. Infantry, of which Nick was a part, was mustered in the courtyard of the Invalides in Paris, where, facing a battalion of battle-scarred *poilus,* they formed an honor guard while the brass, both French and American, made obeisance at the tomb of Napoleon. Then, with ruffles and flourishes and the blaring of the regimental band, they started on the five-mile march across Paris to the Picpus Cemetery, where General Pershing was to lay a wreath on the tomb of the Marquis de Lafayette. How they survived that march, the men of the 16th Infantry were never able to understand. From all sides they were set upon by cheering, weeping, kissing French women of all ages, sizes, and types; they were festooned with flowers and bedecked with wreaths; they were plied with wine and doused with cologne; and in some cases weeping women in black reached out with wispy handkerchiefs to wipe the sweat from the foreheads of the staggering troops. Pershing later observed that "the column, as it moved forward, looked like a moving flower garden."

When they reached the cemetery, the French gendarmes and the Garde Mobile moved in to keep the civilians outside the iron gates, and in the comparative calm the wreath was laid. But then, instead of Pershing's speaking, a captain at his side took two steps forward, saluted, and said three words, the last of which was "Lafayette." The crowd outside the gates shouted and laughed and cheered, and Nick, who had missed the first two words, spoke out of the side of his mouth to Ed Bradley, the man on his left, all the while holding his rigid posture of attention.

"What the hell did he say?" he asked.

"You got me," Bradley replied. "It sounded like 'Good fella, Lafayette.' "

"Impossible," said Nick.

"It was French," hissed the man behind him. "He said, *'Nous voilà,* Lafayette.' "

"Which means?"

"Here we are."

"For chrissakes, anyone can see that," said Bradley.

"Quiet in the ranks!" snarled a sergeant.

By this time the French brass were conferring with Pershing, who finally, and reluctantly, stepped forward and said a few words that nobody could hear, and with that the ceremony was over. The band struck up, the gates were opened, and the troops marched back through the surging crowd to the collecting area at Caserne de Reuilly, where they were dismissed and given passes to go into Paris for the rest of the day.

"I don't get it," Nick said to Bradley, as a group of them made their way in the general direction of the Arc de Triomphe. "Who was that guy who spoke first? And why didn't Pershing do the whole thing?"

"Black Jack don't like to speak," said a corporal, figuratively flexing his stripes among the greenhorns. "He thought he'd push the whole thing off on his buddy Captain Stanton, but the Froggies wouldn't let him. With them it's gotta be straight protocol, or it don't count for sour snail shit."

"Some stupid kind of army," Bradley observed. "No wonder they're in trouble."

To most of the men of the 16th, Paris was a spot on the map, a place referred to occasionally in geography or history lessons, and about as impersonal as, say, Liverpool or Buenos Aires. To the few who had either read or heard of its reputation as a city of lights and romance, it was something of a letdown in 1917; three years of war had drained a good deal of the gaiety out of the French, and a whole generation of Frenchmen had been obliterated to no apparent gain. The strains of the war showed everywhere—in people's faces, their attitudes, and their mourning clothes, and only the arrival of the token Americans had given anyone a spark of hope that things might eventually change for the better. So on this July 4 the festivities at the Picpus Cemetery lingered on into the dusk; people were seen to smile at nothing in particular, and any American in uniform was the subject of almost embarrassing adulation.

Nick, Bradley, and two friends named Langrock and Pinzner decided to start at the Arc de Triomphe, go down one side of the Champs-Élysées as far as the Place de la Concorde, and then back up the other side to the Arc, and let nature take its course after that. They had until six o'clock, which gave them nearly four hours of sightseeing, and with no fixed goal they were, so to speak, drawing to a blind hand.

As they left the Arc, Bradley looked back at it and said, "I heard somewhere that on Napoleon's birthday the sun sets right in the middle of that thing. That's some neat trick, if you ask me."

"When's Napoleon's birthday?" Pinzner replied.

"Search me."

"So far, I'm not impressed," said Pinzner.

"You know what I'd like?" said Langrock, who had just turned eighteen and who came from a farm in western Massachusetts. "I'd like a chocolate frappé. It seems like thirty years since I've had one."

"Well, let's see if we can find a soda fountain," Nick said. "There ought to be one around here somewhere."

"Or even a drug store," said Langrock. "Any decent drug store is bound to have a soda fountain."

"What's the French for soda fountain?" Bradley asked.

"I don't know the French, but I know the Italian," Nick replied. "They can't be too far apart."

"Let's ask these ladies," Langrock said, indicating a pair who had just turned into the boulevard from a side street. "They look as though they live here."

Nick saw two girls in their early twenties, dressed like all Parisians in somber clothes, and while one of them was pale and wan the other had an indescribable quality to her skin, which seemed to glow with some inner light. Her eyes were large, and everything about her was well proportioned. Nick felt suddenly short of breath.

"Mi scusi, signorina," he said, in what he hoped was a steady voice. *"Dove una fontana di soda?"*

Her eyes grew even larger. *"Vous êtes italien?"* she said, incredulous.

"No, sono americano, but I can't speak French."

She laughed. "I can speak English," she said. "A little bit."

"Thank God. We're looking for a soda fountain."

"A–?" The eyes clouded.

"A–" Nick tried to pantomime a chocolate soda, with no success.

"A drug store," Langrock put in. "A drug store will have a soda fountain."

"Una farmacia," Nick said.

"Pharmacie?" The girl looked from one to the other of them. *"Vous êtes malade?* Someone is sick?"

"No, but my friend wants a chocolate soda."

"Chocolate frappé," Langrock corrected.

The girl turned to her companion. *"Tu comprends?"* she asked, and the pale girl shook her head. "We can take you to a *pharmacie,"* the first girl said. "Perhaps the man there will understand."

"We don't want to put you to any trouble," Nick said. "It isn't all that–"

"C'est rien," the girl said. "It is not far. Come." She started off, and Nick managed to slip into step beside her. The other girl was on her left, and after a certain amount of fruitless jockeying the other three Americans fell in behind.

"This is very kind of you," Nick said, as they walked down the block. "We've never been in Paris before."

"It is a bad time," the girl replied. "But now things will be better."

"In what way? By the way, my name is Nick. Nick Baldino."

She smiled. "Marie Dubois."

"Do you live near here?"

"Not near, not far."

"How did you mean, things will be better?"

"With the Americans here, the war will soon be over."

Nick thought of how poorly prepared his group was for anything, much less combat, and hoped they wouldn't be a disappointment. He remembered how one man in his platoon kept his bayonet wrapped in newspaper because there hadn't been enough scabbards to go around, and the idea of unwrapping a newspaper before stabbing a German was so grotesque that he found himself smiling.

"You are amused?" Marie asked.

"Not really. I was thinking of something else."

They turned down a side street, and at the end of the block was a sign saying "Pharmacie–R. LaMotte Prop." Marie looked at him and smiled, and he felt his insides go weak. *"Voilà,"* she said. "And good luck." She started away, but Nick put out a hand.

"Just a second," he said. "I'd like to–uh–send you a little thank-you present. Where should I address it?"

"There is no necessity. I was happy to do it."

"Nevertheless. You were very kind. Please–where could I send it? I just mean something like a flower."

She smiled again. "Rue Arsène Hussaye, 36," she said, and left.

"Somebody give me a pencil and paper, quick!" Nick said, and scribbled her name and address on a slip that Bradley handed him.

"You don't waste any time, do you?" Bradley asked, as Nick returned the pencil.

"There's such a thing as an emergency situation," Nick replied. "Emergency situations call for emergency measures."

When they entered the pharmacy, they realized their mistake. It was a true apothecary's shop, with jars and bottles and vials and various colored liquids, and it smelled of herbs and unguents and antiseptics. A small, wizened man, summoned by the tinkling of a bell over the door, appeared between two colored jars and said, *"Bonjour, messieurs. Comment puis-j' vous aider?"*

"Uh—I don't suppose you'd have such a thing as—" Nick began, then finished, "The hell with it. I'm sorry we bothered you." He herded the other three back into the street, and said, "I guess there's got to be another word for it."

"Rats," said Langrock. "I had my mouth all set for a chocolate frappé."

"I had kind of thought of getting laid," Pinzner said. "But then old Baldino, here, grabbed off the only good-looking one. He strikes like a cobra, that Baldino."

"You'll never get laid if you don't know the language," Bradley said. "The French have to draw the line somewhere."

"I got the words for it." Pinzner pulled a crumpled piece of paper out of his breast pocket, and read: "Voo-lay voo coo-shay avek mwa?" He put the paper back, and as he buttoned the pocket said, "The trouble is, I don't know which word to accent. If I put the emphasis wrong, I may spoil it."

"Put the emphasis on the last word," Bradley told him. "That should give it more force."

"O.K.," said Pinzner. "I'll try it if I get a chance."

Nick looked at his watch. "You guys can do what you want," he said. "I got important business to attend to."

"How do you know she's going to be home?" Pinzner asked. "Remember, we gotta be back at the base by six."

"I'm just going to send some flowers," Nick replied. "The rest can wait till another time."

He searched for an hour without finding a florist, and ended by picking a few roses in the Luxembourg Gardens. A gendarme swooped down on him like a hawk, shouting and gesticulating, and it was only Nick's American uniform that saved him from being arrested. He even managed, in a mixture of Italian, English, and sign language, to mollify the gendarme enough to get from him directions on how to reach the Rue Arsène Hussaye. This took him back up the Champs-Élysées to a narrow cross-street near the Étoile, and when he found 36 it turned out to be a small restaurant. His first reaction was of disappointment, which changed to rage, but then, feeling he had nothing to lose, he pushed through the swinging door and went into the warm darkness inside.

"Fermé, monsieur," came a woman's voice from the rear. *"Nous fermons jusqu'à dix-huit heures."*

"Does Mademoiselle Marie Dubois work here?" Nick asked.

"Marie? Ah, oui. Mais elle est sortie. Elle—"

"Would you give her these, please?" Nick held out the roses, and the woman appeared from the gloom, smiling.

"Ah, que c'est gentil!" she said. *"Et votre nom, monsieur?* How do you call yourself?"

"Nick Baldino. She'll recognize it. Just tell her I brought them." He left, making a note of the name of the restaurant, and found his way back to the Caserne de Reuilly.

That night they were loaded aboard the boxcars aptly marked *"40 hommes 8 chevaux"* and taken eastward to Lorraine for nearly ten months of intensive training. French instructors gave them the essence of trench warfare—the use of the Chauchat and the Hotchkiss machine guns, how to string barbed wire and how to cut through it, the timing of a grenade so it explodes just before it hits the ground, how to get a bayonet into a man so it doesn't jam between his ribs and how to get it out if it does jam, and how a shovel can be used either for digging or for splitting a man's face in two. They had gas-mask practice, patrol practice, and first-aid practice, and at Pershing's insistence they had practice in marksmanship and the use of the rifle in open-field warfare, both items thought to be passé by the British and French.

Nick wrote Marie the day after they'd arrived, and was astounded to receive a reply two weeks later. She thanked him for the flowers and said she wished him well, and that was about all, but the mere fact of her having written was enough to send him straight to his notepaper. He wrote her a long letter—most of which, it later turned out, was cut by the censor—and he continued to write as often as possible, although the rigors of the training schedule were such that he often dropped in a soggy heap at the end of the day. Her replies were sparse, friendly, and noncommittal.

He had one brief leave in the early spring of 1918 and managed to see her twice, and both times she was friendly, but nothing more. He tried to find out if she had a fiancé or lover or boyfriend, but all such questions ran up against a blank wall, and he finally gave up trying. He got to kiss her before he went back to camp, but that was all.

On May 28, the 1st Division mounted the first American assault of the war: they attacked the town of Cantigny, which the Germans had taken in their March offensive, and drove the enemy a half mile or so out of town to the east; they then hung on through three days of savage counterattacks, until the Germans were forced to accept the fact that the town was lost. During that fighting Langrock vanished in a direct hit from a heavy mortar, Pinzner had a leg torn off at the knee by a shell splinter, and Bradley suffered a dislocated jaw from grinding his teeth in terror. Nick was unscathed, and came out of the ordeal feeling that he was protected by some benign force; if he'd lived through that, he thought, he was going to live through anything.

His luck deserted him not quite two months later. On July 20 at Buzancy, on the road between Soissons and Château-Thierry, a machine gun stitched him through the legs and lower abdomen, and he lay by the roadside for an hour before the stretcher bearers could reach him. He was taken first to a dressing station, then to a field hospital, and finally to a large hospital in Paris, where his abdominal wounds could be treated. It was October before the drains were taken out, and early November before he could walk.

Marie visited him every Sunday while he was in the hospital, and gradually her reserve began to thaw. He found out that she alternated her duties at the restaurant with work at an Army clothing depot; that her father was a retired professor of classics at the Sorbonne and her mother worked in a munitions factory; that her brother had been killed at Verdun and her fiancé at the Aisne; and that she had determined not to become attached to any man until the war was over. She saw no sense, she said, in making herself a target for any more grief than she'd already experienced. Nick pointed out that the war was sure to be over soon, and that he was unlikely to be sent back to the front, and she replied that she'd listen to him when an armistice was signed, and not before.

With the grudging permission of his commanding officer they were married November 18, and two days later Nick was shipped back to the States on a hospital ship, the transformed liner *France.* Marie had to wait three months before she could obtain passage.

5

Nick got home the first week in December, to find New York still wallowing in its post-Armistice euphoria. Service men were celebrities wherever they went, and nothing was too good for them—especially the ones who'd been wounded—until it came down to such practical matters as finding housing or a job. Then the prospective employers would clear their throats, talk about inflation and recession and the overcrowded job market, and end with pious pronouncements about how everything possible would be done, while the landlords muttered about the cost of fuel and the necessity of raising rents, and cited the influenza epidemic as the reason for the shortage of low-cost housing. Nick remarked at one point that if a half million Americans had died of the flu, then it should follow that there was that much more housing available, but his argument was brushed aside as showing ignorance of the law of supply and demand. It took him a while to come to the conclusion that all the talk about help for the veterans was just that, and anything that was done for him would have to be done by himself.

Approximately a year earlier, on December 18, 1917, the Eighteenth Amendment to the Constitution, banning the manufacture, sale, and transportation of intoxicating liquors, was submitted to the various states by Congress, and on January 16, 1919, it was ratified by Nebraska, the thirty-sixth and final state necessary for its passage into law. It was to take effect one year from that date, and there was general rejoicing among the members of the Women's Christian Temperance Union, the Anti-Saloon League, those wives who felt their husbands spent too much of their paychecks in saloons, and those industrialists who felt their productivity was hurt by "Blue Monday" absenteeism. The most starry-eyed backers of Prohibition maintained that it would wipe out poverty, disease, crime, insanity, and degeneracy, and that the nation's jails, asylums, and poorhouses could be turned into playgrounds for happy children. Such was the general belief in this tooth-fairy credo that twenty-seven states were dry in 1917, and several others had local-option laws allowing communities to decide whether to be wet or dry. The ratification of the Eighteenth Amendment was, at first blush, considered to be a good thing for the country, and most of the grumbling came from the distillers, brewers, and saloonkeepers.

Nick finally managed to get a job as a waiter in the restaurant where his mother made the pasta, but it was a stop-gap arrangement and served only to bring in a little money until he could find something else. One day, when he was setting up the restaurant's six tables for the evening meal, an old friend named Frank DiMotto came in, and they greeted each other warmly. Nick still walked with a slight limp, and DiMotto noticed this and said, "I heard you got yourself wounded. That's a damn shame."

"I was lucky," Nick replied. "You should have seen some of the others."

"Yeah, I guess so. Is the *padrone* in?"

"He's at home. He says he's got the flu, but I know a hangover when I see one. Can I do anything for you?"

"Well–" DiMotto hesitated, then said, "I want to know what kind of arrangements he wants to make about–you know–the future."

"What do you mean?"

"When this goddam Prohibition starts. Will he still want to get his wine, or what?"

"Are you in the business?"

"Yeah. I thought you knew."

"I've been away."

"I'm a general liquor salesman, and I'm here to tell you I'm going to be up shit creek unless I can work out an arrangement with some of my customers."

"How'll you do it?"

"I don't know. But I've got to find out first who's interested, and then see what I can work out. It's such a goddam stupid law they're never going to be able to enforce it."

"Is wine included too?"

"Everything's included–wine, beer, you name it."

"Well, I'll ask him. When do you need to know?"

"As soon as possible. This kind of thing is going to take organization."

When, some time later, Nick relayed the message, the *padrone* said he'd have to give it some thought, and there the matter rested. He was a large man, who did everything slowly, and nothing could ever hurry him. He pointed out that the law would not take effect for almost a year, and that any number of things could happen in that time. Take it easy, he advised Nick, and you'll live longer. He died of a stroke in August, and his widow took over the restaurant and fired Nick forthwith, claiming she was going to have to cut down on expenses.

Marie had arrived the end of March, and she and Nick were living in his room in his parents' flat. It was a situation that was only barely tolerable, and when Nick lost his job he decided the time had come to make a complete change. Go somewhere else, try something different–anything, so long as it got him out of the rut he thought he'd escaped when he joined the Army.

"We could start a restaurant," Marie suggested one night, when they were sitting on the fire escape to avoid the strangling heat of the flat. "Between us, we must know how to do it."

"We know enough," Nick replied, "but we don't have the money. It takes a lot of dough to start a restaurant, and without liquor I don't know how we'd make it go."

"What do you mean, without liquor?"

"You haven't heard about Prohibition?"

"No."

"Next January, there will be no more liquor sold in this country." He paused, and added, "Legally, that is."

"Well, you don't need liquor for a restaurant. Wine will be enough. People can't taste the food if they have been drinking whisky."

"No wine, either."

"No wine? *Mais, c'est impossible! C'est idiot, ça! C'est barbare!*"

He spread his hands. "That's the law."

"But will anyone obey it?"

"That remains to be seen."

"I cannot believe it. You might as well make–make loving illegal."

"I agree, but–well, we'll see."

"What will we see?"

"I have a friend who may be able to help." Nick had just remembered his talk with Frank DiMotto, and it occurred to him that DiMotto might be a possible partner, in view of his connections with the liquor business and the fact that he probably had access to a certain amount of money. He left a note at DiMotto's home, asking him to be in touch, and a few days later they met in a saloon on Second Avenue.

"I'm sorry about your job," DiMotto said. "That old bitch buried her husband on what she saved by firing you."

"It must have been a shallow grave," Nick replied. "She wasn't paying me enough to bury a hot dog."

DiMotto ordered two glasses of Cinzano, and said, "What's on your mind?"

"This and that," said Nick. "How would you like to be a partner in a restaurant?"

DiMotto was quiet for a moment. "What kind of a restaurant?" he asked.

"A small one."

"Selling liquor?"

"Probably."

"Where's the money come from?"

Nick cleared his throat. "Well, if you could lend me some while we get started," he said, "then I could pay it back in work, and once I got it paid back then we could be partners. And it occurred to me that maybe one of your suppliers might like an outlet, so to speak."

"Who'd do the cooking?"

"Marie worked in a restaurant in Paris. She's a hell of a cook."

"You mean just you and Marie would be the staff?"

"At first, yes. All we need is the place–and the money to get started."

DiMotto was quiet again. "I'll think it over and let you know," he said.

"That's all I can ask," said Nick, and finished his Cinzano. "This next round's on me."

"One thing you gotta learn, if you're going to run a restaurant," DiMotto said, "is the house never buys. The customer pays for everything, including his hat, when he steps through the front door."

"I'm not the house yet," Nick replied, and gestured to the barman for another round.

In October, Congress passed the Volstead Act, which provided for the enforcement of Prohibition and which defined intoxicating liquor as anything with an alcoholic content of more than 0.5 per cent; President Wilson vetoed it, and it passed over his veto and became law on January 17, 1920, the day after the Eighteenth Amendment took effect. Almost immediately, people began to look for ways to circumvent the law, and the violations were so widespread that the authorities could offer no more than a token show of enforcement. The law had spawned an industry that would grow over the next thirteen years until it became the largest single operation in the country; bootlegging and gang warfare and organized crime were a part of the national scene, all as a result of an act that was designed to empty the nation's jails, asylums, and poorhouses. A secondary result was that the nation's drinking habits changed: the profit margin on wine and beer was not fat enough to interest the bootleggers, so hard liquor was the drink, and those who were able to enjoy the lower-proof beverages were those who made their own. Those with access to grain alcohol and juniper could, of course, make their own gin in their bathtubs (the porcelain kept the taste pure), but the penalty for getting wood instead of grain alcohol was either death or blindness, and a person had to have the utmost confidence in his supplier.

At first it looked as though Nick's restaurant idea was doomed; there was a sudden shortage of basement facilities, and the price for an inconspicuous location rose beyond the bounds of sanity. Then one day, when he and DiMotto were sitting in the back room of a restaurant, DiMotto said, "I think I may have a lead on something." DiMotto had clearly come on good times; he wore a double-breasted tan suit, and smoked a cigar with his coffee.

"What is it?" Nick asked. "Does it look good?"

"It's not very big," DiMotto replied. "In fact, it's only one room, but it might do as a starter."

"What's the kitchen like?"

DiMotto paused. "There isn't any kitchen, as such," he said. "It's just a small alcove off the room. But the beauty of it is that—"

"That would never do for Marie," Nick cut in. "She can't cook in a coat closet."

"Well, the cooking might have to wait. She could do sandwiches, and things like that. The beauty of this is it's rent free. Everything you take in is so much gravy."

"How come?"

"It belonged to a guy who–uh–defaulted on a debt. It's all free and clear."

"In whose name?"

"It's in the company's, but I can get it. The thing is, it's a place to start. We serve good booze, and have a homey atmosphere, and pretty soon people will be fighting to get in. Once we get a little cushion, we can move someplace with a kitchen."

"I'll talk it over with Marie and see what she thinks."

"You talk things over with her? You don't just tell her?"

"If she's going to be the cook, she ought to have some say in where she works."

DiMotto shook his head. "You're spoiling her," he said. "First thing you know, you're going to have an American wife on your hands. Now they've got the vote, there's no telling what they'll want next."

Nick smiled. "I'll take my chances."

Marie was not enthusiastic, but when Nick convinced her that it was just a temporary arrangement, she finally agreed. "It's just until we make a little money," he told her. "After two, three months we should be able to get a bigger place."

"I don't want a big place," Marie replied. "I just want a place where I can cook."

"And you'll have it–I promise you."

"What am I to do in this *boîte?*"

"Frank said it would be good for making sandwiches."

She thought a moment, then shrugged. "There are sandwiches and sandwiches," she said, and let the matter drop.

The room had once been a grocery store, and the alcove in back had been where the proprietor kept his cash box and records, and it also had a gas ring on which it was possible to make coffee. There was an icebox and a rudimentary toilet, and that was about all. Nick and DiMotto removed the vegetable bins, and procured chairs and tables, while Marie made curtains to cover the front window and did what she could to brighten up the general decor. She also curtained off the alcove, and put a shade on the naked light bulb that hung by the toilet, and suggested to the men that candles be put on the individual tables, rather than trying to light the whole room by electricity. The effect, when they were finally done, was of an intimate wine cellar, and she suggested they call it *La Cave Intime*.

"Not enough people know French," Nick replied. "They wouldn't know what it meant."

"It sounds like 'The Cave in Time,'" DiMotto added.

"Also, I think we should be a club," Nick said. "If we're going to let some people in and keep some others out, we ought at least to call ourselves a club."

"Why keep some people out?" Marie asked. "Why not let everyone in?"

"Because there are some people who make trouble," Nick said. "And one thing we don't need is any troublemakers." As an afterthought, he added, "Furthermore, if it's known that some people aren't let in, then more people will *try* to get in, because that makes it sound exclusive."

"Would you please say that again?" Marie said. "I must have missed a word somewhere."

"You didn't miss anything," he replied. "It's what's called snob appeal."

She shook her head. "I have a lot to learn about America," she said.

"Just think of a name for the club," Nick said. "Something that will be easy to remember but won't be too specific."

"Specific about what?"

"Well, we can't very well call it the Booze Club," he replied. "That kind of specific."

"Then call it the *cheval de Troie,*" she said. "You know–that wooden horse the Greeks left in front of *Troie.*"

"You mean the Trojan Horse?" Nick said, and she nodded. He thought a moment, and then said, "That's not bad. It's got a kind of sneaky feeling that I like."

"I don't," said DiMotto. "Horses drive me crazy. My father was a white wing."

"We wouldn't have a real horse, for God's sake," Nick said. "This would just be the name of the club."

"Furthermore, it doesn't say it's a club. If you say Trojan Horse Club it sounds like a club for horses, and if you say Club Trojan

Horse it sounds just plain crazy. I say think of something else."

"What about the Club Foot?" said Nick.

DiMotto grinned. "Nertz to you," he said.

"*Qu's'qu' veut dire* nertz?" Marie asked.

"Well," said Nick, "it's Brooklyn for 'nuts.' "

"Like *noisettes?*"

"Not exactly. Think of another kind."

"*Amandes?*"

"No. I saw it on a menu in Paris once. I think they called it *animelles.*"

"Oh!" Marie put her hand to her mouth, looked at DiMotto, and blushed.

"It's the latest expression," DiMotto said. "Don't take it too literally."

"This isn't getting the club named," Nick said. "Unless, of course, we want to call it the Club Nertz."

"What about the Club *Circé?*" Marie suggested. "There is a sort of *double entendre* there."

"I don't get it."

"*Circé* was the enchantress in *l'Odyssée,* who turned men into swine."

"Where do you get all these ancient references? Were you a Greek scholar, or something?"

"No, but my father was a professor. He used to read us the myths at bedtime."

Nick thought about the name. "Not many people would recognize it," he said.

"*Tant mieux*. It could be our little joke."

"I kind of like it," DiMotto said. "It's different, it's short, and it's easy to remember."

So they decided to call it the Club Circe and see what happened. They opened in April, at a time when many colleges were having spring vacation, and there was a big influx of students determined to test the new law. The Club Circe was ostensibly a tearoom—that is, the liquor was served in teacups—and there was always a platter of sandwiches available for those who needed solid nourishment. Marie's first sandwiches were simply baguettes, which had been split lengthwise and filled with either ham or cheese, but after a while she began to vary the menu, adding chicken, sausage, salami, and home-made pâté. The college group seemed to enjoy themselves, and there was a good deal of singing and ad-lib dancing not usually associated with the run-of-the-mill tearoom. Nick had cards printed, giving the club's name and address, and possession of one of these cards was all that was necessary for admission. A tray of cards stood at the door, so that departing customers could take one, and while it was theoretically possible for a card to fall into the wrong hands, none seemed to, and the first few weeks of the club's existence were unmarred by any unpleasant incident.

Then, one night, Nick opened the door and two obviously noncollegiate types came in. One was short and stocky, and had shoulders that seemed to begin at his ears, while the other was taller and thinner, and had a scar that ran from his forehead down to his cheek, narrowly missing one eye. "What can I do for you?" Nick asked, not moving aside.

"We'd like a little talk with you," said the taller one.

"About what?" Nick still didn't move.

"We come to give you protection."

"From what?"

"From accidents."

"Thanks, I don't need it."

"Lucky thinks you do."

"Who's Lucky?"

"You must be new around here. Lucky Livorno. He'll guarantee you don't have no accidents. Otherwise . . ."

"I told you I don't need it. Now, if you'll excuse me, I'm busy."

"You're being very stupid, pal."

"We'll see. Now, please. This is a private club, and only members are welcome. Do you mind?" Nick realized he was unconsciously imitating the inflections of some of the collegians, and as he ushered the two men out he said, "Thanks awfully, anyway," and closed the door.

A few hours later, when he and Marie were making their way home through the darkened, empty streets, two shapes appeared from an alley ahead of them; one of them grabbed Marie and clamped a hand over her mouth before she could scream more than once, while the other, the shorter one, took a cut at Nick. It triggered a reflex in Nick that brought back all his months of combat training; he shot a straight-fingered chop to the Adam's apple, then a kick to the groin, and, as the man fell and his knife clattered on the pavement, Nick aimed another kick that was supposed to hit the temple, but the man rolled and Nick's foot crashed into his mouth. Nick then spun on the man who was holding Marie, dug a thumb into one eye, pulled the man's arm backward and twisted it until he heard the joint crack. The man screamed and fell away, and Nick retrieved the knife. He crouched, shifting the knife from hand to hand, and only then did he realize that every move he'd made had been automatic; he'd done it all without so much as a single thought, and had stopped short of killing them only because he'd suddenly become aware of Marie, who was standing in a doorway, screaming. He straightened up, threw the knife in the gutter, and went to her.

"It's O.K.," he said. "You can take it easy."

"Take it easy?" she replied, her voice rising. "Take it EASY? Those *salauds* were trying to kill you!"

"No, they weren't," he said, holding her by the arm. "They were just trying to frighten me." As they turned toward home he added, "And, come to think of it, they did. They almost made me a murderer."

Two days later the bell rang in the early afternoon, when Marie had gone home for a nap and Nick was the only one on the premises. He went to the door, which had a chain guard, and when he opened it found himself staring into the barrel of a .32-caliber pistol. "Open the door," a voice said. "Take off the chain." Nick obeyed, and a man wearing a gray fedora hat and Chesterfield coat came in, still holding the gun on Nick, and with the other hand closed the door behind him. Nick thought briefly of leaping for the gun and wresting it away, then decided against it. He kept his hands hanging loosely at his sides. "Sit down," the man said, and Nick turned and walked to a table and sat down. The man followed, but remained standing on the other side of the table. "You think you're pretty good with your mitts, don't you?" he said.

"I get along," Nick replied. "I take it you're Livorno."

"Mister Livorno to you. Most people call me Lucky, but to you I'm Mister."

"I'll tell you something, Livorno," Nick said. "You think you can scare me with a lousy .32-caliber pistol, and you're–" He was interrupted by an explosion and a dart of flame from the pistol, and a candle on the table behind him shattered. "You're wrong," Nick continued, his ears ringing, "and I'll tell you why. A .32 is chickenshit compared to some of the things I've had shot at me. You want to know–" Another explosion, and another candle shattered. "You want to know what a Maxim machine gun sounds like when it's shooting at you? Most of the time it's just a clatter, but when it's shooting straight at you there are little flashes of yellow, and it goes BAMBAMBAMBAMBAMBAMBAMBAMBAM! You hear a noise like that, and you get your ass into the ground. And then–" One more shot from the pistol, and one more candle destroyed. "Honest to God, Livorno, you're getting to be a bore with that thing . . . Then there's the heavy mortar; that's the worst, because you can't hide from it. It sails high in the air, and then comes down, down, down, down, ker-BLAM! and you know what it does? It blows you straight out of your clothes. You see bits of naked bodies in the trees, or plastered against a house, and bits of shredded clothing here and there, smoking a little from the explosion. I saw a nice young kid get hit by one of those, and he just vanished, right off the face of the earth. We later found little pieces of him–a shoe in one place, a bit of gut in another–but we never collected enough of him to bury. And now you come around, all full of balls because you've got a .32 in your hand, and think you're going to make me cringe. You are out of your fucking mind, and the sooner you realize it the better. And you can thank whatever it is that gets you called Lucky that my wife isn't here, because she would make you sweep up every last bit of those candles you broke. To sum up the bad news, Livorno, you're not as tough as you think you are, and you'll do yourself and everyone else a favor if you stop cluttering up the place. Now, get out." Livorno hesitated, the pistol barrel wavering, and Nick said, "I said get out. You're lowering the tone of the joint." Livorno turned and went out, slamming the door behind him.

Nick didn't tell Marie about the episode because he didn't want to worry her, and he felt sure he'd never see Livorno again.

He had a different kind of visitor the following week. It was late afternoon, and about a half dozen customers were drinking their Scotch in teacups, when the buzzer sounded and Nick admitted a red-faced, beefy man wearing a blue serge suit, a heavy watch chain with an elk's-tooth pendant, and square-toed black shoes. The word "police" was written all over him, but he displayed one of the club's cards and seemed in a congenial mood, so Nick didn't challenge him. He simply said, "Come in," then closed the door and rechained it.

The man looked around the room and said, "Is there someplace we can talk?"

"About what?" Nick asked cautiously.

"This and that."

"Anything you have to say, you can say right here," Nick replied. "Nobody's going to shoot their mouth off."

The man glanced at the other customers, who were loudly telling one another the same things they'd been saying for the last half hour. They were oblivious to everything else, so he said, "All right," and moved toward a table. Nick followed him, and they both sat down.

"Let's start with your name," Nick said. "Mine's Nick Baldino."

"I know," the man replied. "Mine's McGinty. Lieutenant Aloysius McGinty, Fourteenth Precinct." Nick stiffened, and McGinty went on, "No need to worry–this is a social call. Do you have a drop of something in a teacup to wet an old man's whistle?"

Nick hesitated, then stood up. "What would you like? We have Scotch, Bourbon, or gin."

"Bourbon, if you don't mind. Did you ever think of stocking Irish whisky?"

"There's not that much call for it," Nick said, and went into the alcove. He returned in a moment with a teacup of Bourbon and a chunk of ice, and set it in front of McGinty, then sat down. "Now," he said. "What was it you wanted to talk about?"

McGinty raised his teacup in salute, took a sip, and said, "That's good Bourbon. First rate."

"Thank you," said Nick. "We try to oblige."

"What I was wondering," McGinty said, "was why I haven't seen you around the station. Most of the lads, when they start up a store like this, come around the precinct and make what you might call arrangements, guaranteeing that they're not molested by the law. We'd heard you'd opened up, and we wondered if you had some religious scruples, or something, that was keeping you away."

"I'll be honest with you and say I never thought of it," Nick replied. "I'm new at all this, and it just never occurred to me. I got some pressure from Livorno and his thugs, but I didn't think of the other."

"I'd heard about that," McGinty said. "He swears he's going to get even, but I think the odds are he's a bag of wind."

"He doesn't worry me," said Nick. "As for the–ah–arrangements with the police, we just don't have the money to spread around. Maybe by Christmas we will, but right now I'm working for nothing, so as to pay back my share of the business. Every nickel we take in is already spoken for."

"I can understand that," McGinty said. "These are trying times."

"Let me put it this way," Nick said. "We'll be glad to serve you or any of your men who come in here in civilian clothes, and at Christmas we'll come up with whatever size present we can afford. How does that sound?"

"Nothing could be fairer than that." McGinty finished his drink, and reached in his pocket. "What do I owe you for your excellent Bourbon?"

"My partner told me never to buy anyone a drink," Nick replied, "but I think for this occasion we can say it's on the house."

"That's very gracious of you."

"My pleasure." McGinty rose to leave, and Nick said, "By the way, how did you get our card?"

McGinty smiled. "One of the lads was in here a few days back," he said. "He picked up a card on the way out."

"Who was he?"

McGinty's smile broadened. "From the plainclothes squad," he said. "If I gave away his identity, he'd be dead in a week."

The next day, when Nick and Marie came to open up the place, they found a brown paper bag by the door, and in it was a bottle of Bushmills Irish whisky.

6

The first snow of the winter fell on December 8, 1920, which was unusually early for New York. The sky had been overcast all morning, and there was a sharpness in the air that made people turn up their coat collars and walk a little faster; then, around noon, the scattered flakes began to fall, sparsely at first but finally in a steady, heavy mass that whitened the sidewalks and blurred the outlines of the buildings. Office lights came on, and the sounds of traffic were muted by the accumulating blanket. It was Wednesday, and the theatre district became a tangle of wet and skidding people trying to get to matinees.

At the Club Circe three customers, who had had a lunch of pâté sandwiches and Scotch, paid their check and put on their coats, and when Nick unchained the door to let them out they saw the snow, and stopped.

"Hell," one of them said, "there's no point trying to get back to the office in this. We'll die in a snowdrift before we've gone two blocks."

"I've got a meeting this afternoon," another said. "I ought to take a stab at it."

"Call 'em and tell 'em you can't make it," said the first. "Tell 'em the wolves chased your droshky up to Tuckahoe, and you can't get back."

"What the hell, it's worth a try," the second man said, and turned to Nick. "May I use the telephone?" he asked.

"Sure," said Nick. "It's in the back room." He started to close the door, then saw a small, snow-covered man approaching. He wore a bowler hat and an overcoat with the collar turned up, and on his feet were a gleaming pair of rubbers, obviously new. He hurried toward the door, and Nick opened it but stood in the way, waiting for identification. The man looked faintly familiar, but he couldn't tell from where.

"My name is Hopkins," the man said, with a toothy smile. "Albert Hopkins. I've been here before."

"That's right," Nick said, and stood aside to let him in.

Hopkins entered, brushing the snow from his clothes; he hung his hat and coat on a rack and, sitting down, removed his rubbers. He glanced briefly at the others, then took a table by himself, sitting with his back to the wall. "May I have a Scotch, please?" he said.

"Coming right up," Nick replied, and went into the back room. The man on the telephone was apparently having a little trouble getting a convincing message across.

"Just tell him I won't be at the meeting," he was saying. "Tell him my taxi skidded in the snow . . . No, it's nothing serious . . . I just think I ought not to . . . No, I'm not in the hospital, I'm . . . Look, will you do me a favor? Just tell him I'll see him tomorrow. I'll explain then." He hung up, and wiped his forehead. "Let's have another round," he said to Nick.

Nick filled four teacups with Scotch and ice, put them on a tray, and went into the main room. He gave the three men theirs, then went to the table where Hopkins was sitting. Hopkins had taken a small, thin book from his overcoat pocket and was reading. "Thank you," he said, when Nick put the Scotch in front of him, and then, seeing that Nick was looking at the book, "Do you know Robert Frost?"

"Not personally," Nick replied. "I don't think he's ever been in here."

"He's a poet," said Hopkins. "And an extraordinary one. Listen to this." He held the book up slightly, and read: " 'I'd like to get away from earth awhile / And then come back to it and begin over.' Don't you think that's a marvelous idea?"

"Probably," Nick replied. "Are you a poet?"

"No, I work on Wall Street. Then he goes on: 'May no fate willfully misunderstand me / And half grant that I wish and snatch me away / Not to return. Earth's the right place for love: / I don't know where it's likely to go better.' I think that man really has something."

"What is it you do on Wall Street?" Nick asked.

"Investment banking."

"Do they close down when it snows?"

"No, no. I'm just taking a little breather." He sipped his Scotch, turned a page, and went back to his reading.

The other three men, invigorated by the idea of an afternoon off, were discussing the various possibilities that lay ahead of them. The one who'd just called his office said, "You know what I've always wanted to do? I've always wanted to take a horse and sleigh through Central Park. Up hill, down dale, jingle bells, jingle bells, jingle all the way– Let's go up to the Plaza and rent a sleigh."

"They won't have the sleighs out yet," said the man who'd been first to speak. "It's only just started to snow. You need anyway a good six inches before a sleigh's any good."

"That's a lotta banana oil," said the third man. "You can sleigh on an inch and a half of snow."

"Says who?"

"Says me. My grandfather had a sleigh could run on an inch of snow, if it was packed flat."

"On a lake, maybe. Try that in Central Park and your grandfather'd split his noggin on a rock."

"There's a lake in Central Park, isn't there?"

"I know what let's do," said the man who should have been at a meeting. "Let's take one of those excursion boats to the Statue of Liberty. That ought to be a hell of a sight in the snow."

"Are you sure they're running?" said the first man.

"No, but we could find out." He turned to Nick and said, "May I use the phone again?"

"Go right ahead," said Nick, just as the buzzer sounded, and he went to the door and admitted Marie, who'd been shopping. The shawl over her head was stiff with snow, and snow covered her shoulders, arms, and market basket. Snow lay like diamond dust on her eyelashes.

"*J'suis gelée,*" she said, beating her clothes. "Do we have any cognac?"

"I can make you a hot toddy," Nick replied. "You want it with Scotch or Bourbon?"

"I don't care, so long as it's hot." She took off her outer clothes and hung them up, and went on, "The man at the French market said we should stock up on food. He said this might be a real *tempête de neige*."

"A what?" said Nick.

"What is your word? Gizzard?"

"Blizzard."

"Well, he said we should have plenty of supplies."

She took her market basket into the back room, and Nick followed to heat the water for the toddy. The man at the telephone sounded as though he were about to have a stroke. "Listen, Central," he was saying, "it's that big statue out in the harbor! There's *got* to be a number for it! I've looked under S and I've looked under L, and I've . . ." The line apparently went dead, and he jiggled the hook a few times, then hung up the receiver. "For crying out loud," he said. "If that isn't the payoff!"

"Trouble?" Nick asked.

"Nobody seems to have heard of the Statue of Liberty," the man said in disgust.

"Did you try the Department of Parks?"

The man's eyes widened. "You're a genius!" he said, and picked up the receiver.

There was the sound of the doorbell, and as Nick came out of the back room he heard one of the other two men saying, "I want to tell you, Morris, that Jackie Coogan will break your heart. And when they team him up with Charlie Chaplin, you got a combination that's worth a million dollars. That little kid—that's what they call the picture, *The Kid*—with his ragged little cap all cockeyed on his head" —his voice broke and went up a half octave—"I want to tell you, it just tears your heart apart!" He took a handkerchief out of his pocket and blew his nose.

"Sounds like a kind of a gloomy picture," said the first man.

"It's not gloomy—it's beautiful! It's got all the beauty of love, and bravery, and little children, and Jesus Christ, Morris, I tell you you shouldn't miss it!"

Nick opened the door and saw a young man with a slightly elfin face, wearing a cloth cap and an olive-drab Army greatcoat, with the collar turned up around his ears. "I'm George MacDougall," he said. "I was here with Fred McClain."

"Oh, yes," said Nick, and unchained the door. "Come in." MacDougall came into the room, took off his hat and coat, and looked for a place to hang them. "I'll take them," Nick said, noticing that MacDougall was wearing a bronze service button in his lapel. "What outfit were you with?" he asked.

"Second Division," MacDougall replied. "Ninth Regiment."

"I was in the First," Nick said. "Sixteenth Infantry."

"The Big Red One," said MacDougall. "Were you at Cantigny?"

"Uh-huh. And at Soissons."

"Son of a bitch. That must have been rough."

"I didn't make it all the way through Soissons. A machine gunner did some hemstitching on me."

"You look all right now."

"He was shooting low. What'll you have?"

"Scotch, please." MacDougall looked around and took the table next to Hopkins, and Nick went into the back room. Marie was putting away the groceries and sandwich materials she'd bought, while the water for her toddy simmered on the gas ring. The man on the telephone seemed to be talking into an empty cave.

"Hello, Park Department?" he shouted. "Is this the Department of Parks? . . . I asked Central to give me the Department of Parks . . . Well, actually, I don't want a park, I want the Statue of Liberty . . . I'm not trying to *buy* it—I want to *go* there! . . . Battery Park? . . . Oh, the subway? . . . Look, you can't take a subway to the Statue of Liberty . . . All right, then what can I do? . . . What I want to know is, is the boat running? . . . You don't know? You don't KNOW? Then who does know?" He turned to Nick and said, "Let's have another round, can we?" and when Nick nodded the man went back to his telephone conversation.

Nick made a toddy for Marie and four Scotches; he gave one to the man on the telephone, then took two to the men at the table, and as he put the cups down the one named Morris was saying, "I was just a little shaver at the time, maybe six or seven, and I was wearing a little red tippet, which is what saved my life. I fell in this snow bank, and all that showed of me was the end of my scarf . . ." Nick moved on, put MacDougall's Scotch in front of him, then turned to Hopkins, who was quietly reading his book.

"Can I get you another?" he asked.

Hopkins looked up, as though he'd forgotten where he was, and glanced into his teacup. "No, thank you," he said. "I still have a bit left." He went back to his reading.

"Will you join me?" MacDougall said to Nick, and Nick pulled out a chair and sat down. "Have a drink?" MacDougall asked.

"Thanks just the same," Nick replied. "It's a little early."

"This is a nice place you have here. Do you own it?"

"No. I have a partner."

"You don't need another, do you?"

"Partner?" Nick laughed. "Not unless you've got a lot of money to invest."

"I was thinking of making money, not putting it up."

"We're just beginning. We haven't started to break even yet."

"Well, it never hurt to ask."

"What do you do?"

"At the moment, nothing. I'm trying to get a job on a newspaper, but so far I haven't convinced them I'm worth it."

"Did you have a job before the war?"

"Yeah, but it was on a small-town paper upstate. That doesn't seem to count for anything."

"I know what you mean. The only job I could get when I got out was waiter in a spaghetti house. I wouldn't have got that if my mother hadn't made the spaghetti."

MacDougall laughed. "Nothing's too good for our brave Doughboys," he said. "I hear they're going to give us a bonus, but I'll bet most of us are dead of old age before we get it."

"I wouldn't be surprised. When we were at Soulaucourt, there–"

"My God, were you at Soulaucourt?"

"Hell, yes. We trained there, ten goddam months."

"We went back there, after Blanc Mont. We were supposed to go to Souilly, but some dizzy bastard got the orders wrong, and we wound up at Soulaucourt."

Nick laughed and said, "Did you stay there long?"

"Only long enough to turn around. Longest goddam march I ever made, and me with a hangover you could fire out of a gun."

"I remember one time we–" Nick was interrupted by one of the men from the other table, who asked for their check, and he said, "Excuse me," and got up and went into the back room. The man on the telephone was by now a little hoarse.

"Is this the Mayor's office?" he was saying. "I want to speak to the Mayor . . . That's right. And nobody else . . . It's about the Statue of Liberty . . . I said the Statue of Liberty . . ."

Nick added up the bill and took it to the table, where one man was saying, "I tell you, Morris, if you haven't seen *The Kid* you haven't lived. It's a picture you absolutely gotta see, especially since what happened to you. This Jackie Coogan is . . ."

Nick went back to MacDougall's table and said, "Now. Where were we?"

"Something about Soulaucourt," MacDougall replied.

Nick thought a moment, then said, "Well, I guess it couldn't have been important. I haven't talked Army in so long my stories are all confused."

"I have the same trouble." MacDougall finished his drink and set the cup down.

"Would you like another?" Nick asked.

"Uh . . . I guess I'd better not."

"You need something against the cold. You're not due anywhere, are you?"

"No, but . . . Well, to be honest with you, I can't afford it. Until I get some steady kind of job, I'm walking a very thin wire."

Nick took a deep breath, remembered DiMotto's advice, and said the hell with it. "Pay me when you can," he said. "There's no rush about these things."

"I thought you weren't breaking even."

"We're not, but a buck or two here and there isn't going to make any difference."

MacDougall smiled. "Thank you," he said. "In that case, I would like one."

Nick stood up. "How about a sandwich, too? Marie makes a very superior sandwich."

"Yes, please."

At that point the other two men rose from their table and began to get into their coats. As Nick let them out, the one named Morris was saying, "This is just like the snow we had when I was a little kid. Did I ever tell you about the time I fell in a snowdrift? I was just a little shaver at the time, and . . ."

Nick chained the door behind them, picked up the money and the empty cups from the table, and looked at Hopkins. "Is there anything I can get you?" he asked.

"No, thank you," Hopkins replied, not looking up.

Nick went into the back room, where Marie was sipping her toddy while she arranged the material for sandwiches. "Feeling any warmer?" he asked.

"Much, thank you," she replied.

"We've got an order for one sandwich. He didn't specify, so give him a little of everything."

"That's a full meal."

"I know. That's what I meant." Nick put the money in the cash box and poured another Scotch.

The man at the telephone shouted, "And that goes for you too!" into the mouthpiece, and slammed down the receiver. "All right," he said, picking up the directory. "I'll try just once more . . . Navy . . . Navy Yard . . . How do I find the Brooklyn Navy Yard?"

"Your pals just left," Nick told him.

"That's their worry," the man replied. "I'm going to get to the Statue of Liberty if it kills me."

The snow had apparently clogged traffic all over town, because very few people came that afternoon. MacDougall and Nick reminisced about the Army while MacDougall had his sandwich and another Scotch, and then MacDougall left, muttering something about finding a job shoveling snow. The man who wanted to get to the Statue of Liberty finally gave up, and when he had gone only Nick and Marie and Hopkins were left. They heard a snowplow rumble through the street outside, and the scraping of shovels on the sidewalk, and Nick figured that eventually, when the snow had stopped and the streets been cleared, business might pick up. He parted the front curtains a crack and saw a Sanitation crew out front, but by now it was dark and he was unable to make out any details. He closed the curtains and went back to Marie.

"I guess it wouldn't hurt to have a short one now," he said. "Can I get you something?"

"I wish we had some cognac," Marie replied. "Whisky gives me—what do you call it? Hot heart?"

"Heartburn," Nick said. "Then try some gin."

"Is it impossible to get wine?"

"No, but there's no point selling it. I can get some for you, if you'd like. My father makes it in the basement."

Marie made a gesture of regurgitation and said, "Then a small whisky, please."

"I'll get wine for you tomorrow," he said, as he poured two Scotches. Hopkins put his head through the curtain.

"I hope I'm not keeping you people up," he said.

"Not in the least," Nick replied. "We'll probably have a busy evening, as soon as the snow stops."

"Then I would like one more Scotch, and a ham sandwich if you have it. Then I'll be on my way."

"No hurry," said Nick, as Marie began to make the sandwich. "I gather your schedule is a flexible one."

"At the moment, yes. I've just finished the Frost book, and now I'd like to get into Edwin Arlington Robinson. I understand he has a new one out, called *The Three Taverns*. Did you know he worked in the Customs House, here in New York?"

"Ah–no," said Nick. "That's news to me."

"Back in 1905. Teddy Roosevelt liked his poems and got him this job."

"Seems like a strange job for a poet," said Nick, handing Hopkins his cup of Scotch.

"Well, it was better than what he'd been doing."

"I hope you don't mind me saying this, but for an investment banker you sure have a lot of outside interests."

Hopkins smiled. "Most of the time I'm like all the rest," he said. "Then, come the first snow"–a far-off look came into his eyes–"I just have to get away from it. I don't know what it is, but the first snow always makes me restless. I have to get out, and sort of wander."

"What do you tell your office?"

"They understand. Sometimes I'm gone for as much as three days, and nobody says anything. They know it's important to me, I guess. Or maybe they don't miss me. I've never been able to figure out which." He took a sip of his Scotch and watched Marie as she made the sandwich. "You do that awfully well," he said.

"Thank you, *m'sieur,*" she replied.

"Have you ever been up to Grant's Tomb?" Hopkins asked.

"I went up there once, as a kid," Nick said. "I don't think Marie's been north of Fourteenth Street."

"There's a little gravestone, just down the hill from the tomb. It says on it: 'Erected to the memory of an amiable child, St. Clair Pollock, died 15 July 1797 in the fifth year of his age.' I go up there often, but I've never seen it in the snow."

"You're not going up there tonight?" Nick said, incredulous.

"I don't know where I'm going tonight. I just let my feet lead me. But that ought to be quite a sight on a dark and snowy night."

Nick thought a moment, then said, "Are you married?"

Hopkins smiled again. "Define marriage and I'll tell you," he replied.

"Voilà, m'sieur," Marie said, handing him his sandwich. *"Bon appétit."*

"Thank you." He took the sandwich and the Scotch to a table, and as he sat down he said, "You know, this is quite the nicest place in town. There's a homey atmosphere that you don't find anywhere else . . . At least, anywhere that I've been."

"That's nice to hear," said Nick. "That's what we're trying to do."

Hopkins finished his sandwich and his Scotch, and no other customers appeared. Nick looked at his watch and saw that it was ten-thirty, a time when, most nights, the club was beginning to fill up. He concluded that the snow had clogged traffic all over town and people were staying home. It seemed incredible that *someone* wouldn't be out, but the fact remained that they might as well have been sealed in a tomb as far as any visitors were concerned. When, finally, Hopkins asked for his check, Nick thought seriously of closing the place and taking Marie home.

"You going up to Grant's Tomb now?" he asked, as he handed the bill to Hopkins.

"That'll all depend," Hopkins replied, taking out his wallet. "I don't like to commit myself too far in advance, because something better might always turn up." He put the money on the table, then retrieved his rubbers and, grunting slightly, bent over and snapped them onto his shoes. "I guess I should have worn galoshes," he said. "But when I started out I didn't think it was going to snow this much. I keep a pair of galoshes in my desk drawer, just in case, but today I thought if I bought a pair of rubbers that would be enough. It just goes to show." He put on his overcoat, slipped the volume of Frost into a pocket, then took his bowler hat off the rack. "This has been a real pleasure," he said, and they shook hands. He bowed to Marie, said, "My compliments on your sandwich," and as Nick unchained the door he put on his bowler, turned up his coat collar, and prepared to go forth into the night.

The door opened and revealed a solid wall of dirty snow, flat and seemingly as hard as concrete, which completely sealed off the exit.

"What in the hell—" Nick pressed against the snow but it was heavy and didn't move. He rushed to the front window and pulled the curtain all the way back, and by cupping his hands beside his eyes was able to look out and see that the Sanitation crew had apparently shoveled all the nearby snow into a mountain against the door to the club. "Those stupid sons of bitches!" Nick said, then realized it couldn't have been done by mistake; it was intentional, and had obviously been done at someone's orders. The pile was too big, and was put too specifically in front of his door, to have been an accident. Hopkins and Marie stared at the wall of snow, stunned into silence.

Nick went into the back room, picked up the telephone, and called the Fourteenth Precinct. "I want to speak to Lieutenant McGinty," he said, when the desk sergeant answered.

"About what?" the sergeant asked wearily.

"About the Sanitation Department blocking my door. I'm sealed in, and I can't get out."

"Call Sanitation," the sergeant said, and hung up.

Nick fluttered the hook, got the operator, and placed the call again. "God damn it, listen to me!" he said. "This is Nick Baldino, calling from the Club Circe, and I want to speak to Lieutenant McGinty!"

"Whyn't you say so?" the sergeant replied, and in a few moments McGinty came on the phone. Nick explained the situation and put forth his conclusion that it had been intentional.

"That bastard Livorno," McGinty muttered. "All right, we'll send someone around to dig you out."

"What's Livorno got to do with it?" Nick asked. "It was the Sanitation Department that dumped it on us."

"Yeah, I know. Sit tight, and we'll send a crew around."

McGinty hung up before Nick could pursue the subject any further, and after about ten minutes there came the sounds of men digging at the snow. It was a half hour before the first shovel broke through the doorway, scattering snow onto the floor. It was followed by a man wearing overalls, galoshes, and a policeman's cap, and then another, and a third, and in a few minutes the exit was clear.

"I want to thank you all," Nick said, as the three officers began to clean the floor. "We'd never have gotten out without you."

"That's all right," said the first man. "It's all in a night's work."

Nick paused, then said, "Do you consider yourselves in uniform?"

The officer looked at him for a long moment, then took off his cap and flung it through the door. "Not now, I don't," he said, and the other two did the same.

"Splendid," said Nick. "What'll you have–Scotch, Bourbon, or gin?" They all opted for Bourbon, and while Nick made the drinks Marie passed out some of the sandwiches she'd made.

A half hour later the first man drained his teacup, wiped his mouth, and pushed back from the table. "Whoever said a policeman's lot is not a happy one?" he said, with a broad smile. "Come on, lads, we'd best be getting back, or Nanny McGinty will be wondering what happened to us."

"He knows," said the second, stubbing out a cigarette. "I'm only surprised he didn't offer to lead us here."

"He thinks he's in line for captain," said the first. "He doesn't want to spoil his chances for promotion."

"If a character reference from me would help, I'd be glad to give one," Nick said, and everyone laughed. The officers were still laughing as they retrieved their caps from the snow, got in their truck, and drove off into the night.

7

Christmas Eve can be a lonely time in New York. People with distant relatives have left the city; those with families nearby are gathered in their homes; and the restaurants and theatres and public places are largely populated by the singles, the strays, and the unwanted. Theatre and movie box offices report more single seats sold than at any other time, and the police and hospitals are busy with those for whom the season is one of desperation rather than joy. Christmas Day can be just as bleak, but at least there is the knowledge that in another twenty-four hours life will return more or less to normal.

For Christmas Eve, Marie had made three *bûches de Noël,* long, cream-filled cakes, rolled and covered with chocolate icing to resemble Yule logs, and while a slice of *bûche de Noël* did not go particularly well with whisky or gin, it added a welcome air of festivity to the occasion. She had also tied red bows around the candlesticks and put sprigs of holly over the front curtain and a twig of mistletoe over the door, and she had persuaded Nick to concoct a punch made of rum (especially procured from DiMotto's bootlegger), hot tea, sliced fruits, and spices, a variation of a French Navy beverage known as *grog.* All in all, the Club Circe was as Christmassy as any of the department stores, and a great deal friendlier.

People began to arrive in the late afternoon, some having been doing last-minute shopping, others to get a stiff drink or two before boarding a train for the suburbs, and still others because they had no place else to go. The tables were soon filled, and people stood around as at a party, or between the acts at the theatre. As Nick moved through the room, dispensing drinks, he caught snatches of conversation: A man saying to the woman beside him, "My wife doesn't understand that I sometimes need time to myself," while a tall girl in a cloche hat said, "I admire short men–they have so much to put up with," and behind her one man said to another, "The thing I don't get is how you pin the goddam diaper without stabbing either yourself or the kid," while a woman shrieked with laughter and said, "Your grandmother warned me about you, but I didn't believe her!" "My grandmother talks too goddam much," a man growled, and a girl at one of the tables said, "I promised myself I'd never do it on a religious holiday."

Between tending the door and making the drinks Nick had more than he could handle, and Marie had to be pressed into service to help. Even then they were almost overwhelmed, and Nick decided that as soon as they could afford it they'd have to get a man to tend the door, or the bar, or both, and that would inevitably lead to a larger establishment. So long as the attendance was moderate they were all right, but as soon as the room became crowded they needed help and needed it badly.

By six o'clock all the commuters but one had gone; a short man, with a Chesterfield coat and a battered brown felt hat, was staring at a present he'd bought about which he'd had second thoughts and now was beginning to get cold feet. It was a black lace nightgown, with a transparent top and imitation rosebuds on the straps, and he kept picking it out of its tissue paper and asking people their opinion. "What do you think?" he said, holding it up for a bosomy girl who wore her hair in an unattractive Dutch bob. "Would you wear that if it was given to you?"

"Honey, I'd wear it all day if I could fit into it," she replied.

He turned it around and examined it for what might have been the fiftieth time. "I just don't know," he said. "People simply don't wear things like this in Red Bank."

"Your wife may love it," the girl said. "She may have wanted something like that all her life."

The man gave a hollow laugh, wrapped the nightgown loosely in the tissue paper, and crammed it back into its thin, flat box. "I'm afraid my position is hopeless," he said. "Hopeless, hopeless, hopeless." He caught Nick's eye and gestured for another drink.

Around eight o'clock Lieutenant McGinty arrived, in civilian clothes. He shook hands with Marie, and then with Nick, and in a low voice said, "The boys are all very appreciative of their Christmas present."

"I'm very appreciative of what they did for me," Nick replied. "I'm glad we were able to afford a present."

"And a very handsome one it was, speaking for myself."

"I'd like to talk to you sometime about Livorno," Nick said. "I was interested in what you said over the phone."

McGinty cleared his throat. "A slip of the tongue," he said. "Think nothing of it. Do you happen to have a spot of Irish whisky on the premises?"

Nick smiled. "It just so happens," he said, "we found a bottle of Irish a while back. I've been saving it for the right person."

"And very thoughtful of you, too," said McGinty. "I'll have just a dram and then be on my way. I have a lot of territory to cover tonight."

The next to arrive were George MacDougall and a short, dark-haired girl he introduced as Mrs. Peters. She was as wide-eyed as a child at its first party, and while she took in all that was going on she concentrated most of her attention on MacDougall. She seemed to melt a little every time she looked at him.

"Why are you being so nice to me?" she asked. "What can you possibly see in me that you don't see five times over, every day of the week?"

"I don't know you well enough to analyze it," MacDougall replied. "Just put it that there's a potential there that fascinates me. Will you settle for that right now?"

Her eyes turned moist, and she looked up at him from under her dark bangs. "Those are the sweetest words I've ever heard," she said. "I think I may cry."

"Don't for God's sake start crying," MacDougall said quickly. "We're here to have a good time."

"Oh, I can cry out of happiness just as well as sadness," she said. "I can cry at the drop of a hat."

"Well, try not to. People might get the wrong idea."

Her eyes moved away from him and came to rest on the man from Red Bank, who with one hand was clutching the torn Christmas wrapping around his package, while with the other he groped for a place to put his teacup. She looked at him for a moment, then said to MacDougall, "There is the perfect picture of Christmas gone wrong. I don't know what's happened to him, but I can tell he wishes he were dead. Should we ask him to have a drink?"

"Sure," said MacDougall. "Why not?"

She went to the man, who looked at her nervously, and said, "Excuse me, but Mr. MacDougall and I would like you to join us in a drink. Would you do us the honor?"

The man glanced at his watch, made a mental calculation, and said, "That's very kind of you. I ought to make a phone call first—may I join you in a couple of minutes?"

"Take all the time you want," said Mrs. Peters. "We're going to be here all evening."

She rejoined MacDougall and said, "He has to make a phone call. You know what I bet? I bet he's missed the last train for the country."

"How can you tell that?" said MacDougall.

"I don't know. He just has that look. He knows Christmas is shot, and he's trying to salvage what little he can by calling home. He makes me want to cry."

"Oh, no."

"It's when people are being brave that I really cry. That just dissolves me into a puddle."

"Maybe he isn't being brave—maybe he's being shifty and is lining up an assignation."

"Maybe, but it's not the way to bet."

Slowly the crowd began to thin out, as those who had someplace to go went wherever it was. The man from Red Bank joined Mrs. Peters and MacDougall for one drink and then hurried out into the night, still clutching his rumpled present under his arm, and as he was leaving Albert Hopkins came in, smiling and faintly glassy-eyed.

"Welcome!" Nick greeted him. "Did you go up to Grant's Tomb that night?"

Hopkins laid one finger alongside his nose in a gesture of secrecy. "I did even better," he said. He spotted the remains of a *bûche de Noël* on a table and picked up a slice and popped it in his mouth. He swallowed, paused a second, then said, "You know what my stomach just said?"

"What?" said Nick.

"It just said, 'Well, I'll be a son of a bitch.'"

Faintly, from somewhere outside, Nick heard the thin, brassy sound of a trumpet playing "Silent Night." He went to the door and opened it, and the sound became louder, the trumpet being accompanied by the throaty notes of a trombone. He went out, avoiding the piles of snow still left beside the door, and when he looked toward Third Avenue he saw a Salvation Army trio playing under a streetlight. Two men in caps and greatcoats were playing the trumpet and trombone, while a bonneted woman made a jangling noise on a tambourine and sang the lyrics in a reedy soprano. Some hunch, or instinct, prodded Nick into going down the street, and when he reached the trio he put a dollar bill in the tambourine. The woman thanked him, and he said, "How would you like to play where it's warm, and pick up some real money?"

"Where?" she asked, disbelieving.

"Follow me." The others stopped playing, and followed Nick as he led the way back to the club. When they got inside, he clapped his hands for silence and said, "Ladies and gentlemen, we have some musicians here who have graciously consented to play a few numbers. Those who feel like singing may join in, and those who want to show their appreciation may do so by putting a token in the young lady's tambourine. Here." He took the tambourine and started it around the room, while the musicians played "God Rest You Merry, Gentlemen," "O Little Town of Bethlehem," "Adeste Fideles," and "Silent Night," and everyone sang except Mrs. Peters, who was weeping so hard she couldn't speak. The tambourine came back piled high with bills, and there were loud calls for encores. Nick offered the musicians a drink; the woman and the trumpet player declined, but the trombonist, saying his doctor had told him to take whisky to ward off the flu, accepted a cup of Scotch, which he downed in one massive gulp. They played three more numbers, then turned and trooped out into the dark street, followed by the ringing cheers of the customers.

Christmas Eve in Roland Butterworth's flat was somewhat more subdued. Sarah gave the baby her six o'clock bottle, then put her to bed in the dresser drawer that served as a cradle until the rest of the furniture could be shipped down from Massachusetts. She made supper for herself and her husband, a repast of fishcakes and beans that she had tried to make festive by putting candles on the kitchen table and by substituting Christmas wrapping paper for a tablecloth. It was only a partial success, because the wrapping paper kept curling and skidding, but the candles were a decidcd improvement over the naked bulb that hung from the kitchen ceiling. Sarah tried to keep a sprightly conversation going, but it was uphill work because Butterworth was preoccupied and answered in little more than monosyllables.

"I should think Mr. Reid would make up his mind pretty soon," she said. "If he said to come around after the first of the year, that's only a week away, and he must have *some* thought of hiring you or he wouldn't have said it."

"I understood I'd already been hired," he replied. "I wouldn't have brought you down here if I didn't think I had a job."

"I know, but that was just a misunderstanding. Besides, if he was encouraging enough to make you think you *did* have a job, then he must have something in mind or he'd have given you a flat 'no.' "

"We'll see," said Butterworth.

"And it isn't as though his was the only job in the world. There are lots of papers besides the *Tribune,* and Mr. Prentiss did give you a fine recommendation."

"Uh-huh."

"Don't say 'Uh-huh' as though it were nothing. It was a splendid recommendation, and you know it."

"There's a difference," he said, "between a splendid recommendation from the owner of a company house organ and a splendid recommendation from a real live newspaperman."

"Just because Mr. Prentiss's company makes paper boxes doesn't mean he doesn't know talent when he sees it."

"As I said, we'll see."

"Well, I think you're destined for great things, and I'm only sorry you can't see it that way yourself."

"It's not that. I just don't believe in fooling myself."

"If you're not careful, you can fool yourself in the wrong direction."

He laughed and put his crumpled paper napkin on the table. "I'm sorry," he said. "I'm not being very Christmassy. I guess we need to have a reading."

"I was hoping you weren't going to forget that. Now, of all times, is the time we should hear it."

They went into the adjoining room, where Sarah had set up a miniature Christmas tree on a card table. It was about eighteen inches high, and she had decorated it with tinsel and imitation candy canes, and for lack of a Star of Bethlehem she'd cut an angel from a Christmas card and affixed it to the top of the tree with adhesive tape. Sarah liked to think she could "make do" in almost any circumstances, and if the results were not always of professional quality they at least gave evidence of determined effort.

"Before we start, would you like some coffee?" she asked.

"No, thanks." Butterworth rummaged around in a packing case, which had been pushed out of sight behind the Morris chair. "I'd rather do this without any stimulants." He picked a battered book from the packing case, dusted it off, then sat in the Morris chair and adjusted the reading light. His face, which was thin and serious, took on a serene expression, almost one of contentment, as he read: " 'Marley was dead, to begin with. There is no doubt whatever of that. The register of his burial was signed by the clergyman, the clerk, the undertaker, and the chief mourner. Scrooge signed it. And Scrooge's name was good upon 'Change for anything he chose to put his hand to.' " Sarah settled on the floor at his feet and rested her head against his knee as he read. She knew the words almost by heart—he'd read *A Christmas Carol* to her every Christmas Eve for the last five years—and the knowledge of what was coming didn't in any way detract from her pleasure at hearing the story. When Scrooge said, "Let me hear another sound from *you*, and you'll keep your Christmas by losing your situation!" she flinched in terror for Bob Cratchit, and when the Ghost of Christmas Yet to Come showed Scrooge his own neglected grave, she all but clapped her hands in delight. Then, at the end, when Scrooge became carried away by the spirit of Christmas, she felt her throat tighten, and when, finally, came Tiny Tim's "God bless us, every one!" she was weeping, and she could tell by the crack in her husband's voice that he was doing the same. She blew her nose, pressed her cheek against her husband's leg, and stood up.

"Thank you," she said, and went into the kitchen and began to wash the dishes.

Butterworth blew his nose loudly, put the book away, and followed her. "Do you want me to warm the bottle?" he asked.

She looked at the alarm clock over the sink, which showed nine-thirty. "There's still a half hour," she replied. "We might's well let her sleep."

Butterworth stood to one side, watching her as she put the dishes in the sink. "Should I dry them for you?" he said.

"Thank you, my love, there's no need. Why don't you find something else to read?"

"I don't know. I just feel kind of useless."

"That'll change, as soon as you get a job. Make the most of your leisure while you can."

"I know what–I'll write in my diary." He went back to the living room, got out his red-bound diary, and took it to the card table. He opened to the date, which was Friday, December 24, and wrote:

> Cold & overcast–smell of snow, but none fell.
>
> Up with the baby at 6, then after breakfast walked to 42d Street for the exercise. I find lack of exercise in the city makes me sluggish, which I can ill afford. Thought of dropping by the paper to see if anything had opened up, but decided it might look too anxious. If Mr. R. said after the first of the year, then that's what it shall be. (Just realized that Jan. 1 is Saturday, so Jan. 3 will be the earliest.) Solved the problem of S.'s Christmas present by skipping lunch, and with the money saved bought her a bunch of flowers. They're not much, but I hope she realizes how much love goes with them. Here, of course, is the trouble with Christmas: too much depends on the material presents, and not enough on the spiritual ones. Spent the afternoon making a list of possessions & the order in which we'll sell them if it becomes necessary, then after supper read *Christmas Carol,* crying, as usual, not at the sad parts, but at the parts that are so glad that they shut off your wind. Bed shortly after the 10 o'clock bottle, hoping that the New Year, soon to come, will bring a sharp change of fortune.

He closed the diary, stood up, and looked into the kitchen, where Sarah had just finished cleaning up and was starting to warm the baby's bottle. The overhead light made her blond hair shine, and he wondered briefly if there was a story in a twentieth-century Madonna, bending over a kitchen stove . . . Stop it! he told himself, suddenly embarrassed. That's what comes from reading too much Dickens. You've got to get out in the world and see things unsentimentally, or you won't be worth one thin dime as a reporter. Try to be tough, and try to be cynical, and . . . He couldn't think of another adjective, and the whole idea was so preposterous that he laughed out loud.

"Something funny?" Sarah asked, drying her hands.

"Yes," he replied. "Looking at it one way, I suppose you could say it's funny."

"That's good," she said, as she hung up the towel. "I knew that sooner or later you'd feel better."

It was the middle of January before Butterworth was hired by the *Tribune*. He was taken on as a city reporter at fifteen dollars a week, and on his first day at work the city editor, one Robert Forsburg, looked at him as though he were an odd species of weed that had suddenly grown up through the floor. "Ever done any reporting?" he asked.

"Not as such," Butterworth replied uneasily.

"Then as what?" said Forsburg.

"As a house organ editor," Butterworth said. "I was in the paper-box game."

Forsburg looked at him closely to see if this was some kind of joke, but Butterworth maintained a straight face, and after a moment Forsburg said, "I suppose there are worse ways to start. I'll have someone show you the ropes." He looked around the city room and spotted a reporter who appeared to be doing nothing. "Mr. MacDougall!" he called, and the man jumped to his feet and came toward the city desk. "This is Mr.–ah–Butterworth," Forsburg said. "Will you show him around?"

"Yes, sir," MacDougall said, as he and Butterworth shook hands. "Anything special you want him to see, sir?"

"We can do without the 'sir,'" Forsburg told him. "You're not in the Army anymore. You can start by showing him the men's room, so he won't get lost." He glanced at the assignment sheet and added, "Then take him with you to the Paper and Pulp lunch. He's an old paper-box man himself, so he ought to feel right at home."

"Yes, sir." MacDougall motioned for Butterworth to follow him and returned to his desk. "I don't know why he's asking *me* to show you around," he said, as he took some sheets of copy paper, folded them horizontally into three sections, and put them in his pocket. "I've only been here ten days myself."

"What's this lunch we're going to?" Butterworth asked.

MacDougall sighed. "The forty-third annual convention of the American Paper and Pulp Association," he said. "And it's a 'must,' because the paper's delivered free to all conventioneers, and they've got to see their names in print. It's a royal pain in the ass."

They stopped in the men's room on the way out, and as he stood against one of the urinals MacDougall said, "This is always a good idea before one of these luncheons. They last forever, and if you have to take a leak it's that much worse."

"There's more to this reporting than I thought," Butterworth said, following MacDougall's example. "I thought you just went to fires, and things like that."

MacDougall laughed. "In two years on the Elmira *Bugle,* I never covered a single fire. That's why I joined the Army—to see some excitement."

"And did you?"

"If you call it exciting to be bored stiff most of the time, and scared shitless the rest."

They took the elevator, then walked along Park Row and headed for the Waldorf-Astoria. The Grand Ballroom was teeming with men wearing name badges, and the air was blue with cigar smoke as MacDougall led Butterworth across the ballroom to a table marked "Press." Two other reporters were sitting there, their faces blank with resignation, and MacDougall introduced them as Trexler of the *Times* and Fishbein of the *World*. He then picked up one of the Mimeographed press handouts that were at every place, glanced at it quickly, and put it in his pocket. "This is Butterworth's first day," he said to the other two. "Forsburg figured to hit him with the worst he could right away."

"You think this is the worst?" Fishbein said. "I go from here to a Girl Scout cherry-pie baking contest."

Trexler gave a hollow laugh. "I stay here," he said. "I have to do in-depth interviews after the session is over."

"You poor bastard," said MacDougall.

Trexler shrugged. "All the news that's you know what," he said.

The luncheon consisted of fruit cup, chicken croquettes and white sauce, green peas, and vanilla ice cream, with saltine biscuits on the side. There were also hard rolls, but when Butterworth tried to break his open it shattered, strewing fragments of crust all over the table and into his lap. By the time he'd cleaned it up his plate had been taken away, and the ballroom began to echo with the clatter of coffee cups being served. The toastmaster rose, and the speeches started.

Butterworth marveled later that MacDougall was able to make a coherent story out of what followed, because he took very few notes and seemed to be on the point of falling asleep. The first speaker made a strong plea that the government mind its own business and leave the governing of the paper and pulp industry to the experts; the second praised the research in the field, which he said had raised the nation's standard of living; and the final speaker went all out for forestry conservation, without which, he maintained, there would be no paper in the country in fifty years. Not one speech contained anything that was, in itself, newsworthy, but MacDougall had to find enough words—about a thousand—to fill an entire newspaper column.

"It's simple," MacDougall explained, as they headed back toward the paper. "You put the gist of it in the lead, then repeat and expand the various parts of it in different words until you have the space filled. This being a 'must' story, they'll run every word you write."

"Supposing it weren't a 'must'?" Butterworth asked.

"Then you tell the desk man what you think it's worth, and he tells you to go ahead. In this case it would be about a stick, if that."

"A what?"

"A stick of type." MacDougall indicated about four inches with his fingers. "A couple of paragraphs. And another thing—the desk changes at five, so it's best not to come in till after the night desk takes over. Let *them* tell you how much to write."

"I don't understand," said Butterworth.

"The day desk gives you the assignment, and he wants to have a lot of copy ready when he turns it over, so he'll tell you to do a column, or three quarters, or whatever. By the time you get it done the night man will be on, and he'll say, 'What is all *this* crap about?' and tell you to boil it down to one paragraph. It's simpler to kill time till five-thirty and then do what the night man tells you. Go to a movie, go to a burlesque—whatever you want. You can even get laid, if you're quick about it."

"I'm married," Butterworth said.

"Then go to a speak."

"I don't drink."

MacDougall grinned. "You've got a problem, don't you?"

"Not really."

"It's none of my business. Just don't go in before five, five-thirty."

"I must say, for someone who's been here only ten days you've picked up a lot of information."

"You'll find you learn fast. Like in the Army—you've got to develop an eye for cover, or one day you find yourself without a head."

"I'm afraid I'd have been no good at that."

"It's surprising what you learn when you have to."

That was on a Monday. On Tuesday, Butterworth did three one-paragraph obituaries, telephoning the next of kin listed in the classified death notices and eliciting from them whatever further details seemed pertinent; Wednesday was his day off, and on Thursday he did six obituaries, two of which were used. On Friday he was sent to Freeport, Long Island, to interview a couple named Brown who, in spite of being divorced, were living next door to each other; Mr. Brown, it turned out, liked to collect midgets as drinking companions, and Mrs. Brown was living next door simply because she couldn't find another place to go. Butterworth tried to slant the story as an example of the evils of drink, and was told to rewrite it straight, without any editorializing. He worked on it until midnight, when it was spiked.

On Saturday he covered a Girl Scout outing in the Botanical Gardens section of the Bronx, and on Sunday he was sent down to the St. Nicholas Hellenic Church, at 155 Cedar Street, to observe the celebration of the Feast of the Epiphany. This involved an hour-and-a-half performance of the rites of the liturgy, then a parade down West Street to the Battery in the teeth of an icy gale, while the congregation sang psalms in primitive Greek chants. On arrival at Pier A the presiding Bishop of the Autocephalous Greek Orthodox Church sang the gospel for the day in Greek, and then cast a wooden crucifix into the water, symbolic of the baptism of Christ. According to tradition, several Greek youths were then supposed to jump into the water and race to see who could retrieve the cross, but the weather was such that nobody had volunteered, and the Bishop was forced to recover it by means of a long ribbon, one end tied to the cross and the other looped around his wrist. There followed the playing of the Greek and American national anthems, and then everybody headed for cover.

The next day, Butterworth was astonished to see that his story had run exactly as he'd written it, and was illustrated by a two-column cut from the Associated Press photo service. When he reported for work, Forsburg said, "Nice piece," and gave him a fistful of classified obits.

He got home around ten o'clock that night, to find Sarah in tears. She ran to him and threw her arms around his neck, and his first thought was that something had happened to the baby. "What's the matter?" he asked, feeling her wet face against his. "What happened?" She shook her head and said nothing, and he tried to peel her arms away so as to look at her. "What *happened?"* he said again.

"Nothing," she replied into his ear. "I just missed you." She backed off, blew her nose, and said, "I'm sorry. It just seemed like thirty years since I'd seen you, and then I got thinking of all the terrible things that can happen in the city, and after a while I convinced myself you'd been run over, or—or worse, and then I just kind of lost control. I'm sorry."

"If you're worried, you can always call the paper," he said. "They'll know where I am."

"I couldn't do that. I'd feel like an idiot. I guess I'm just not used to the city; I get lonely, and then my mind begins to work, and before I know it I'm in pieces. I'll try to do better—I promise I will."

He tried to think of something comforting to say, but could come up with nothing. "You needn't worry about me," he said at last. "You're the one we should worry about—you don't get out enough."

"I get out all I want. It'll be better in the spring, when Nancy can stay out longer."

"Isn't there someone you could leave her with? That Mrs. Nussbaum seems like—"

"I wouldn't leave her with anybody. Every day you read about heaters that explode, or babies that suffocate in their cribs, and half the time their mothers have left them alone, or with a neighbor's daughter, or who knows what. I'm not going to leave my baby with just anyone."

"Well, it's up to you. I just think it might help."

"I'll be perfectly all right as soon as I learn to control my imagination. That's my only problem, and that's something I'll have to figure out for myself."

"O.K. Whatever you say."

"Did you have any interesting assignments today?"

"Obits. But Forsburg congratulated me on the Epiphany piece."

"I should think he would. Sooner or later, he'll learn you're worth more than just obits."

"I can't complain. It's a job, which is more than I had two weeks ago."

"I hope you don't let him think you're satisfied, taking just any old assignment."

"It's not a question of whether *I'm* satisfied. It's a question of whether *he's* satisfied with my work."

"You're going to let him walk all over you, just the way you did with Mr. Prentiss."

"Honey, you don't *let* anyone do anything to you. You simply do as he tells you, or you look for another job."

"I wouldn't mind being left alone all the time if I thought it was going to lead to something, but it seems to me you're up against a blank wall. Unless you do something about it, they'll have you writing obits the rest of your life."

"Look–I've had the job exactly one week. Let's give it a little time before we start forecasting the future. O.K.?"

Her chin began to quiver. "Please don't snap at me. I have quite enough to worry about, without you taking my head off every time I make a suggestion."

"I didn't snap. I simply said–"

"I think I know when I've been snapped at and when I haven't!" She buried her face in her hands and fled to the bathroom, where she locked the door and turned on both taps. Butterworth started to follow her, then his shoulders sagged and he hung up his overcoat and sat down at the card table. After taking his diary from the packing case, he unscrewed his fountain pen and began to write:

Monday, January 24
cold & raw–snow flurries around noon, clearing later

Took the 6 o'clock bottle detail, then back to bed & lazed around for ½ hr or so. Spent the morning trying to get the flat ready for the arrival of the furniture, which they promise "in just a couple more days." Gave S. my first paycheck, which she used to buy some much-needed groceries, & while she was gone I made a cheese sandwich for lunch & set some soup on to heat for her. Checked in at the paper at 1, where Forsburg complimented me on the Epiphany piece & gave me a dozen or so classified obits to write up. That took the rest of the day, what with some people being unavailable to the phone (at the undertaker's most likely) & others not wanting to talk. I hate butting in on people who are in grief (is there such a phrase?) & wish there were some other way to do it, but I suppose in cases like this the news comes first, & people's sensibilities second. That's as may be, but I still hate it. Got home around 10, to find S. highly distraught, so far as I can figure out for no other reason than being alone all day. Tried to convince her she should get out more, but she seems to have a hatred of the city that outweighs everything else. It would be nice if we could move, but that of course is out of the question. The move here has used up every available penny, & it will be a long time before we can afford anything else.

A week later, he and MacDougall were two of three reporters sent down to Wall Street to cover a bomb explosion. The previous September an anarchist's bomb had killed thirty people and injured a hundred, and although the first reports did not indicate that this one was as serious, the city desk took no chances and dispatched three reporters and a photographer to the scene. The reporters were to interview any eyewitnesses, find out the extent of the damage, and get whatever theories they could about the perpetrator; they were to phone their findings in to a man on rewrite, who would have got from the police and the hospitals the names of the casualties, and he would do the wrap-up story. Lenzner, the third reporter, had been on the paper for ten years, and he would give specific directions to Butterworth and MacDougall.

As they took the subway down to Wall Street, Butterworth reflected that this was the first time he'd been assigned to this kind of job and for some reason he was nervous. There would be no press handouts here and nobody at the other end of the telephone to give him the facts; whatever he got he would have to get on his own. He hoped the dead and injured would have been taken away before he got there, but if they weren't he'd simply have to brace himself and try to pretend it was all in a day's work. He almost wished he were back doing obits, although there was an undeniable excitement to this story that made him willing to risk whatever unpleasantness might be involved. Both MacDougall and Lenzner looked bored; Lenzner, however, was an old hand at such stories, and MacDougall had been in the Army, where sudden death and injury were a way of life. He, Roland Butterworth, was undergoing an initiation of some sort, and he both dreaded and welcomed it, hoping that he wouldn't be sick, or faint, or do something stupid.

The area of the blast had been cordoned off, but by showing their police cards the four *Tribune* men passed through the barriers and approached the damaged building. Several windows had been blown out, and the street was littered with broken glass; beyond that, it was hard to tell just what the bomb had done. Then Butterworth saw a horse-drawn ambulance at the curb, and as he watched two men came out of the building carrying a stretcher on which was a blanket-covered form, and they opened the back doors of the ambulance and slid the stretcher inside.

"Well, there's one casualty," Lenzner said. "Butterworth, go see if you can find out his name."

Butterworth approached the ambulance, showed his police card to one of the attendants, and said, "Who was that?"

"Who was what?" the attendant asked, pulling another stretcher from the rack.

"That. The person you just put in there. Do you have a name?"

"Buddy, we just load the meat, we don't tag it," the attendant replied. "Ask the cops, or the Bellevue morgue."

"Thank you," Butterworth said, and went back to where Lenzner and MacDougall were entering the building. "No name," he reported.

"Well, rewrite'll have it," Lenzner said. "See if you can scare up any eyewitnesses."

The bomb had exploded in an office off the lobby of the building, and the air was thick with plaster dust and cordite fumes. There was a good deal of shouting, some people giving instructions and other people asking for them, and everyone seemed to be in a hurry to get someplace else. Butterworth stopped one man and asked him if he'd seen the explosion, and the man laughed and said, "No, thank God!" and moved away, and it occurred to Butterworth that he was looking in the wrong place: any eyewitness in the building would probably be dead or injured, and the place to look was outside, where a passerby might have seen it and still be hanging around. He went out, glad to be in the fresh air, and approached the police barricade, on the other side of which the crowd stood, silent and wide-eyed, as though waiting for another explosion. "Did anyone see it happen?" Butterworth asked, and for reply got only bovine stares. He moved down the line, repeating the question with the same result, and the third time he asked, a man put up his hand and said, "I did!"

"You did?" Butterworth saw a man of medium height with pince-nez glasses, wearing a bowler hat and a woolen scarf. "Your name?" he said, taking out his copy paper.

"Newton Masterson," the man replied.

"Address?"

"My legal address is Tuskegee, Alabama, but at the moment I'm staying with my mother in Brooklyn Heights." Feeling he was already a celebrity, he added, "She recently underwent surgery for perforated diverticulosis, and my wife and I—"

"Your age, Mr. Masterson?"

"I'll be forty-eight on my next birthday, but since I was born on Leap Year I have a birthday only every four years. So my next birthday isn't really my forty-eighth, because—"

"I understand. Just tell me what you saw."

"Where?"

"Here. Did you see the bomb go off?"

"Not the bomb itself. I saw the smoke coming from the windows. I'd just turned the corner from Pine Street, where I'd been having a meeting with my mother's banker. You see, the nature of her operation is such that—"

"Excuse me, but let's stay with the explosion."

"I was getting to that. My mind was on my banking problems—or, rather, on my mother's banking problems—so I was looking at the ground—the sidewalk, really—as I walked, and not paying much attention to where I was going. I heard someone shout, and then a loud BOOM! and when I looked up the street was full of broken glass, and smoke was pouring from those windows. It was then I realized there'd been an explosion, and I—"

"Did you hear what was shouted?"

"When?"

"Just before the explosion. You said you heard someone shout."

"Oh, yes. No, it was just a shout, like 'Hey!' or—well, you know. The kind of shout you give when someone steps on your foot."

"Did you see anyone doing anything suspicious?"

"Well, as I said, I was looking at the sidewalk, thinking about my mother's trust fund. There's an interesting complication there, that–"

"Please–let's stay with the explosion."

"That's what I'm doing. But this explains why I wasn't paying as much attention as–"

"Did you see anything suspicious, or not?"

"I didn't actually *see* anything, but I do believe I heard someone running. That would be suspicious, wouldn't it?"

"If you actually saw someone running away from the building, yes."

"Well, I know I heard someone running, but I couldn't swear which way he was going."

"Thank you, Mr. Masterson," Butterworth said, and put away his copy paper.

"If I think of anything else I'll give you a call," Masterson said. "What's your name?"

"Just ask for the editor of the *Tribune,*" Butterworth replied. "He's the one in charge. If you can't get him, ask for Mr. Reid."

He went back to the building and found Lenzner, who was talking to a police lieutenant. "Did you get anything?" Lenzner asked him.

"No," said Butterworth.

MacDougall joined them, having been talking with the head of the firm whose office had been bombed. "No dice," he said.

"No theories?" Lenzner said. "No disgruntled employees, nobody who's been fired recently?"

"Nope. He just says it's anarchists, and lets it go at that. I have a feeling he'd have blamed Sacco and Vanzetti, if they weren't already in jail. He mentioned them as the types who'd do it."

"Swell," said Lenzner. "All theory, no fact." Turning to Butterworth, he said, "You were talking to someone back there. Who was it?"

"Newton Masterson," Butterworth replied. "Of Tuskegee, Alabama. Forty-eight years old. Saw smoke following the explosion, but that was all."

"What's he doing in New York?"

"You don't want to know."

"Supposing we say it *was* Sacco and Vanzetti," MacDougall suggested. "Then we'd have a hell of a story."

"Yeah, and a better one if it was Edith Bolling Wilson," Lenzner replied. "For the moment, however, let's stay with the facts." He looked at his notes and said, "Well, I'll call this in and see what they say. You two stick around."

"I could use a drink about now," MacDougall said, when Lenzner had left. "I don't suppose you brought anything with you." Butterworth shook his head, and MacDougall said, "That's right. I forgot."

"Why would you want a drink now?" Butterworth asked, honestly curious. "Don't you want to stay as alert as you can?"

MacDougall tried to think of an answer, then laughed. "I'm sorry," he said. "Forget I spoke."

"No, I mean it. What possible good would a drink do?"

"I can't explain it," MacDougall said. "Someday you may find out."

In a few minutes Lenzner reappeared, tearing two pieces off his copy paper. He handed one to Butterworth and one to MacDougall, and said, "Here are the names and addresses of the two who were killed. Go see their families, get whatever facts you can, and try to get a recent picture. Steal one, if you have to. See if you can get it in in time for the bulldog."

Butterworth glanced at his piece of paper in dismay. The address was in the Forest Hills section of Queens, but worse than trying to get there was the prospect of confronting the bereaved family and badgering them for a picture and obit material. He and MacDougall took the subway to Grand Central, and as he changed to the Queens-bound train Butterworth knew that, if he were the bereaved one, a reporter would be the last person he'd want to talk to. The more he thought about it, the surer he was he couldn't go through with the assignment. Besides, he told himself, it was pointless to go to their home because they would undoubtedly be at the morgue, or a funeral parlor, or some such place, so he was simply wasting time and money trying to track them down. He changed trains at Long Island City and came back to Manhattan and then, remembering MacDougall's advice, went to Times Square and caught the last part of Douglas Fairbanks's film *The Mark of Zorro*. At six o'clock he called the city desk, said there'd been nobody home but a maid who had refused him admittance, and the desk man told him to keep trying until eleven. He had supper at the Automat, called Sarah and told her he wouldn't be home until late, then saw Conrad Nagel and Anna Q. Nilsson in *The Fighting Chance*. At eleven he called the desk and reported no luck, and got his good-night. He went home feeling as though he'd robbed a bank. It was, to the best of his knowledge, the first time he'd ever lied to anyone.

Next day the *Times* had a half-column obituary, with cut, of the man Butterworth had been told to track down, and when Forsburg silently showed it to him Butterworth laughed. "I'll be a son of a gun," he said. "I thought he was just kidding."

"Who was?" said Forsburg.

"The *Times* man. He said this guy was his uncle. I naturally thought he was pulling my leg, but I guess he was on the level. The maid said she was to let nobody into the house except members of the family."

Forsburg studied the *Times* story for a few moments, then dropped it in the wastebasket. "Son of a bitch," he said.

9

The address that Lenzner had given MacDougall was in the east fifties, and as Butterworth headed for Grand Central on his way to Queens, MacDougall joined him on the Lexington Avenue I.R.T.

"I hate the idea of this," Butterworth said, as they got on the last car and sat down. "Suppose I have to break the news to them?"

MacDougall shrugged. "Just make sure you have the right house, he said. "It's a hell of a thing to break the news to the wrong people. I did that once, in Elmira." He laughed, and said, "God damn, what an afternoon *that* was!"

"That's a big help," Butterworth replied.

"Nothing's as bad as you think it's going to be—except, of course, in those cases when it's a lot worse. That's all I can tell you."

"Thanks a lot," said Butterworth, with a tight smile.

Butterworth changed for the Queens train at Grand Central, and MacDougall rode the local one more stop, to Fifty-first Street. He walked to the address, which was a brownstone house between Lexington and Third, and after checking the slip once more he went up the front steps. Someone inside the house was playing "Humoresque" on the piano, and when MacDougall rang the bell the music stopped. A maid came to the door, and opened it cautiously.

"Is this the residence of Preston Bostwick?" MacDougall asked.

"He's dead," said the maid.

"I know. Uh—is Mrs. Bostwick in? I'm from the New York *Tribune*."

"Just a minute." The maid vanished, and MacDougall had the odd feeling he'd detected a note of satisfaction in her voice. She reappeared in a minute and said, "Come in." He took off his hat and entered, and as she led him to a room in the back of the house he smelled furniture polish, dusty rugs, and the distant smell of cooking.

Mrs. Bostwick was, he guessed, somewhere in her forties, and her rust-colored hair was pulled straight back and tied with a small black ribbon. She wore a black dress with a black lace shirtwaist, and her only jewelry was a small gold brooch at her throat. There was a piano behind her, and a copy of *Vanity Fair* on the desk from which she'd just risen. She clasped her hands in front of her, and waited for MacDougall to speak. The maid closed the door silently, and left.

"My name is MacDougall, Mrs. Bostwick," he said. "I'm from the *Tribune*."

"So I was told," she replied. Her voice was low, and sounded faintly seductive.

"I'm very sorry about your husband," MacDougall said. "I hope you don't mind my coming at this time."

"Not in the least. I was rather expecting you."

"Oh?"

"I assume you want some facts about my husband—excuse me—my late husband."

"As a matter of fact, yes. And a picture, if you have one."

She turned back to the desk and picked up a sheet of paper, on which were written the salient facts about Preston Bostwick's life. Born in 1875, educated at Andover and Yale, served with Colonel Roosevelt's Rough Riders in 1898, and then a succession of jobs in various financial firms. It was a solid, respectable, and, after 1898, dull career. "As for pictures," Mrs. Bostwick said, while MacDougall skimmed through the outline, "I don't know what you want. Here's one when he was playing polo at Yale, or this one with the Rough Riders—of course, he doesn't have a horse, since they were dismounted— Oh, here's one, taken when we were on vacation in the Thousand Islands. We're the fifth and sixth from the left. Or—"

"I'd like something a little more recent, if you have it," MacDougall said. "A studio portrait, preferably."

"I don't think I have one," she said, "All his pictures have to do with Yale—or most of them, anyway. To the best of my knowledge he hasn't had a picture taken in–well, since the banquet when he won his 'Y' in life."

"I beg your pardon?" said MacDougall.

She smiled a sweet, indulgent smile. "It's quite an honor, really. Anyone who is deemed to have–how shall I say it?–made a killing in his chosen profession is said to have won his 'Y' in life and is honored with an elaborate banquet and speeches."

"I see. Well, then, let's settle for the polo picture. Mr. Reid was on the water-polo team at Yale, so that ought to ring a bell with him."

"Which Mr. Reid?"

"Ogden."

She thought a moment, then said, "I don't remember Preston mentioning him, but I don't suppose that proves anything."

"Probably not." MacDougall gathered up the outline and the picture, then said, "Oh–do you have any plans for the funeral?"

"Not yet," said Mrs. Bostwick. "After all, this only happened three hours ago."

"Yes, of course. I'm sorry." MacDougall found it hard to believe that this was a newly and suddenly widowed woman, and he could only conclude that she was still in shock. Later she'll fall apart, he told himself; she'll have to.

"By the way," she said, as he turned to leave, "was anyone else–ah–hurt in the explosion?"

"Yes," he replied. "One other man was killed; I don't know how many injured."

Her lips lost all color, and she said, "What was his name–the one who was killed?"

"I don't know," said MacDougall. "It'll be in the paper."

She seemed to totter slightly, then recovered herself. "It's a terrible thing," she said. "Terrible. These anarchists should all be taken out and shot."

"Well, nobody knows who did it." An idea was beginning to form in MacDougall's mind, but it was so wild that he tried to suppress it. "It could have been almost anyone," he concluded.

"But that was an anarchist last fall, and then this Sacco and Vanzetti–it just seems there are anarchists everywhere you look."

"It does that. Well, thank you, Mrs. Bostwick, and again my condolence."

"You're very kind. The maid will show you out."

All the way to the paper MacDougall tried to tell himself that he was crazy; that the idea of a woman's having someone plant a bomb in her husband's office was so preposterous that anyone who even entertained it would have to be deranged. He went back over everything, from hearing the sprightly strains of "Humoresque" when he arrived, to her obvious scorn for the winning-one's-"Y" ceremony, to his jolting her with the news of another man's death, and no matter how hard he tried he couldn't make it fit the picture of a woman mourning her husband. When he got to the city desk he showed them the picture and gave them a rundown on Bostwick's life, and when the desk man asked for a half column MacDougall took a deep breath and said, "Also, I think I know who may have done it."

"Who?" said the desk man, marking the picture and tossing it in a basket.

"Mrs. Bostwick," MacDougall replied.

The desk man looked at him with curiosity, then said, "For Christ's sakes, Mac, this is no time for jokes."

"I'm not joking!" MacDougall listed all the things that made him suspicious, but the desk man simply shook his head and began editing a sheet of copy.

"Go back and do the obit," he said. "We want to get it all in the bulldog if we can."

"Will you at least let me look into it?" MacDougall said. "Will you let me snoop around and see if I can find anything concrete?"

"And get the paper sued for a million dollars? Not on your life. We're a family newspaper, not a scandal sheet."

"We won't be sued if we print the truth! And think what a story it'll be if we're right!"

"For the last time, MacDougall, are you going to write that obit or aren't you?"

"Of course I'm going to write it, but—"

"Then hop to it. You haven't got all night."

He went back to his desk and hammered out a half-column summary of Bostwick's life, then realized he'd neglected to get the names of any children. He looked up the Bostwick number in the phone book and put through a call. He expected the maid to answer, but instead there came the unmistakable, dulcet tone of Mrs. Bostwick's voice saying, "Yes?"

"Mrs. Bostwick?" MacDougall said.

Her voice changed, and she said, "Who's this?"

"This is George MacDougall, from the *Tribune.*"

"Oh, yes." The voice was now flat.

"I forgot to ask you if you had any children, or if there are any other survivors, like a brother or sister, or whatever."

"Oh. Ah—no. No other survivors. I'm the only one."

"All right, then, thank you. Sorry to have bothered you."

"Not at all."

She hung up, and MacDougall slowly replaced the receiver on the hook. I wonder whom she was expecting, he thought. Whoever it was, she sure as hell wasn't expecting me. He turned in his copy, then went back to his desk and called Dorothy Peters. "Hi, there," he said, when she answered. "This is the big butter-and-egg man from Setauket. How would you like to snap at a whisky sandwich?"

"You can't fool me," she said. "You're Rudolph Valentino."

"I turn into Rudolph Valentino at midnight. Until then, I'm just out for laughs. Shall I pick you up, or do you want to meet me at the Circe?"

"I'll meet you there. What face do you want me to put on—sad, glad, or seductive?"

"A mixture of the last two would be nice."

"That may take a little time. I'll meet you there in forty minutes."

"Done and done." He hung up, looked at his watch, and decided there was no point trying to kill time; he could go directly to the Circe and have a few drinks before she arrived. The way he felt now he could drink a whole fifth, just out of frustration.

An impromptu musicale was being held at the Circe when he arrived. Someone had brought a saxophone, and someone else had a comb and toilet paper, and they were belting out the strains of "If He Can Fight Like He Can Love," while a third man kept time by striking two spoons against assorted bits of crockery, and a girl sang the lyrics in a throaty alto. Nick grinned as he admitted MacDougall, and said, "You're just in time. How many verses of 'Hinky Dinky Parlez Vous' do you remember?"

"None that I could sing here," MacDougall replied. "Do you know any clean ones?"

"Only 'The General got the Croix de Guerre.' I don't think anybody'd mind the last line—not in this crowd, anyway."

"All right, let's do it."

Nick told the saxophonist, and then he and MacDougall sang the verse, the last line of which was 'But the son of a bitch was never there,' and there was general laughter and applause. Then, before anyone could come up with some of the gamier verses, Nick asked the man with the sax to play "Swanee," the George Gershwin song that Al Jolson had popularized, and everyone joined in the singing. After that they did "Nobody But You," and they were halfway through "Everybody Swat the Profiteer," which Gershwin had written for *George White's Scandals of 1920,* when the buzzer sounded, and Nick gestured for silence. He went to the door, which now had a peephole, and saw Dorothy Peters standing outside.

"Warren Gamaliel Harding sent me," she said.

Nick recognized her and laughed, and unchained the door. "He's already here," he said.

As she came in she saw the saxophonist and the man with the comb, and said, "You needn't have stopped for me. I could hear you halfway down the block."

"It's time we took a break, anyway," the sax man said. "I haven't had a drink in all of six minutes." He drained his teacup and gestured to Nick for a refill.

Dorothy saw MacDougall, who was standing in a corner talking with Marie, and she went across and said, "You two look as though you're plotting something."

"Only how to get the most nourishment out of a single sandwich," MacDougall replied. "Marie thinks it should include a couple of squares of chocolate, but I think beef would be better. What do you think?"

"It's academic," she said. "I've already eaten."

"I don't mean for now. Tonight, I'm having Scotch for dinner." He emptied his cup and said to Marie, "Would you ask the *patron* if we could have two of his special Scotches?"

"Better than that, I'll get them for you," Marie replied, and she went into the back room, while MacDougall and Dorothy took a table.

"What's eating you?" Dorothy said. "You look as though you're intending to drink the joint dry."

He told her about his interview with Mrs. Bostwick, and the follow-up telephone call, and concluded, "It isn't as though I wanted to print anything without proof. These bastards won't even let me look for evidence."

"You must remember, the *Tribune*'s a respectable paper," she said. "It can't print anything that smacks of s-e-x."

"I don't care what it prints. I just want to get at the truth, and they won't let me."

She thought a moment, then said, "Did it ever occur to you that Mrs. Bostwick might have good and sufficient reason for wanting him killed?"

"What do you mean?"

"From what you say about his life he sounds like an insufferable prig, I believe the word is, with a hard 'g.' Also, he sounds like a Bones man, and as the ex-wife of one of those I can testify that a bomb in the lap is often too good for them."

"What makes you think he was Skull and Bones?"

"You mentioned a group picture in the Thousand Islands. That's where they go for their vacations, business meetings, and whatnot. Believe me, I know. You should go easy on this little lady, because she may have justice all on her side."

"I don't think the law would–"

"I didn't say the law; I said justice. There's a difference."

Marie brought their drinks, and MacDougall took a big swallow of his. The musicians had started another medley of songs, and he brooded silently while Dorothy sang those lyrics that she knew. She sang more to herself than anything else; she didn't join the chorus so much as she trotted along after it, like a small dog following a parade.

"You know what?" she said at last.

"What?" said MacDougall, finishing his drink.

"I think you're sweet."

He smiled briefly, and looked around for Marie.

"I'm not just saying that," Dorothy said. "I really mean it. You're as sweet as anyone I ever met."

"I'm not feeling so sweet right now," he said.

"That'll pass. You know something else?"

"No." He caught Marie's eye and gestured for two more drinks.

"Not for me," she said, putting her hand over her teacup. "This is fine."

"You'll need another one sooner or later," he replied. "That's not the last drink you'll ever have in your life."

"No, but. Ah, well . . . What was I saying?"

"Don't look at me. You asked if I knew something else."

"Oh, yes. Your ears have little points on them, like a satyr's, and your mouth and your eyes have a kind of pixie quality, and I must be drunk as a skunk to be saying all this. That's why I didn't think I needed another drink, because if I'm saying all this now on my first drink, think what I'll be saying on my second."

He suspected she must have had something before she arrived but saw no point in saying so. "I don't know," he said, "but it might be kind of interesting to find out."

"No, it won't, because on my third drink I usually want to adopt any animal I see, and on my fourth I go all out for horses. The only way to avoid this is not to have the second, because then the rest follows as the night the day, and Mummy is weeping over a milkman's horse. Believe me, I know; I've been through it all too many times to be mistaken."

"You must wake up with some interesting souvenirs."

"Only cats. The other animals manage to escape. But, my God, do I have cats."

"Do you keep them?"

Marie brought their drinks, and Dorothy stared into the dregs of her first Scotch, stirring it with her finger. "That's the trouble," she said. "I can't keep them because I can't take care of them, so I have to turn them loose again." Her eyes began to puddle, and she said, "And that makes me feel like a perfect heel. A complete and utter bitch."

"No reason to. It's better to let 'em go than to keep 'em penned up where they can't be cared for." He found he was having to enunciate clearly to keep from slurring his words, and he moistened his lips and took a sip of his new Scotch. "After all, nature takes care of them better than people can."

"But then I shouldn't promise them a home," she replied. "To promise a kitty a home and then turn it away is like—like—well, almost like murder."

"Like sending a bomb to your husband's office."

"Nothing whatsoever. I would bomb fifty Wall Street offices before I would intentionally harm one little kitty, and whoever says differently would suck eggs. How do you like that?"

"I think it's an interesting theory. It also gives me an idea."

"About what?"

"You know the line in *Hamlet:* 'The play's the thing / Wherein I'll catch the conscience of the king'?"

"Act Two, Scene Two," she said. "What else is new?"

"Suppose I write a play, about a woman who has her husband's office bombed, and put in all the things I think Mrs. Bostwick probably did. Then, when she sees it, her reaction'll show whether I'm right or not."

"What makes you think she'll see it?"

"The reviews. When she reads what it's about she'll *have* to see it, out of curiosity if nothing else."

"Have you ever written a play?"

"No, but that doesn't mean I can't."

"Possibly, but it's the way to bet."

"Why? There has to be a first time for everything."

"I don't think of you as a playwright. I think of you as a satyr, frolicking through a woodland glade, with little rabbits and fieldmice dancing in your wake."

"What did I ever do to give you that impression?"

"This and that. It's your looks, mostly."

He was aware that Marie had brought another round, although he didn't remember ordering it. He was having to speak more and more slowly, in order to keep his speech clear, but it didn't really matter because Dorothy was doing most of the talking. She was saying something about horses, and the miserable life they led, and even when he tried to make an observation she didn't seem to be listening. At one point he lost track of where they were: the candlelit tables reminded him of a restaurant in Paris during the war, and Marie's voice in the background was French, or partly French, and he wondered if he was on a seventy-two-hour pass, or leave, or what. He didn't want to be picked up by the MPs if he was over leave, but then he realized he was in civilian clothes, so they'd probably never recognize him. The night air was cold, but instead of waking him up it made him sleepy, and he closed his eyes, and when he opened them everything was dark and he was in bed; Dorothy's arms were around his neck and her legs were around his thighs, and they both were naked and were performing a slow, almost stately, act of intercourse. Totally astonished, he disengaged himself and sat up, trying to make out where he was. He could dimly see some clothes on the floor, but the room was unfamiliar and smelled of perfume, and he could only conclude it was Dorothy's. He shook his head to clear it, then looked back at her. She was staring up at him, and her eyes in the dark were enormous, like those of some nocturnal animal.

"How did I get here?" he asked.

"By taxi," she replied. "Don't you remember?"

"That's right," he said, remembering nothing. "Of course." He leaned down and reached for his drawers.

"Where are you going?" she asked.

"I suppose it's about time I went home."

"Why? What is there at home that isn't here?"

He paused, then said, "Now that you mention it, nothing." He lay back and pulled up the covers, and almost instantly was asleep.

When he got to the paper that afternoon, the desk man gave him a baleful look. "Where were you last night?" he said.

"Here and there," MacDougall replied. "Why?"

"For your future guidance, you should stick around until you get your official good-night."

"I figured there was nothing more to do, once I'd finished the obit."

"Well, this time it didn't matter, but we like to know where you are."

"What happened? Did I miss something?"

"I gather you didn't go to the Club Circe from here."

"As a matter of fact, I did. At any rate I started out there. Why?"

"It was torched last night."

"It was *what?*"

The desk man handed him a piece of City News copy, which stated simply that the Club Circe had been destroyed by a fire of probably incendiary origin in the early hours of the morning. There were no known casualties, but firemen were still searching through the wreckage.

"You're a buddy of Baldino's, aren't you?" the desk man said.

"I know him, yes," MacDougall replied.

"Suppose you trot on down there and see what he can tell you. See who his enemies are, or who might want him out of business."

"O.K." As MacDougall pocketed the City News copy and went back to his desk, he remembered his idea of writing a play to trigger some sort of reaction in Mrs. Bostwick. In the cold light of day it didn't seem quite as sensational as it had last night, but he wondered if somewhere, between the bombing of Bostwick's office and the torching of the Circe, there might be a thread, or a theme, that could be dramatized. The country seemed to be entering a new and violent era, and he wanted somehow to chronicle the transition. The war to end all wars had given way to a spate of private, parochial wars of all sorts, wars that could not be stopped by the mere signing of a treaty, and were therefore that much more dangerous. He felt as though he were enlisting all over again, this time with a chance of doing something worthwhile, although just how he would go about it was something to be determined later.

10

When MacDougall and Dorothy Peters had left the club, Nick chained the door and went into the back room, where Marie was making sandwiches for the saxophonist and his friends. "How did Mac get so drunk?" Nick asked. "He was absolutely pie-eyed."

"He insisted on ordering more Scotch," Marie replied. "I tried to get him to eat, but he wanted none of it."

"Next time, ask him if he's sure he wants another. Then, if he insists, give him a watered one. That at least will slow him down."

"I don't think he'll do it again. There was something special on his mind tonight."

The buzzer sounded, and Nick went to the door, opened the peephole, and admitted Albert Hopkins. "Welcome!" he said. "I haven't seen you since Christmas."

"I've been to Europe," Hopkins replied, taking off his coat. "Just got back yesterday."

"A business trip?"

"Not really."

"Boy, I wish I was an investment banker. Take off for Europe any time I felt like it . . . Where'd you go?"

Hopkins cleared his throat. "Cherbourg."

"Then where?"

"New York."

"Not even Paris?"

"I wasn't allowed off the ship." Nick stared, and Hopkins went on, "I went down to see a friend off on the *France,* and what with one thing and another I woke up next day at sea. I didn't have a passport, so I had to stay aboard. Longest damn trip I ever took. May I have a Scotch?"

Nick brought him a cup of Scotch and said, "This one's on the house—a bon voyage and welcome home present."

"Thank you." Hopkins raised the cup in salute and drank.

"What did your wife say?" Nick asked.

"I didn't tell her. What she doesn't know won't hurt her."

"You mean she didn't miss you?"

"We keep our own hours. She hasn't asked, and I see no reason to bring the subject up. She'd just jeer at me for not having taken my passport."

Nick tried to think of something to say but couldn't. Insanely, he found himself asking, "Do you have any children?"

"Three," said Hopkins. "Of varying ages." He took another sip of his Scotch and looked at the man with the saxophone. "Do you know 'Red Lips Blues'?" he asked.

"No, but if you hum a few bars I can fake it," the sax man replied.

Hopkins took a quick drink, then set the cup down and, in a bell-clear tenor, sang:

I got them red lips blues
I got them red lips blues
Bluer than my baby's eyes

The sax man picked up the tune, and the comb-and-toilet-paper man made a buzzing background accompaniment, and gradually all the customers joined in, some tapping spoons on tables, some clicking crockery, and some getting up and improvising dances, and by the time Hopkins reached the last verse, which ended:

If I can't have them red lips now
I'll lay me down and die

the song had reached the proportions of a musical-comedy production number. There was wild applause, and cries of "Encore!" but Hopkins demurred and lifted his teacup in acknowledgment.

"You're wasting your time on Wall Street," Nick told him. "You ought to be with a band."

"I know, but I need the security," Hopkins replied. "Musicians are a pretty footloose group."

Nick started to say something, then decided against it. His attention was drawn to the front door, where it appeared that someone was trying to get in. He went and opened the peephole, and saw two men he didn't recognize standing in the darkness outside. "What do you want?" he asked.

"Frank sent us," one of them said.

"Frank who?"

"Frank DiMotto." The man produced a card, and Nick took it through the peephole and examined it. When Frank gave out a card he always marked it with a code, indicating how the bearer should be treated, and this card was unmarked. Nick passed it back.

"Sorry," he said. "We're full."

"Don't give me that shit," the man said. "We're friends of Frank."

"Tell him to bring you around in person." Nick closed the peephole and went back into the room, wondering what the men had had in mind. If they just wanted a drink that was one thing, but there were plenty of places where they could get a drink, so they must have had a specific reason for wanting to come to the Circe. It wasn't hard to get hold of a card—it was, if anything, too easy—but to invent a friendship with Frank, and to be truculent when turned down—Nick's thoughts were interrupted by a crash, and a shattering of glass, and the front curtains leaped as a brick came through the window and thudded to the floor. A woman screamed, and Nick ran to the front door, but by the time he had unchained it and gone outside the street was deserted. He stood there for a few moments but saw nothing, and he finally turned and went back in, chaining the door behind him. Marie was already sweeping up the broken glass, and Nick picked up the brick and examined it, as though by staring at it he could find some clue. It told him nothing, and he looked around for a place to put it.

"Don't throw it away," Marie told him. "It will be useful in making pâté."

He stared at her, then at the brick, then shrugged and took it into the back room. "I guess there's tricks to every trade," he said, putting the brick by the gas ring. He looked around for something to cover the broken window but could find nothing, and when he returned to the front room he found that the festive mood had vanished, and people were getting ready to leave. "I apologize for all this," he said. "I think we'll have to put up a grill, to protect our windows."

"Is there anything I can do to help?" Hopkins asked, as Nick started adding up the checks.

"Not unless you're a glazier," Nick replied, and added, "Which wouldn't surprise me a great deal."

"As a matter of fact, I almost took up glassblowing once," Hopkins said. "But then, come summer, I had to quit."

"Why?"

"Hay fever. Bitched up all my designs."

"You've led a varied life, I'll say that for you," Nick said.

"Jack of all trades, master of none . . ." Hopkins sighed. "If it weren't for investment banking, I'd probably be a bum."

When everyone had left Nick and Marie cleaned up, then lifted a floorboard in the back room and hid the bottles in a recess that had been cut out for the purpose. Nick replaced the floorboard, stamped on it, then picked up the cash box, which he took home with him every night. "I wish there were some way we could seal off that window," he said. "It's like leaving the door open to go off with it like that."

"Unless you want to sleep here, I can think of no answer," Marie replied. "And if you want to sleep here, I'll see you tomorrow. My bones are crying for a bed."

"The hell with it. Nothing can happen between now and tomorrow. Let's go."

They walked through the quiet streets toward home, their footsteps sounding loud against the pavement. Nick had the cash box under one arm and Marie's arm in the other, and the fingers of their hands were intertwined. "It's a long way from the Champs-Élysées," he said at last.

She squeezed his hand and laughed. "And you never found your soda fountain, did you?"

"I found something a great deal better."

"So did I."

"Will you tell me something?"

"Of course."

"Is this what you thought the United States would be like?"

She was quiet, then said, "No."

"Are you disappointed?"

"No . . . I don't know what I expected, but–well, yes, I do, but that was idiotic."

"Tell me. I'd like to know."

"Well . . . I thought there'd be red Indians with feathers in their hair, and we'd have to close the stockade gates at night, and–oh–"

"In New *York?*"

"I wasn't thinking New York, I was thinking America. That's what French children think, when they think America."

"I'll be damned. You *must* have been disappointed."

"Not really. Well, perhaps a little. I'd like to see a red Indian, just once."

"I'll find one for you. First chance we have to take a vacation, we'll go out west."

"When will that be?"

"That'll depend on business. It could be a year, it could be five. It could be never. In case you hadn't noticed it, our trade is full of surprises."

They had managed, with the first money they'd taken in, to move out of Nick's family's flat and into one of their own. It was a third-floor walkup with two rooms and a bath, and while there was no telephone there was at least an adequate kitchen, and it served their needs until they could afford something else. Messages were delivered through the superintendent, who lived on the ground floor.

Nick had no idea what time it was when he was awakened by a pounding on the door. "Mr. Baldino!" the superintendent was shouting. "Mr. Baldino, wake up! The place is on fire!"

Nick reached over and shook Marie, who was lying as though she'd been shot, and called, "All right! All right! We're coming!" then leaped out of bed, turned on the light, shouted at Marie, "Get up! Fire!" and began to throw on his clothes. He could smell no smoke, nor could he hear any of the sounds of fire, but as he and Marie raced about, bumping into each other as they picked up their belongings, he felt it was only a matter of time before smoke began to seep into the room. He flung open the door, and still there was no smell or sound, and he began to wonder if he'd dreamed the whole thing. He ran downstairs, with Marie following, and knocked on the superintendent's door. There was a muttering and stamping behind the door, and then it opened.

"*Now* what the hell?" the superintendent said.

"Where's the fire?" Nick asked. "You told me we're on fire, didn't you?"

"I said the place is on fire—your place. The speakeasy."

"My God," said Nick. "How'd you know?"

"Your partner called. Now, if it's all right with you, I'm going back to bed." He closed the door.

Nick turned to Marie. "I'd better get over there," he said. "There's no need for you to come."

"I want to come. I'll just get rid of this stuff." Her arms were full of random items of clothing she'd grabbed on the way out—her best dress, a summer hat, seven shoes, and assorted lingerie—and she took them back upstairs and returned in a few minutes.

"I don't imagine there's much we can do," Nick said, as they started out. "Until we see how bad it is, there's just no way to do anything."

"Except stop thinking about a vacation," she replied. "As you said, our trade is full of surprises."

"We may have a longer vacation than we want, but we're not going to think of that right now."

The fire engines were still at the scene when they arrived, and the firemen were hosing down the pile of smoking rubbish that had been the Club Circe. Marie blew her nose and began to weep quietly, and for a while Nick was so stunned he could say nothing. Then he saw Frank DiMotto talking with a Fire Department lieutenant, and he went over and greeted DiMotto.

"Any idea how it started?" DiMotto asked.

Nick shook his head. "A couple of hoods came around, and busted a window when I wouldn't let them in. They might have done it, but there's no proof."

"Who were they?"

"No idea. They said you sent them, but there were no marks on the card so I figured they'd swiped it someplace."

"I know who you mean. They're a couple of Livorno's boys."

"I wonder what they wanted."

"Bust the place up—intimidate the customers—that sort of thing."

"Well, they busted it up, all right. What do we do now?"

"I've got a couple of ideas. I'll scout around and let you know what I find. How're you fixed for money?"

"We're O.K., for the moment. I took the cash box home."

"Well, let's let the son of a bitch think he's put us out of business, and in the meantime I'll make some inquiries."

"What'll I tell people who ask? We've got a lot of loyal customers."

"If they're all that loyal, they'll wait. Tell 'em we don't know what we're going to do next, and at the moment that's the God's honest truth."

"It seems to me McGinty ought to be able to do something. What are we paying all this police protection for?"

"For protection against the police. That, and no more."

Nick thought a moment, then said, "A little while ago I promised Marie I'd take her out west, to see some Indians. It looks like you can be scalped without ever leaving New York."

"Brother, you just said a mouthful." DiMotto turned back to the Fire Department lieutenant and said, "Tell the boys if they should find any unbroken glassware in the wreckage, they can keep it."

The lieutenant grinned. "Thank you," he said.

"Not that they wouldn't have, anyway."

"Well, it's always nice to have permission."

Later that afternoon, MacDougall found Nick and Marie sifting through the wreckage. A sour, smoky smell hung over everything, and the debris was wet and spongy. They had found a metal teakettle, about two dozen unbroken teacups, and the twisted remains of the gas ring, but beyond that, and a few warped and blackened kitchen utensils, there was nothing that was readily identifiable. Nick saw MacDougall watching them and went over to join him.

"Some mess, huh?" he said.

"There was a lot of heat there," MacDougall replied. "Do you know what they used?"

"No idea. Whatever it was, it did the trick."

MacDougall looked at the buildings on either side, which were unharmed except that some of their windows were cracked and blackened from the heat. "It could have been a fire bomb," he said. "Bombs seem to be all the rage these days. Any idea who did it?"

"None that we could prove," Nick replied. "We have suspicions."

"Like what?" MacDougall brought out his copy paper.

"Like"–Nick hesitated, not knowing if he should mention Livorno or not–"well, just say it was underworld elements."

"What did they have in mind?"

Nick gave a short laugh. "To put us out of business."

"You mean it was competition?"

"Not exactly."

"Then what?"

"They were extortionists who couldn't extort."

"What do you mean?"

"They tried to hit us for protection money but I wouldn't play, so they did this to get even."

"Then you must know who it is."

"Well—we have no proof."

"Can I say whom you suspect?"

"Look, Mac, I'll level with you, but we don't want it in print. O.K.?"

MacDougall sighed. "O.K."

Nick filled him in on Livorno's extortion attempts, and concluded, "We hope we'll be able to set up someplace else, but for the moment we want the bastard to think he's beaten us. So say anything else you want, but just remember we don't have a speck of proof it was his guys who did it."

"You say he's got his hooks into the Sanitation Department?"

"So I gather, but you'll have to find that out for yourself. Just leave us out of it."

"It's O.K. to mention your fire? I mean, that's the reason for my being here."

"Oh, sure." Nick looked at the ruins and laughed. "We can't very well keep that a secret."

"Oh—what should I call you?"

"What do you mean?"

"How do I identify the club? I can't very well call it a speakeasy."

Nick thought for a moment, then said, "Well, we were supposed to be serving tea."

"O.K.," said MacDougall, smiling. "I'll call it a tearoom."

Back at the paper, MacDougall sat down at his desk and wrote:

> The Club Circe, a tearoom at 214 West Eighth Street, was destroyed by fire of suspicious origin early yesterday morning. There were no injuries, the club having been unoccupied at the time of the fire, and police estimated the damage at $150,000. The entire stock was declared a total loss.

He handed the item in to the city desk, and the desk man read it and said, "That's all?"

"That's all," MacDougall replied.

"He has no enemies? No theories on who might have done it?"

"No theories. All he would say was 'underworld elements.' "

"Then he must have some idea."

MacDougall shrugged. "None he'd tell me."

"I thought you were a buddy of his."

"I know him, that's all."

The desk man looked at the copy again, marked it with his pencil, and tossed it in a basket. "For someone who was going to solve the Bostwick bombing," he said, "you sure as hell don't have much initiative."

11

A week after the fire, Nick and DiMotto met in a Greenwich Village restaurant, run by a friend of DiMotto's. It was primarily a pasta house, specializing in a variety of spaghetti sauces, but friends of the management could have wine in teacups if they so desired. The wine, like the spaghetti sauce, was made on the premises.

DiMotto took a sip of would-be chianti, rinsed it around his front teeth, and swallowed. "Not bad," he said. "Everything considered."

Nick sampled his, and said, "Marie's been after me to stock some wine, just for her. I wonder if this guy would let me have a couple of gallons."

"I can get you better stuff than this," DiMotto replied. "I don't think the French are too crazy about homemade dago red."

"Well, we're not in a position to be too fussy," Nick said. "At the moment, we don't even have a place to store it."

"I think I've found a place."

"For storage?"

"For the club. It's the ground floor of a brownstone, in the east forties."

"Does it have a kitchen?"

"It used to *be* the kitchen. There's three rooms, with a front and back door."

"What about a basement?"

"I don't know. Why?"

"We've got to have a basement, to store the stock. And it's got to be good and secure, so nobody can break in. Ideally, we should have it camouflaged."

"Who do you think is going to try to break in?"

"You never can tell. We can't buy everyone off, and that son of a bitch Livorno is going to be on our necks as soon as he hears we've opened up."

DiMotto shrugged. "Do you want to see it?"

"Sure. When could we move in?"

"We can have it the first of the month, but when we open will depend on how much you want to do."

"I just think it makes sense. It'd be a shame to open up, and then get hit and lose all our stock. We've got to be able to hide it so's nobody can find it."

"Any idea how?"

"In general, yes. Like fake doors, and maybe a brick wall that opens up."

"Jesus, you'll need an engineer for that. Think of something simple."

"If it's simple, it'll be no good. I think it's worth waiting, if we can get it right."

"Well, let's go look at it. Maybe something'll come to you when you see it."

They paid their check and went uptown, and when they reached the brownstone house they found a moving van out front, and men were coming down the front steps carrying beds, sofas, and dressers.

"Do we get the whole house?" Nick asked, incredulous.

"No," said DiMotto. "A decorating firm is taking over the top part, and they'll have no need for the kitchen. We'll block off the stairway and have the kitchen to ourselves." He waited for a break in the stream of movers, then went up the front steps, followed by Nick. A man was standing in the front hall, directing the flow of traffic. He looked at DiMotto, who with brisk authority said, "We're the kitchen inspectors. How do we get downstairs?"

"Around the corner to your right," the man replied, and they went where he directed and down to the cave-like ground floor. The window shutters were closed, and in the near-total darkness Nick could sense rather than see the layout of the rooms. DiMotto turned on an overhead light, making everything a jumble of glare and shadows, and for a moment Nick had the sensation they'd entered an Etruscan tomb that had been cleaned out by vandals.

"My God," he said. "When was this place last used?"

"Don't ask me," DiMotto replied. "But I'd hate to cat anything that was cooked here."

"Let's see if we can find the cellar," Nick said. "We can worry about the rest later."

They found the cellar, in one corner of which stood a coal furnace, and Nick realized that the furnace area would have to be separate from the liquor storage bins, so that the janitor could go about his business without knowing the real function of the place. This would involve a certain amount of reconstruction, but was certainly not an insurmountable problem if done by the right person.

"I know who we can get!" he said, as a sudden idea struck him. "Why didn't I think of it before?"

"Who?" said DiMotto, peering up the coal chute.

"Fred McClain is an engineer, and this sort of thing would be right up his alley. He'd be perfect for it."

"How much would he charge?"

"Never mind that; he's got a mind that would have a field day with this."

"Is he trustworthy?"

"Of course he is. Why?"

"The guy who sets this up has got us by the short hairs, you realize that. Any time he cares to rat to the Feds he can wipe us out, and he can also blackmail us to make sure he *doesn't* rat. What we're doing is putting our knockers in a vise and giving him the handle."

"I think Fred was our fourth customer. They don't come any more loyal than he is."

"O.K. I just hope you know what you're talking about."

"I do, believe me. What about the police? Are they likely to make trouble?"

"We're on the upper edge of McGinty's precinct. No problem there."

They went back into the kitchen, and Nick surveyed the room and said, "It doesn't look like much now, but Marie can take care of that. In a week she'll have it looking like the palace at Versailles."

What with one thing and another, it was three months before the club was ready to reopen. McClain was a man with good ideas but he moved slowly, as though afraid that speed might upset his calculations. He'd been a naval aviator during the war, operating out of Bay Shore, Long Island, in Curtiss flying boats, and the regularity with which these machines had dumped him into Great South Bay had made him cautious in the extreme about anything mechanical. His tendency was not to think of a new machine in terms of what it might do, but rather what might go wrong with it, and this built an inevitable delay into his plans. However, he finally came up with a security system for the Club Circe's liquor cellar that involved hidden doors, a movable brick wall, a dumping system for the bar, a concealed staircase, and several dummy closets, these last to create confusion in the mind of anyone trying to visualize the entire layout.

"As I see it, there's only one thing that can go wrong," he told Nick, as they were examining the final drawings. "If some bastard gets down there with a tape measure and starts measuring actual against potential cubic footage, he's going to realize you've got a lot of dead space that isn't accounted for. And if he's the suspicious type he's going to think that dead space is full of booze, which of course it will be."

"I guess that's a chance we'll have to take," Nick said. "Can you think of a way around it?"

McClain was a large, handsome man, who looked something like the J. C. Leyendecker advertisements for Arrow Collars. He leaned back, put his feet on his desk, and smiled. "Yes," he said. "Buy the houses on both sides of you, and put the booze in them."

Nick laughed. "Thanks a lot," he said. "Next question: Do you know any reliable workmen, who can do this for us without blabbing?"

"Yes. They've done–uh–some other stuff for me, and they're reliable."

"Which brings us to the last question: What about your fee?"

McClain looked at the ceiling. "Supposing I were to be your consulting engineer," he said. "On a permanent basis, that is. In exchange for that, you pick up the tab for whatever I may eat or drink in your place. How does that sound?"

"You mean forever?" Nick said.

"As much as there is a forever. As long as I'm your consulting engineer."

"Suppose we don't need any more engineering?"

"That's the chance you take. If, however, you do need something done, then I've got to do it for you free. That's the chance I take."

Nick paused. "I'll have to ask Frank," he said. "As a rule, he's against the house picking up the tab."

"Then I'll just charge you what I'd charge anyone else. For a job like this, that would be a bundle of dough."

"As I said, I'll ask Frank."

"Do it whichever way you please. It's all the same to me."

They eventually settled on the exchange that McClain had proposed, and the alterations started as soon as the previous tenants were off the premises. From experience Nick knew he'd need at least two men to help him with the larger establishment, and after scouting around and interviewing several people he settled on Charles Kestrow, who'd been a bartender at the Hotel Brevoort, to tend his bar, and Max Feistel, a onetime Pinkerton detective, to guard the door. Marie refused any help in the kitchen, saying she was perfectly capable of doing it herself, and Nick decided to wait until she asked before he hired anyone there. Two new paychecks were all he figured the budget could stand, anyway.

The opening was scheduled for mid-June, and as many of the old customers as possible had been notified. Marie had tried to keep the wine-cellar atmosphere of the old place, but certain changes had had to be made: candles on the tables were now impractical as well as a fire hazard, and their effect had to be simulated by the use of indirect lighting. The red-check tablecloths were retained, and a conscious effort had been made to decorate the walls in a manner appropriate to the situation. There was, for instance, a framed copy of the classic French cartoon showing a small boy micturating into a pond over the caption *"Ne buvez jamais d'eau,"* and next to it, as a sly reference to the teacups in which the drinks were served, was a large print of the Boston Tea Party. Framed copies of newspapers, detailing the ratification of the Eighteenth Amendment and the onset of Prohibition, were interspersed with shots of the Statue of Liberty, Niagara Falls, and the Grand Canyon, and directly over the entrance door was the James Montgomery Flagg recruiting poster saying "Uncle Sam wants YOU." A large copper samovar stood to one side of the bar with a teacup beneath its spigot, and on the wall behind it was the sheet music for the song containing the lines: "Come, come, come and make eyes at me / Under the Anheuser Busch." The decor was, in a word, eclectic, and if some of the atmosphere of the original establishment was lost, a great deal was gained in the way of diversity.

The opening hour had been set for five in the afternoon, and Nick stood with Max by the door to help familiarize him with the regular customers. Charlie was peeling his oranges and lemons behind the bar, and in the kitchen Marie went from pot to pot, inspecting the dishes she'd prepared. She had a thick, country *potage,* made primarily from potatoes and leeks, and she had a chicken casserole, a recipe of her mother's, that included onions, tomatoes, garlic, parsley, white wine, herbs, and ripe olives. Also, simmering on a third burner, was a beef *bourguignon,* which she'd made the day before and allowed to stand overnight, to improve the flavor. She was equipped to handle a few special orders, such as small club steaks or chops, but she was relying on her casseroles to handle most of the traffic. To occupy her time until the customers arrived, she filled a large wooden salad bowl with lettuce, poured in some oil, vinegar, and salt, and sampled it. She added a bit of dry mustard and sugar, tossed the leaves, and sampled it again, then began to peel a clove of garlic.

Standing at the door with Max, Nick looked at his watch and saw that it was seven minutes past five. Nobody had arrived so far, but that didn't disturb him; at the old place it was sometimes six o'clock before the first customer appeared. He'd set five as the opening time so that people wouldn't get sidetracked in some other speakeasy, and he realized that the majority would barely have left their offices by now. It was just too early to expect anyone, and he told himself to relax. He adjusted the white carnation in his buttonhole, pressed the lapel flat, and shot his cuffs. His mouth was dry, and he went to the bar and asked Charlie to pour him a ginger ale.

At quarter to six there were still no customers, and Nick began to wonder if the notices had been mailed. He went into the kitchen, where Marie was standing by the salad bowl, a glass of red wine in one hand and a salad fork in the other. "Did you mail those notices out?" he asked.

"What notices?" said Marie.

"The letters I gave you last week. The notices of our opening."

"Oh, those." She sampled a piece of salad, then held out a leaf to him. "Tell me what you think."

"Listen—I said did you mail those notices? It's a simple question—did you, or didn't you?"

"Oh, yes. I guess I must have."

"What do you mean, must have? Don't you know?"

"Ne te fâche pas, choux. I must have because I put them on my dresser when you gave them to me, and they're not there now. So I must have mailed them. What do you think of the salad?"

He took the lettuce leaf she offered him and swallowed it. "Not bad," he said. "Are you sure—"

"It needs something, but I don't know what." She took a sip of wine, then poured some in the salad, and stirred it around.

The buzzer sounded before Nick could say anything more, and he turned and hurried to the front door, where Max was peering through the peephole.

"It's a Mr. McClain," Max said, as Nick came up. "He says you know him."

"I certainly do," Nick replied, opening the door and shaking hands with McClain. "Welcome to our first customer." A thought struck him, and he added, "Even if he is a nonpaying one."

"I can't do that to you," McClain said, coming into the bar. "I'll buy the first drink, provided you frame the bill." He brought out a dollar, put it on the bar, and said, "I'll have a Scotch."

"Done and done." Nick turned to Charlie, who was pouring Scotch into a teacup, and said, "After this, Mr. McClain's drinks are on the house. Don't ask me why, because I think I got screwed."

"Come the first raid, you'll see whether you got screwed or not," McClain replied. "I think you got the better of the deal."

"We'll see," said Nick, and tapped his knuckles on the bar.

McClain raised his cup, said, "Here's mud in your eye," and took a sip. He set the cup down, looked at it for a moment, then said, "Does it make much sense to use teacups at a bar? I mean, it was all right when you sat at a table, but to stand with your foot on a bar rail, drinking out of a teacup, seems to me a bit ludicrous. Do you think anyone'll be fooled?"

"Of course not," Nick replied. "It's just that we've got so many teacups we've got to do something with them. Besides, I feel kind of sentimental about them—they're what got us started." He saw Marie peering through the kitchen door and said, "Are you going to be eating here tonight?"

"I hadn't thought of it," said McClain. "Why?"

"Marie's done a lot of cooking, and she'll cut her throat if nobody eats it. She's as nervous as a bride."

"I may have something later. It's a little early for dinner right now."

There came the sound of the buzzer, and Nick went to the door and admitted Albert Hopkins, introducing him to Max as he did. Hopkins smiled, looked around, and said, "This is a nice place you have here. Whoever burned down the other one did you a favor."

"If you want to look at it that way," Nick replied. "I gather you got our notice."

"What notice?"

"Of our new address. We mailed them out last week–or at least I think we did."

"I wouldn't know–I've been away. I got your address from the police. Did you know McGinty made captain?"

"No. I've been all tied up with work here. Are you sure you didn't get a notice? We sent it to your office."

"I haven't been through all the mail yet." Hopkins looked at Charlie and said, "May I have a Scotch, please?"

"Where'd you go this time?" Nick asked.

"Oh–here and there. The company's thinking of setting up an office in Cleveland."

"Well, Cleveland's not as far as Cherbourg. At least you stayed in the country."

"Oh, I didn't *go* to Cleveland. I was scouting around." He took his drink from Charlie, said, "To crime," and drank. Out of the corner of his eye he saw Marie peering in from the kitchen, and he said, "Is Marie still making those wonderful sandwiches?"

"You should see what she's made. Potato soup, chicken casserole, beef stew, salad–you can have a whole meal, as good as you'll get in France."

"Actually, I had my mouth set for one of her ham and cheese sandwiches. I didn't have lunch, and I've been looking forward to it all afternoon."

"Well, I'll ask her. I guess she'll do it, seeing it's you."

"This isn't in place of dinner, mind you. I just need a blotter of some sort, to keep from getting cockeyed."

"Oh, sure. I understand." Nick went into the kitchen, and Marie looked at him expectantly. She had refilled her tumbler with red wine and was chewing on a scallion that she'd prepared for the salad.

"Does he want the *potage* first?" she asked.

"He wants a ham and cheese sandwich," Nick replied, and then, seeing her face, he added, "He may have dinner later, though. He says this is just a blotter."

"Idiot! Crapaud! Salautier! What kind of appetite will he have after eating a ham and cheese sandwich? If he wants a blotter why doesn't he buy a loaf of bread, and pour his whisky into that? Why doesn't he pour his whisky into his hat, and pull it down over his ears?" She went to the refrigerator and brought out the ham and cheese, then snatched a *baguette* from a basket and halved it with one savage slice of a carving knife.

"Easy does it," Nick said. "He's a good customer."

"Anyone who pays his bill is a good customer," Marie replied, buttering the bread and slamming the sandwich together. "That doesn't entitle him to special orders. Supposing he wanted *crêpes suzettes?* Supposing he wanted *escargots?* Would that mean I'd have to go out and–"

"Look," Nick said. "It's only a little after six. He's got all the time in the world to have this sandwich and a few drinks, and *then* have dinner. Nobody eats before seven-thirty, even if they're going to the theatre."

Marie put the sandwich on a plate, said, "There's his Lordship's *hors-d'oeuvre,"* then took a big gulp from her wine tumbler. She looked at the leftover ham and cheese and on a sudden whim diced it all into small squares and tossed it in the salad bowl. Then she poured in a splash of wine and a flop of mayonnaise and stirred it vigorously. Nick took the sandwich out to the bar and gave it to Hopkins.

"Here you are," he said. "She was glad to do it for you."

"She's a treasure," Hopkins replied. "And you can tell her I said so."

"I'll do that," said Nick.

The next to arrive were MacDougall and Dorothy Peters. McClain, who was standing at the bar, spotted MacDougall and greeted him warmly. "Well, look who's here!" he said. "Where've you been keeping yourself?"

"Hi, Fred," MacDougall replied. "I got a job. Fred, I'd like you to meet Dottie Peters. Mrs. Peters, Mr. McClain."

"How do you do?" McClain said, noticing that Dorothy was clinging tightly to MacDougall's arm.

She saw his look and said, "I'm Mrs. in name only. Mr. Peters is in another part of the forest."

"I see," said McClain. Then, to MacDougall, "What kind of job did you get?"

"I'm a reporter at the *Trib*. I started in January."

"Great! Let's have a drink to it. What'll you have?"

MacDougall and Dorothy glanced at each other, and after a short pause MacDougall said, "Scotch, please. We'd both like Scotch. But let me get it. I–"

"Nonsense!" McClain gestured to Charlie, who poured two Scotches and set them on the bar. "My tab is taken care of by the house."

"How'd you work that?" MacDougall asked.

McClain remembered the vow of secrecy he'd given Nick when he drew up the plans, and said, "I'm a consultant. I take my fee in booze instead of money."

"Boy," said MacDougall. "I wish they'd consult me."

"Who knows? Maybe you could be their press agent."

Dorothy, who'd been studying McClain in silence, said, "What do you do, Mr. McClain?"

"Please call me Fred. Ah–technically I'm an engineer, but I have a number of sidelines."

"I'll bet you do," she said.

He glanced at her to see how the remark had been intended but could tell nothing from her expression. All he could see were large brown eyes looking at him from under a curtain of bangs, and they were absolutely neutral, as though she were studying a bulletin board.

"Any time," he said.

They had another round, which MacDougall paid for, and then he said, "Fred, would you excuse us? I think we'll sit down and have a bite to eat."

"Sure thing," said McClain. "Thanks for the drink. Nice to have met you, Mrs. Peters."

"Likewise, I'm sure," said Dorothy. She took MacDougall's arm as he led her to a table in the far corner of the room. They sat down, and he motioned to Charlie for two drinks. In a low voice she said, "I don't like your friend."

"I sensed that," he replied. "That's why I got us away. Why don't you?"

"He's too pretty. I think his face has gone to his head."

"Actually, he's a nice guy. He was the one who brought me here—or, rather, to the old place. He introduced me to Nick."

"Have you known him long?"

"A couple of years."

"Just don't let him come between us."

"How could he possibly do that?"

She put out her hand, palm up, and he took it in both of his. "It was a bad joke, my love," she said. "As far as I'm concerned, nothing could ever come between us."

"All right, then."

There was a pause, and she withdrew her hand. "Excuse me," she said.

"Excuse you for what?"

"I didn't mean to embarrass you."

"I don't know what you're talking about."

"Well, forget it. It's of no consequence."

Nick brought their drinks to the table and said, "Would you folks care for something to eat?"

MacDougall looked at Dorothy, who shook her head. "I guess not right now," he said to Nick, then added, "Wait a minute–I suppose we ought to have something, because I told Fred we were going to have a bite. I'll have a—a roast-beef sandwich."

Nick cleared his throat. "Marie has made a special menu for tonight," he said. "Potato soup, either chicken casserole or beef stew, and salad. It's as good as any restaurant in town."

"That sounds like an awful lot. Couldn't she just make me a roast-beef sandwich? Or a ham and cheese, if she doesn't have roast beef?"

Nick took a deep breath. "To be honest with you, she's not in a sandwich-making mood. She's spent so much time on the special menu that that's all she can think of."

MacDougall hesitated. "We should be polite," he said. "All right, then, let me have a small portion of beef stew. Dottie? Are you sure you don't want anything?"

Again Dorothy shook her head, and Nick went into the kitchen. "One beef stew," he said to Marie, who had just sprinkled some capers into the salad.

"It is not beef stew!" she replied. "It is *boeuf bourguignon,* and the next person to call it beef stew gets the casserole dumped on his head!" She moved her empty wineglass, got a plate, and ladled out a large portion. Then she tossed the salad two or three times and filled a salad plate.

"He didn't order salad," Nick said. "He just wanted the beef—"

"He gets a salad whether he wants it or not," said Marie. "This is not what you call a one-arm lunch joint."

At the table, MacDougall said to Dorothy, "All right, now. Tell me what you were talking about."

"When?" said Dorothy.

"Before Nick brought the drinks. You were sore about something, and I have no idea what."

"Let it pass."

"I will not let it pass! If it was important enough to make you sore, then it's important enough for me to know. You said you'd embarrassed me, and I want to know how."

She sighed. "I said as far as I'm concerned nothing could ever come between us, and this apparently embarrassed you because you said nothing."

"I did not say nothing!"

"You said, 'All right,' or something steamy like that. That's as good as nothing."

Nick brought the food, and when he'd left MacDougall said, "That is absolutely insane! The fact that I said, 'All right,' meant I agreed with you, didn't it?"

"How would I know? I can't read your mind."

"Oh, God."

"And you don't need to swear at me. I can take a hint without your having to invoke the Deity."

"Will you listen to me? Just for a minute?"

"I'll listen better with another Scotch. This one seems to have evaporated."

MacDougall turned in his chair and said, "Charlie, another Scotch, please." Then to Dorothy, "I agree with you completely that nothing can ever come between us. I feel as though you're as much a part of me as my—my right hand."

"Then how come you haven't proposed marriage?"

"How come? How come? Well—in the first place, I'm not making enough money. I mean—well—"

"What you mean is I'm good enough to go to bed with but not good enough to be your partner for life—in spite of the fact that I'm as much a part of you as your right hand. What's your left hand doing these days?"

"Oh, come on, now. Just—"

"You come on. How do you think it makes me feel?"

Nick appeared with the Scotch and said, "Is everything all right?"

MacDougall, who hadn't touched his food, looked up and said, "Yes, thank you. Just fine."

"Fine and dandy," Dorothy said. "Couldn't be better."

"Marie'll be interested in how you like the food," Nick said.

MacDougall took a bite of *bourguignon,* swallowed, and said, "It's swell. My compliments."

"Thank you." Nick went into the kitchen, where Marie had refilled her wineglass and was tasting the salad. "He says it's swell," he said.

"What does that mean, swell?" she replied. "I don't know the word."

"In America, something is either swell or it's lousy," Nick said. "If it's swell it's good, and if it's lousy it's bad. He said the beef was swell, so it means he likes it."

"What about the salad?"

"He hasn't got to that yet. He's having a little trouble with the madam, and it's cut in on his eating."

He heard the buzzer and went out to the front door, where Max was talking to someone through the peephole.

"It's two guys who want to sell you insurance," Max told him. "I think they're hoods."

Nick stepped to the peephole and saw two shadowy figures outside. "This is a private club," he said. "Whatever it is, I'm not interested." He started to close the peephole, but one of the men spoke in a voice that was faintly familiar.

"We thought you might be interested in some fire insurance," the man said. "We hear you had a little trouble with fire recently."

"If it's the kind of insurance I'm thinking of, you can forget it," Nick replied.

"You're kinda stupid," the man said. "A slow learner, like."

"Not that stupid," said Nick, and slammed the peephole shut. Damn, he thought. It didn't take them long to find out where we are. He saw McClain at the bar and went over and stood beside him. "I may have another job for you," he said.

"What's that?" said McClain.

"How hard would it be to make this place fireproof?"

McClain thought a moment, then said, "That would depend."

"Well, give it some thought, will you? Charlie, Mr. McClain's about ready for another round here."

"I think I know who got screwed," McClain said, with a smile. "And I don't think it was you."

By eight o'clock there were twenty or more people in the bar, and Nick had managed to convince a few of them that they should try the food. All those who ate were loud in their praise, and there were special hosannas for the salad. At one point Nick went into the kitchen and said to Marie, "How's the salad holding out? Suddenly everybody wants some."

Marie looked into the bowl. "A few more servings," she said. "Maybe six." Her glass was empty and she looked around for the bottle to refill it, but that was empty too.

"Well, you'd better make some more," Nick said. "We don't want to run out."

Marie went to the lettuce bin, took out a handful, and then stopped. *"Merde,"* she said. "I can't remember what went in it."

At the corner table, Dorothy had subsided into quiet weeping. "All you have to do is tell me," she said. "Just say the word, and I'll leave. One word is all I need."

"I don't want you to leave," MacDougall replied. "You just don't seem to be having a very good time."

"What kind of time am I supposed to be having? When you've as good as said you don't love me, am I supposed to put garlands in my hair and leap about with a lyre?"

"I never said I didn't—"

"Put it this way: did you ever say you loved me? Did you ever come right out with those three little words?"

"I must have. I mean—"

"When? Name me the specific time, and I'll be happy. God knows it's little enough to ask."

"I can't name you the specific time because I don't remember. But that doesn't mean I—"

"I don't think we need carry this any further." She blew her nose and stood up. "I'll just leave and save you the trouble of inventing anything. You must be tired enough as it is." She picked up her purse, and crammed her handkerchief into it.

MacDougall rose. "I'll take you home," he said.

"I'd rather you didn't."

"Don't be silly. I wouldn't hear of–"

"Don't *you* be silly. I'm a big girl now, and I can find my own way about town. I'm sure if I let you take me home you'd think I was trying to seduce you."

"I mean it. I–"

"So do I. Thank you for everything. It's been, as they say, just swell." She walked quickly from the room, and MacDougall could hear the door close as Max let her out. He took a deep breath, exhaled slowly, and went to the bar, where McClain was standing.

"Trouble?" McClain asked.

"Not really," MacDougall said. "It might better be termed a close call."

"Close, but no cigar," McClain said, and they both laughed.

When she got to her apartment, Dorothy turned on the overhead light and locked the door. The glare of the light seemed to magnify the disorder in the room, picking out the ashtrays piled high with lipstick-stained cigarette butts, the pair of stockings trailing over the edge of the wastebasket, and the glass, perched miraculously like a bird on the arm of the sofa, holding the watery remnants of a Scotch in which a cigarette had disintegrated. The room was, God knew, familiar to her, but it no longer seemed a part of her; it was just something she had to pass through on the way to the bathroom. It's going to be somebody else's worry from now on, she thought; it's all theirs and they can have it, along with a big, wet kiss from Aunt Dorothy.

She turned on the light in the bathroom and opened the medicine cabinet. She had some trouble focusing, but she could recognize the Nembutal bottle, and she opened it and tipped it into her hand. Two pills rolled out, and she stared owlishly at them, returned them to the bottle, and put it back on the shelf. She saw the small, brown iodine bottle with its skull and crossbones, and rejected that almost immediately. Finally, after staring into the cabinet for several minutes, she took her safety razor, unscrewed it, and lifted out the rusty blade. Then she pulled up a bathroom stool, sat at the sink, and turned on both faucets. With calm deliberation she brought the razor blade to her left wrist, pressed the edge into her flesh, and jumped at the pain. She tried once more and produced only a few drops of blood, then held her breath and made a quick slash. The pain was like a thin line of fire, and she dropped the blade and instinctively put the cut to her mouth. There was blood this time, but she'd missed the artery and severed only a few of the small, blue veins, and suddenly the whole thing seemed more trouble than it was worth. She applied a facecloth to the cut, bound it in place with a towel, and then, with the faucets still running, she put her forehead on the edge of the sink and wept.

12

On May 5, 1920, Nicola Sacco and Bartolomeo Vanzetti, self-proclaimed anarchists, were arrested for the murder of a paymaster and guard in South Braintree, Massachusetts, three weeks earlier. More than a year later they were brought to trial before Judge Webster Thayer of the Massachusetts superior court, sitting in Dedham, and on July 14, 1921, they were found guilty. The verdict caused an immediate outcry in liberal circles, where the feeling was that the men had been convicted for their political beliefs rather than any proof of having committed a crime, and an appeal was filed for a new trial. It failed, and periodically new appeals were submitted, all with the same result. Sentencing was postponed, pending outcome of the litigation.

On Friday, July 14, 1922, Roland Butterworth reported for work as usual at the *Tribune*. In the more than eighteen months he had been on the paper his assignments had consisted of preparing obituaries on people not yet dead; of covering conventions, testimonial dinners, banquets, and communion breakfasts; and of doing feature stories on such events as the annual outing of the Institute for the Crippled and Disabled, the awarding of the S.P.C.A. Medal of Honor to a dog named Spot for having alerted its master to the fact that the bed was on fire, and the arrival in New York of a man who had walked all the way from Beloit, Wisconsin, carrying a banner urging the repeal of the Nineteenth Amendment. He was, in short, a well-rounded city reporter, able to hammer any mass of trivia into the appearance of a news story. The important stories were entrusted to men with more experience.

"Here's something you can really sink your teeth into," the desk man told him, as he came up to get his assignment. "What does July 14 mean to you?"

"Bastille Day," Butterworth replied. "It's also the day my grandmother got hit by an ice wagon in Worcester, back in '95."

The desk man looked at him for a moment, then said, "More recently, it is one year since Sacco and Vanzetti were found guilty."

"True," said Butterworth. "I'd forgotten."

"Well, let's see how many other people have."

"What do you mean?"

"The Bolshies made a big stink when the jury came in with that verdict. They screamed to high heaven. Let's see how they feel about it now, after a year. They can't bleat about their men being railroaded, because their men are still alive–they haven't even been sentenced. My hunch is there'll be a lot less screaming, now that a year has passed."

Butterworth hesitated. His conscience still hurt about the way he'd ducked out of the bombing interview, and he wanted to atone for it by doing a good job on this assignment, but he was uncertain just how to begin. "Where would I find these Bolshies?" he asked.

The desk man closed his eyes and pinched the bridge of his nose, almost as though praying, then said, "Try Little Italy–Union Square –Greenwich Village–any of those places."

"Socialist Party headquarters?"

"God, no. They'd feed you a lot of party propaganda. This should be interviews with ordinary people, not professional rabble-rousers."

"Ordinary people, or ordinary Bolshies?"

"God damn it, I don't care whom you get! The point is to show that all the hysteria has died down!"

"Supposing it hasn't?"

The desk man gave him a cold stare. "Do you want to be a reporter, or don't you?"

Butterworth was on the point of saying it made no difference to him, but checked himself and said, "Of course I do. I just want to know what's expected of me."

"I've told you what's expected of you. Now, hop to it."

As he went out of the building and into the glaring sunlight on Park Row, Butterworth reviewed the question of whether he wanted to be a reporter, and had the uneasy suspicion that the business was not for him. He didn't like intruding on people's privacy, he was incapable of injecting himself where he wasn't wanted, and he had no interest in writing stories he didn't believe. The bulk of his assignments had been innocuous, to say the very least, but he couldn't spend the rest of his life covering conventions and Girl Scout meetings, and at the same time he felt an aversion to the grittier side of reporting. The only thing to be said for it was that it was a job, now paying him twenty dollars a week, and that was nothing to be given up lightly.

Little Italy, which had once been on the Upper East Side, had now eased gradually south, encompassing an area in the east twenties and thirties, with outposts as far south as Mulberry Street. As he headed east from Park Row, Butterworth rehearsed the various gambits he might use, such as: "Pardon me, sir, but are you aware that Sacco and Vanzetti were found guilty one year ago today?" or, "Excuse me, have you thought much about Sacco and Vanzetti recently?" or perhaps, "In the year since Sacco and Vanzetti were found guilty, have your feelings on the matter grown stronger, or don't you care?" He could imagine what the answers would be to any one of those questions, and the odds were that they would all be unprintable. Taking a new approach, he thought of simply saying, "Remember Sacco and Vanzetti?" but that might run the risk of getting him locked up as a public nuisance, perhaps even as a lunatic. No matter what phraseology he thought of it didn't sound right, and he decided the only answer was to let nature take its course. Rehearsed conversations never followed the original script, anyway.

On Second Avenue he found a small Italian market and decided it was as good a place as any to start. An awning shielded the fruits and vegetables from the sun, and in the dark interior hung long salamis, prosciutto hams, and balls of provolone cheese. It was like a grotto, with stalactites of food dripping from the ceiling, and he wouldn't have been surprised to see some woodland deity—a satyr, perhaps, or a garlanded nymph—appear from the darkness in the rear. Instead, a short, fat man, reeking of garlic and wiping his hands on a dirty apron, came forward and gave him an inquiring look.

"Si, signor?" the man said.

"I—uh—am from the *Tribune,*" said Butterworth. Then, skirting the main question, "Do you have any artichokes?"

"*Si, signor*. How many?"

"Two, I imagine. There are only two of us, and I don't think we'll eat more than one apiece." He tried to remember if Sarah liked artichokes, but couldn't think. He'd asked for them only because he saw them in a bin.

The man picked out two and said, "Anything else?"

"Yes, as a matter of fact—" Butterworth cleared his throat, aware that he could stall no longer, and said, "Do you realize Sacco and Vanzetti were found guilty a year ago today?"

The man stared at him for what seemed like a long time, then said, "And so?"

"I just wondered—" Butterworth cleared his throat again. "I mean, the paper is doing a survey, to see what people think."

"About what?"

"About—well, what was your reaction a year ago, and what is it now?"

"I think it stinks. I thought it stunk a year ago, and I think it stinks now."

"I see. Well—thank you." Butterworth started to leave.

"Do you want your artichokes?" The man held them out, and Butterworth laughed.

"Yes, of course," he said. "How much do I owe you?"

"Ten cents."

Butterworth groped in his pocket for a dime, and the man shook open a paper bag, dropped the artichokes in, and handed them across. "Thank you," Butterworth said. "Thank you for everything."

The man said nothing and returned to the back of the store.

Well, *that* was certainly a dud, Butterworth thought, when he was once more on the street. If I can't do any better than that, I might as well give the whole thing up. The trouble was, he realized, that the reaction he'd just run into was probably a typical one, and no Italian, accosted by a stranger, was likely to say anything more. Unless the man was a friend, he wouldn't— Butterworth stopped, as he remembered Nick Baldino, whom he'd met a little over a week ago when MacDougall had taken him to the Club Circe. He couldn't count Nick as a friend but he was certainly an acquaintance, and he might be the exact person he was looking for. At least he'd be willing to talk, which in itself would be a step forward.

He had a little trouble finding the club, because it had been dark on his previous visit, and all the high-stoop brownstones looked alike. But after two mistakes—one when the door was opened by a Swedish cook, and one that was very obviously another speakeasy—he finally got the right number. When Max opened the peephole, Butterworth said, "Hello, Max, I'm Roland Butterworth. I don't have a card, but I was here last week with George MacDougall, and—" He didn't get to finish the sentence, because the door swung open and Max said, "Good afternoon, Mr. Butterworth. Glad to see you back." As he walked inside, Butterworth had an odd feeling of importance, and pleasure at being recognized. Everything was as he remembered it except that it was virtually empty, with only one customer standing at the bar and two sitting at a table in a far corner. Nick came toward him, and greeted him warmly.

"Welcome back!" he said. "You want your usual ginger ale and steak?"

Butterworth was flattered that Nick, as well as Max, remembered him, and he decided that the least he could do was order something. "Actually, I'd like to talk to you," he said. "But I might just as well have a ginger ale while I'm doing it."

Nick signaled to Charlie for a ginger ale, then pulled out a chair for Butterworth. "Do you want to check your parcel?" he asked, indicating the paper bag.

"Those are artichokes," Butterworth replied. "I got them more or less by mistake."

Nick looked interested. "How do you do that? I generally buy them on purpose, or not at all."

"It's a long story. Sit down and I'll tell you."

Nick took the ginger ale that Charlie had produced, and sat at the table. Butterworth explained his assignment, and when he was through Nick thought for a while, then said, "In the first place, I think it's a mistake to ask just Italians. That isn't going to prove anything, because they'll all have pretty much the same reaction."

"I was going by what the city desk told me," Butterworth said.

"I know. But they're trying to concoct a story, and I'm not sure there is one. Whatever people felt a year ago they're going to feel the same today, so right there your story goes out the window."

"True."

"But since you've got to do something, why not get a cross section of opinion? That'll at least fill up your space."

Butterworth considered this. "Of course," he said. "I should have thought of that."

"You would have, in time."

"One more thing. Do you know where I could find a raging, dyed-in-the-wool Bolshevik?"

Nick gave the question some thought. "That ought to be easy," he said. "But just when you want one, they're never around. I'd say go down to Union Square and see if you can find someone making a speech. The odds are he'll serve your purpose. Of course, if this were the first of May you'd have to beat 'em off with a stick."

Butterworth finished his ginger ale and stood up. "I guess I'd better get going," he said. "I've got a lot of territory to cover. What do I owe you?"

Nick shrugged. "Fifteen cents should cover operating costs," he said. "Let me know how you make out with the story."

"I'll do that." Butterworth put the money on the table and said, "A dime for artichokes, fifteen cents for ginger ale–I should be on an expense account."

"Is it all right to ask why artichokes are part of the story?"

"Conversational ice-breakers. They make a man let down his guard."

"Oh." After a moment's thought Nick said, "I guess there's more to this reporting than meets the eye."

"If you find out what it is, I wish you'd let me know." Butterworth picked up his bag of artichokes and started out.

"Remember," Nick called after him, "give me a report on what happens."

Union Square, baking in the glare of a July afternoon, bore a faint resemblance to siesta hour in a Spanish *plaza.* Shirtsleeved men sought the shade of store entrances, while the equestrian statue of George Washington seemed to radiate the reflected heat of the sun. On the southeast side of the square, near the bend in the old cable-car tracks that was known as Dead Man's Curve, a man wearing an undershirt, dark trousers, and sandals was haranguing a group of perhaps a half dozen people in the shade of a nearby building. He was hoarse, and shouting as though he were addressing an audience of thousands, and as Butterworth moved closer the man's words slowly became intelligible.

"And always remember the congress of 1883," he was saying. "The congress of 1883 set forth the fundamental principles of anarchism, which are: first, the destruction of the existing class rule by all means—and that means energetic, relentless, revolutionary, and international action; second, the establishment of a free society, based on co-operative organization and production; third, free exchange of equivalent products by and between the productive organizations—"

Butterworth listened while the man detailed the fundamental principles, six in all, and when he paused for breath Butterworth said, "What about Sacco and Vanzetti?"

"Shut up," the man replied. "Don't interrupt while I'm talking." He went on with his harangue, getting hoarser by the minute, and finally he cleared his throat, spat, and pointed at Butterworth. "You had a question, comrade," he said. "What was it?"

"I said what about Sacco and Vanzetti?" Butterworth replied, wishing he'd phrased it a little better.

"What about them?" The man's eyes widened, and his face turned dark red. "What *about* them? Martyrs! Sainted, blessed martyrs, broken on the rack of capitalist greed!" Thus warmed up, he began a nearly incoherent tirade, and Butterworth saw that the passage of a year had brought about no cooling of his passions. He tried to edge away, but the man was shouting directly at him, and there was nothing to do but ride it out like a ship in a storm, figuratively taking in his sails and streaming a sea anchor. Then two of the audience drifted off and Butterworth followed, leaving the orator making sounds like a rutting elk.

Looking at his notes, Butterworth saw he had very little on which to build a story, but in the interest of getting a cross section of opinion he decided to go to the opposite extreme, from Union Square to the Union League Club. He had no illusions about being allowed in to interview the members, but there was an outside chance he might see someone who at least would give him a quote. By now he had lost some of his fear of intruding on people, although he still lacked the ingenuity to get around their defenses. It came to him that this was the only time, except for the Bostwick bombing, that he hadn't been given a publicity handout, and the technique of reporting was as different as night from day. Perhaps that was why they'd given him the assignment: perhaps they were gradually easing him into big-time journalism, and with that as a prod to his initiative he boarded the subway for Thirty-fourth Street. Normally he would have walked, but he didn't want to appear at the Union League Club looking as though he'd just completed a cross-country run.

The club was on Thirty-seventh Street, near Madison Avenue, and as Butterworth surveyed its grim exterior he felt as though he were about to storm the Bastille single-handed. He mounted the steps, still clutching his bag of artichokes, and went through polished mahogany doors into the dim, cool interior. A black steward, wearing a livery waistcoat, approached him.

"Yes, sir?" the steward said.

"Has Mr. Larrabee arrived yet?" Butterworth said, picking a name at random.

"No, sir, Mr. Larrabee's in Wisconsin," the steward replied.

"That's funny. He told me to meet him here this afternoon." At least there *was* a member named Larrabee, so Butterworth felt on somewhat firmer ground.

"If you'll wait in the visitors' room, sir, I'm sure he'll be along shortly." The steward was clearly puzzled but was in no position to call Butterworth a liar. He went to the board, where members' names were listed with "in" or "out" pegs next to them, and checked to make sure that Larrabee's read "out." Then he looked at the entrance door, as though expecting Larrabee to be coming through.

In the visitors' room, just off the lobby, Butterworth riffled through a copy of *The Spur,* trying to decide what to do next. He saw members come in, singly and in pairs, but none of them stopped at the visitors' room, and he knew he could wait only so long until his pretense of waiting for Larrabee began to evaporate. Finally he straightened his tie, clutched his bag of artichokes, and went back into the lobby.

"Excuse me," he said to the steward, "could you direct me to the washroom?"

"It's that door on the left, sir," the steward replied, nodding his head in the direction of an unmarked door.

Butterworth went through the door and into a small, white-tiled washroom that smelled of witch hazel and bear grease. He used the urinal, washed his hands and face, then put some bear grease on a comb and ran it through his hair, running through it twice to make sure that the part line was straight. He retied his bow tie, tugging the ends tight and flat, splashed witch hazel on his cheeks and forehead, and was trying to think of other ways to kill time when the door opened, and a portly man in a rumpled white suit came in and stood at the urinal. Butterworth took a paper cup from a stack, poured mouthwash into it and gargled, then dabbed at his mouth with a towel and examined his teeth in the mirror. Then, throwing the towel in a wicker hamper, he said, "You know, I just realized–it was a year ago today that Sacco and Vanzetti were found guilty."

The portly man seemed to be experiencing a slight blockage, because he said nothing for a moment, then let out his breath in a kind of sigh and said, "You don't say."

"You'd think that after a year they'd at least get around to sentencing them," Butterworth went on. "It seems pointless to just keep them sitting in jail."

"They should've strung 'em up the minute they caught 'em," the man replied. "Couple of goddam anarchists–jail's too good for the likes of them."

"That's one way of looking at it, certainly," Butterworth said.

"It's the only way. It costs the taxpayers money to keep 'em in jail, and for what? A couple of bomb-throwing bastards who'd as soon run a knife into your back as look at you."

"I didn't know they'd done any bombing," Butterworth said mildly.

"Where've you been the last few years? That bomb on Wall Street a couple of years ago–"

"I meant Sacco and Vanzetti," Butterworth said. "Did they throw any bombs?"

The man flexed his knees, bent forward slightly, and began to button his trousers. "They all throw bombs," he said. "The whole goddam bunch. They ought to be wiped out."

Before Butterworth could say anything more, the door opened and the steward put his head in. "Excuse me, sir," he said, "but are you sure Mr. Larrabee said to meet you here today?"

"That's the way I understood it," Butterworth replied. "Why?"

"I checked his box, and there's a letter there says to hold for his return the twenty-fourth. That's ten days from now."

"Then it must have been my mistake. He must have said the twenty-fourth, and I wrote down the fourteenth. How very stupid of me."

"That's all right, sir. It could happen to anyone."

He held the door open, and Butterworth went out saying, "Thank you–if you hadn't checked the box I might very well have spent the night here."

The steward chortled. "No, sir," he said. "I doubt if you would."

Once more on the street, Butterworth looked at his watch and saw that it was quarter to five, too late to get the story done before the desk changed. He decided to kill an hour or so at the Circe; fill Nick in on how the assignment had gone, and possibly talk with someone who might be able to add a few details. The place should be filling up within the next hour, and there ought to be a wide variety of opinions. It was, he reflected, a nice thing to have a place like the Circe, where he could pass his spare time in congenial company and meet people he might otherwise never have known.

There were several people at the bar, although the place was by no means full, and Butterworth ordered a ginger ale and studied the customers. They all seemed to be sober, quiet businessmen, and they looked no more like law-breakers than they did like choirboys. Not one of them showed any sign of excess, and while Butterworth realized it was early and the drinking had hardly begun, he still found it hard to reconcile his scorn for drinkers with the people he saw here. He was pondering this when he realized that Nick was standing beside him.

"How'd it go?" Nick asked.

"About the way I expected," he replied. "Nobody has changed his mind in the last year."

"There was something I forgot to tell you," Nick said. "I don't know whether it would fit into your story or not, but there was a guy from Worcester in here the other day, and he said the judge had shot his mouth off during the trial and said he was going to get those red bastards good and proper."

"He did?" said Butterworth. "What's his name?"

"The judge's name is Webster Thayer."

"I mean the guy who told you."

"I don't know. He was with McClain, who was showing him the town. I'll ask Fred, next time I see him."

"And what was it he said?"

"He said he'd been in the locker room of the Worcester Golf Club while the trial was going on, and the judge was holding forth about Sacco and Vanzetti, calling them 'those bastards down there,' and saying he was going to 'get them good and proper.' He said Thayer had said he was getting a lot of pressure from the radicals and that he was going to 'show them and get those guys hanged,' and that he'd also 'like to hang a few dozen of the radicals.' "

"And those were his exact words?"

"As close as I can remember."

"Wow."

"It's not what your paper was asking for, but you might be able to squeeze it in. It's certainly part of the story."

"I should say it is. I just wish I had this guy's name."

"As I said, I'll ask Fred next time I see him."

When he got to the paper Butterworth went to the night desk man, who looked up and said, "Get anything good?"

"I think so," Butterworth replied.

"O.K. Let's have a column."

"Actually, nobody's changed their minds very much. But there's some stuff I'd never heard before, and—"

The desk man dismissed him with a wave of the hand. "Write it, don't tell me about it," he said.

Butterworth went back to his desk and called for a copy boy to bring him a stack of flimsies—sheets of onionskin and carbon paper, packaged into books of six each, which made an original plus duplicates of his copy; the duplicates were subsequently sent out to the paper's news services and affiliates. He took a book of flimsies, rolled it into his typewriter, put his name and the slug "sacco x local" in the upper left-hand corner, rolled about half the page through, and then sat, trying to think of the lead. Finally, after considering a number of approaches, he typed out:

> A year ago yesterday, July 14, 1921, Nicola Sacco and Bartolomeo Vanzetti were found guilty of a payroll murder in South Braintree, Mass., and opinions were sharply divided as to whether or not they had received a fair trial. A survey by the New York Tribune showed yesterday that the opinions are still sharply divided, and that those who hold them are, if anything, firmer in their beliefs than ever before.

He realized he hadn't got the name of the Italian grocer, but that was of less importance than padding out the interview to make it take up the required space. The same was true for the Union Square orator and the Union League Club man, but he found that by using phrases like "typical of this approach was an East Side greengrocer who wished to remain anonymous," and "one of the most vocal proponents of this theory, a prominent midtown clubman," and the like, he was able to squeeze out three quarters of a column of copy. Then, leading into the windup, he wrote:

> Of considerable interest to those who maintain that the trial was unfair is the testimony, recently revealed, showing that Judge

Webster Thayer expressed extreme prejudice against the defendants while the trial was still in progress. Witnesses who heard him in the locker room of the Worcester Golf Club report that

He concluded with the account that Nick had given him, using the quoted phrases as nearly as he could remember them, and after rereading the piece he made the # mark at the bottom and took the original to the city desk, leaving the flimsies to be collected by a copy boy. The night man was busy reading another story, so Butterworth left his piece on the desk, went to the water cooler and had a drink, then returned to his desk and began preparing to leave. He was interrupted by a shout of "Mr. Butterworth!" from the city desk.

"Sir?" He looked up and saw the desk man beckoning to him, and he hurried across.

"What in the name of God is all this?" the man said, holding out the final page of copy.

"Just that," said Butterworth. "This guy from Worcester told–"

"What testimony? Recently revealed where? What witnesses?"

"This guy from Worcester was in the locker room–"

"What guy? What's his name?"

"I don't know his exact name. He was with a man named McClain. I may get the name in a–"

"Where'd you hear this?"

"Actually, it was at the Club Circe. But–"

"Jesus, Mary, and Joseph, man, don't you know anything about the laws of libel?"

"Well, this guy certainly wouldn't have made it up. I mean, there has to be something to it, and if the papers can quote 'usually reliable sources,' I see no reason–"

"No reason why you can't quote some anonymous bum in a speakeasy? Are you out of your mind?"

"No. I was simply trying to make a story out of an impossible assignment."

"What was impossible about it?"

"The assignment was to prove that all the radical shouting about the case had died down in the last year, when actually it hasn't at all."

"The assignment was to do a survey, and you come out with some wild-eyed statement attacking the judge. We're supposed to be impartial in this, you know."

"Is it impartial to try to prove all the shouting was for nothing? That's just as slanted as taking the other side and, as you put it, attacking the judge."

"It may be slanted, but at least it's slanted on the right side."

Butterworth almost stopped breathing, and he felt his face getting red. "Next time, tell me how I'm supposed to slant things," he said. "It helps if I know which side to be impartial about."

"If there is a next time," the desk man replied, slamming the story on a spike. "Good night."

Butterworth picked up his hat, swung his typewriter down into the desk well, and went out to the elevators. He was trembling, and for reasons he was later unable to explain the only place he wanted to go was the Club Circe. He felt if he went home he'd probably shout at Sarah, but why the Circe seemed the best place was beyond him. A few months ago he'd have taken out his frustration by walking, fast, from one river to the other, but tonight he wanted to be with people and to give vent to his feelings in words.

The club was crowded when he arrived, and loud with the noises of conversation and laughter. Somebody shouted, "Whoopee!" and somebody else replied with "Nertz to you!" and a girl who was surrounded by three men at the bar said, "I'm told I'm known as an easy mark, but I can't see why because I know so few people." Butterworth ordered a ginger ale and downed it in three swallows, then set the glass on the bar and asked for another. Nick appeared beside him and said, "You look ready to eat a tarantula. What happened?"

"Give me ten minutes to get a grip on myself," Butterworth replied. "Then stand well back."

"What you need is a drink. That'll relax you and make you feel better."

"I thought drinks were supposed to pep you up," Butterworth said, downing half of his new ginger ale in one gulp.

"No, no. They calm you down. Try one and see. If you don't do something, you're going to explode."

Butterworth thought for almost a minute, then finished his ginger ale and said, "You're serious? You wouldn't kid me?"

"Honest to Pete. If it doesn't make you feel better, it's on the house."

"All right. I'll try just one, but make it weak. I don't want to fall on my head."

"You won't if you take it slowly. What do you want—rye or Scotch?"

"I wouldn't know the difference. Whichever is easiest."

"Charlie, give Mr. Butterworth a Scotch," Nick said. "And lots of ice."

Charlie set the teacup in front of him, and Butterworth looked at it as though it were hemlock. He felt like a man about to leap off a cliff, and as he raised the cup to his lips he was struck by a strange, familiar odor. His mother, he remembered, had once given him whisky in a tablespoon when he'd fallen through the ice, but this was something else; this was a person, who seemed to be wafting up out of the cup at him. Then it hit him, and in utter amazement he said, "Uncle Albert!" He set the cup down as his mind went back to his Uncle Albert Grinnell, who always seemed to have something to do out in the barn; he was forever going out to curry the horses, or polish the harness, or paint the wagon spokes, and what Butterworth had assumed was Uncle Albert's personal bouquet had been, in fact, a cloud of whisky fumes. Uncle Albert had been quietly cockeyed most of the time.

"Drink it down," Nick told him. "It won't do you any good sitting on the bar."

Butterworth raised the cup, and Uncle Albert came out of it and enveloped him as he took his first drink. He swallowed and felt the whisky make a warm path to his stomach. He shuddered. "Blaugh," he said.

"The first one always does that," Nick said. "Take another."

Butterworth obeyed, and found that this one went down more easily. The whisky tasted medicinal at first, then just faintly unpleasant. "Isn't there a way to make it taste better?" he asked.

"Sure, if you want to mix it with something," Nick replied. "Would you like to try a sour?"

"Anything, to get this taste out of my mouth," said Butterworth.

"A Scotch sour for Mr. Butterworth," Nick told Charlie. "On the tart side."

"Coming right up," Charlie replied. He poured lemon juice and a dash of sugar into a shaker, then added a large splash of Scotch, and ice, and shook it briskly, holding the shaker on a level with his right ear.

Butterworth sipped the new drink and found it a pleasant mixture of tastes. "That is more like it," he said, setting the cup down. "That, if I may say so, is the cat's meow."

Nick laughed. "I thought you might like it," he said. "Now, tell me what happened at the paper."

Butterworth waved a hand in dismissal. "It's too sordid to talk about."

"Did they go for the business about the judge?"

"They went for it, all right. They spiked the whole piece."

"Why?"

Butterworth described what had happened, but by now some of his rage had left him, and nothing seemed quite as important as it had before. "The hell with them all," he concluded. "I've a good mind to resign, before they fire me. I'm not cut out to be a reporter, anyway."

"Don't do anything you'll regret."

"What is there to regret? They want the news written their way, no matter what actually happens. To me, that's dishonest."

"It may be, but it's a job."

"I'll tell you one thing–if I could find a job that paid me ten cents more, I'd take it in a flash. I'd forgotten how much a new baby costs."

"How many do you have?"

"Two. Nancy will be two next month, and Lionel–I still can't get used to calling him that. I can't even remember why we *named* him that, except that Sarah's mother once knew a man named Lionel, who– Where was I?"

"I think you were telling me how old Lionel is."

"Oh, yes. He's seven weeks. He eats more than Nancy does."

"It doesn't seem like the best time to quit your job."

"Well, if you hear of anything let me know. I'm serious–I'll dig ditches, if it'll bring in more than twenty dollars a week." He finished his sour and set the cup down. "And now, I guess I'd better toddle along. How much do I owe you?"

"Did the drinks help?"

"They seem to have. I'm no longer homicidal."

"Then two dollars ought to square the account."

Butterworth produced one dollar bill, and counted out the rest in change. "There you are," he said. "To the penny."

"You can sign for it, if you'd prefer," Nick said. "I don't want to leave you flat."

"This is no time to run up bills," Butterworth replied. "I believe in paying on the spot. And remember—I'm in the market for any kind of job, up to and including work on a flying trapeze."

"I'll remember," said Nick. "You'll be the first to know if I hear of anything." Butterworth started out and Nick said, "Oh—do you want your artichokes? You left them here."

"No," said Butterworth. "I never want to see them again."

Sarah was in bed when he got home, and he undressed in the living room so as not to wake her. He went to the bathroom and performed his usual ablutions, and was on his way into the bedroom when he remembered he'd neglected to write in his diary. He thought of all that had gone on during the day, and the length of time it would take to record it, and decided it could wait until the morning. I'll be a little more objective then, he thought. Just let the dust settle a bit first.

He got into bed without turning on the light, and realized Sarah was awake. "Sorry to wake you," he said.

"You didn't," Sarah replied. "I was just lying here."

"Everything all right?"

"I guess so. How about you?"

"It has been, to use the word lightly, one hellish day. I can't go through it all now; I'll tell you tomorrow."

"Where'd you have supper?"

He stopped, and realized he'd completely forgotten to eat. "I didn't," he said. "There was too much else going on."

"Is there any trouble?"

"I don't think so. I'll know better tomorrow."

"I wish you'd tell me what it is."

"Love, it's simply too long a story. Don't worry—everything will be all right." He rolled over, fumbled for her briefly in the dark, and kissed her. "Now, go to sleep. Good night."

There was a pause, then she said, "Roland, have you been drinking?"

My God, he thought. She must have smelled it. "Not really," he replied. "Not in the usual sense of the word."

"What is that supposed to mean?"

"I wasn't drinking for the fun of it. I had one Scotch, for—for medicinal purposes."

"Where?"

"At the Circe. Nick told me it would relax me, and as it turned out he was right. I was about to jump out of my skin. But I had to force myself to gag it down."

She said nothing. Butterworth thought of explaining the entire situation, then decided not to provoke a dialogue that might end in a tantrum. If she was content to be quiet, then so was he. He rolled back, closed his eyes, and pulled the pillow up around his ears, feeling as he did so a strange buzzing in his head. As he drifted off to sleep he could sense that she was lying, rigid and wide-eyed, in the bed beside him.

"I love you," he said, but there was no reply.

13

As it turned out, the matter of Butterworth's staying at the *Tribune* was decided not by him, but by the management. When he arrived for work the next day Forsburg, the city editor, beckoned him aside. The day desk man suddenly became immersed in a pile of papers in front of him and didn't even look up. There seemed to be a hush in the city room, and Butterworth felt like a man ascending the steps to the guillotine.

"Follow me," said Forsburg. He turned and led the way into the office of Grafton Smedley, the managing editor, and Butterworth saw Smedley and another man, a hawk-nosed individual he took to be Ogden Reid, the paper's owner, sitting at the conference table. Butterworth had technically been hired by Reid but had always dealt with an underling and had never actually seen him. Nobody said a word, and Forsburg closed the door quietly. There was a silence of possibly thirty seconds, which to Butterworth seemed like an hour, and then Smedley said, "Now. About that Sacco-Vanzetti story."

Butterworth moistened his lips. "Yes?" His voice was a dry croak.

"That part about the judge. Where'd you get it?"

"I told Mr. Hoskins. It came from a guy from Worcester, who'd heard the judge sounding off in the locker room."

"Who told you?"

"Nick Baldino."

"He sounds Italian," observed the man Butterworth assumed to be Ogden Reid.

"He is, sir."

Reid shrugged, as though that ended the matter.

"Sir, if I may ask," Butterworth said to Smedley, "what difference does this make now? The story was spiked, wasn't it?" He had, after all, seen it spiked, and there'd been no sign of it in the edition of the paper he'd read that morning.

"Are you in the habit of using speakeasies as your news sources?" Smedley asked, not answering the question.

"No, sir," Butterworth replied. "I mean, not usually. I don't even *go* to speakeasies–or, rather, I didn't use to. I'm not what you'd call an habitué."

"Yet you took Baldino's word about an anonymous man from Worcester, who claimed to have been in a locker room with Judge Thayer. How much had you had to drink?"

"Nothing, sir. I don't drink–or didn't, until after the story was spiked."

"And then?"

"And then I had a Scotch, which I followed with a Scotch sour to get rid of the taste."

Nobody said anything, although someone at the table made a sound of quiet strangulation. Butterworth could see no reason for the inquisition, since he'd already told Hoskins, the night man, the entire story, and he felt he was being interrogated more out of sadism than out of any attempt to get at the facts. "I still don't see what this is about," he said. "If the story was spiked it was spiked, so why are we going through it all again?" He was aware he sounded arrogant, but there had to be a limit somewhere. "If you want to know *why* I wrote it," he went on, "it was, as I told Mr. Hoskins, an attempt to get a story out of an impossible assignment."

"Oh?" said Smedley. "What was impossible about it?"

"It was supposed to prove that all the shouting about Sacco and Vanzetti has died down, when in actual fact it hasn't. It was a silly premise to begin with." Butterworth knew he'd gone too far but was past caring.

"I'm sorry to hear you say that," Smedley said quietly. "It was my idea."

This time the silence seemed endless. Butterworth could feel his heart pounding in his ears; the rest of him seemed to be miles away, as though he were watching the scene from another building. Then Forsburg touched him on the arm and led him out of the room. As they left, he heard Smedley say, "I'll tell the cashier to have your paycheck ready."

"I'm sorry about that," Forsburg said, when the door had closed behind them. "I suppose I should have warned you."

"I'd have probably said it anyway," Butterworth replied. "I still don't see the point in flogging a dead horse like that. What difference does it all make now?"

"More than you might imagine. Somehow, the flimsies of that story got on the wires, and every paper on our news service has run it. We've been getting queries all morning, asking for more fill-in."

"Oh," said Butterworth, and then again, "Oh."

They parted at the city desk, and Forsburg said, "Let me know if you ever find out the name of that guy from Worcester."

"I'll do that," Butterworth replied. "I guess that's the least I owe you." He went to his desk and cleaned out his personal belongings, then took his old used notes off the spike and threw them in the wastebasket. He was pocketing some stray rubber bands and paper clips when MacDougall came over and sat on the edge of the desk.

"Is it true?" MacDougall asked.

"If you mean did I get fired, yes," Butterworth replied.

"Jesus, I'm sorry."

Butterworth shrugged. "In a way it's a relief," he said. "It saves me from having to make the decision."

"What are you going to do?"

"I don't know. Nick said he'd keep an eye out for anything, but other than that I haven't thought. Right now I'm going to wait for my paycheck, and then I'll probably go to Nick's. I've got a certain amount of thinking to do, and that's as good a place to do it as any."

"Have you become a regular there?" MacDougall asked, with a faint trace of amusement.

"I see no harm in it. I even had a drink last night, to help me unwind."

"Well, congratulations. I wish I could join you, but I've got a murder wrap-up to do. There were five murders last night, all within twenty blocks of Times Square."

"The way I felt, I could have made it six. It's probably just as well I was at Nick's."

It was after two by the time Butterworth got to the Circe. He had his final week's paycheck, a few paper clips and rubber bands, five sharpened pencils, and as much copy paper as he'd been able to fit in his inside pocket. His first move, he knew, ought to be to call Sarah, but he wasn't sure just how he was going to break the news to her, and he wanted a little time to sort out his thoughts. He went to the bar and looked around to see who was present. Two or three people looked familiar, but the only ones he was sure of were Nick, who was sitting at a table and talking with a large, brassy-looking blonde, and Dorothy Peters, who was with an unidentified man at a table in the far corner. Charlie approached him, wiping the bar as he came.

"Yes, sir," Charlie said. "What can I do for you?"

Butterworth noticed that a man down the bar was eating a sandwich, and said, "Are you serving lunch these days?"

"Sandwiches only. Marie's got about all she can handle with the dinner trade."

"Then I'd like a ham and cheese, if I may."

"Right. Anything to go with it?"

"I guess a ginger—no, the hell with it. I'd like a Scotch sour."

Behind him, Butterworth heard Nick say, "I'm sorry, Miss Guinan, but I can't think of a thing at the moment. This is pretty much a family operation, and we just don't have any need for a hostess. But if I hear of anyone who does, I'll be glad to give him your name. Where can you be reached?"

"That's right nice of you, sugar," the blonde replied, and she wrote something on a slip of paper and handed it to Nick. He looked at it for a moment.

"You come from Waco," he said. "Is that near any place I might have heard of?"

"I don't rightly know," she said. "It's in McLennan County on the Brazos River, about eighty miles south of Dallas or Fort Worth, whichever you prefer. That do anything for you?"

"Enough. And here in New York you're staying at the Webster. Ask for Mary Louise Cecilia—"

"Just plain Texas will do," she put in. "Texas Guinan. I tossed in all those other names to show I'm legitimate."

"All right, then. I'll pass the word around." The blonde picked up her beaded purse and straightened her cloche hat, and Max let her out. Nick went to the bar, where Butterworth was taking the first sip of his sour. "That's a strange one," Nick said.

"What is?" Butterworth replied, shuddering slightly.

"That dame wants to be a speakeasy hostess. I can't imagine what she'd do."

"Well, if you find out let me know, and I can be a host."

Nick stared at him for a moment, then said, "Did you quit?"

"I didn't have to. I was fired."

"Because of the judge business?"

"Not exactly. I was indiscreet enough to tell the managing editor he was silly. Or, rather, that his idea was."

"Were you nuts?"

"I didn't know it was his. But by that time I didn't really care."

"Do you have anything lined up?"

"This only happened about an hour ago. My chair in the city room is still warm." Butterworth's sandwich arrived, and he inspected it, took a bite, and said, "Better eat while I can. It may be a while before I do it again." He took another bite and said, "I'll have to teach Sarah how to make these."

"Look," said Nick. "I feel kind of responsible for all this. It's only—"

"Don't be silly. You had nothing to do with it."

"Nevertheless, I don't want you to stay away from here just because you think you can't afford it. I—"

"Who's staying away? Do I look as though I were boycotting the place?"

"Listen to me. We'll keep a tab on what you spend here, and you pay as much or as little as you can, when you can. Just don't ever feel that you owe us anything, that it's a bill like any of the others."

Butterworth thought this over, and found he had trouble speaking. "That's very good of you," he said.

"Forget it. Or, rather, don't forget it. Keep it in mind."

"I shall." Butterworth raised his cup in salute, said, "Here's to turning over a new leaf," and drank. It warmed him as it went down, and the lemon juice gave him an agreeable puckering sensation. "Hello, Uncle Albert," he said.

"I beg your pardon?" said Nick.

"Nothing. I was just talking to an old relative." He bit into his sandwich and laughed. "If only he could see me now."

"Do you know anything about the theatre?" Nick asked, after a moment.

"What kind? Beaumont and Fletcher? The Globe Theatre? Grand Guignol?"

"I mean modern theatre. Broadway."

"I regret to say I've never seen a Broadway show. I'm a little boy from backwoods Massachusetts, and the last theatre I saw was when I played Puck in the Terence F. Gibson High School production of *A Midsummer Night's Dream.*" Turning to Charlie, Butterworth said, "May I have another sour, please?" and then, back to Nick, "Why? Who wants to know?"

"You know William A. Brady, the producer? Or have you heard of him?"

"No."

"His general manager was in here last night, and it seems they need a press agent."

"I wouldn't know where to begin."

"But you're a reporter."

"I was."

"If you've been around newspapers, that's all they want."

"There's got to be more to it than that."

Nick shrugged. "I thought you were looking for a job."

"I am, but– How much does this pay?"

"I have no idea. I just know he said he was looking for a press agent."

"Where do I get hold of him?"

"At the Brady office, I suppose. That would seem the logical place to start."

"Do you know his name?"

"What's the matter with you, anyway? You once told me you'd dig ditches if it'd pay you more than twenty bucks a week, and now you're dragging your ass about a job that might get you fifty or seventy-five. If you want the job, call the Brady office and tell them you hear they need a press agent–what's so hard about that?"

"You said you had no idea what it paid."

"I'm guessing, but it can't be *less* than twenty bucks a week."

Butterworth took a sip of his new sour. "I'm not really dragging my ass," he said. "It's just that I never thought about a job like that, any more than I thought about being a–prizefighter. Press agents are a kind of pushy lot, aren't they?"

"Some are, some aren't. You don't have to be."

"Well, I'll think about it. Thanks for the tip, anyway."

"If I were you, I'd get on the phone this minute. Jobs like that don't just float around in the air, you know."

"Is it O.K. if I finish my sandwich first?"

Nick smiled. "I guess it can wait on that."

"I don't mean to sound ungrateful, mind you. If I get the job, I should give you a commission."

"Get it first, and then we'll see."

There was the scraping of chairs, and Dorothy Peters and her companion rose from the far table. He was thick-set and balding, and carried a cigar between his knuckles as though it were a weapon. As they passed the bar he said, "Can I drop you anywhere?"

"No, thank you," she replied. "I think I'll stay here for a few minutes."

"As you wish. And–I'm sorry about all this. You realize there's nothing personal."

"Of course." Her voice was soft and gentle as she added, "It's as impersonal as a hysterectomy."

"Whatever that may be." He nodded at Nick, stared briefly at Butterworth, and left.

"Will you join us?" Nick said to Dorothy. "Have you met Mr. Butterworth?"

"Yes, we've met," she replied. "You were with George MacDougall."

"That's right," Butterworth said. "I was an ardent Prohibitionist. And look at me now." He raised his cup and added, "Would you care for anything?"

"I certainly would. Charlie, I'd like a–I don't know. What's an appropriate drink for someone who's just been fired?"

"You too?" said Butterworth in amazement.

"The very same. By that courtly gentleman who just left us. Don't tell me you're in the same boat."

"I am indeed. I'm having a Scotch sour, but then that's the only drink I like."

"I'll try a Scotch sour, then, Charlie. Maybe it'll settle my stomach."

"What happened?" Nick asked.

"Foundations are no longer the thing," she replied. "All the girls have given up corsets, so there's no longer any need for a foundation editor."

"Is that what you were?" Butterworth asked.

"In a manner of speaking. I wrote touching little bits of prose about the undergarment world for *Vogue.* My luncheon companion was the business manager or something for Condé Nast, who brought me here to explain how they couldn't afford to keep on an unnecessary department. The poor darlings–he almost made me weep." She groped in her bag for a cigarette, extracted one from a pack, and put it in her mouth. Nick lighted it for her. "What happened to you?" she asked Butterworth, letting out a long breath of smoke.

"Nothing, really," he replied. "I simply questioned the judgment of a man named Grafton Smedley. That's the essence of it."

"I'd question his judgment just on hearing his name. No man with a name like that could judge a sack race."

"I don't say I was wrong. It's just I was in no position to give my opinion."

"I know what you mean." She took the drink that Charlie gave her, said, "Mud in your eye," and sipped it. "Delicious," she said, with a shudder. "What made you settle on this as your favorite drink?"

"I don't like the taste of Scotch." Nick had moved on down the bar, and Butterworth added, "I saw George just before I left the paper. He'd be down here now, only he's got a big murder wrap-up to do. It's possible he'll be in later."

"Oh?" she said. "Did he tell you to tell me?"

"No, no. I just thought you might be interested. I thought–well, I thought you might like to see him." She said nothing, and Butterworth realized he'd got into deeper water than he'd intended. "Actually, it's none of my business," he said. "I don't know why I brought it up."

"Don't feel badly," she replied. "If you hadn't I suppose I would have."

"Well, nevertheless." He could think of nothing else to say, so he pushed the remains of his sandwich aside, took a sip of his drink, and said, "You know what Dr. Coué says–'Day by day, in every way, I'm getting better and better.' "

For some reason this struck her as funny, and she sagged against the bar, helpless with laughter. Finally she straightened up, wiped her eyes, and said, "I think I'll have that tattooed on me, so I can look in the mirror and face the day."

"You'll have to have it printed backward, to read it in a mirror."

Butterworth felt flushed with pleasure at having said something comical, and he wanted to keep the subject going.

"I'll let you do the tattooing," she replied.

"Thanks, but I'm a married man."

"I didn't say where I'd let you tattoo it."

He felt that the joke was about to get out of hand, so he said, "It's only fair to warn you, I do nothing but Gothic script," and then, "How's your drink? Are you ready for another?"

"Yes, but I think I'll have a plain Scotch this time. The lemon juice makes my fillings sing."

An hour later Butterworth stared owlishly at his watch and saw that it was a quarter to five. "I guess I ought to be getting on home," he said. "I've got to tell the little woman I'm unemployed."

"Wouldn't it be kinder to let her guess?" Dorothy said. "That's an awful thing to say in so many words."

"I can't think of a euphemism for it," he replied, enunciating carefully. "There is no other word."

"What about a cup of coffee?" asked Nick, who'd been hovering in the background.

"Probably not a bad idea," said Butterworth, and hiccuped. "Oh—oh," he said. "I must have eaten my sandwich too fast."

"I'll get you the coffee," said Nick, and went into the kitchen, and at the same time Charlie began making something at the bar. On a plate he put a slice of lemon, piled it high with sugar, then soaked the sugar with bitters.

"Here," he said, passing the plate to Butterworth. "Eat that."

"All of it?" Butterworth asked, trying to strangle a hiccup. "Just like that?"

"In one bite. Down the hatch."

Butterworth took the lemon and ate it quickly, and as it passed down his throat he felt a relaxing sensation. He waited a moment, breathed deeply, and smiled. "I'll be damned," he said. "Thank you."

"Any time," said Charlie.

Nick arrived with a tray and two cups of coffee, setting one in front of Butterworth and one in front of Dorothy. She pushed hers toward Butterworth and said, "Don't confuse the issue. I don't have to go home."

"This really isn't necessary," Butterworth said, blowing on the scalding coffee. "It's just what you'd call a precaution."

"Be quiet and drink up," she replied. "You've got two cups to finish."

He took a sip and laughed. "Wouldn't it be a scream if we were raided? The Feds would think I was drinking hooch in these coffee cups, and when they came to test they'd find it was really coffee!" He laughed some more, then found he was alone in his amusement, and straightened up and took another sip.

"Stick with it, Dr. Coué," Dorothy said. "Just keep plugging."

By the time he'd finished both cups Butterworth's head had cleared, and he buttoned his jacket, dusted the sandwich crumbs from his lap, and said, "There, now. Fit as a fiddle. May I drop you somewhere?"

"No, thanks," she replied. "I think I may stay around awhile and take the waters."

"Very well. Charlie, may I have my check, please?"

Charlie put the bill in front of him, and a pencil beside it, and as Butterworth was reaching for his wallet Charlie said, "You can sign that, you know. Mr. Nick said you were to have an account."

Butterworth hesitated, preferring to pay in cash, then remembered he had no more paychecks coming in and decided it would be the better part of wisdom to keep as much cash on hand as possible. He signed the check and, as a gesture of largesse, added a ten per cent tip. "There you go," he said. "And thank you very much."

"Thank you, sir," Charlie replied, putting the check in the till. "Come again, any time."

The pavements still radiated the heat of the day, and the asphalt in the streets was soft and spongy. As Butterworth walked toward the subway he experienced a strange, disembodied sensation, and he wondered if the drinks he'd had were still with him. It was the first time he'd ever felt the effects of too much liquor, and he resolved that, now that he knew what his limit was, he'd never let it happen again. Have no more than two, or at the most three, and there'd never be any trouble. He realized he might have a hard time convincing Sarah of this, and concluded the best thing would be not to bring the subject up at all. To make sure she didn't smell it on his breath again, he sought out a small grocery store, bought a Bermuda onion, and peeled it with his penknife, then took a large bite. It made his eyes water but it tasted strangely sweet, and he took two more bites and then threw the remains in a trash can. That should take care of that, he thought, as he went down the steps into the Grand Central subway. It was the evening rush hour, requiring him to stand jammed among the other straphangers, and he detected baleful glances cast his way by those nearest him. He smiled at one woman, who was glaring at him as though he'd stepped on her foot, and she said something under her breath and looked away. He thought he caught the words "Dago bastard," but he wasn't sure.

When he got home, Sarah was feeding the baby while Nancy tried to spoon dry cereal into a Teddy bear. Sarah looked up, smiled, and said, "*You're* home early. No night assignment?"

Butterworth cleared his throat. "That's right," he said. "As a matter of fact, no assignment at all. No more assignments." He put his hat in the closet, aware of a sudden silence in the room.

"What do you mean?" Sarah asked.

"I was fired."

"Why?"

"It's a long story. What it boils down to is that I never should have tried to be a reporter in the first place."

"But what did they say? Did they give a reason?"

"The reason was I didn't like Grafton Smedley's idea, and told him so."

"Was that what you were upset about last night?"

"Partly."

"I wish you'd tell me the whole story."

"It's too long, and it's idiotic. They wanted one thing, and I couldn't make myself do it. It's as simple as that."

"Have you been drinking? Or had you?"

"That had nothing to do with it. If you're wondering what you smell now, I ate an onion on the way home."

"You mean a plain onion?"

"That's right."

"Why?"

"I just had an urge for an onion. I can't tell you any more than that."

Sarah was quiet for a moment, then said, "I wish I knew what's changed you."

"Changed me how? What's different about me?"

"I don't know. You've never had a whim to eat an onion before."

"Look, honey, it's been a long day," Butterworth said. "If it's all the same to you, I'd rather not go into the whys and wherefores of having an urge to eat an onion. O.K.?"

"That's what I mean. This isn't like the old you."

"All right. I've changed. We all change. The human body has a complete change of cells every seven years. I just–"

"Who told you that?"

"I don't know. I read it somewhere. My point is–"

"I think you're saying that to change the subject. I think you've been to that speakeasy, and ate the onion so I wouldn't smell the liquor on your breath."

"Oh, come on. In the middle of the day? Give me credit for a little sense, will you?"

"I can't help what I feel."

Butterworth made a couple of attempts to form a sentence but wound up just opening and closing his mouth. "I'm not going to argue this anymore," he said at last. "It leads nowhere but to insanity."

Sarah put the empty nursing bottle down, arranged a diaper over her shoulder, then lifted the baby and began to rub his back. He made a noise that sounded like a small grunt, and drooled onto the diaper. "What are you going to do?" she asked.

"Me?" said Butterworth. "What do you mean?"

"For a job. Do you have any ideas?"

"Not at the moment. All I can think of is–" He stopped, as he remembered the publicity job with William Brady. "As a matter of fact, there is one thing," he said, "but I don't hold much hope for it. I'm going to make a call tomorrow–or I guess the next day. Tomorrow's Sunday."

"Is it all right to ask what it is?"

"Of course. It's with William Brady, the producer. He's apparently got an opening for a press agent."

"Then it would be working in town."

"I assume so."

Sarah sighed. "I suppose it would be too much to hope you could find something in the country."

"At the moment," said Butterworth, "I'll settle for anything. We'll worry about the country later."

14

William A. Brady was a large, heavy-set man with pince-nez glasses and an unnaturally high-pitched, cracked voice. His office, above the Playhouse on Forty-eighth Street, was piled high with play scripts, billboards, and posters, the largest of which advertised plays in which his wife, Grace George, had appeared. When Butterworth came to be interviewed, Brady examined him for a while in silence, as though waiting for him to change shape.

"What kind of experience have you had?" he asked at last, in a voice that made Butterworth jump.

"City reporter on the *Tribune,*" Butterworth replied.

"How long?"

"Two years—a year and a half—well, nineteen months."

"Ever done any theatre work?"

"Not as such, no, sir."

"What do you mean, 'as such'?"

"I've never written for the theatre, but I've been—around."

"How much do you think you're worth?"

Butterworth remembered Nick's guess about the salary, and decided to take a chance. "I'd like to get seventy-five," he said.

"That doesn't answer my question. What are you worth?"

"Well, sir, if you give me seventy-five, I'll try to be worth it."

Brady considered this. "All right," he said. "Just remember–there are no clocks on this job."

"Yes, sir–no, sir–I mean yes, sir."

"See Brown. He'll tell you what to do."

Clarence J. Brown was Brady's general manager, and he was more specific in spelling out Butterworth's duties. "It's a little bit of everything," he said. "You get out press releases, take care of the ads, the road publicity, and the advance billings, and in general you hang around and make yourself useful when the boss wants you. You–ah –occasionally have to track him down to get his O.K. for something, but there's no real trouble about that. He has a set list of places he goes, and you'll catch on to that with no trouble."

"He said there were no clocks," Butterworth replied. "I gather that means I work at night."

"You sure as hell do. When there's an opening, you stay around and pick up whatever comments you can afterward, and you just kind of–well–you sort of shepherd things along."

"Uh-huh," said Butterworth. "With my little shepherd's crook."

Brown gave him a thoughtful look. "That's about the size of it," he said.

"For seventy-five dollars a week I would join the castrati choir in Rome," Butterworth said. "I think I can probably handle this."

"That's the ticket," said Brown. "Chin up, stiff upper lip, and all that." He turned to his desk, sorted through a pile of pictures, and handed one to Butterworth. "See what you can do about that," he said.

Butterworth looked at the picture, which was of a young lady in an evening gown, standing in a doorway and gazing pensively offstage. "Who is it?" he said, looking for a caption.

"That is the boss's daughter, Alice. She and her mother are to be accorded the widest possible press coverage."

"What am I supposed to do about this?" Butterworth asked.

"Read the back."

Butterworth turned it over and saw that Alice had written: "There is a highlight across the bust that makes me look large–see if you can fix it–but you can use it anyway–only if possible try to fix." He looked at the picture again but could see nothing overly developed in the bust area. "How do I fix it?" he asked. "Or what do I fix?"

"The exact question your predecessor asked," Brown replied.

"Only he was a little more profane. His last words upon resigning were, 'You can tell Alice to fix her own goddam boobs.' "

"He sounds kind of high-strung," Butterworth observed.

"Some people get that way, after a while." Brown reached out and took the picture back. "There's nothing much can be done with it," he said. "I just showed it to you to give you an idea of some of the things you can expect."

"Thanks," said Butterworth.

"Now," Brown said in a more businesslike way. "Have you ever seen a play in rehearsal?"

"Well, yes and no. I was in a high-school production of *A Midsummer Night's Dream.*"

"I think we can count that as a 'no.' It might be a good idea if you knew how the business works."

"I agree."

"All right, then. We've got a play going into rehearsal next week, and you just tag along and see how it's done. If anything newsworthy happens, so much the better."

"What's it called?"

"It's called *Swifty,* and it's by John Peter Toohey and W. C. Percival. John Cromwell is the director, and Hale Hamilton the star. The second lead, I'm unhappy to say, is some friend of Alice's who she's convinced can be an actor. She badgered her father into giving him a job."

"What's it about?"

"It's about an ex-prizefighter, and a girl who got–ah–deflowered in a cabin in the Adirondacks by some social squirt."

"That sounds kind of racy."

"Well, we'll see. Things are loosening up in the theatre these days, and you can deal with subjects that were impossible before. Some people say it's the letdown of the moral standards that came with the war, but that may be too glib an answer. I think it's just that the American public is growing up."

"Does it say in so many words that this girl has been deflowered?"

Again, Brown studied Butterworth for a moment before answering. "I forget the exact wording," he said, "but the meaning is clear."

"Wow," said Butterworth.

The first rehearsal was called for eleven o'clock Monday morning. The assistant stage manager had arranged a semicircle of chairs under a work light for the cast, and they sat, their scripts in their laps, facing Cromwell.

"All right," he said, when everyone had settled down, "let's go through it once, just for the words."

Listening to the toneless recitation of the lines, Butterworth tried to estimate the acting abilities of the various players, but it was virtually impossible because they all sounded more or less alike. He was able, however, to guess the identity of Alice's friend when a pleasant-looking young man, with dark hair and a faint trace of a lisp, put up his hand and said, "May I ask a question?"

"Go right ahead," said Cromwell.

"Which way do I face when I speak—toward the audience, or toward the other actors?"

"I tell you, Humph, we'll go into that when I start blocking," Cromwell replied. "In general, it's a good idea to face the person you're supposed to be talking to, but you have to project your voice so the audience can catch it, too."

"Oh," said the young man. "It just occurred to me to wonder."

Butterworth glanced at the cast list to see who might be called Humph, and the only name he could find was Humphrey Bogart, who played the part of Tom Proctor, the seducer. I see now why Brown was nervous, he thought. I'll bet this guy is replaced within a week.

He was, however, reckoning without Alice's influence on her father. One day during the second week of rehearsals Brady and his daughter came into the theatre and sat in back, listening as the actors groped their way through their first attempt to do the play without scripts. Suddenly, after young Bogart had delivered a particularly inept reading, Brady's voice shattered the quiet. "God damn it, Alice, what have you done to me?" he said.

"Nothing that a good script wouldn't cure," Alice replied.

"But this son of a bitch lisps!"

Alice said something in a low voice and Brady subsided, muttering, but his outburst had done nothing to soothe the nerves of an already apprehensive cast. Like horses smelling the first smoke of a stable fire, they knew there was something wrong but were unable to pinpoint the trouble, and the more nervous they became the more the trouble seemed to grow. Cromwell tried to reassure them, saying that once they had their lines learned they would achieve a pace that would make everything play better, but this was a cosmetic argument where surgery was needed, and they all knew it.

The first hint of anarchy came when the actors started rewriting the lines. Hale Hamilton, the lead, was supposed at one point to say, "Little did I know, when first I met you, that I would ever find myself doing this," and every time he came to the line he stumbled. He tried dodging it by saying, "I never guessed, when first we met, I'd ever find myself doing this," but it gave the line a sort of hobbled rhythm, and John Peter Toohey, one of the co-authors, objected.

"Try to read the line the way it's written," he said, from his seat in the fifth row.

"I can't," Hamilton replied. "It sticks in my throat."

Toohey shrugged, as though to suggest another actor be given the part. "In that case–" he said, and left the sentence unfinished.

Hamilton flushed, and Cromwell, to avoid a scene, said, "Can you think of a line that would be easier?"

"Almost anything," Hamilton replied. "How about–well–supposing I say, 'I never thought I'd find myself doing this.' "

Cromwell looked at Toohey. "Is that all right?" he asked.

Toohey shrugged again. "Anything to make it easier for him," he said. "So long as he doesn't change the meaning."

With that, the other actors began having ideas about their lines. They would open by saying, "In the interest of clarity, do you think it might be better if I said," or, "As I see it, this character would react more forcefully," or, "I'm only thinking of the play, mind you, but," and there would ensue a discussion of the line in question that would sometimes end in a change, and other times in the playwright's insisting that it remain as written, and its being read by a disgruntled actor. In either event, a lot of time was wasted on trivia, when the basic problem lay far deeper. Of them all, Bogart was the only actor who read his lines as they were originally written–not well, but at least without any embroidery of his own. Butterworth noticed this, and wondered if he was just being agreeable, or didn't know enough to complain. He suspected it was the latter.

Then one afternoon Butterworth saw a thin, lemur-eyed man in a straw hat sitting quietly in back during a rehearsal, and when the rehearsal was over Cromwell came back and sat with him. They talked for a few minutes, and then Cromwell went down front and addressed the cast.

"That'll be all for today," he said. "You may have some new sides to learn tomorrow, so there's no point going on until we get the changes." To the stage manager he said, "Let's have a ten o'clock call tomorrow morning, and be prepared to work on into the night."

Butterworth had noticed that neither of the co-authors was in the theatre, and on looking more closely at the man in back he saw it was Ring Lardner, who had apparently been called in to do repair work on the script. The mere fact that a change was being made gave the cast a lift in their spirits, and as they filed off the stage they were anticipating whatever changes Lardner might make.

"I think this may be our salvation," Hamilton said. "I never liked the idea of working with two authors, anyway."

"I think one author is too much," replied Willard Holden, who had a minor part. "I think the author should be barred from the theatre the minute rehearsals begin."

"They're a necessary evil," said Hamilton. "But if you must have one, you couldn't ask for a better one than Lardner."

Helen Scott, the ingenue, turned to Bogart. "May I ask a personal question?" she said.

"Go right ahead," Bogart replied.

"How did you get that scar?"

Bogart touched the pink scar on the right side of his upper lip. "I was in the Navy," he said.

"You mean, it's a war wound?" Her eyes opened wide.

"You could call it that."

Butterworth had overheard the conversation, and it occurred to him there might be something here that could be used for publicity. He drew Bogart aside and said, "May I speak with you a moment?"

"Sure thing," said Bogart. "What can I do for you?"

"That scar. Is there any–ah–good story that goes with it? Anything we could use, I mean?" He suddenly felt as he had when he was a reporter, asking people questions that were none of his business.

"Use how?" Bogart said, puzzled.

"For publicity purposes–or in your program biography. Was there any–uh–exploit connected with your getting it?"

Bogart considered this a moment, then said, "Do you want the real story, or something you can use for publicity?"

"Well, as I said, my main interest is in the publicity."

"Then you can say it was a piece of shrapnel–or maybe a splinter from the deck. I was a quartermaster on the *Leviathan,* and we were in a surface battle with a German sub."

"Say, that's great," Butterworth said, reaching for a pencil. "Let me get that down."

"Now would you like to hear the real story?" Bogart asked.

"Is it very different?"

"I was doing Shore Patrol duty, taking a prisoner from Norfolk to Portsmouth. When we changed trains in Boston he asked me for a cigarette, then slugged me across the mouth with his handcuffs. Damn near tore my lip off."

Butterworth stopped writing. "Then you weren't on the *Leviathan?*"

"I was, but I didn't report aboard until sixteen days after the Armistice."

"And you never saw any action?"

"None. I'd just been kicked out of Andover that spring."

Butterworth looked at his notes, then at Bogart. "Why'd you have to tell me that?" he said.

Bogart shrugged. "Use whichever story you want," he said. "It's all the same to me."

Butterworth sighed and put his notes in his pocket. "When I was a reporter there'd have been no question," he said. "I'd have insisted on the true story, or none at all. Now that I'm a publicity man, I may have to think it over. The truth isn't all that important anymore."

"Sorry to have put you in a dilemma," Bogart said, laughing. "Why don't we have a drink and see if we can cook up a really good story?"

Butterworth looked at his watch, and saw that it was a quarter to six. "I'll have to check with Mr. Brady first," he said. "I never know when he's going to want something."

"Well, it was just an idea."

"Do you know the Club Circe?"

"No. I usually go to the Puncheon Grotto."

"Go to the Circe and tell Max, the doorman, I sent you." Butterworth had a pleasant sensation of importance as he went on, "Nick is the owner, and you tell him I said he should be good to you. I'll get there if I can; if I can't, I'll give you a call."

"O.K. Where is this place?"

"Just across town." Butterworth gave him the address, then went up to Brady's office. Brown was going through a sheet of advertising copy, and he looked up as Butterworth came in.

"Rehearsal all over?" he asked.

"Yes," said Butterworth. "They're waiting for the new material from Lardner."

"Then you can take care of these."

"What are they?"

"The boss wants a change in the ad copy. Take these new sheets to the *Times,* the *Trib,* the *Herald,* the *News,* the *Mirror,* the *Sun,* and the *World;* tell them to kill the old copy and substitute this."

"Is this for tomorrow's papers?" Butterworth asked, taking the sheafs of paper.

"That's right. You'd better hurry."

"But they'll be all locked up now. It's too late."

"Tell 'em the old man won't pay for the ad unless they make the change."

"Well, I'll try. I've got to make a phone call first."

Butterworth called the Circe and left a message for Bogart with Nick, then spent the next three hours trying to persuade the various papers to kill the old copy and substitute the new. He was successful with the first two, but by the time he got to the third it was too late, and then only the afternoon papers would listen to him. It was after nine when he got through, and he returned to the Playhouse to find Brady belligerent and glassy-eyed.

"Where the hell have *you* been?" Brady asked.

"Out trying to get the papers to change their ad copy," Butterworth replied, through tight lips.

"What took you so long?"

"A couple of them wouldn't listen to reason. They refused to replate for—and I use their words—a lousy fifty-dollar ad."

Brady flushed. "Which ones?"

"They're on the list here." Butterworth handed him a slip of paper, and was about to close up his desk when Brady stopped him.

"Get me Ogden Reid," he said.

"You mean *now?*" Butterworth could hardly believe what he'd heard.

"I mean this minute."

"But, sir, he won't be at the paper, and—"

"Call the paper and get them to tell you where he is. I want to talk to the son of a bitch, and I want to talk to him now."

"But–"

"Listen, Butterworth, or Buttersquirt, or whatever the hell your name is, do you understand English?"

"Yes, sir. I'm just–"

"Then get me Ogden Reid, or get the hell out of here."

Butterworth was about to take up his hat and walk out, when he remembered he would also be walking out on seventy-five dollars a week. "Yes, sir," he said, and sat down and picked up the telephone. When the *Tribune* operator answered he asked for Reid and, as he had known would happen, the operator said Mr. Reid and his secretary had both left for the day, and she asked who was calling. Butterworth was about to reply when Brady grabbed the telephone out of his hand.

"Hello!" Brady shouted into the mouthpiece. "Hello! Who's this?" The operator identified herself, and Brady said, "Well, this is William A. Brady, and I want to speak to Ogden Reid." Butterworth could smell the liquor fumes surrounding Brady as the operator went through her routine, and then Brady slammed the receiver back on the hook, saying, "A hell of a way to run a newspaper!" Brady turned and looked at Butterworth as though seeing him for the first time. "You used to work on that sheet, didn't you?" he said.

"Yes, sir," Butterworth replied. "In a manner of speaking."

"Then you get him for me tomorrow. You must know where he hides out."

Butterworth started to protest, and realized it would do no good. To change the subject he said, "I think we may have material for a news release on Humphrey Bogart. He was in the Navy during the war and apparently had quite a time. He's got that scar on his lip to prove it."

"I don't know anything about a scar," Brady replied. "All I know is the son of a bitch lisps. You can forget any news releases about him." Then, as though the subject had never been changed, he said, "When I come in tomorrow morning, I want you to have Ogden Reid on the phone, waiting."

"Yes, sir," said Butterworth. "What time will that be?"

"It doesn't matter what time. When I come in, I want him to be on the phone."

"Yes, sir. Is that all for tonight?"

Brady thought for a moment, then said, "It might as well be. Go on home."

Butterworth went home by way of the Circe, where he had two Scotch sours to take the edge off his rage. Bogart had been there but had left, and Dorothy Peters was there with a man he didn't recognize, so after finishing his second sour he signed the check, then went home and undressed in the dark, so as not to wake Sarah. He wasn't sure if she was asleep or not, but decided not to take the chance.

Brady arrived at the office at ten-thirty the next morning, greeted Butterworth warmly, and made no mention of Ogden Reid.

Swifty was scheduled to open in mid-October, and as rehearsals progressed it became increasingly obvious there was something the matter that could not be fixed by superficial tinkering. The changes Ring Lardner made had been good but not deep enough, and when one act was improved the other two suffered by comparison, in a never-ending struggle for equilibrium. Those who were close to the play were blinded by familiarity, and while they knew something was wrong, no two of them could agree on exactly what it was. This led to a state of wishful thinking that perhaps it wasn't as bad as they thought, and the company stumbled toward the October 16 opening in a state of nervous expectation, hoping for one of those miraculous performances when everything goes right. On opening night Butterworth, pacing the rear of the theatre in a rented tuxedo, was as nervous as any of the actors.

The first review to appear, around midnight, was by Burns Mantle of the *News,* and there was momentary elation at the post-opening party when the review turned out to be favorable. Then came the review of Alexander Woollcott, critic for the *Herald,* and the elation was quickly shattered. He called the play "a consistently incredible piece, a little more gauche and artless than the average of similar endeavors which slip past the tryouts in the suburbs," and of Bogart, whom he had earlier referred to as "a young sprig of the aristocracy," he wrote: "The young man who embodies the aforesaid sprig is what is usually and mercifully described as inadequate." The other reviews were along the same general line: Heywood Broun, in the *World,* called it "cheap and implausible," and Alan Dale, in the *American,* wrote that "Willard Holden and Humphrey Bogart gave some rather trenchant exhibitions of bad acting."

Swifty quietly folded, and the actors went looking for other plays. The night of the last performance, Butterworth went to the Circe on his way home after the show, and there found Bogart standing at the bar. "It didn't take you long to get here," Butterworth observed.

"It didn't take long to clean out my dressing room," Bogart replied. "Did Brady have you working tonight?"

"He has me working every night, whether or not there's anything to do." Butterworth ordered a Scotch sour, then saw Dorothy Peters coming down the bar toward him. "Hi, there," he said. "Mrs. Peters, do you know Mr. Bogart?"

"How do you do?" said Dorothy. "I saw your play."

"Why?" said Bogart.

"Line of duty. I'm a reviewer."

Butterworth looked surprised. "When did this happen?" he asked.

"A week ago. A deranged magazine editor took me on."

"What magazine?"

"I blush to say it's one of the Hearst stable. Beyond that, I'd rather not be specific." Turning back to Bogart, she said, "For what comfort it may give you, your play was at least better than *Abie's Irish Rose*."

"Why did you have to see *that?*" Butterworth asked. "That opened last May."

"I know, and the fact it's still running is some kind of phenomenon. They thought I should see it as an example of the public's taste."

"Did you see what Woollcott wrote about me?" Bogart asked, and then, grinning, produced a clipping of the *Herald* review and went on, "He said I was 'what is usually and mercifully described as inadequate.' That, in the circumstances, is what I'd call a rave review." He showed it to Dorothy, who returned it with a look of quiet admiration.

"The world needs more people like you," she said.

"That's going to have to be the world's worry," Bogart replied, returning the clipping to his wallet. "I'm having enough trouble keeping myself going."

"What do you usually do?" she said.

"How could you ask? I'm an actor."

"Tell her how you got your scar," Butterworth put in. Bogart glanced at him, and Butterworth said, "The knife fight on the poop deck."

"Oh, that." Bogart put his drink on the bar and launched into a story of a midnight fight at sea, with German U-boat sailors swarming up the sides of a ship and engaging the crew in hand-to-hand combat. He did it so well that even Butterworth was half-convinced, and Dorothy was openmouthed with awe.

"By God, you are an actor, aren't you?" she said, when he'd finished.

"That was nothing," he replied, picking up his drink and taking a sip. "You should see me do *Little Women.*" He turned to the bartender and said, "Charlie, let's have a round for my uncle and aunt, here."

It was one o'clock by the time Butterworth got home, and as he walked from the subway he saw a lighted window that he realized, with growing unease, was in his apartment. That could only mean one of the children was sick, or . . . His mind began to race ahead as he hurried the last half block and almost ran up the stairs, and when he entered the apartment he saw Sarah, sitting silently in a chair and staring at the window. She was in her nightclothes, and her feet were bare. "What's wrong?" he asked, gasping for breath. "What are you doing?"

She turned her eyes toward him and looked at him without expression. "Hello," she said.

"What's the *matter?*" Butterworth ran to her and knelt down beside the chair. "What are you doing up at this hour?"

She looked back at the window. "I was just thinking," she said.

"About what? What in God's name could keep you up at this hour of the night?"

"Any number of things. You, for instance."

"What about me? What have I done?"

She paused, then said, "Nothing, I guess. Maybe it's all just a part of the city."

"Look, honey," he said, "in a little while I may have enough money so we can think about moving. I promise you, as soon as it makes any kind of sense we'll start looking for something in the country, but right now it's simply out of the question. I haven't forgotten; I just can't do anything about it."

"I know," she said. "I know."

"But I promise you–"

She reached out and put a hand over his lips. "You've already said it once," she said. "That's all I need to hear."

15

Sunday was usually a slow day in the city room at the *Tribune*. The routine news events, such as conventions, banquets, testimonial dinners, and the like, were not held on Sundays, and the bulk of the local news consisted of obituaries, accidents, and sermons by prominent clergymen. One or two publicity men had found that the sure way to get good space was to stage an event or time a release for Sunday, because there was virtually no competition.

For George MacDougall, Sunday was a day only marginally different from any other. He had become the paper's unofficial murder expert—why, he could never figure out, unless it was as a result of his theory about Mrs. Bostwick and the bombing—and any homicide that was at all out of the ordinary was tossed his way. There were usually more homicides on Saturday night than at any other time in the week, but they were the routine kind that could be handled by the police reporters or district men, and only if there were complications or the hint of a bigger story were they given to MacDougall. Thus his Sundays were usually spent mulling over his notes on unsolved cases, doing odd bits of rewrite, and every now and then writing an experimental scene for his play. He hadn't forgotten Mrs. Bostwick, but he hadn't been able to give her his full attention either.

On Sunday, December 31, he reported at the usual one o'clock, and Findlay, the desk man, said, "You can take it easy this afternoon. You've got Times Square tonight." Findlay was a thin, balding, lugubrious man, who looked superficially like a sick crane.

"Oh, no," MacDougall said. "What have I done to deserve that?"

"There'll be four of you," Findlay went on. "You and Lenzner take Times Square itself, Rackham will cover the theatres, and Fullmer the so-called supper clubs. Lenzner will do the wrap-up."

"Happy nineteen twenty-three," said MacDougall.

"Same to you, Sherlock," Findlay replied. "By the way, was there ever any follow-up on that double murder in Jersey?"

"Which one?"

"You know–the minister and the choir singer." The previous September, the Reverend Edward W. Hall, rector of the Protestant Episcopal Church of St. John the Evangelist, in New Brunswick, had been found murdered in a local trysting spot known as DeRussey's Lane, along with Mrs. Eleanor R. Mills, wife of the sexton of the church and a singer in the choir. They had both been shot, and her throat had been cut, and love letters from her to him lay scattered about. His calling card had been propped against one of his shoes. His wife, Mrs. Frances Stevens Hall, and her two brothers, Willie and Henry Stevens, had been questioned, but no indictments had been handed down. A Mrs. Jane Gibson, known to the press as "the pig woman," had delivered shrill, garbled testimony that tended to implicate Willie Stevens, but his alibi was impeccable, and the case had foundered for lack of an indictment.

"Oh, them," MacDougall said. "No, nothing new."

"If you ask me, there's more to that than meets the eye," said Findlay.

MacDougall laughed. "I couldn't have put it better myself," he said, and went back to his desk. He sat there for a while, shuffling through various piles of notes and spiking those that were out of date or irrelevant, and at the same time pondering various approaches to the Bostwick play idea. For some reason, Mrs. Bostwick led him to think of Butterworth, who had struck out on his assignment that day, and that brought up the idea of Butterworth as a possible character. The naïve country boy, the Puritan who frowns on sinful city ways, caught up in a murder that was masterminded (mistressminded?) by a socialite who wants to do away with her husband. It sounded more like a comedy than a mystery, but there was probably nothing wrong with that. If you could do a good comedy about murder, you might have something that for sheer novelty would knock the public over backward. Smiling with the pleasure of a new idea, he took a piece of copy paper and began to list the various aspects of Butterworth's character that could fit into such a plan. The more he thought the more he became carried away by the idea, and the next time he looked up it was five o'clock, and the night desk men had arrived and were being filled in on the schedule for the evening. I guess I'd better get something to eat, MacDougall thought. It looks as though it's going to be a long night.

He went over to Lenzner's desk, arranged to meet him in Times Square at ten o'clock, then put on his Army greatcoat, a scarf, and a hat, and went out and headed for the Club Circe. An icy wind cut through the streets, and he decided to borrow a bottle, or a flask, or something from Nick to keep him warm during his cold and pointless vigil. Just for a moment he let his mind run on ahead, and pretend that his play had opened and was a smash hit, and brought in enough money so that he could afford to give up reporting and become a playwright. That may be a long way off, he told himself, so you'd better live for the moment, and anything good that happens will be so much gravy.

In this pleasantly unbuttoned state of mind he rang the bell at the Circe's iron gate, and heard the click as the peephole slid open. "Happy New Year, Max," he said, and the door swung ajar.

"Happy New Year, Mr. MacDougall," Max replied. "I have a present for you here."

"For me?" MacDougall couldn't imagine who might have sent him a present to the club.

Max reached back to a shelf and produced a package the size of a small book, wrapped in green tissue paper and bound with red ribbon. "Here," he said. "They say there's a card inside."

MacDougall opened the package and saw a leather-bound flask, curved so as to fit comfortably into a hip pocket. A card fluttered to the ground and he picked it up and, holding it under the light at Max's desk, read:

Here's mud in your eye.

x

d

The "d" had to stand for Dorothy Peters, but the last thing he expected from her was a Christmas present. He hung up his hat and coat and went into the bar, which Marie had decorated with every bit of Christmas trimming she could find. Mistletoe hung over the entrance, sprigs of holly sprouted along the back bar, and the bar itself was festooned with strings of small Christmas balls. She had originally wanted to deck the bar with pine and spruce cuttings, until Nick pointed out the obvious fire hazard, so she had hung the cuttings from the ceiling, out of range of the customers' cigarettes, and had put centerpieces of holly on each table. Red bows and ribbons filled what extra spaces were left, and on a table at the far end of the room were three *bûches de Noël,* surrounded by pinecones and more holly, and as a centerpiece there was a large fruit and rum cake, decorated with the legend *Bonne année 1923.*

The bar was fairly crowded, mostly with people who had stopped by for a New Year's drink before going on to other festivities, and at the far end MacDougall saw Dorothy standing next to Nick, who was talking with Fred McClain. He went to her, and her eyes brightened as she saw him. He produced the flask, kissed her on the forehead, and said, "That was a very dear thing to do. There was no call for you to give me a present."

"I know that. I just wanted to."

"Well, thank you. May I buy you a drink?"

She glanced in her cup and said, "I still have some, thank you."

"Well, finish it off. Are you alone?"

She inclined her head toward McClain and said, "Fred brought me."

"McClain?" MacDougall lowered his voice. "I thought you didn't like him."

She shrugged and said, "Any port in a storm. Do you have any better ideas?"

"I have to work tonight. Otherwise . . ." He let the sentence trail off.

"Coward," she said.

"What do you mean?"

"You might at least have said otherwise you'd be happy to squire me about. Since you're safe from being taken up, you might at least have made the gesture."

"Oh, come on," he said. "Cut it out. You're his date, and that's the end of it."

"Did Lochinvar care whose date was who? Not a bit of it. He came out of the west, swept the bride-to-be from the altar, and made off with her. There was a man for you, that Lochinvar. They don't make them like that anymore."

MacDougall could see she was just faintly drunk, and he decided to get off the subject as quickly as possible. "This flask arrived in the nick of time," he said. "I have to see the New Year in in Times Square, and this is going to be a lifesaver."

"In God's name, why do you have to do that?" she said. "I thought you specialized in murders."

"This in itself is a form of murder," he replied. "The murder of all human sanity." Holding the flask out to the barman, he said, "Charlie, will you fill that with Scotch to go, please? And then give me one on the side."

"Right you are," said Charlie, and took the flask.

"I also have to get something to eat," MacDougall said. "I need every bit of sustenance I can get."

"I'm not sure this is going to be the place to eat," Dorothy replied. "Things are in something of an uproar tonight."

"What are you talking about?" MacDougall looked at the *bûches de Noël* and the cake, which appeared to be the work of a master confectioner. "I don't see anything wrong."

"Nick decided to give Marie a New Year's present," Dorothy said. "As a big surprise he hired a chef to help her in the kitchen, and she's so mad she can hardly spit. You'll probably get dinner, but there just may be a little blood around the edges."

"Oh." MacDougall thought a moment, then said, "Is this a permanent gift, or just for the holiday?"

"It's intended to be permanent, but I wouldn't put any bets on it."

Nick, who had apparently finished whatever he was discussing with McClain, greeted MacDougall and then moved on down the bar. He had a sprig of holly in his buttonhole and was wearing a double-breasted pinstripe suit that accentuated the width of his shoulders. His mere presence at the bar guaranteed good behavior on the part of the customers.

"He's handed me a nice problem," McClain said, after Nick was out of hearing.

"What's that?" MacDougall replied. "Have a drink."

"You forget—I drink free here. And it looks as though I'm going to earn it. He asked me a while back to see how I could make the place fireproof, and while that's no great problem I can't do the whole building, because he doesn't own it. So anyone who wants to torch this place can do it by firing the decorator's shop on the upper floors, and it'll fall through into here."

"Has anyone tried?"

"I don't think so, but he's had threats."

"Livorno again?"

"I assume so."

MacDougall thought for a moment, then said, "As I see it, he has two choices—he can either reinforce the ceiling here, and make it fireproof, or he can buy the building and turn it into a fort. I should think the first would be the easier."

"That's what I told him, but he's got some bug about wanting to own the whole place. If he can raise the money, more power to him."

"If I had my tambourine, I could raise it in a trice," Dorothy said. "Did you ever see my flamenco shimmy?"

"Is flamenco a noun or an adjective?" MacDougall replied.

"Nertz to you, big boy," said Dorothy, and finished her drink.

They had two more rounds, then MacDougall excused himself and went to a table. "I hear we have a pair of chefs tonight," he said, when Nick approached. "Do you have any recommendations?"

Nick put his hands to his temples and said, "*Mama mia,* what a headache! You'd think I'd taken on a mistress."

"Why don't you? That'll get her mind off the chef."

"I may be stupid, but I'm not that stupid. No, this will simmer down after a while. She was working herself too hard but doesn't like to admit it."

"Is there a house special?"

"Let me put it this way: Louis' special is veal scallopini, and Marie's tonight is chicken tarragon. You can also have steak, chops, or a roast of beef. For certain customers, Marie will do an omelette."

MacDougall considered the choices, then said, "I somehow feel it would be wise if I had the chicken tarragon. What do you think?"

Nick bowed and smiled. "I think *monsieur* has made an excellent choice," he said.

As it turned out it *was* an excellent choice, and MacDougall had a glass of the house red to go with it. By the time he was finished the place was crowded, and more people were appearing in the doorway every minute. It was like a college fraternity house before a football game: there was a sense of anticipation and a shared excitement, and most of the people knew everyone else, at least by sight if not more intimately. The collegiate atmosphere was heightened by a scattering of coonskin coats, and all that was missing were Harvard or Yale or Princeton pennants, carried over the shoulders of the celebrants. My God, MacDougall thought, if it's like this here this early, what is it going to be like in Times Square at midnight? I guess there's only one way to find out, and that's the hard way. He managed to get one more drink at the bar, then with difficulty found his coat and made his way out into the night.

He found Lenzner at the appointed place, in front of the Times Building. Times Square had been closed to traffic, and mounted policemen as well as foot patrolmen were stationed around the perimeters to govern the flow of pedestrians, of whom there were only as yet a few thousand. They milled about and blew horns, and one or two, who'd had an early start on the celebration, were already being sick in the gutters. Gradually, as more appeared down the side streets and out of the subways, the police began to herd them into a moving circle, going north on the east side of the square and south on the west side, but always moving, like a slow, gigantic whirlpool.

"All right," Lenzner said after a while, "you go stand in the middle, where that police captain is sitting on his horse, and I'll work the edges. I'll see you back at the paper as soon after midnight as I can get there."

"O.K.," said MacDougall. "Anything special you want me to look for?"

Lenzner gave him a baleful stare. "You know better than to ask a question like that," he said. "This is simply a crowd story. Human fucking interest. Oh—one thing—it's always good to ask the captain for his estimate of the size of the crowd. His name is Grandle and he always says a million two hundred thousand, but ask him just the same. He likes to see his name in print."

"Right," said MacDougall. He moved into the crowd, edging his way toward the center of the square, and when an officer tried to herd him to the east side he showed his police card, and the officer nodded and let him proceed. It wasn't easy, because the whirlpool was picking up in density and strength, but he finally managed to reach the little island in the center, where Grandle and some of the higher police brass were stationed. Grandle glanced down at him, and he again showed his police card and said, "I'm from the *Tribune,* Captain. My name is George MacDougall. Anything unusual happened so far?"

The captain grunted. "It's a little early yet," he said. "Hell don't really break loose till midnight."

MacDougall looked into the crowd and saw a man blowing a snake-like noisemaker against the back of a girl's neck, at the same time trying to encircle her hips with both his hands. "It's a funny thing," he said, "I could have sworn there was a law against alcoholic beverages in this country."

The captain stared at him, then said, "Woddaya think you are—a wise guy, or something?"

"Only asking," MacDougall replied. "No offense intended."

"That kind of stuff is up to the Feds," Grandle went on. "If they want to dry up this crowd, let 'em try."

"My sentiments entirely," said MacDougall. "I believe in the broad view of things."

A man from the *Times,* whom MacDougall knew slightly, appeared through the crowd, nodded to Grandle and the other officers, then said, "What happened? Are you in the doghouse too?"

"What do you mean?" MacDougall replied.

"In our shop, this is a doghouse assignment. I won it by showing up cockeyed at a Lucy Stoners' luncheon."

MacDougall laughed. "As far as I know, I'm not in the doghouse. I won it by not having anything else to do today."

"Did you get the crowd estimate?"

"I figured it was too early."

"Let's ask him anyway, and compare it with what he says later." To Grandle, the *Times* man said, "Captain, what would your estimate be of the crowd right now?"

Grandle started to say something, then checked himself and gazed out over the swarming sea of heads. He squinted his eyes and after a pause said, "I'd say about eight hundred thousand, maybe eight fifty. They're coming in pretty fast."

"Thank you." The *Times* man checked his watch, and made a note.

The celebrants were now converging on Times Square like a moving mass of lava, filling the side streets and bubbling up from the subways, forcing their way into the slowly circulating pool in the center. Most of them had noisemakers of some sort, and many wore paper hats festooned with Christmas ornaments, but the icy wind soon clawed the frills to shreds and forced the people to retract their heads into their collars, like turtles. Looking at them, MacDougall wondered what had drawn them of their own free will into such an orgy of mass masochism, and he concluded that they were people who, throughout the rest of the year, lived drab and uneventful lives in the suburbs or the low-rent areas and who, this one night, felt the need to kick up their heels and act like children. A girl darted out of the crowd, kissed Grandle's horse on the nose, and vanished before MacDougall or the *Times* man could get her name, and MacDougall decided he'd been right: all through the coming year she would have the distinction of being the one who kissed the police captain's horse in Times Square, and nobody in Mount Vernon or Newark or Long Island City or the Bronx could say the same. She'd probably wake up with a hangover, possibly even in the wrong bed, but there was one thing she'd done that put her in a category apart from everyone else. He found it cheerful, though the picture as a whole was more than a little depressing.

As midnight approached, all motion in Times Square stopped, and people turned and looked at the light atop the flagpole on the Times Building, on the south side of the square. Even the noisemakers subsided until, at five seconds before the hour, the lighted ball began to drop, and then there was a roar and a clattering and a ringing of bells and blowing of horns that made all the previous noises sound like the mewling of mice. People kissed one another, hugged total strangers, shouted, and in general behaved as though all their debts had been forgiven and disease had been eradicated from the face of the earth. MacDougall could remember no comparable celebration; even the Armistice, which had gone into effect while his company was on the way to attack the fortress city of Metz, had been notable more for its sudden quiet than anything else. A few idiots had shot off their rifles; there was some ragged cheering, and one man had shouted "Hot shit!" but the overall sensation was one of silence, and an unwinding of tension that left people limp rather than excited.

MacDougall went over to Grandle and said, "Captain, what would you say the crowd is now?"

Grandle took a perfunctory look around the square and said, "I'd say a million—a million two hundred thousand."

"Would you say it's the largest ever?"

"Well—one of the largest." MacDougall made a note, and Grandle went on, "And my name is Grandle, not Grundle. Roscoe F. Grandle."

"I know that, sir," said MacDougall.

"Well, last year your paper printed it Grundle. See if you can't get it right this time."

"That was just a typo, but I'll tell them to be careful. Thank you, sir."

The *Times* man, who had been doing some calculating, said, "Based on the earlier estimate, four hundred thousand people came into the square in an hour and a quarter, which means that five thousand three hundred and thirty-three and a third people came in every minute. Would you say that was an accurate guess, Captain?"

"I would," said Grandle, and nudged his horse away from the reporters.

It was more than an hour before MacDougall could get back to his paper. It was impossible to buck the flow of traffic along the side streets, and he had to go where the crowd took him, with no more control than a leaf in a millrace. By the time he got to Fifth Avenue he was able to head downtown, and when he arrived at the paper he felt as though he'd been run through the high-speed roller presses. A man named verPlonck had the desk Sunday nights, and when MacDougall came in verPlonck opened his bottom desk drawer, took out one of a dozen or so shot glasses of Holland gin, and handed it to MacDougall, saying, "Happy New Year."

"Happy New Year to you, Pete," MacDougall replied, and downed the drink. It was warm and syrupy and tasted terrible, and for a moment he thought it was going to come right back up, but he swallowed hard, wiped his eyes, and felt his stomach begin to glow. "Good stuff," he said.

"Get anything worthwhile?"

"Not much. Some dame kissed Grandle's horse, and that's about all. I'm glad I don't have to write the story."

"Leave that to Lenzner. Give him what you've got, and then good night."

"Thank you, Pete. Good night to you." He could still taste the Holland gin, and he was anxious to get to the Circe and some good Scotch.

When he got there, the crowd seemed almost as dense as it had in Times Square. Marie had left the kitchen and donned an evening gown, and she gave him a *bonne année* kiss that, under other circumstances, might have rerouted his whole train of thought for the evening.

"Welcome, *mon petit!*" she said. "We thought you had forgotten us!"

"I was working," he replied. "Trampled by one million two hundred thousand of the biggest boobs this side of the Alleghenies." Looking at her he could see that her eyes were brighter than usual, and he guessed that Nick had managed to get enough wine or champagne or whatever into her to ease her out of her earlier mood. "You look ravishing tonight," he said, not entirely as an afterthought.

"Merci," she replied, with a slight curtsey. "Tonight is, how you say, my night to howl."

Nick came up behind her and put an arm around her waist. "It took her a while to get used to the idea," he said to MacDougall. "Now I'm probably going to have to use whips to get her back into the kitchen."

"Sez you, big boy," Marie replied, in a bad imitation of an American accent. "Tomorrow that Louis will be a *sous chef* again."

Albert Hopkins came out of the crowd and formally shook hands with Nick, Marie, and MacDougall. "Happy New Year, Happy New Year, Happy New Year," he said. "May you all have the best of all possible fortune in the year to come."

"The same to you," Nick replied. "Where'd you come from? I didn't see you earlier."

"I was at some deadly party," Hopkins replied. "I happened to look out the window and see that it was snowing, so I put on my hat and coat, made my excuses, and left."

"What about your wife?" Nick asked.

"Oh, she stayed. She's having a whale of an old time." Hopkins went to the bar, and the crowd closed in around him.

The noise level was such that few complete sentences could be heard, but snatches of conversation rose like rockets and then died out, and they had the superficial profundity of statements made under the influence of alcohol. "I think loyalty is the most important thing," a woman said. "Loyalty to a school, an ideal, the flag–I don't care what, so long as you're loyal–" A man's voice drowned her out, saying, "When you look at the broad sweep of history, you'll see that those who have lived by the sword have–" and his next words were lost in a wild outburst of laughter from four people who had obviously just heard an off-color joke. "I think the next few years are going to be as crucial as any our country has been through," another man said, and a woman shouted, "Whoopee! There goes my girdle!"

Four youths, with their foreheads almost touching, started singing Yale songs; and the woman who believed in loyalty said, "The Whiffenpoof Song always makes me cry, no matter where I hear it." Another woman said, "It was the most hideous weekend I've ever known–it lasted from Thursday to Tuesday, and I loathed every second of it." "You think that's funny?" a man said, "I know a better one than that." "I'd like you to meet my fiancée, Miss Evans," said another man, and a woman said, "Oh? Didn't I see you out with Buster Fetterman?" "You did not," replied Miss Evans. Suddenly, and unmistakably, MacDougall heard Dorothy Peters' voice saying, "It's the little people who break my heart–the ones who try to be brave." He looked around, and it was a few moments before he could spot her. She was standing at the bar, a college youth on one side of her and a paunchy, middle-aged man on the other, and the college youth was doing his best to peer down the front of her dress. MacDougall made his way toward her, and she glanced around and saw him coming.

"There you are, you old bastard," she said. "I thought you'd never get here."

"Where's Fred?" MacDougall asked.

"You mean Lochinvar McClain? He was taken with an acute case of the drunks and has gone beddy-bye."

The college youth gave MacDougall what was supposed to be a challenging stare, but the effect was lost because his eyes were out of focus. "Do I know you?" he asked.

"No, and if your luck holds you'll keep it that way," MacDougall replied, taking Dorothy by the arm. "Come on," he told her. "How would you like a nice, long walk in the snow?"

"Delighted," she replied, picking up her purse. "I've never been had in a snowdrift." She finished her drink, then put her forefinger in the chest of the paunchy, middle-aged man. "Just remember what I told you, Buster," she said. "The little people are going to take just so much from you Wall Street shits, and then they're going to rebel. And when they do, God help you."

"Come on," MacDougall said. "Let's go."

A light snow was falling, and the city was quiet. Most of the sounds of revelry had died away, with only an occasional, lonely blast on a horn to break the silence, and Dorothy clutched MacDougall's arm tightly as they walked toward Madison Avenue. She said nothing for perhaps four minutes, and then, in a voice that seemed to come from someone else, she said, "Why did I have to do that?"

"Do what?" MacDougall replied.

"Sail into that old fool. He wasn't doing anyone any harm—he just wanted to have a good time. But would I let him? No. Not little Nell, here. I have to go at him like some flaming pinwheel—I ought to be ashamed of myself. I ought to have my mouth washed out with soap."

"I did think you came on a little strong," MacDougall said. "What had he said to you?"

"That's just it—he hadn't said anything. He just came up all smiles, and I—I don't know. I guess I thought he was being condescending."

"How long ago did McClain fold up?"

"Oh, I don't know. Sometime around midnight. Nick put him in a cab and paid the driver."

They walked on awhile, and then suddenly Dorothy stopped. "I'm going back," she said.

"Back where?" said MacDougall.

"To the club. I'm going to apologize to that poor old poop."

"Oh, come on. He's probably forgotten all about it by now."

"I don't care. I won't sleep tonight unless I apologize. Why I should take it upon myself to ruin a man's evening—"

"You *haven't* ruined his evening! I told you, he's forgotten all about it!"

"Well, I haven't, and I'm the one who needs the sleep." She tried to pull away, but MacDougall gripped her arm tightly.

"Listen to me," he said, "this is nothing to do on the spur of the moment. At least think it over awhile before you go back."

"I have thought it over."

"Not enough. You come to my place, and we'll have a drink and talk it over, and then if it still seems like a good idea I'll take you back. How does that sound?"

She hesitated. "Just one drink?"

"As many as you want. As many as you think are necessary. No more, no less."

She stood still, swaying slightly, and then said, "All right. Just one. Then I'll go back and apologize, and then I'll sleep like a babe."

"Fine. Let's go."

She began to weep as they walked, and her voice was high and squeaky. "When I think of all those people trying to have a good time," she said. "All those people all over the world . . . blowing horns . . . dancing . . . and for what? Just so they can go through another lousy year . . . and I have to spoil it for one old poop who was only trying to be nice . . ."

"Cut it out," MacDougall told her.

"It's all very well for you to say," she replied. "You're never anything but nice to people. You must be the nicest person there is in the whole world. I mean that. I mean it sincerely."

"There's no need to go overboard," MacDougall replied.

"Yes, there is. There's every need in the world. And when we get to your place I'm going to show you just how nice I think you are. I'm going to show you so that it'll be burned forever in your brain, and every time you look in the mirror you'll be able to say, 'I'm the nicest person there is in the whole world.' That's what I'm going to do."

"That's quite an order. I'm not sure I'm up to it."

"You will be, Oscar. You will be."

MacDougall was the first to awake. He saw Dorothy sleeping beside him, the bedclothes snarled around her in a haphazard manner that revealed as much as they covered, and for a few moments he studied the breast that seemed almost to be staring at him. Then he slid quietly out of bed, got a dressing gown from the bathroom, and went into the kitchenette to make coffee. He lighted a cigarette and stamped it out after one drag, then opened the icebox door and peered inside. It was a depressing sight: a mangled stick of butter with toast crumbs on one end, two oranges that were beginning to develop soft spots, a third of a bottle of milk, a lamb chop wrapped in butcher's paper, a half loaf of bread, and three lemons. He took out the bread and the butter and was cutting a slice from the loaf when Dorothy appeared in the door. She had wrapped the sheet around her like a toga, and her hair looked like a wig that had been put on backward, producing an effect that was more reminiscent of Halloween than anything else.

"I had a hat when I came in," she announced. "And I'm not leaving this joint until I find it."

16

It was in April that Butterworth began looking for a house in the country. His job with Brady precluded his doing any extensive house-hunting on his own, so he studied the real estate sections of the Sunday newspapers, and finally made contact with an agent who said he had just what he wanted and would be happy to show it to him at his convenience. It turned out to be a renovated barn in Connecticut, an hour and a half by train from the city, and heated by a kerosene stove with an attached boiler for hot water. The smell of kerosene permeated the house, almost but not quite masking the residual odors from the time when it was a barn. The agent next produced something in White Plains, a city that Butterworth immediately nicknamed "Night Pains," which had as its sole advantage the fact that it was within decent commuting range of New York. Finally, the first week in May, the agent called and said he had precisely the house Butterworth had been looking for, and the tone in his voice implied that it was a take-it-or-leave-it situation; this was all there was in Butterworth's limited price range. Butterworth said he'd come out the following Sunday and have a look. If it hadn't been for his promise to Sarah he would probably have given up by now; as it was, he felt that this one last try was necessary to prove his good intentions.

The house was in Crestwood, a small community between Tuckahoe and Scarsdale, nestled near the bosky banks of the Bronx River about fifteen miles from New York. The Sunday trains were all locals, which meant more than a dozen stops between Grand Central and Crestwood, and since Sarah had not been able to find anyone with whom to leave the children, they'd been brought along, Sarah holding the baby and Butterworth more or less in charge of Nancy. By the time the forty-five-minute trip was over, the baby was in obvious need of a change of linen and Nancy had just asked her father, for the forty-seventh time, when they were going to get there. The idea of commuting had never appealed very strongly to Butterworth, but now, descending the train steps with Nancy in his arms, he felt that commuting would be a breeze compared to the trip he had just made.

The agent met them on the platform and escorted them over the footbridge to the southbound part of the station, where his slope-nosed Franklin touring car was parked. He was a short man with large ears, and was wearing plus-four knickerbockers and fringe-tongued golfing shoes. The air smelled of moist earth and new greenery, and bursts of yellow forsythia brightened the borders of the turn-around area. There was no parking space as such, because most of the houses lay within easy walking distance, and those people who did have cars would never have considered leaving them at the station. A car was to be driven, and polished, and cosseted, and paraded in front of those envious neighbors who had yet to own one.

Sarah breathed deeply and smiled. "Oh, my," she said. "I'd forgotten such heavenly smells existed."

"Crestwood is noted for its clean air," the agent replied. "The river purifies it."

"How about mosquitoes?" Butterworth asked.

The agent smiled condescendingly. "Not here," he said. "Above the dam, at Scarsdale, there are millions of mosquitoes, but the river runs so fast here they don't have a chance to breed. They're just swept away by the current."

Butterworth glanced down at the river, which at this point looked more like a muddy brook. "Ah, yes," he said.

The agent opened the doors to his car, as though demonstrating how well they worked. "But we're not here to talk about the river," he said. "We're here to look at your dream house. And I can promise you, that's exactly what it is. Just wait until you see it."

As it turned out, it was one of several almost identical houses, on a street lined with sycamore and maple trees; the exterior was stucco and the interior dark wood paneling, and the thing about it that appealed most to Sarah was the space for a small garden out back. "Oh, it's perfect!" she said. "We can have a playpen for Puddin and maybe a sand pile for Nancy, and I can grow vegetables and things, and–it's just *perfect!*"

"I knew you'd like it," the agent said, glancing at Butterworth.

The sights and the smells of spring had taken his mind back to his boyhood in Massachusetts, and he was remembering the cold-flowing brooks, the skunk cabbage in the woods, and the gelatinous clusters of frogs' eggs among the pond grasses, and it took him a moment to realize the agent was waiting for him to say something. "It seems fine," he said. "What's the rent?"

"Forty-five dollars a month."

"Does that include utilities?"

"No, but they're negligible. The electricity might be another five or ten, and the phone is on a party line so you save there. Then, of course, in the winter there's the coal."

"You mean I have to pay for the heating, too? I've never heard of that before."

"Well, in this case–"

"Roland, please," Sarah said, clutching his arm. "I don't care what it costs–please, let's take it."

"Wait a minute," Butterworth replied. "I just want to find out what this is going to add up to. There'll be the electricity, the telephone, the train fare–"

"You don't use any electricity in the daytime," the agent said. "The rooms are really quite bright. And as for–"

"Roland," Sarah said again, but he ignored her.

"I'd like your estimate," he said to the agent, "of just how much extra all these things are going to cost."

"Negligible, really," the agent replied. "Perhaps another fifteen, twenty–"

"So that brings the price of the house to sixty or sixty-five dollars a month, at the very least."

"Well–"

"And now you want to add the heating on top of that, which is something no landlord I've ever heard of has had the gall to do. How much will the heat come to?"

"I'll tell you, Mr. Butterfield–"

"Butterworth."

"Excuse me. I'll tell you, Mr. Butterworth. I'll talk to the owner, and I'm sure we can come to some sort of agreement."

"You didn't answer my question. How much will the heat come to?"

"Well, that will be immaterial, if he decides to pay for it."

"You mean, this was all a dodge, to see if he could get me to pay for the coal?"

"Not in the least. But I feel sure that, in the circumstances, he'll be glad to take that on himself."

"I see," said Butterworth. "In that case, we'll take the house."

On the train going back to New York, Sarah was silent, staring out the window as the countryside merged gradually into the upper reaches of the Bronx. "What are you so quiet about?" Butterworth asked her. "I should think you'd be happy as a lark."

"I am happy," she replied. "I'm delighted."

"When are we going to get home?" Nancy asked.

"Then what are you so quiet about?" Butterworth said to Sarah.

"It was just a side of you I've never seen," Sarah replied.

"What was?"

"Talking to the agent that way. I thought for a minute you were going to punch him in the mouth."

"Daddy," said Nancy.

"I wasn't going to do any such thing," Butterworth said. "I just saw what he was trying to do to us, and decided I wouldn't let him get away with it."

"That's what I mean. I've never seen you do that before. You were a completely different person."

"Daddy!" said Nancy. "Daddy, Daddy, Daddy!"

"Be quiet!" Butterworth said. "We'll get home when we get there, and not a minute before!"

"There you go again," Sarah said.

"Where do I go? What are you talking about?"

"You snapped at Nancy, just the way you did at the real estate agent."

"I didn't snap at him! I was just trying to keep him from cheating us! Don't you understand?"

"Daddy!" Nancy cried, in a shrill voice. "I have to go to the bathroom!"

"Why didn't you say so?" Butterworth took her by the hand and guided her down the aisle, aware of sympathetic smiles from a few of the other passengers.

Sarah returned to the subject that night, when they were in bed and had turned out the light. She reached out in the darkness and found his hand, and held it while she said, "I didn't mean to sound complaining today."

"About what?" he replied.

"About you. The way you talked to the agent."

"Oh."

"But it was just so different from the usual you that I couldn't help remarking on it."

"How would the usual me have handled it?"

"You wouldn't have been so—well, so forceful."

"I don't see what's forceful about not wanting to be cheated."

"Well, you wouldn't have mentioned it. Not that way, at least."

"You mean the usual me would have padded along and got cheated?"

"I don't know. Maybe."

"What you're saying is that the usual me is a sucker?"

"Now, don't start taking offense. I didn't mean—"

"I'm not taking offense. I just find it interesting to know what you've thought of me all these years."

She was quiet for a moment, then said, "I've always thought of you as kind and dear and wonderful, and not—well, not one to be suspicious."

"In other words, a sucker."

"I wish you wouldn't put words in my mouth. No, not a sucker. Just a love. Until . . ."

"Until what?"

She was quiet again, and finally said, "Until you started drinking."

"Oh, come on. Drinking had nothing to do with this."

"I didn't say it did."

"That certainly is the way I heard it."

"It's not what I meant. I meant it's brought a change in you."

"In what way, for God's sakes?"

"For one thing, you never used to swear at me."

"I didn't swear at you! I simply asked what the change was."

"If you don't call taking the Lord's name swearing, then we have nothing to talk about."

"I agree with you. This is getting us nowhere." He withdrew his hand, turned on his side, and tried to feign sleep, but the knowledge that she was still awake acted as a stimulant. He had the sensation that a large bird was hovering over the bed, ready to swoop down the minute he closed his eyes.

They moved in the first of June. Work at the Brady office had tapered off somewhat, since no new plays were expected until the fall, and Butterworth had time to help Sarah with the apparently endless list of things that had to be done. They didn't have enough furniture of their own to make the move a complicated one, but the matter of moving from a small apartment to a house revealed unexpected areas that needed attention. In the apartment there had been room only for a crib for Nancy and a bassinet for Puddin; he now needed the crib and Nancy needed a bed of her own, but that could be arranged only by putting her in a separate room, an idea that brought forth her loud disapproval. A packing case had been perfectly adequate as a piece of makeshift furniture in the apartment, but in the house it looked ludicrous, and no amount of covering it with rugs or runners could disguise it. And the increased size of the rooms required more lights (the rooms were not, as the agent had insisted, bright; on an overcast day they took on a grotto-like appearance), and while candles would have helped, Butterworth vetoed the idea of any lighted candles in the room with a three-year-old child. A further problem was the fact that none of the rugs was big enough to fill its assigned space, so they had to be scattered about, in some cases wrinkling around the legs of chairs and creating tripping hazards. One afternoon, when Sarah was out with the children, Butterworth decided to make himself useful by writing labels for all the empty jars in the pantry, and by the time she got back he had completed more than a dozen, with neatly lettered labels such as "Salt," "Pepper," "Mustard (hot)," "Mustard (regular)," "Cloves," "Thyme," "Marjoram," "Mandrake Root," and so on. It turned out that Sarah had been saving the jars for grape jelly in the fall.

He had been keeping up his diary, but the entries were terse, consisting of notations like "worked around the house," "more moving chores," and such. Finally, about a week after they'd moved, he decided it was time to do an introspective report, so after Sarah had gone to bed he took his diary to the dining room table and wrote:

Friday, June 8, 1923 warm & sunny

We seem to be fairly well moved in by now, and I think it's a good thing all around. It will be wonderful for the kids—which is, after all, what the whole business of living is about—and I must admit there's something about the country that reaches very deep inside me. I guess (what do I mean, I guess? I know) I'm still a country boy at heart, and if there were some way to make money in the backwoods, I'd probably be there like a shot. Well, maybe not backwoods, but on a farm. Is it wrong to like the smell of cows? I certainly hope not. This whole move, of course, was originally for S's benefit, and I hope and pray it will work out well for her. There is no reason why it shouldn't, because it's exactly what she's been asking for, but there seems to be something nagging at her that keeps her from enjoying everything to the fullest. She has said it's because I take a drink now and then, but I honestly think there's something worrying her that she just doesn't want to talk about. Her nerves were in pretty bad shape by the time we left the city, and it's possible she got herself worked up to a point where she was hating everything. Once she settles down in the country, I think she'll be able to relax and enjoy life a little more. I'll do everything *I* can to help, so one way or another it's bound to work out.

He reported for work at the Brady office on Monday and found that Brady had taken off for the country, looking for a possible location for a summer theatre. The New York theatres, with nothing more than creaking fans to cool them, were hell pits during the summer, and even some of the biggest hits suspended their runs until September. This left a lot of actors out of work, and the idea was growing that some sort of theatre might be possible in rustic surroundings, either in the open air or in some structure with natural ventilation. Brady was off scouring the woods, and Brown, his assistant, was left to run the office. When Butterworth came in, Brown was going through a stack of publicity pictures, sorting them into two piles.

"Anything I can do?" Butterworth asked.

"That's what I'm looking for," Brown replied. "Something for you to do." There was an odd note in his voice that made Butterworth suddenly apprehensive.

"Just name it, and I'll do it," he said.

Brown looked at a few more pictures. "A lot of these are out of date," he said. "You might sort through them and weed out the oldest ones, then see if you can't arrange to have some new ones made."

"Yes, sir!" Butterworth tried to make it sound like the reply to a military command, but since he'd never been in the military it didn't quite come off. The tone of Brown's voice still worried him, and he didn't know quite how to define it. He went through a few pictures, most of which were of Grace George or Alice Brady, and stopped when he came to one of Alice, dressed in what looked like a fringed curtain from a San Francisco bordello, holding a Chinese fan at arm's length. The caption told him it showed her in *Drifting,* a melodrama of two seasons past. "Now, this picture," he said, holding it up for Brown to see. "Do you think she'd want to be remembered like that?"

Brown glanced at it and said, "She okayed it. That means it stands." As an afterthought, he added, "Incidentally, Alan Dale, of the *American,* called that play 'strangely protuberant.' Make of *that* what you will."

"O.K., then," Butterworth said. "Since Alice or her mother must have okayed every one of these, what is there to throw away? And as for having new ones made, does that mean we've got to find the old costumes, and re-create the sets? I just don't know how to go about it."

"You have a point there," Brown said. He stared at the pile of pictures for a moment, then said, "I tell you what—you can bring their scrapbooks up to date. There's a lot of stuff that hasn't been pasted in yet. In the meantime, I'll try to think of something else."

"What is this sudden need for me to work?" Butterworth asked. "Do I have to give proof that I'm employed here?"

"In a sense, yes," Brown said, after a moment. "Before he left, the Old Man said that unless you pulled your weight around the office, I should let you go. I'm just trying to think of ways to give visible evidence of your work."

"Oh," said Butterworth. "I see."

"Don't worry about it. I'll think of something."

"Sure."

He spent the day doing odd jobs around the office, trying to think of something so spectacular that it would revolutionize the world of press agentry, but all he could come up with were variations of assorted college pranks he'd either heard of or been involved in, and he discarded them almost immediately. A good press agent, he'd been told, should focus attention on his client rather than on himself, and at the same time should make the attention seem natural rather than forced. The press agent should always be in the background, ready to give out whatever information was needed, but he should arrange it so that the press wanted the information and did not feel it was being forced on them. The more he thought of it the more contradictory and impossible the job seemed, and he wondered what he was doing in the business anyway. The answer came as soon as he'd asked himself the question: he was in it for the seventy-five dollars a week, which was just barely enough to support himself and his family in their new circumstances. The only thing that guaranteed him food during the week was the fact that he could charge at the Circe; he paid cash whenever he could, but when he was down to nickels and dimes he could always go to the Circe and be assured of a good meal.

Unlike most commuters, he had no fixed train that he took home in the evening. If a play was opening, or there was work to be done, he might not get away before midnight; if it had been a routine day with no problems (which it seldom was) he could sometimes make the 5:19, or even the 5:08. The last train left at 1:00 A.M., and if he missed that it meant looking for a bed in town. MacDougall had offered him a spare bed any time he wanted, but he couldn't always find MacDougall, and he hesitated to barge in on him late at night. Just once he had called the apartment around midnight, looking for information about a person MacDougall had interviewed for the paper, and had heard the unmistakable sounds of a young lady in the background. For reasons he was never able to explain, Butterworth knew from the sound of her voice that she was undressed.

This particular evening he could probably have caught the 5:08, but Brown's message had so unsettled him that he didn't feel like going home; he wanted to stay within reach of the office in case something important turned up. It was an irrational urge; he simply felt that in his precarious position he had better take no chances. Any slip would be his last, and any good he could do would give him that much more help. He called Sarah and told her he'd probably have supper in town, then put on his boater with the college hatband and went to the Circe.

It was early, and there were only about a half dozen people at the bar. Butterworth ordered his usual Scotch sour, then looked at the man next to him and found himself staring at the flawless, classic, left profile of John Barrymore, an actor whose work in *Justice, The Living Corpse, The Jest,* and *Richard III* had earned him considerable acclaim. Barrymore rolled his eyes toward Butterworth, examined him for a moment, and said, "How now, cousin? A bit of wine for thy stomach's sake?"

"My stomach isn't the problem," Butterworth replied. "It's my job."

Barrymore nodded, and took a sip of his Scotch. "I'm told that happens to everyone," he said. "Of course, I've never had what you'd really call a job, so I wouldn't know. My calling is to smear paint upon my face and pretend to be someone else."

"Do you happen to know William A. Brady?" Butterworth asked.

Barrymore's eyes widened. "Wee Willie Brady?" he said. "I do, indeed. And I think I understand your problem, if he's your employer."

"He is. Or was, the last I heard."

"You have my sympathy. My only advice is never to see him in the same state of sobriety twice running. When sober, he will make all sorts of announcements that he promptly forgets the minute his wits leave him, and when foxed by the grape he is a veritable fountainhead of bombast circumstance, horribly stuffed with epithets of war. Catch him in his alternate moods, and you need fear nothing."

Butterworth tasted his sour and said, "That's easy to say, but when you work in the office it's not always possible."

"Then stay away from the office. Dream up projects that will take you to the far reaches of Yonkers, and by the time you return he's bound to be in a different mood from when you left."

"I'll see what I can do. Thanks for the thought, anyway."

Barrymore waved a hand in dismissal, and handed his drink to Charlie for a refill. "There are tricks to every trade," he said. "Some of them more devious than others. When last did you see *Hamlet?*"

"I can't even remember," said Butterworth, who had read the play but never seen it produced.

"Do you recall who did it?"

"No."

"I thought not. These mountebanks who play Shakespeare all read their lines as though they were reciting the Koran, and you're lucky if you can distinguish any of the words, much less understand them. I have an idea for a whole new approach, so simple that it will stun the general, make mad the guilty, and appall the free."

"What's that?"

"Read the lines as though they were everyday English. Let people understand what you're saying and thinking. The boudoir scene, for instance, will take on a wholly new dimension, fairly bristling with Havelock Ellis."

Butterworth, whose knowledge of *Hamlet* was superficial, had let his mind wander back to his problems with Brady, and when Barrymore stopped speaking he felt it was his turn to say something, if only out of politeness. "Which part are you going to play?" he asked.

There was dead silence for a moment, and then Barrymore said, "Ophelia. What else?"

Butterworth's mind suddenly snapped into focus, and he said, "I'm sorry. I'm afraid I was wool-gathering. It sounds like a splendid idea."

"Anyone who works for Wee Willie Brady has a right to become comatose," Barrymore replied. "Finish your drink, and then we can take to our heels."

"Where to?" Butterworth wondered if he'd missed anything else.

"Do you know Tony Soma's?"

"No."

"It's a splendid watering hole, not far from here. It's always good to have an alternate oasis, in case your favorite one is raided."

They finished their drinks, had one round for the road, and then went to Tony's, which was somewhat reminiscent of the Circe, although different in decor. The sours were more acid than those that Charlie made, and Butterworth found it was easier on his digestion if he had plain Scotch and water. In this case "digestion" was not the exact word because he'd had nothing to eat, and he had a faint memory of Barrymore's feeding him a sandwich, then taking him to Grand Central and putting him on a train. He slept through to White Plains, and had to wait an hour for a train to take him back to Crestwood. It was nearly midnight when he arrived, and as he climbed the hill from the station he felt that he was sober, but for all practical purposes he might just as well have stayed in the city.

17

The Circe's closing hours were flexible, and depended on the amount of business at any given time. Some nights the place would be empty by twelve o'clock, in which case Nick and Marie would close up and go home; at other times the customers would be in a singing and carousing mood, and Nick would have to clear them out at three. Marie usually closed the kitchen at midnight—at least that was when Louis went home—and what the customers ate after that depended on Marie's mood and the state of the larder. Sometimes she could be persuaded to make sandwiches; at other times she simply took off her apron and had a brandy in the front room. Until midnight a person could expect to be reasonably well fed; after that, most of them didn't care what they ate anyway.

It was the quality of the food that set the Circe apart from most of the other speakeasies. Between them, Marie and Louis managed to turn out a menu that was at once varied and dependable, and if there was a new dish on the bill of fare you could be sure that it had met Marie's critical standards. After her initial disapproval, she had accepted Louis as a part of the kitchen, but she tasted every dish he turned out, and felt free to make whatever suggestions occurred to her. Louis, who was a Burgundian with his own ideas about cooking, accepted the insult in silence, telling himself that only among Frenchmen could this sort of criticism be tolerated. If Marie had been anything but French, he would have thrown his apron at her feet and walked out. Also, there was something about her that stirred memories of his youth, and while he knew better than even to think of any carnal contact, he enjoyed working in her presence and every now and then letting his mind drift back to the days before the war, when he had known any number of girls in the Biblical sense of the word. She reminded him particularly of a girl in Auxerre, whose legs were those of a cross-country runner and who could imprison a man between them for as long as she chose. He had once remarked to this girl that the man in the iron mask was a *boulevardier* compared to anyone locked in her limbs, an observation that she mercifully took as a compliment. Had she taken offense, she could have broken him in half.

One Thursday night in July, when those who could escape the city's heat had already taken off for protracted weekends, Marie looked out of the kitchen and saw Charlie adding up the money in the till, while Nick rearranged the chairs and Max dozed over his law books at the front door. She glanced at the clock and saw it was eleven-thirty.

"Are we closing?" she asked.

"Not quite yet," Nick replied. "We'll give it another half hour."

She went back into the kitchen and said to Louis, *"Va-t'en, choux.* No need for you to stay."

Louis shrugged. "I like it here," he said. "This is as much home as anywhere else." He was short and wiry, and wore a dark chin beard that somehow made his face look like the figurehead of a ship. His biceps, bulging beneath his skivvy shirt, were still those of an artilleryman, and the only soft thing about him were his eyes, which were an unexpectedly bright blue. With his eyes closed, he could have been taken for a Neapolitan; with them open, he was almost Nordic.

"Comme tu veux," Marie replied. "In that case, let's change into our society clothes and have a drink with the gentry."

They removed their aprons, and Louis put on a shirt and jacket, and they went into the front room. *"Deux cognacs,"* Marie said to Charlie, who had just finished sorting the money.

"Who's buying?" Charlie asked. "Is this on the house?"

"Who's here except the house?" replied Marie. "Don't ask foolish questions."

Charlie reached for the cognac bottle just as the door buzzer sounded.

"Ah, merde," said Marie. "Wouldn't you know." She started to get up, but Nick stopped her.

"Wait a minute," he said. "Let's see who it is."

"If it's *les gangsters,* I'm not here," said Louis. "Tell them I just went home."

"What do you know about *les gangsters?"* Marie asked. "Where did you ever see any?"

"I know enough," Louis replied, and kept his eyes on the door.

Max opened the peephole, then swung the door wide to admit George MacDougall, who came in with his jacket on one arm and his hat on the back of his head. "Jesus, it's hot out," he said. "I hope you didn't all wait up for me."

"What does it look like?" said Marie. "We were hoping the Mayor would be here to give you a formal welcome."

"I'm sorry, but I just got through work." MacDougall turned to Charlie and said, "May I have a Tom Collins, please?"

"For you," said Charlie, "but for you only."

"I get the impression this has been a tough day," MacDougall said.

"Not really," Nick replied. "Just in fits and starts. Brother Barrymore was in earlier, and that always makes the day seem a little longer."

"I have an interesting assignment, which I'd like to talk to you about," MacDougall said, lowering his voice slightly.

"You don't have to whisper," said Nick. "This is all family here."

"I'm sorry. The nature of it is such that—well, the hell with it. How do you get your hooch?"

"That's Frank's department," Nick replied. "Why?"

"I've been assigned to make a pick-up run with a bootlegger. Do you think you could arrange it?"

Nick thought for a moment, then said, "They're pretty touchy about their sources. I don't think they'd want it advertised in the newspapers."

"Obviously, there'd be no names used. Or places, either. I simply want to know how it's done, and some of the problems they run into. Just for instance, do they bring it across the border, or does it come in on boats? And what about the Feds, and the Coast Guard, and things like that? It looks like a growing business, and it could make a good story."

Nick thought some more, then said, "I just don't know. I'll have to talk to Frank. I know when Prohibition first came in they used to haul it across the border—that's what it was called, hauling—but they had to stick to the roads, and that made it easier to be ambushed. They'd have maybe four trucks, or cars, and—"

"Ambushed by whom?"

"Anybody. The Feds—hijackers—whoever. There are just so many roads into Canada, and the word gets around. If the Feds caught you, they confiscated the cars as well as the stock, but you could always buy the cars back at public auction; if it was hijackers that ambushed you, you lost everything, including maybe two or three people, so it was always preferable to be caught by the Feds. At any rate, that's what I've been told."

"Well, there's no great hurry on this. But if you'd sound Frank out on the chances, I'd appreciate it."

"I'll be seeing him in the next day or so. I'll do what I can." The door buzzer sounded, and Nick looked at the clock. "So it's going to be one of *those* nights," he said. "No action from eight until quarter to twelve, then hell breaks loose."

"I think I'll go home while I can," Louis said, finishing his cognac and rising. "*À demain, messieursdames.*" He went into the kitchen, and after a moment they heard the lock snap as the back door closed behind him.

From the darkened entrance hall came Fred McClain, who looked at the nearly empty room and said, "Am I too late for a drink? I feel as though an owl had slept in my mouth."

"In that case you can have something," Nick replied. "We're open for emergencies only."

McClain ordered a gin sling and turned to MacDougall, who was just finishing his Tom Collins. "Will you join me in a slug?" he asked.

"Why ever not?" MacDougall replied. "It's a long time till sunrise."

"Are you celebrating something?"

"No. I just got through work."

"Me too, but it was a different kind of work. I seem to have bedded down with some silly flapper who'd just seen *Blood and Sand*. She wanted me to act like Valentino."

"That's a tall order."

"You don't know the half of it. She wanted sand in the bed."

"Oh."

There was a short pause, then McClain said, "Seen anything of Dottie recently?"

"No," MacDougall replied. "Have you?"

"Not really. I still haven't made up for that crash dive I took New Year's Eve."

"She told me about that."

"What did she say?"

"Just that you'd gone teepy-bye, or words to that effect."

"That's the nicest way she could have put it. I became a public charge." There was another pause while they tasted their drinks, and then McClain said, "Do you know anyone who's seen her around—or heard of her?"

"Not that I can think of. Why?"

"I hear she had a you-know-what."

"You mean an abortion?"

McClain nodded. "That's what I heard."

"Who told you?"

"Well, it wasn't in so many words, but Angela Fenwick said Dottie'd asked her, 'for a friend,' if she knew a doctor who'd do it. Angela gave her the name of a guy, but she wasn't taken in by that 'for a friend' gag. I just wondered if you knew anything about it."

"Why should I know?" MacDougall had been trying to remember the last time he'd seen Dottie, and the last time he'd been to bed with her, but the dates were blurred and, for this purpose, meaningless. "She doesn't tell me everything," he said, realizing that that, if nothing else, was the truth.

The buzzer sounded, and Nick called to Max, "Whoever it is, tell him we're closed. No more customers tonight."

Max opened the peephole and then unlocked the gate, and Nick started to say, "Goddammit, Max," when he saw that the person who'd been admitted was Louis. Louis' face was expressionless as he came to Nick and said, "Can I see you in the kitchen?"

"Sure," said Nick. "If it's all that important."

He followed Louis into the kitchen, and Louis turned and in a low voice said, "Boss, we're being watched."

"What do you mean?"

"By a couple of hoods. I went out the back door, and saw a guy crouching in the alley there, so on a hunch I went around to the front, and there's another guy posted across the street. They're not doing anything; they're just hiding in the shadows, waiting."

"How do you know they're hoods?"

"Look, Boss, I know. Don't ask silly questions."

"What are they waiting for?"

"My guess is they're waiting for you. There's nobody else here that's worth their time."

Nick remembered the night he and Marie had been set upon by Livorno's hoods, and the comparative ease he'd had dispatching them. "You say there're only two?" he said.

"Yes, but I think they're just lookouts. I think they probably got a hit car cruising around somewhere."

"Oh." Nick thought for a moment, then said, "All right, we'll go out two by two. You take Marie out the back, then George and Fred will go out the front, and finally Charlie and Max will go out the back. You take Marie home, but don't go straight—take a roundabout route."

"What about you?"

"I'll stay here."

"Is that very smart?"

"Who knows? I'll just turn out the lights and wait and see what happens. I can wait as long as they can."

"You got a heater?"

"A what?"

"A rod—a gun. You don't speak as good English as I do."

"No. I never thought it would be necessary."

"Take this." Louis reached in an inside pocket and brought out a snub-nosed .32 revolver. "It won't do much damage, but it's better than nothing."

Nick took the gun, flipped open the cylinder and saw it was fully loaded, then snapped the cylinder shut and put the gun in his pocket. "Thanks," he said. "I hope I won't have to use it."

Louis crossed himself and said nothing.

They went back into the bar, and Nick explained the situation as calmly as he could, trying to make it sound like a rehearsal for a Christmas pageant. Nobody spoke for a few moments after he'd finished, and then, in a quiet voice, Marie said, "I'm not going."

"Yes, you are," Nick replied.

"I am not. If you stay then I stay, and that's all there is to it."

"Wouldn't it be better if we all stayed?" McClain said. "That way, we'd have them outnum–"

"Will you please listen to me?" Nick cut in. "The more people stay here the worse our chances will be, and anyone who insists on remaining is only making it more likely someone gets hurt. If I have to run for it *I* can probably dodge them, but if we go out like a flock of chickens we'll all be screwed. I have a gun but it's good for only one person, and that person is me. I'm the one they're after, so they won't bother the rest of you if you're on your own. Now, let's all knock off the chatter and get with it. Marie, you and Louis go out the back."

"I'm not moving," Marie said through tight lips.

"Have you heard what I've been saying?" Nick shouted. "Are you deliberately trying to get someone shot? Because if you are, I've got a cure for that too–I can have Louis slug you one, and carry you out of here like a drunk. What's it going to be–are you going to walk out, or are you going to be carried?"

Marie shifted her gaze to Louis, who ran his tongue across his lips and said nothing. "Would you really slug me?" she asked.

"I will do what Monsieur Nick says," he replied. "He pays my salary."

"En ce cas," said Marie, *"allons-y."* She took Louis by the arm, and they went out the back door and into the night. As the door closed behind them she said, "Those Italians–they have no more chivalry than toads."

Nick let the next pair out the front door, and finally, after waiting a few minutes, let Max and Charlie out the back. Then he double-locked both doors, turned out the lights, and took a position behind the bar. He reasoned that if they tried to get in to torch the place, he'd be in the best position to hold them off. He couldn't see the back door from the bar, but it was within leaping distance if he had to get there in a hurry. A silence settled down, as thick as the darkness surrounding him, and the only thing he could hear was his own breathing. He was reminded of the sensation that had enveloped him while waiting to jump off in the attack on Soissons, when his senses were alert to the smallest detail, but his body seemed paralyzed. It occurred to him that it would be perfectly possible to spend the night here–and all the next day, for that matter–but that would only postpone the confrontation and settle nothing. It would be much better to take some sort of action now and get it over with.

Finally, after about a half hour he came out from behind the bar, checked the lock on the back door and slipped the chain in place, then went to the front door and opened the peephole. He could see nothing except the immediate area, so he opened the door a crack. There was nobody in sight. He went out, closed and locked the door, locked the iron gate, then took a deep breath and started walking down the darkened street, one hand on the gun in his pocket and his eyes searching the opposite side of the street for any sign of movement.

He had almost reached the corner when he heard the sound of an automobile engine behind him and, looking back, he saw the black shape of a touring car approaching without lights. He let it come a little closer, then instead of running away he turned and dived down the steps of an entrance to a brownstone house. He saw a flicker of yellow lights from the car and heard the clatter of the gun and the smack of bullets into the brownstone, and as the car gained speed he pulled himself up carefully and peered at the street through the iron railing. From the deep shadows on the other side a figure came out and started toward him, and he breathed deeply and braced his elbows, aware that the accurate range of his gun was probably not more than twenty yards. The man approaching him must have thought Nick was dead, because he came casually, almost nonchalantly, and held his gun loosely in one hand. When he was about fifteen yards away, Nick held his breath and squeezed off a shot aimed at the left knee, and the man shouted and fell down, holding his leg and writhing in agony. Nick rose from his hiding place and picked up the gun the man had dropped.

"Hello, pigshit," he said cheerfully. "Does your mother know you play with guns?" The man made an incoherent, strangled reply, and Nick, aware that the other lookout would have been alerted by the gunfire, decided to head for home. As he left, he said, "Tell your chums they should always aim low. A submachine gun rises when you fire it."

The next day Nick sought out Frank DiMotto, who had an office in what was ostensibly a furniture warehouse. There was a lot of furniture in evidence, but there were also crates and packing cases, stenciled with such designations as "Desk," "Davenport," and "Bedroom Suite," and it didn't take much imagination to guess the actual contents. DiMotto was on the telephone, so Nick had time to look around the office and make a rough guess as to the amount of money involved. It was impressive.

DiMotto finished the phone call, hung up, and smiled at Nick. "How are things at the store?" he asked.

"Only so-so," Nick replied. He filled DiMotto in on the events of the previous night and on his long-standing feud with Livorno, and concluded, "It looks like we're going to need some kind of protection. I can handle them one at a time, but when they start using shock troops I've got to have help. I can't fight them and run the store at the same time."

DiMotto considered this for a few moments, then said, "What kind of protection were you thinking of?"

"I thought you might have an idea. I'll consider anything except paying the bastard money."

"Well, I'll look into it," DiMotto replied. "I'll ask around."

"One other thing," Nick said. He detailed George MacDougall's request for a trip with the bootleggers, and when he was through DiMotto shook his head.

"Impossible," DiMotto said. "I don't see them agreeing in a million years."

"Well, ask, will you?" Nick said. "This guy is honest–he's totally trustworthy, and all he wants is a general picture of how it works. He won't mention names or places, or anything like that, so I don't see what possible harm it could do."

DiMotto continued to shake his head.

"Look at it this way," Nick said. "This is a chance for the boots to look like heroes. Nice American boys, doing their countrymen a favor by short-circuiting a stupid-assed law. They're putting their butts on the line to see that the public gets what is its rightful due, and all the thanks they get is to get shot at by the Feds."

"They make a buck or two on the side," DiMotto put in.

"So more power to them. But they shouldn't be treated as criminals, and this will be their chance to put their case before the public. As I see it, it's an opportunity they should jump at, not try to duck."

DiMotto was quiet for a few moments. "I'll ask," he said at last. "But don't expect anything to happen."

18

Ten days later, MacDougall was in the Circe with Roland Butterworth, who had stopped by for a rum Collins before catching the 6:23 for Crestwood.

"How do you like being a commuter?" MacDougall asked. "Is the country life worth the train ride?"

"This time of year it is," Butterworth replied. "But come winter it'll be something else again. Those midnight trains are a pain in the neck."

"You can bunk with me any time you like," MacDougall said. "I've got an extra bed that's never used—well, very seldom. Call it occasionally."

"I might take you up on that. How much advance notice would you need?"

"That depends. But I'm sure we can work it out—first man in leave a note on the door, or something like that."

"By the way, have you seen Dottie recently?"

MacDougall looked at him sharply. "Why do you ask?"

"No reason. I just haven't seen her for a while."

"I had a long session with her last night. We decided, among other things, that I'm not the Lochinvar she's had in mind all these years."

"Oh. Sorry to hear it."

"I'm not."

"What's she had in mind?"

"That's part of the problem. I don't think she knows. She's all for being swept off her feet, but then there's always a–if you'll excuse the expression–fly in the ointment."

Butterworth sipped his drink and said, "All this is kind of beyond me. Where I come from, if you liked a girl you took her out for a while and then asked her to marry you; if she said yes, then fine, and if she said no, you looked for someone else."

"It's simpler that way, God knows," said MacDougall. "Or so I would imagine."

"Yes and no. Some guys I know are still looking for the right girl."

"And not having any fun on the side?"

"I wouldn't know."

"You New Englanders are a close-mouthed bunch, I'll say that for you."

"My grandmother used to say if you don't talk, then everyone else will have to guess, and nobody pays off on guesses."

"Your grandmother sounds like quite a person."

"She was. She hated oak trees because they live longer than people, but other than that she kept a pretty even disposition."

"Son of a gun," said MacDougall. "You've got to admire an old lady who hates oaks. Nothing trivial for her, hey?"

"Oaks and postmen. She said postmen brought only bad news."

Nick came in from the kitchen, and motioned MacDougall to one side. "Are you doing anything tonight?" he asked.

"Today's my day off," MacDougall replied. "I'm free as a breeze."

Nick gave him a slip of paper and said, "Be at this warehouse at nine o'clock, and wear something warm."

"*Warm?* In this weather?"

"I'm told it gets chilly on the water."

"Oh." MacDougall looked at the paper and said, "Whom do I say sent me?"

"Frank's got it all arranged. They'll be looking for you."

"Well, thank you. I'd sort of given up hope."

"Don't thank me, thank Frank. And also, don't mention this to anyone–and that means anyone."

"Do you think I'm crazy?"

"No, but it never hurt to throw in a reminder."

"O.K." MacDougall looked at his watch, which showed not quite six o'clock. "I've got time to finish my drink, go home and get a jacket—"

"And don't be late. They leave the warehouse on the dot of nine."

"I'll be there." MacDougall put the paper in his pocket and went back to the bar, where Butterworth was talking with two men, one of whom was dark-haired and handsome, although with slightly prominent teeth and the remains of a scar on his upper lip. The other man was thin and prim-mouthed, and seemed to be observing rather than joining in the conversation.

"Mr. MacDougall," Butterworth said, "do you know Mr. Bogart? Humphrey Bogart—George MacDougall." They shook hands, and Butterworth added, "And Mr.—I'm sorry—"

"Webb," said the other man. "Clifton Webb." He and MacDougall shook hands.

"We are the co-stars of that Broadway smash hit *Meet the Wife,*" Bogart said, grinning. "Ably supported by the lovely if somewhat plump Mary Boland." Webb smiled a tight little smile, and Bogart went on, "I was just telling Roly, here, about my disgrace."

"What's that?" MacDougall said.

"I forgot I had an entrance in the third act, so after the second act I took off my makeup and went home, leaving Mary with a big hole in the stage. Next day the stage manager asked me where the hell I'd been, and I couldn't think of anything to say so I hit him in the mouth. Mary hasn't spoken to me since." He laughed, and took a sip of his Scotch. "Drink up, Webbie," he said. "We still have time for one more."

"I ought to call Mother," Webb said. "She worries if she doesn't hear from me."

"There's a phone in back. I'm sure Nick'll let you use it."

Webb left the bar, and Butterworth said, "It seems to me that stage manager lacked imagination. When you didn't show up he should have brought a phone onstage, said, 'It's for you,' and handed it to Mary and let her ad-lib a few lines. That would at least have given her something to play with."

Bogart looked at him with interest. "You have a fascinating turn of mind," he said. "Did you ever think of writing for the stage?"

"I think he ought to be an actor," MacDougall said, "but I can't go into that now. I've got an assignment." He finished his drink and put money on the bar.

"I thought today was your day—" Butterworth began, then looked at his watch and saw it was ten minutes past six. "Oh, my God," he said. "I've got a train to catch!" He downed his drink and ran out into the street looking frantically for a taxi, but the evening rush hour was on and there was none to be had. It had been raining when he left Crestwood that morning, and his rubbers now made running a nightmare, squeaking and seeming to clog his steps as he raced for Grand Central Station. He shot down the stairs to the Lower Level, squeezed through the gates of the 6:23 just as the trainman was closing them, then raced down the ramp toward the train. His extra speed, which appeared to be approaching the velocity of light, caused his rubbers to wrench loose and fly clear in a shuddering arc across the platform, and by the time he had retrieved them the train was moving. Panting and exhausted, he watched it go, then turned and trudged back up the ramp and through an open gate to the concourse. The next train was the 7:15, which wouldn't get him home until after eight o'clock, and rather than ask Sarah to wait supper he went to a phone booth and called her, and said he'd be out around ten. Then he went back to the Circe and ordered a rum Collins.

Bogart and Webb had left, but there were several familiar faces at the bar, including that of Fred McClain. He was sporting a new cane, ebony with a silver top, and he smiled when he saw Butterworth, and made a saluting gesture with the cane.

"Ah, there, old bean!" he said. "Up to Ascot for the races?"

"I race trains, not horses," Butterworth replied. "And usually lose. What's got into you?"

"Let me show you," McClain replied. "It's the cat's whiskers." He unscrewed the top, thereby making it into a small cup, and from the hollow inside of the cane he poured a couple of ounces of whisky and held it out. "Have a nip," he said. "Right off the boat."

"No, thanks, I'm having rum," Butterworth replied. "But I must say it's a fine idea. Where'd you get it?"

"A present from an admirer, but I'm told you can get them almost anywhere. Abercrombie's–Brooks–you name it. There are female versions, designed like garter belts." As an afterthought, he added, "Of course, those are somewhat harder to drink from."

"Not if you're short enough," said Butterworth.

McClain was about to say something more when he saw Dorothy Peters coming through the entrance hall. She was large-eyed and quiet, and she looked around the room as though afraid to enter.

Then she saw Butterworth and McClain, and smiled and came toward them.

"We've got to stop meeting like this," she said. "People are beginning to talk."

"To which of us are you speaking?" McClain asked.

"To whom it may concern." She glanced once more around the room.

"He left," Butterworth said. "He had a sudden assignment."

"I don't know what you're talking about," said Dorothy.

"Are you doing anything this evening?" McClain asked her.

She laughed. "I guess that all depends. Why?"

"I'd like to make up for my New Year's Eve disaster, if you'd let me."

"I've never known a man with such a conscience. You weren't all *that* bad."

"From what I gather, I was."

She smiled and said, "In that case, you may feel free. Where do we start?"

"I'd say this is as good a place as any. Would you care to drink from my cane, or from the bar?"

"Let's save the cane till later. I've heard the whole thing may soon become illegal."

George MacDougall got to the warehouse in Brooklyn at ten minutes to nine, and found it apparently deserted. Not a light showed inside, and when he tried the door to the front office it was locked tight. He went slowly down the block, looking for another entrance, but found none so returned to the office door and knocked. He had the sensation that he was the character in Walter de la Mare's "The Listeners," knocking on the door of a house full of ghosts. From somewhere in the back he heard footsteps, and then the heavy clunk of the bolt being turned, and the door opened a crack.

"Woddaya want?" said a voice.

"My name is MacDougall," he replied. "Frank DiMotto sent me."

There was a pause, then the door opened wider. "Come in," the voice said.

MacDougall stepped into the blackness and waited, hoping for some sort of light. He heard the door being closed and locked behind him, then the voice said, "Follow me."

"Where?" MacDougall asked, trying not to sound plaintive. "I can't see a goddam thing."

"Just keep going. You'll be all right."

MacDougall heard footsteps ahead of him, and as his eyes became accustomed to the dark he could see a faint hairline of light, apparently coming from beneath a door. Then the door opened and his guide beckoned him through, and he found himself in the presence of a towering, canvas-topped truck, which looked as big as a battleship in the gloom. The only light came from a lantern on the other side of the truck, where someone was tinkering with the engine. The room smelled of oil and kerosene and old rubber. The lantern cast an eerie, distorted light that made the walls swim and jump, and when MacDougall glanced at his guide it looked as though the man were wearing a Halloween mask. They studied each other for a moment, and then the man said, "Is this straight–you're from a newspaper?"

"That's right," MacDougall replied. "The *Tribune*."

"And you think you're going to write about us?"

"Not in any detail. I just want to get the broad picture."

"Son of a bitch. I guess it just goes to prove you never know." He paused, then added, "You must be pretty palsy with Frank."

MacDougall shrugged. "Enough."

The other man slammed down the hood of the truck, locked the catches, and lifted the lantern. "O.K.," he said. "She's as good as she's going to be."

"We better get going, then," said the first. "Benny, this is Mr. MacDougall. He's a friend of Frank's."

Benny nodded. "You got the heater?"

"It should be in the back of the truck. That's where I left it."

"Jesus, Morris, that's no place to leave a heater," Benny said, climbing into the truck. "Supposing someone should come along and find it?"

"Who's gonna come along?" Morris replied. "Besides, I left it in the well."

Benny fumbled around for a while, then produced a submachine gun and put it on the seat. "You're never gonna shoot nobody with the heater in the well," he said. "Come on, let's go."

Benny started the engine, and Morris went around and pulled on a chain hoist that lifted a large metal door into the ceiling. Benny backed the truck out and waited, without lights, while Morris closed the door and locked the warehouse. Then, at Benny's direction, Mac-

Dougall climbed up onto the truck seat and sat between the two men, and they started off. Morris sat on the right side, the submachine gun held loosely between his knees.

"What's this well you're talking about?" MacDougall asked. "I never heard of a well in a truck before."

Morris hesitated. "It's a manner of speaking," he said. After another pause, he went on, "We got a double bottom in the truck bed. We can lift the top, put in a load of booze, then put back the top and cover it with any kind of crap we want. Unless the Feds wanna tear the truck apart, they won't find nothing."

"Good idea," said MacDougall.

"It's better than a touring car. On a touring car, the load'll show in your springs–like if you're riding low on the springs it's a cinch there's booze hidden somewhere–but with truck springs–" He stopped and said to Benny, "How come you're going through Flatbush?"

"It's the quickest way to Jamaica," Benny replied. "You know any quicker?"

"No, but remember what happened last time. I think by way of Coney Island'd be safer."

"So we get picked up again–so what? They won't find no more'n they did the last time."

"Well, I ain't gonna get caught with this." Morris took the submachine gun from between his legs, reached around, and after some difficulty managed to get it stowed in the hollow part of the truck bed.

"It's a matter of philosophy," Benny replied. "You're either prepared, or you ain't."

"I'll be prepared, if I have to. I just don't wanna do a weapons rap for nothing."

They went through the hot, sultry streets of Flatbush and then on to Jamaica, where the first trees gave a hint of the countryside ahead. The trees became thicker at Valley Stream, and as they took the road toward Lynbrook and Rockville Center, MacDougall could smell the clean, earthy air of the farmlands, with a hint of the sea in the distance. By the time they got to Oceanside the salt smell of the ocean was unmistakable, and the sky above was aglow with stars. MacDougall imagined he could hear the sound of the surf, although the truck engine drowned out all but the most immediate noises.

"How do we know where to find the boat?" he asked. "Does it land in some special place?"

"Sometimes yes, sometimes no," Morris replied. "What they call Rum Row is a few miles offshore, just outside the limit. The ships from Canada and England and the Bahamas and whatnot lay off there, in a line that can go from Sandy Hook to Montauk, or even up the New England coast, and then the shore boats go out and meet 'em and take the stuff off. Where they land it depends on the Coast Guard." He looked at the stars and said, "I wisht we had some cloud cover. All them goddam stars make it bright as Times Square."

"You ever been shot at?" MacDougall asked.

"Once or twice. The Coast Guard get frustrated when their boats can't go as fast as us, and every now and then they snap off a few shots. But I never heard of nobody getting hit."

"What kind of boats do they use?"

"Cutters, picketboats–small stuff, mostly. Nothing to sweat about."

They were now approaching the shore, and Benny switched off the lights. They went on in the dark, following a rutted road, and then finally Benny stopped, and turned off the engine. MacDougall could hear the lapping of the water on the sand, and in the glow of the starlight he could see the loom of several islands nearby. Somewhere a dog barked, and then was quiet. Benny took a flashlight, and got out of the truck.

"Where are we?" MacDougall asked.

"There ain't no name, exactly," Morris replied. "See that blinking light off there? That's Jones Inlet, and beyond that's the Atlantic Ocean. These islands here got a number of names, but no two people call 'em by the same one. What one guy'll call Walnut Island, another'll call Pissant Island, and so on. We got our own names for 'em, but that's for business purposes. What Benny's blinking at now, we call Hog's Mother Island. Then there's Gertie's Garter, and Fat Ass, and–well, you name it. With us it's a kind of code, like."

MacDougall looked out and saw that Benny was blinking the flashlight at one of the islands. After a minute or so he saw a response, two quick dots followed by two more. Benny came back to the truck. "O.K.," he said. "He's coming."

Morris got out of the truck, and motioned MacDougall to do the same. "You might's well get going, then," he said to Benny. "We'll try to be back here by three, but don't wait more'n a half hour if we're not. We'll stash it in the barn and come back later."

"Right," said Benny. He handed the flashlight to Morris, got in the truck, and drove off into the darkness. The truck looked like a waddling elephant on the rutted road, then after a few minutes the sound of its engine died away, and only the small noises of the water remained. The distant dog barked again.

"Where's he going?" MacDougall asked.

"Up the line a ways, to make a pickup. Last time we went out the Feds had the truck spotted, and we had to bury the load. If his timing is right, he can dig it up and get back here in time to take on our load."

"And if his timing isn't right?"

Morris shrugged. "There's an 'if' in every business," he said. "We take care of it when we come to it, and try to take as few chances as possible." Then he snapped his fingers and said, "Son of a bitch."

"What?" said MacDougall.

"I forgot to tell Benny I unloaded the heater. It drives me nuts to leave one of them things lying around loaded." He looked in the direction the truck had gone, but could see only the dim and scattered lights of Oceanside. "Oh, well," he said. "That's the way it goes."

They heard the throaty muttering of a boat engine, and after a while MacDougall could see a black shape moving across the water. Morris blinked the flashlight once; there came an answering blink, and the boat swung toward them. Morris guided MacDougall to a makeshift dock, constructed out of planks that had been nailed across half-sunken barrels, and as the boat slid alongside Morris said, "Jump in." MacDougall scrambled over the gunwale and Morris followed him, saying to the boatman, "We got a passenger tonight, Artie–a friend of the Boss." Artie, whom MacDougall could see only as a silhouette, said, "Hi," then nudged the throttle, and the boat moved away from the shore.

The boat, as much as MacDougall could see of it, appeared to be a regular fishing boat, thirty or so feet long and broad in the beam, with a cabin trunk forward and a half-enclosed wheelhouse to shelter the helmsman. Fishnets and barrels and assorted gear covered the decks, and MacDougall found it hard to imagine where any great amount of liquor could be stowed. But it was hard to get an accurate impression in the darkness, and he reasoned there must be more stowage space forward than it seemed.

"Did you get your new engine?" Morris asked, as the boat began to thread its way among the islands.

"Did I?" said Artie. "Just wait'll we get outside and you'll see. There ain't nothing gonna catch us now."

"That's the way I like it," Morris said. "The farther we stay from trouble, the happier I'll be."

Artie laughed. "We like to please our customers. Our motto is, 'A happy customer is a steady customer.' "

"You know, looking at it one way Prohibition isn't all bad," Morris said. "You'd never of got a new engine for your boat if it wasn't for Prohibition, and I sure as hell wouldn't be able to buy me a Reo runabout. There's lotsa guys living a lot better, just because some crazy-ass old ladies decided the country shouldn't drink."

"My old lady still don't know what I'm doing," Artie said. "Or she tries to make out she don't know. She knows goddam well that fishing don't bring in this kind of money, but when people ask her how I'm doing she just says the fish have been biting mighty good lately. The first time I come home and give her a fifty-dollar bill she looked at me kind of funny like, but she didn't say nothing, and you can be damned sure *I* didn't say nothing, and that's the way we left it. She gets to buy a few things for herself now and then, which is more'n she did when I was really fishing, so I guess you could say she's another one who's got some benefit out of the crazy goddam law. Maybe we should all be thankful the Congress is crazy, or we'd all be up to our asses in misery." Turning to MacDougall, he said, "What do you do, mister? Are you in this business too?"

"No," replied MacDougall. "I'm a reporter."

"A *reporter?* Jesus H. Christ!" Artie turned to Morris and said, "Is this some kind of a joke or something?"

"I told you, he's a friend of DiMotto's," Morris replied. "He's just gonna do a story in like what they call generalities. No problem."

Artie glanced at MacDougall in the darkness, then returned his attention to the helm. They passed the flashing green light that marked the entrance to Jones Inlet, and as the boat dipped into the ocean swells Artie switched on the running lights.

"Why'd you do that?" MacDougall asked.

"Protection, for one thing," Artie replied. "It can get a mite crowded out here, and it's nice not to be run down. I turn 'em off when we get to the Row, but between here and there it's better to look like a strictly kosher fishing boat. If you run dark, it's an advertisement you don't wanta be seen."

"Let's see what your engine can do," Morris said, and Artie reached for the throttle. There was a roar and the boat lurched forward, almost knocking MacDougall off balance, and as the speed built up explosions of spray flew over the bow, forcing Morris and MacDougall to take cover beside Artie. "Son of a bitch, that's something," Morris said. "What are we doing now?"

"Close to twenty, I figure," Artie replied. "Maybe a little less."

"What's the engine?"

"A Packard Liberty. It come off an airplane." Artie closed the throttle slightly, and the engine noise abated. "Don't want to run her at full speed for too long," he said. "She might split a plank or jump her blocks, or who knows what."

"Well, it's nice to know you can do it if you have to," Morris said.

"I say amen to that," replied Artie.

They headed south, in the general direction of Ambrose Lightship, taking care to remain clear of the inbound shipping lane. The sea had a restful effect on MacDougall, and for a while he forgot about his assignment and became lost in contemplation of the stars. He felt as he imagined Leif Erikson must have felt, approaching the shores of a strange country, not knowing what lay ahead but secure for the moment in the total peace that surrounded him. He wondered how Roly Butterworth, the domesticated commuter, would react in a similar situation, but he could no more imagine Butterworth on a rumrunner than he could on an aerial trapeze. This led him, inevitably, to the Butterworth he was trying to make into a dramatic character, and suddenly a whole new area opened up. If somehow his character, aside from being involved in a murder, could become entangled with a group of rumrunners, he would have a lot more room to move around in, and a lot more chances for comedy. Cheered by this new idea, he decided to make his notes on two levels: one for the piece in the *Tribune,* and one for the character in the play. He heard Morris and Artie talking in low voices, and moved closer to catch their words.

"You get a piece of laundry soap," Artie was saying, "and you smear that good and thick on the bottom of the bottle. Then you heat up a soldering iron, and you press it into the soap, and pretty soon you'll have a nice little hole in the bottle. You run a wire through that, and put a regular light fixture in the neck, and you've got yourself a lamp. Easy as falling off a log."

"Son of a bitch," said Morris. "I'll have to try it. The old lady's always saying she needs new lamps around the house."

"If she's finicky, make it with a champagne bottle," Artie said. "That'll give it a touch of class."

After perhaps a half hour Artie snapped off the running lights and brought the boat onto an easterly heading. He slowed the engine and said, "All right, now. Everybody keep his eyes peeled. We're looking for the *Dorothy.*"

"What's she look like?" MacDougall asked.

"She's a Down East fishing schooner. Full name *Dorothy M. Smart,* out of Digby, Nova Scotia. There'll likely be some other schooners too, and the steamer *Vaudreuil,* out of Montreal. But the *Dorothy*'s the only one we'll be doing business with."

MacDougall stared into the darkness ahead, trying to make out the line where the stars stopped and the sea began, but there was a slight haze that blurred the horizon, and he couldn't be sure if he was seeing anything or not. He found, oddly, that he saw better with his peripheral vision than he did straight ahead, and he kept turning his head in the hope of picking up some movement.

"There's the *Vaudreuil,*" Artie said quietly.

"Where?" said MacDougall.

"Port bow. Big as a house." MacDougall looked, and suddenly where there had been nothing he saw the loom of a steamer, looking every bit as large as Artie had said. "There'll likely be some little ones around," Artie went on. "Keep an eye out for them."

They went past the *Vaudreuil,* and the assorted small craft that were taking on their cargoes, and the next ship they came to was a schooner, her sails furled, rolling gently in the swell. "That's either *Tom August* or *Veronica,*" Morris said, from his lookout post on the starboard bow. "They got that weird long bowsprit."

"We'll be getting to the *Dorothy* soon," Artie replied. "They usually anchor together."

They passed two more ships before they came to the *Dorothy M. Smart,* and as they neared the ship Morris made a signal with his flashlight. It was answered, and Artie swung in and headed alongside, slowed the engine, and then backed down, coming to a gentle stop against a fender board that had been lowered over the side. Morris threw a line to a man on deck, and Artie threw one up from the stern. "Have a good trip?" he called.

"None better," came a voice from above.

"Coast Guard give you any grief?"

"Nah. You ready to load?"

"Give us a minute. Morris, you take the forward part; I'll open up back here. Mister"—this to MacDougall—"you better stand in the wheelhouse, outa the way."

MacDougall did as he was told. Morris went down into the cabin, and Artie took a flashlight and screwdriver and lifted the deck boards on either side of the engine hatch. They came up in one piece on each side, exposing a gaping hold that was two feet deeper than might have been imagined. Morris, who had been performing the same operation forward, came out of the cabin and said, "All set. Let's go."

"Aren't you forgetting something?" said the voice from the schooner.

"Oh. Sorry." Morris produced a roll of bills, held together by a rubber band, and tossed it up to the man on deck. "Count 'em if you want," he said. "They're all there."

Instead of being in wooden cases, the liquor was in diamond-shaped burlap sacks, six bottles to a sack, and as MacDougall helped the other two load the cargo he realized the value of the arrangement. They were easy to carry and easy to stow; they were sewed tightly enough so there was virtually no breakage, and in case they had to be jettisoned they could be tied to a stake, or a buoy, and be recovered later. He wondered who had first thought of doing it this way, and concluded that progress would always be made by those trying to outwit the law, rather than those trying to enforce it. A poor situation, but there it was, and the longer the idiotic law remained in force the more ways would be found to circumvent it.

They finished loading and replaced the deck boards. "Anything you want us to do for you ashore?" Artie called, as he started the engine.

"I think Victor has some mail," the man on deck replied. "Hold on a sec." He disappeared, and returned with a packet of letters, which he dropped down to Artie. "That's from Victor," he said. "And if you know anyone coming out here in the next coupla days, we could use some fresh oranges and a coupla cartons of fags. Oh—and bumwad. We're all out."

"I'll see what I can do," Artie said, hefting the package. "That Victor is some letter-writer."

"He just got married last month. Writes her twice a day."

"He'll get over that. See you in church." Artie nudged the throttle, and the boat moved away. In a couple of minutes the *Dorothy M. Smart* was just a dark shape against the horizon, and then she vanished. Artie headed northwest, toward the inlet, and gradually inched the throttle open until the boat was making about eight knots. He didn't want to draw attention by going too fast unless he had to, and once he was away from Rum Row he switched on his running lights and tried to assume the pose of a legitimate fishing boat. He ran that way for about twenty minutes, and then Morris said, "Lights ahead."

MacDougall looked out and saw a green running light and a white masthead light, moving toward them from the port side.

"He's a big bugger, whoever he is," Artie said. "But we got right of way, so I'm gonna hold course and see what happens."

"How do you know he isn't Coast Guard?" MacDougall asked.

"He's bigger'n any Coast Guard I ever see around here," Artie replied. "Mostly, they're those little twenty-eight-footers. The biggest are the eighty-three-footers."

The ship's lights continued to approach, and then a long, low silhouette began to show, with a high bridge forward and a line of four stacks running aft. It changed course slightly and headed straight at them, so they could see both its red and green running lights.

"Holy Jesus, it's a destroyer!" Artie said, and at the same moment a siren shrieked, and a beam of white light hit them and made their boat glow like a fireball.

A hollow, megaphone voice came over the water, saying, "Ahoy, on the fishing boat! Heave to!"

"For chrissakes get going!" Morris said, from a crouching position. "Whaddaya waiting for?"

"I'm gonna head for his stern," Artie replied. "He's got such a big turning circle he'll never catch us, once I get behind him." He took the engine out of gear and let the boat wallow, pretending to obey the destroyer's orders, and as the destroyer slowed to come alongside Artie put the wheel over, bringing him onto a reciprocal course, and waited. When the destroyer was so close that he could see the men on deck, he opened the throttle wide, turned off his running lights, and shot down the destroyer's side and into the blackness astern. They could hear men shouting, and the thunder of screws as the destroyer tried to back down, and then as they opened the distance the destroyer became a pinprick of light and a wildly groping searchlight beam, and that was all.

"Let me know if you can tell which way he turns," Artie said. "I can't beat him in a flat-out race, but I can dodge faster'n he can."

"He's coming left," said Morris. "I can see his red light now."

Artie also came left, and slowed his engine so as not to make a visible wake. Then he described a wide circle, keeping well out of range of the spotlight, and waited until the destroyer had passed; after that he swung into its wake, and followed it toward shore. When, finally, it gave up the chase and turned east, Artie ran straight into shallow water, then turned left and headed for Jones Inlet. As they passed the flashing green light, MacDougall felt as though he'd been holding his breath for the last half hour. He let it out, and realized he was shivering.

"Isn't there an easier way to make a living?" he said.

"Easier, maybe," Artie replied, "but it don't pay so good." He thought a moment, then added, "That destroyer could get to be a royal pain in the ass, though. Nobody told me they'd lost their sense of humor."

The sky was gray as they came through the deserted streets of Flatbush, and by the time they had put the truck in the garage the gray had begun to turn to pink.

"This is calling it too close," Morris said, as he lowered the garage door. "We might's well be operating at high noon."

"Don't look at me," said Benny. "I was there on time."

"It was that goddam destroyer," Morris replied. "I'm afraid we're gonna need a faster boat, but I don't have the heart to tell Artie." He scratched himself and yawned. "But that ain't up to me," he said. "Thank God, that's up to the powers that be." Then he looked at MacDougall and said, "You might tell that to DiMotto, next time you and him are taking tea together."

MacDougall got to the paper at one o'clock that afternoon and began to tell Forsburg his story. "There's a lot we can't use, such as place names and all that," he said, "but there's still enough to make a hell of a good background piece. These guys aren't gangsters; they're just regular people like you and me, earning an extra buck or two. And believe me, they work for it."

Forsburg had been chewing thoughtfully on a pencil, set crossways in his mouth like a horse's bit, and he now took it out and examined the tooth marks on it. "Let's put that aside for a while," he said. "I got something else for you to do. I suppose you heard about Harding."

"I haven't heard anything since late yesterday afternoon. What about him?"

"He died, out in 'Frisco. First he got ptomaine, then pneumonia, then an embolism, then bang."

"I'll be damned."

"This Coolidge, his Vice-President, is a Vermonter. He got the word at home, and had his old man, who's a j.p., swear him in as President. Used the family Bible. Kind of a nice sidelight."

"Yeah," said MacDougall, wondering what this had to do with him.

"Let's do a roundup on all the Vice-Presidents who've succeeded to the office and see what they were doing when the Boss kicked the bucket. There might be something kind of spicy there, for all we know."

"If there is, how do we print it? I thought we're supposed to be a family newspaper."

"We'll worry about that when you've done the research. There aren't too many of them, you know–maybe five or six at the most." MacDougall turned away, trying not to show his exasperation, and Forsburg added, "By the way, speaking of kicking the bucket–didn't some friend of yours have a run-in with Lucky Livorno?"

MacDougall looked back quickly. "Yes," he said. "Why?"

"You can tell him to relax. Livorno was found under a pier in the East River this morning."

19

Butterworth worked in the Brady office all summer, doing the small, routine jobs that could almost have been performed by the janitor. Brady was away a good part of the time, and Brown took the month of August in Amagansett, so Butterworth had the premises pretty much to himself. He would take the 9:57 in from Crestwood, open the mail, answer those parts of it that needed answering, then go to the Circe for a light lunch around 12:30. He would spend the afternoon in any number of ways, sometimes at the office and sometimes not, and then close up in time to get the 4:26 for home. It was an easy life, in spite of the heat of the city, and he always had the country to return to, with the smells of the earth and the trees and the flowers, and the sight of the pale glow of the gas streetlights, seen dimly through the sycamore trees at night. He went to sleep to the sound of cicadas, and awoke to the cawing of crows in nearby trees, and his life was as sylvan as any Elizabethan poet could have asked for.

His first out-of-doors job had been to dig a garden in back for Sarah's vegetables, and with this accomplished he looked around for other projects. He thought of putting a miniature waterwheel in a nearby brook for the children's amusement, but this was vetoed on the grounds that anything that lured them toward water was dangerous, and to be avoided. He then thought of making a swing, to hang from the limb of a tree, but Sarah killed this by pointing out that

Nancy could climb into it when no one was around and fall off on her head. He volunteered to make a trellis for climbing flowers, but Sarah said she hated climbing flowers and would prefer a cutting garden instead. So he spaded the ground for a cutting garden, and thereafter confined his outdoor activities to mowing the lawn every two weeks. To mow the entire lawn took him a half hour at the most, after which he would go indoors, lie on the couch with the theatre section of the paper, and fall asleep. Sundays he and Sarah would occasionally have a picnic lunch on the porch and then take the children for a walk. After that, he would have his nap. It was suburban living at its most basic, with no frills and few surprises, and Sarah loved it. There was no question the children were happy, and young Puddin seemed to thrive on the occasional worms and grubs he managed to eat while his mother was gardening.

Then, with Labor Day over and the new theatre season approaching, Butterworth's life became more active. Brady had three plays scheduled for fall production, with Alice starring in one and Grace George in another, and the advance and out-of-town publicity had to be organized with the precision of a military campaign. Butterworth had to supervise the road publicity as well as that in New York, and if he wasn't writing a press release he was arranging an interview for one or another of the stars. His country life vanished, and if he got out to Crestwood at all it was on the 1 A.M. local, which gave him about five hours' sleep before he had to be up and getting ready to go back to the city. A good deal of the time he slept in MacDougall's apartment, and eventually started leaving clothes there, so as not to look too slovenly the following day.

One morning, when he had arrived at the office before anyone else and was opening and sorting the mail, he heard Brown come in, and from the ensuing silence he knew there was trouble. Brown usually had some form of greeting, either cheerful or cynical, with which he started the day, but today he seemed preoccupied, and answered Butterworth's greeting with no more than a nod. Finally, after glancing through the mail that Butterworth had put on his desk, he said, "Where were you last night?"

"Home," Butterworth replied, with slight surprise. "Why?"

"What time'd you go home?"

"Early. I took the midnight instead of the one o'clock."

"The Boss was looking for you. He was–should we say?–disturbed when he couldn't find you."

"What time was that?"

"Sometime after midnight."

"Well, for God's sakes–"

Brown held up a hand. "I know, I know. But he said he'd told you when you took the job there were no clocks here, and he meant it."

"You mean I'm being fired?"

"No. I mean he says he wants you immediately available at all times, unless he specifically says you're through for the day."

"What brought all this on?"

"He ran into Eugene O'Neill at Tony's last night, and seems to think he's signed him up to do a play. He wanted an immediate press release, to go in today's papers."

"Did he really sign him?"

"I'd be inclined to doubt it, but the point was that he couldn't find you. That's what drove him wild."

"In other words, I should stand ready to send out a release, no matter whether or not there's any truth in it?"

"Not exactly. You're just to be available."

Butterworth looked out the window, trying to phrase what he wanted to say. He was tempted to stand up, take his hat, and leave the office for good, but then he remembered his seventy-five dollars a week, and that made him think a little more carefully. Furthermore, if he was going to resign he should do it to Brady's face; none of this was Brown's fault, and it would be unfair to say to him what should have been said to Brady. Butterworth continued to stare out the window, and finally said, "The only answer to that is to get a room in town. Do you think he'd go for another fifteen dollars a week?"

"I doubt it like hell," said Brown.

"Well, I'll see if I can work out something with MacDougall, then. He's offered to let me share with him, but I feel kind of like an intruder there. A duenna I guess would be closer."

"Work out whatever you want, just so long as the Boss is able to find you when he wants you."

"The only surefire way would be to go live with him. Do you think I should suggest that?"

"I'd be careful about that. He might take you up on it."

When, a half hour later, Brady came into the office, Butterworth held his breath. Brady hung up his battered felt hat, sat at his desk, then removed his pince-nez glasses, pinched the bridge of his nose, and in his strange, high voice, said, "Christ."

"Is there anything I can do, sir?" said Butterworth, hating himself for his eagerness.

Brady shook his head, replaced his glasses, and picked up a Manila envelope. "What time is it?" he asked.

Butterworth looked at his watch. "Quarter to eleven."

"Thanks. I seem to have left my watch somewhere last night." Looking at Brown, he said, "Where were we, anyway?"

"Tony's," said Brown. "And Eugene O'Neill has your watch."

"What the hell is *he* doing with it?"

"You bet him that *Our American Cousin* was originally written as a minstrel show."

There was a long silence, and then Brady said, "Butterworth?"

"Sir?" Butterworth replied, half out of his chair.

"Do you think you could rush the growler?"

"Could– I beg your pardon?" Butterworth had visions of wrestling a live bear.

"Rush the growler–go to a suds shop–rustle up some booze."

"Oh, that." Butterworth looked at his watch again, wondering if the Circe would be open yet. "I think so, sir. I can try."

Brady opened his desk drawer and produced a large, silver flask, which he handed across. "See if you can get that filled," he said.

"Yes, sir," Butterworth replied, taking the flask. "With what?"

"I don't care. Scotch." Brady turned to Brown. "What were we drinking last night?"

"I was drinking Scotch," Brown replied. "You were drinking Irish. Bushmills."

"That's right." To Butterworth, Brady said, "See if you can find some Bushmills. Otherwise, Scotch will be all right."

"Yes, sir." Butterworth put the flask in an inside pocket of his coat and went out into the bright autumn sunshine. What few trees he saw had started to change color and lose their leaves, and they reminded him of the trees along the Bronx River, and the smell of burning leaves. For some reason Crestwood seemed a long way away, and he wondered how he was going to tell Sarah of the necessity of his staying in town. He could probably get out to the country on weekends–at least on Sundays–but if he was going to keep his job that would be about all. In the back of his mind he wondered if he could strike out on his own and be a press agent for whomever he chose, and in that way free himself of the job of playing wet nurse to a drunk. It was a tempting thought, but offhand he couldn't think of anyone who needed his services, and there was always the matter of food and rent for his family. Maybe, sometime in the future, he could be his own agent, but for the moment he needed all the security he could get. And if that meant playing wet nurse to a drunk, then so be it.

When he rang the bell at the Circe he said a silent prayer that someone would be there, because this was the only speakeasy where he was well-enough known to buy liquor. There was a short wait and then the peephole slid open, and he heard Max say, "Mr. Butterworth! I thought it must be the Federals!"

"I'm just running errands," Butterworth replied, as the gate swung open. "This isn't for myself." He went through the dark entrance hall and into the bar, and there, at the far end of the room, saw Fred McClain and Dorothy Peters sitting at a table, each with a coffee cup. It was clear they were still wearing the clothes of the previous evening: McClain's collar had developed a crease around the neckline, and Dorothy's black sequined jacket all but shouted *diner à deux*.

"Well, look who's here!" she cried, as she spotted Butterworth. "Come in for a bit of the hair of the dog?"

Butterworth smiled. "Running an errand for the Boss," he said, and held out the flask to Charlie. "Do you think you could fill that with Bushmills?"

"I'll have to ask Nick," Charlie replied, and then, as Nick came in from the kitchen, "Mr. Butterworth wants to know if we can sell him some Bushmills. I've only got a fifth, and I like to keep that handy in case Captain McGinty should drop around."

"This isn't for me," Butterworth said. "It's for Mr. Brady, and he needs something very badly. It seems he was on the town last night."

"I'll say he was," Nick replied, and then, to Charlie, "Let him have it. McGinty probably won't be around until Christmas, and I'm ordering a case next shipment anyway."

"Will you join us in a whisky sour?" McClain said to Butterworth, as Charlie took the flask to fill it. "It's the best way to get the day started."

"Thanks, it's a little early," Butterworth replied. "Besides, I've got to get Mr. Brady's mother's milk to him as fast as possible."

"One little sour isn't going to hold you up," said McClain. "Charlie can make it with one hand while he fills the flask with the other."

"Well—" Butterworth hadn't had a sour in what seemed like a

long time, and the idea sounded suddenly appealing. "I really shouldn't," he said.

"You act as though it were going to kill you," Dorothy said. "You know what it does, don't you? It turns you into a raging, red-hot lover boy, is what it does. Ask my friend Mr. Twombly, here. He becomes three different people."

"Four," said McClain, and they both laughed.

"Here you are, sir," Charlie said, as he capped the flask and handed it back to Butterworth. "Should that go on your account, or Mr. Brady's?"

"Put this on Mr. Brady's account," Butterworth replied. "He can afford it a good deal better than I can."

"If you'll join us for just one little drink I'll tell you a secret," Dorothy said. "A secret so dark and deep that very few people even know it exists."

A year ago, Butterworth would have cited these two as examples of how liquor turns a person into a blithering idiot; now, he was faintly intrigued to see what Dorothy had in mind. "O.K.," he said. "What's the secret?"

"I won't tell you unless you sit down and join us. You've got to order a drink first."

Butterworth sighed, and looked at Charlie. "All right," he said. "A Scotch sour, but make it a quick one."

He sat at the table next to Dorothy, and when his drink was brought to him he took a sip and said, "Whistle the patter."

Dorothy leaned her head close to his, and in a voice that was cracking with laughter said, "Achilles was a fairy."

Butterworth thought for a moment, then said, "Achilles who?"

"The great warrior. A big, leaping fairy."

"I don't know what you're talking about."

Dorothy drew back and studied him. "You've heard about Oscar Wilde?"

"Of course."

"Well, he was another."

"Who told you this?"

"My friend Twombly, here. He knows everything."

"How do you know?" Butterworth said to McClain.

"Look at the story," McClain replied. "He kept this Patroclus around as his bugger boy, and when Patroclus was killed he went out of his mind. A clear case of bereaved love."

"He's been reading Havelock Ellis," Dorothy said in a confidential tone. "He knows all about s-e-x."

Butterworth took another swallow of his drink and said, "Well, I guess it's just something I never thought a lot about before."

"You ought to," said Dorothy. "There's more there than meets the eye."

For some reason this struck both her and McClain as funny, and they laughed until they were helpless. Butterworth finished his sour and stood up.

"Thank you for the drink," he said. "I really have to be going."

"Just remember," said Dorothy, wiping the tears from her eyes, "beware of Greeks wearing skirts."

This started them off on another peal of laughter, and they were still laughing as Butterworth went out into the glare of the noonday sun. It had been dim and restful in the Circe, and now the sunlight, plus the drink he'd bolted down, seemed to make everything slightly askew. He had the feeling he was walking two inches off the ground, and the tops of the buildings were undulating. The flask in his pocket felt as heavy as an anvil, and every policeman he passed seemed to be looking straight at him. It would be just my luck to pass out, he thought, and have them find it on me when they picked me up. *That* would be an interesting phone call to make to Sarah: "Hello, honey, I seem to be in jail. I was arrested for transporting liquor." My, what a hit that would be! Almost as good as the call he was going to have to make, announcing he'd be living in town from now on. Not from now on–think of a better phrase than that . . . For the time being? No. Well, something would come to him. It would have to.

"You took your time," Brady said, when Butterworth handed him the flask.

"It's not easy to find Bushmills," Butterworth replied. "It's not every place that has it."

"I said Scotch would be all right."

"Yes, but I knew you preferred Irish."

"I preferred a goddam drink, is what I preferred."

"I'm sorry, sir. Next time I'll remember."

"And we can do without the 'sir.' Get a glass."

Butterworth's jaw tightened as he went to the washroom and found a glass, rinsed it out, and took it to Brady. He handed it across in silence, and Brady poured an inch of whisky in it and handed it back.

"Here," he said. "Your messenger fee."

"No, thank you," Butterworth replied. "Not during working hours."

"Take the goddam drink and stop being so prissy," Brady said. "Here!"

Butterworth took it and returned with it to his desk. He took a sip, shuddered, and found the taste somewhat more wooden than Scotch, although not at all unpleasant. He took another sip and began to have a good idea for something, although he wasn't quite sure what.

In the end, he decided that a phone call was no way to tell Sarah about his new living plans; he'd have to wait until he saw her in person. He took the midnight train to Crestwood on Saturday, and next day began to search for a way to open the subject. He had rehearsed so many gambits that his mind was a jumble of ideas, and no matter what he said it was bound to sound rehearsed. He sat with his breakfast coffee and looked out the kitchen window at Sarah, who was puttering in the garden, while Puddin rattled the bars of his playpen and Nancy rolled in piles of fallen leaves. He decided that after lunch he'd rake the leaves into one large pile and burn them, if for nothing more than to savor the smell of the smoke. It was a long time since he'd smelled it, and the mere idea of it conjured up scenes of his childhood, of fallen apples and pumpkins ripening on the ground, and hoarfrost in November, and . . . Cut it out, he told himself. This is no time to be getting sentimental about the country.

Sarah came in the back door with some bronze chrysanthemums she'd cut; her eyes were sparkling, and her cheeks glowed. "You should be outside!" she said. "On a glorious day like this, it's a crime to stay in the house!"

"I was just finishing my coffee," Butterworth replied. "I thought I might rake the lawn after lunch. Get a nice big leaf-fire going."

"Don't burn them all," Sarah said. "Nancy would die if she didn't have leaves to roll in."

Butterworth glanced out the window at the trees. "There are still plenty left," he said. "I just thought I'd make a start."

Sarah put the flowers in the sink and looked for a container. "It's up to you," she said, taking down a china teapot. "Just leave her a little something to play in." She filled the pot with water and began to arrange the flowers in it, cutting those stems that were too long. There was a short silence, and then Butterworth cleared his throat.

"I was almost fired last week," he said.

She turned and looked at him, her eyes wide. "Why?" she said. "What did you do?"

"I came home."

"What do you mean?"

"Whenever it was–Tuesday–Wednesday–I came out on the midnight. Remember?"

"Yes. It was Wednesday. And you stayed in town the next three nights." Sarah was holding a chrysanthemum in one hand and a pair of scissors in the other, but she made no move to cut the stem. It was as though her hands were frozen in front of her.

"Well, it turned out that Brady wanted me for something that night and was furious when he couldn't find me. Apparently I am to be immediately available at all times–or at least that's the way Brown put it."

"How can he expect you to do that? You have to sleep sometime, don't you?"

"He doesn't mind my sleeping. I just have to be–as I said–available. That means I have to sleep in town."

"All the time?"

"Well–during the theatre season anyway. And even then, I can probably manage to get out here Sundays."

Sarah stared at the flower stem, rolling it slowly between her fingers. "Where are you going to stay?" she asked at last.

"Mac has said I can stay with him. It's not the most convenient thing in the world, but I can't afford a room of my own."

Another pause. "And I'll only get to see you Sundays?"

"Not in the least. You can come in any time you want–I get free theatre tickets, after all–and we can have dinner, go to a show–whatever you say. It's just that I have to be where Brady can reach me when he wants me."

Sarah was silent once more, then said, "And it doesn't matter whether or not I want you."

"You're not paying my salary. If you could give me seventy-five dollars a week I'd never leave your side, but the fact remains that we have to eat. I shouldn't have to tell you that."

Her mouth twisted into a smile. "You don't," she said. "I'm aware."

"All right, then. All we can do is make the best of it."

Sarah hesitated, then her hand with the scissors darted out like an adder and cut two inches off the flower stem. "That's right," she said, and put the rust-colored flower in the pot.

He was raking the leaves that afternoon, when he was aware of someone watching him from the sidewalk. He looked, and saw a man of about his own age, wearing a dark pullover sweater and corduroy knickers and smoking a pipe. The man didn't move, so Butterworth said, "Anything I can do for you?"

"Are you Butterworth?" the man replied.

"That's right."

"My name is Thatcher. Mark Thatcher." The man put out a hand and came toward him. "We live down the next block. It's good to meet you."

"Thank you," Butterworth said, as they shook hands.

"My wife and I were wondering if you and Mrs. Butterworth would like to come by for a cup of tea. Or, if you don't like tea"–he made an elaborately casual gesture–"I happen to have some dandelion winc I made last spring."

"I'll have to ask–" Butterworth began, just as Sarah came out the front door. "Dear, this is Mr. Thatcher," he said.

"Yes, we've met," said Sarah.

"The Thatchers want to know if we'd like to drop by for tea later on."

"I have no one to leave the children with," Sarah said to Thatcher. "Why don't you come here?"

"Bring the children with you," he replied. "We have plenty of room. Violet says when it comes to children, the more the merrier."

"Well–" Sarah hesitated.

"Good. That settles it. We'll see you at four-thirty."

He left, and Butterworth watched him as he strode briskly down the street. "Where'd you meet them?" he asked.

"Not them, him," Sarah replied. "Just the way you did–I was out here and he came past, and we got to chatting. He really seems quite pleasant."

"That makes me feel better," Butterworth said. "If I'm not going to be out here much, it's nice to know you have congenial neighbors."

20

The combination of Butterworth and MacDougall, as roommates, was one of those phenomena that occur, like Halley's comet, only once or twice in any given century. When living their separate lives they were unremarkable–Butterworth was a quiet, domesticated New Englander, and MacDougall an elfin, footloose son of an Ohio insurance broker–but when they decided to room together some mad chemical reaction took place, and they found themselves doing things that would never have occurred to either one of them alone.

There was, for instance, the time they left the Circe after an early lunch, MacDougall to go to the paper and Butterworth to return to the Brady office, and in the street in front of the club they saw a white-uniformed Sanitation worker, commonly called a white wing, morosely pushing his brush and trailing a wheeled cart full of horse droppings. MacDougall approached him.

"Excuse me, pal," he said, "do you get time off for lunch?"

The white wing looked at him without expression. "Wodda you, a wise guy?" he replied.

"Not in the least. I simply wondered if you'd had lunch."

"I eat when I get through. I got no appetite during working hours."

"Then how about a beer?"

The man gave him a hard stare. "You must be crazy," he said, and went back to his sweeping.

"You think I'm crazy? Come with me."

"I can't. I'm working."

"We'll fix that. Give me your cap." MacDougall took the man's cap and put it on Butterworth's head, then thrust the broom in Butterworth's hands, grabbed the man by the arm, and took him into the Circe. At the bar he said to Charlie, "This is an old Army buddy of mine. Give him anything he wants."

"Right," said Charlie. "What'll you have, sir?"

For a few moments the man was too stunned to speak. Then, as though dipping a toe in hot water, he said, "I don't suppose you have any Calvados?"

"Sorry," said Charlie. "We have cognac, though."

The man ran the tip of his tongue over his lips, and said, "I'll have a little cognac, then." Turning to MacDougall, he said, "What outfit were you with?"

"Second Division," MacDougall replied. "Ninth Regiment."

"I was in the Big Red One. Sixteenth Infantry."

"You were? That's the Boss's outfit!" Turning to Charlie, MacDougall said, "Tell Nick to come out here–there's someone he might like to talk to!"

Outside, Butterworth set the Sanitation Department cap low over his eyes, squared his shoulders, and stabbed briskly at the pavement with the broad-headed broom. In short order he had collected enough debris to shovel into the wheeled cart, and as he did it occurred to him to wonder what good it did a horse to eat oats, if they came through the digestive tract as apparently unscathed as they did. From all outward appearances the horse might as well have consumed a bag of BB shot, but there must be some chemical property in oats that made them worthwhile. He was pondering the chemistry of equine digestion, and wondering if there was any conceivable tie-in with theatrical publicity, when he heard someone call, "Yoo-hoo!" and he looked up and saw Dorothy Peters and McClain coming across the street.

"Darling!" said Dorothy in a fake society voice. "You're having a *garden* party! How unutterably chic!"

"Hi, there," Butterworth replied. "I'm just minding the store for a friend."

"What did you do, lose a bet?" McClain asked.

"Mac will tell you all about it," said Butterworth. "And you might ask him to hurry things up—I've got to get back to work."

"You know what they say," said Dorothy. "All work and no play makes Jack a dull boy." She and McClain vanished into the Circe, and Butterworth looked down the block to see if anyone else he knew was in sight. All I'd need right now would be to have Brady come along, he thought. Then an idea struck him, and he almost wished Brady *would* appear. Brady would very naturally ask what he was doing, and he could say he was gathering material for his next press release. He'd be fired, of course, but it would be going out in a white-hot blaze of glory, and almost worth it. He thought of the Marine during the war who, when pinned down by machine-gun fire, jumped up and shouted to his men, "Come on, you sons of bitches! Do you want to live forever?" and he somehow felt a transient kinship with the anonymous hero. He was lost in this and other dreams of glory when he saw MacDougall coming out of the Circe, and he started to take off his cap.

"Not quite yet," MacDougall told him. "He's having a sandwich with Nick. I've got to be at the paper by one."

"I just hope he doesn't forget me," Butterworth replied. "The novelty of this job wears off pretty quickly."

"I told Nick you were standing in. He won't let him forget."

MacDougall left and Butterworth continued his sweeping, not as briskly as before but with a certain dogged persistence. Maybe this is a good object lesson, he thought. Maybe the next time I'm tempted to quit I'll remember how some other people make a living, and be glad with what I've got. Gradually he became aware that people were stopping to watch him, and this puzzled him until he realized he was wearing a double-breasted business suit, a black-and-white polka-dot tie, and a white Sanitation Department cap, and looked no more like a white wing than he did a member of the Swiss Guard. Also, he had been making designs with his sweepings, as though laying out a baroque courtyard, and the overall effect was of a figure skater gone mad. Ignoring the audience, he concentrated on his work, trying to devise some fitting climax, and he was interrupted by a loud voice from the door to the Circe, shouting "Atten—HUT!" He looked, and there was the white wing, standing at attention. Butterworth came to attention and presented arms with the broom; the white wing strode up and took his cap and they exchanged salutes; the white wing then kissed him on both cheeks and resumed his sweeping, and Butterworth marched off to a patter of applause from the bystanders.

What in the name of God have I been doing? he thought, after he'd gone a couple of blocks. I must be out of my mind—stark, raving crazy.

He brooded about it, on and off, throughout the afternoon, but then, when he ran into MacDougall later that night at the Circe, he had come to the conclusion it was funny. A number of things could have happened that didn't, and he had been skating on the thin rim of disaster, which in itself was slightly exhilarating. "You should have stayed around," he said to MacDougall. "I was promoted to sergeant, and given the Legion of Honor."

"I wish I had," said MacDougall. "It was a bleak day at the paper."

"How come?"

"There's some talk of a merger, and nobody knows who's going to end up where. Nobody dares say 'Boo' for fear he'll be dropped when the merger comes."

"Who're you merging with?"

"The story is it's the *Herald*."

"Well, with your connections you can always get a job with the Sanitation Department," Butterworth said, and they both laughed.

But a bigger story than the merger broke in February. Two years previously, Albert B. Fall, Harding's Secretary of the Interior, had secretly turned over two large Navy oil deposits, one at Elk Hill in California and one at Teapot Dome in Wyoming, to the Doheny and Sinclair oil interests, at a cool $400,000 profit to himself. In February of 1924 a Washington correspondent for the St. Louis *Post-Dispatch* dug out the facts and gave them to Senators Thomas J. Walsh and Gerald Nye, who made them public. Fall and Edwin M. Denby, the Secretary of the Navy, were forced to resign, and Fall and Sinclair were subsequently sent to prison, but the *Post-Dispatch* story was the first hint of the corruption that had infested the Harding regime. The day the story broke, Grafton Smedley, the managing editor, called MacDougall into his office.

"How would you like to go to Washington?" he asked.

"And do what?" said MacDougall. He and Butterworth had closed the Circe the night before, and he kept seeing what looked like newts in his peripheral vision.

"There's a lot more to this oil thing than meets the eye," Smedley said. "I have a hunch that whole Ohio gang were stealing left, right, and center, and I'd like to have someone come up with the proof."

"What about the boys in the Washington bureau?" MacDougall said. "Wouldn't they be the logical ones?"

"It's so long since they've had to dig for a story they've forgotten how. They've been living on press handouts."

MacDougall thought for a moment, then said, "Now that I think of it this began to break last year, but nobody recognized it."

"What do you mean?"

"Remember when Jess Smith committed suicide?"

"Who's he?"

"Legal adviser to Forbes, of the Veterans' Bureau."

"Oh, yes."

"Forbes resigned because he was caught with his hand in the till, and Smith committed suicide. They were all part of the Ohio gang you mentioned, and I'll bet they're part of this story."

"And that's exactly why I want you to go to Washington. If the boys in the bureau had been on their toes, we'd have beaten the *Post-Dispatch* by a year."

"How long do you want me to stay there?"

"As long as it takes."

MacDougall hesitated, then said, "O.K. I guess my roommate can get along without me."

"Tell her you can see her weekends."

"It isn't a her. It's Roly Butterworth."

"I thought he was married."

"It's too long a story to go into. When do you want me to leave?"

"As soon as you can."

"Expense acount?"

"So long as you keep it within reason. You're there to uncover graft, not contribute to it."

The day after MacDougall left, Butterworth had dinner at the Circe and then, with nothing specific to do for Brady, went back to the apartment. For the first time since he'd moved in town he felt lonesome, and as he looked around the sparsely furnished flat he realized how badly it needed a woman's touch. Everything in it was functional and slightly tacky: the Morris chair in the living room looked as though it had come from a college dormitory, and the runner atop the table seemed to have had mice nibbling at its edges.

Most of the flat surfaces were scarred with cigarette burns, and the lampshade on the main reading light bore a circular brown spot where it had rested against a hot bulb. On an impulse, he picked up the telephone and called Sarah.

"How would you like to spend the night in town?" he said, when she answered.

"What night?" she replied.

"Tonight. Any night."

"I have nobody to leave the children with."

"Bring 'em along. They can sleep on the couch."

"Roland, have you been drinking?"

"No–well–no. I'm not drunk, if that's what you mean."

"Then what's the point of this call?"

"I miss you. Does a man have to be drunk to miss his family?"

"There are plenty of trains. You're more than welcome out here."

"We've been through all that. You know I can't."

"Are you trying to tell me Brady might want you tonight?"

"I never know when he might want me."

"Well, I thank you for the invitation, but it's out of the question. I can't just haul the children around as though they were peanut butter."

"*Peanut* butter? What is that supposed to mean?"

"You know what I'm trying to say. They're people, not things."

"I'm perfectly aware they're people. That's why I'd like to see them. And you."

"Well, I'm sorry."

There was an odd quality to her voice, and he said, "Is there someone with you?"

"Yes," she replied. "The Thatchers are here. We've been playing three-handed bridge."

"Oh," he said, and glanced at his watch, which showed ten minutes past ten. "Well, give them my best."

"I'll do that."

"Talk to you tomorrow." He hung up, looked around the room, then put on his hat and coat and went back to the Circe.

The *Herald* and the *Tribune* merged on March 24, and MacDougall was brought back from Washington. By that time there was no need for investigative reporting; the Teapot Dome scandal had, so to speak, taken the lid off the corruption of the Harding administration, and people were resigning right and left. Some were brought to trial, but very few were convicted; as Will Rogers put it, it was hard to get a jury to convict a man for criminal corruption when most of the jurors secretly admired those who got away with it.

The first night MacDougall was back in New York, he and Butterworth had dinner at the Circe, and it was as though he'd been away for five years. Nick brought out a bottle of Chianti classico, Marie produced a cheesecake adorned with French and American flags, and she and Louis and Raoul, the newly acquired busboy, sang *"Auprès de ma blonde,"* in an approximation of three-part harmony. Fred McClain and Dorothy Peters, at their table in the corner, furnished the percussive accompaniment, he tapping his teacup with a spoon and she drumming on the table with the high-heeled shoes she'd removed when she sat down. Other customers joined in as the mood struck them, although most of them were unaware of the reason for the celebration. What with one thing and another, dinner lasted until ten-thirty.

When they got outside, MacDougall was ebullient. "Let's go someplace," he said.

"All right," replied Butterworth. "Where?"

"Would you like to take a boat ride? I know some guys who have a boat."

"Where does it go?"

"Just out and back. But come to think of it, they'll have left by now."

"You know what I'd *like* to do—I'd like to take the Boston night boat. We should do that some time."

"Hey, I know! The *Paris* is sailing at midnight—let's go down and see her off!"

"You mean, just wave from the dock?"

"Hell, no! Go aboard and crash some of the parties!"

"Can you do that?"

"I don't see why not. We'll never find out if we don't try."

"All right." Butterworth was doubtful, but MacDougall's enthusiasm was infectious, and no matter what happened the evening would be a novel one.

Butterworth had never seen an ocean liner from close up before, and as they approached the French Line pier he was stunned into silence by the size of the ship. The three lighted funnels, red with black tops, seemed to tower into the night sky like castles, and the lighted windows and portholes along the ship's side gave the impression that a gala ball was going on. Porters were trundling baggage across the dock while passengers, dressed in heavy coats and hats against the cold, lined up to have their passports and tickets examined. MacDougall led Butterworth around this line and straight to the foot of a covered gangplank. He produced his police card, said, "Press," to the man who stood guard, and they were waved up the gangplank and into the side of the ship. Another officer was standing just inside, and when he stepped forward MacDougall again produced his police card and said, "We're looking for B-324."

"Two decks up," the officer replied. "On the port side, aft."

MacDougall thanked him; the officer saluted, and they started up the carpeted staircase to the decks above.

"Who's in B-324?" Butterworth asked, as they reached B Deck.

"Haven't the faintest idea," MacDougall replied. "It was just a way of getting aboard."

They went down a paneled passageway, which smelled of brass polish and furniture wax, and saw other people looking for staterooms, or emerging to call to friends, some of whom were arriving with picnic baskets that clanked. Since the ship's bar wouldn't open until they were beyond the three-mile limit, all the celebrating had to be done with domestic liquor. There was one stateroom from which issued the sounds of what appeared to be a full-fledged orgy, and MacDougall stopped and listened, then said, "We might as well start here," and rang the buzzer. Several people shouted "Come in!" and he opened the door into a double stateroom that contained about a dozen people, some standing, some sitting on the berths, and some lying down. One man had already gone to sleep in a chair, a half-empty glass in his lap.

"I'm sorry," said MacDougall. "I'm looking for Ambrose Bierce. Has he been here?"

"He just left," said a young man with his hair parted in the middle. "The captain wanted to ask him some advice. What'll you drink?"

"Well, since you put it that way, a drop of Scotch would be nice. Just to wet the whistle."

A girl with a cloche hat and bobbed hair came up to Butterworth and put an arm through his. "You're cute," she said. "What's your name?"

"Bierce," Butterworth replied. "I'm Ambrose's brother Yorick."

"What'll you have?" said the apparent host. "Scotch?"

"That would be fine," said Butterworth.

The conversation, which had died down with MacDougall and Butterworth's entrance, now picked up again, and the decibel count rose sharply. The man who'd been asleep suddenly woke up, shouted, "Christ!" and dashed out the door.

"Who's he?" Butterworth asked the girl, who was still clinging to his arm.

"Oh, him?" she said. "That's Scott. He's the one we're seeing off."

"One thing you must remember when you get to Chartres," a man was saying to a blonde with beads that reached her hips, "is to avoid the bistro called *Aux Cheveux du Chien.* They make the worst martinis in all of Europe."

"I'm not going to Chartres," the girl replied. "But I'll remember anyway."

"No Europeans can make a martini," another man said. "They put in too much vermouth."

Butterworth tasted his drink, which was made with straight Scotch and no ice, and it almost gagged him.

"Here," said the girl with the cloche hat, "let me fix that." She lifted her skirt, removed a flask from a holster arrangement that was slung across her thighs, poured a splash in Butterworth's glass, then replaced the flask. "There," she said, straightening her skirt. "That should taste better."

"What is it?" Butterworth asked, raising the glass.

"Gin," she replied. "Gin always takes the curse off Scotch."

Butterworth hesitated, the glass at his lips, then said, "The hell with it," and took a sip. It tasted terrible, as he'd expected, but he managed to get it down. "Frishcraft," he said, with a shudder.

"How's that?" the girl said, putting her head closer.

"I said 'frishcraft,'" Butterworth replied. "It was an involuntary word, like 'aargh,' or 'erk.'"

"I think it's cute," the girl said, and stepped on his feet. Or he stepped on hers; he wasn't sure which. One minute she seemed to be close to him, their noses almost touching, and the next she was far away, at the end of a tunnel, while people all around shouted and screamed with strange, muted voices. Butterworth had an overpowering urge to sit down, and he found the corner of a bunk and perched himself upon it. A gong began to ring, far away at first and then closer and closer, and its echoes filled the cabin and blended in with the noise of the people, and then slowly faded away. Somewhere a throaty whistle blew, and the air in the cabin trembled. The gong returned, and the people screamed, and the whistle blew again.

Someone was shaking Butterworth, and shouting at him, and as his consciousness returned he realized it was MacDougall, saying, "Get up, Roly, get up! We're at sea!"

"We're–" Butterworth struggled to a sitting position and said, "What happened?" The cabin was empty except for the two of them, and glasses and paper cups and cigarette butts lay strewn about the deck.

"We've sailed! We're going down the harbor!"

Butterworth got to his feet and almost fell forward, but MacDougall caught him. "What can we do?" Butterworth asked. Insanely, he found himself about to say, "I can't speak French," but stopped in time. "Do we swim?" he asked.

"They're going to put us off with the pilot," MacDougall replied. "It's all set. We just have to be ready."

"Where were you when we sailed? Why didn't you wake me?"

MacDougall cleared his throat. "I found a little lady who wanted to show me her cabin," he said. "I seem to have missed the going-ashore alarm. Actually I heard it, but it didn't seem terribly important at the time."

Butterworth went to the bathroom and splashed cold water on his face, then dried himself and combed his hair. "Well," he said, coming back into the cabin, "you asked earlier if I'd like to take a boat ride, and it seems we're doing just that."

"It made for a different sort of evening," MacDougall said. "I like to work in a little variety wherever possible."

The pilot boat put them ashore at the Battery around two-thirty, and it was another hour before they got back to the apartment. When, at ten o'clock that morning, Butterworth reported to the Brady office, Brown looked at him without expression.

"All right," Brown said. "That did it."

"Look, I was at the Circe until–" Butterworth began, but Brown put up a hand.

"Don't bother with the explanation," he said. "Just clear out your desk as fast as you can. If I were you, I wouldn't be here when he arrives."

21

Butterworth's first thought was to go back to the apartment, pack his belongings, and take the train to Crestwood. Then he realized that the most important thing was to find a new job, and he wasn't going to do that sitting in the bosky glens of Westchester County. He'd have to stay in town, at least until he found something, and then decide where he was going to live.

He took the personal contents of his desk to the apartment, and arrived just as MacDougall was making himself a cup of coffee. MacDougall was unshaven, and his hair was in his eyes, and the hand that held his cigarette trembled as though an electric current were passing through it. "That turned out to be quite an evening," he said.

"It was an even more interesting morning," Butterworth replied. "I've been fired." He detailed what had happened, and MacDougall's eyes grew large with concern.

"Why, the son of a bitch," he said. "He can't do that to you."

"He just did," Butterworth replied. "And I can't say it breaks my heart."

"What are you going to do?"

"That's something else again. I don't know."

"I feel this is partly my fault. Would you like to see if they'll take you back on the paper?"

"No, thanks just the same. I think I should find something I'm better at than I was as a reporter."

"Well, we'll think about it. I'll get dressed and we can pop down to the Circe for an eye-opener, and maybe something'll come to us."

While MacDougall was dressing, Butterworth went to the telephone and, after thinking for a few minutes, put through a call to Crestwood. "Hi, there," he said, when Sarah answered.

"Hello, dear," she replied.

"How are things?"

"Fine."

"The children?"

"They're fine." Pause. "What did you do last night?"

"Oh–Mac and I went down and saw some friends off to Europe."

"Anyone I know?"

"As a matter of fact, I don't think so."

"Well, that must have been fun."

"Yes. I'd never seen an ocean liner from close up before. You can't imagine how big they are."

"Which one was it?"

"The *Paris*. French Line. We should take a trip on her some day."

"That would be nice."

"How are the children?"

"You've already asked that. They're fine."

"Of course . . . I–oh, I knew there was some other news. I may be changing jobs."

"You mean you're leaving Brady?" Her voice took on a note of hope.

"Most likely. A lot will depend on just what my next job will be. There are several–"

"Then you'll be able to live at home?"

"That again will depend. There are several things that have to be ironed out, and as of this minute I can't say anything definite. But I just thought you'd like to know."

"Oh, I do! It's the most glorious thing I've heard all year!"

"Well, don't get your hopes too high. As I say, I'm not sure about anything."

"No, but just to have you away from Brady is enough! I feel that you were more married to him than you were to me."

"Well, you needn't worry about that, believe me."

"Oh, love, this is beautiful news! When will you know for sure?"

"I wish I knew, but believe me, you'll know as soon as I do."

"Oh, thank you, thank you, thank you! I think I'll go out in the garden and plant a sunflower, just to greet you when you come home."

"Please–I said I don't know–I may have to be in town more than I do now."

"I don't care, so long as you're clear of Brady. That's all that matters to me."

"Well, I think I can safely promise you that."

"Then I don't need to know any more. Good-bye, my love, and thank you for calling."

He hung up, loathing himself more than he had ever believed possible.

When Butterworth and MacDougall reached the Circe, Bogart was standing at the bar, looking sourly into a teacup that had once held a martini. His face brightened when he saw them, and he said to Butterworth, "How's the mighty drumbeater these days?"

"My drum is, for the moment, muffled," Butterworth replied, and explained the reason.

"Damn," said Bogart. "I was hoping to work with you next fall."

"On what?"

"Young Bill Brady is producing a play, written by Johnny Farrar and Steve Benét. I'm going to be in it, along with Paul Kelly, Mary Phillips, Ken McKenna, and some others. I think Ken's brother, Jo Mielziner, is going to do the sets."

"Well, if a Brady is producing it, I guess you can count me out," said Butterworth.

"What are you going to do?"

"Right at the moment, I don't know. It only happened a couple of hours ago."

"Well, I'll ask around. If I hear of anyone who needs a press agent, I'll say you're available."

"Thank you. Every little bit is going to count."

"Let's start by having a round on me. What'll it be, gents?"

Butterworth ordered a Scotch sour and MacDougall a Rob Roy, and after a moment's thought Bogart ordered another martini. "Don't put so much sugar in it this time," he said to Charlie, and Charlie laughed. "I'm not kidding," Bogart said. "That vermouth is straight sugar."

"I have an idea publicity is going to be the coming thing," MacDougall said to Butterworth. "I think if you can get a good, solid start in the business, you can do great things with it. In another few years everyone's going to need a press agent just to be noticed."

"I've got the start in it," Butterworth replied. "I just don't think it's too solid."

"Of course, I still think you ought to be an actor," MacDougall said, and then, to Bogart, "Don't you think he'd be good on the stage?"

"God, no," said Bogart. "There are too many actors as it is. Don't try to ring in any more."

"Wait'll my play's done, and then we'll see."

"Are you writing a play?" Bogart was suddenly interested.

"I'm working on one."

"Well, don't forget your old friends. You'll find me under 'B' in the phone book."

"It's not that far along, believe me." Turning to Butterworth, MacDougall said, "I just had an idea—how would you like to be a publicity agent in reverse?"

"What do you mean?"

"Keep things out of the papers, instead of getting them in."

"Things like what?"

Turning to Charlie, MacDougall said, "Is Nick around?"

"Yes, sir," Charlie replied. "He's in the kitchen."

"Would you ask him to step out here a minute?"

Nick appeared in a moment and greeted the three men. "I thought I heard familiar voices," he said.

"Our friend Butterworth, here, is out of a job," said MacDougall. "I told him there might be an opening for a press agent in reverse." Nick looked at him blankly, and MacDougall went on, "Tell him what you were telling me last night."

"Oh, that." Nick shrugged. "I don't know how you'd go about it, because it's mostly word of mouth."

"Tell him, anyway."

"Well—it's a strange goddam spot to be in, but we're getting too successful. The way to make out as a speak is to be like all the others and don't draw attention to yourself, but it seems like everybody in town knows about us. The Feds don't have enough men to close down *all* the speaks, but they sure as hell can swoop down on any one that gets too famous. I wish we were back in the old days, before the fire."

"What did the fire have to do with it?" Butterworth asked.

"That was the first time we were mentioned in the papers. By now, as I said, it's word of mouth, but that's what got the ball rolling."

"I know one way to stop it," Bogart put in. "Close down."

"Thanks," said Nick.

"I mean it. Get the word around there's bubonic rats in your kitchen, and close down for a few days, then open up under another name. The regulars'll come anyway, and that'll get rid of the riffraff."

"I wish I believed it," Nick said.

Bogart shrugged. "I was only trying to be helpful." Then, to Butterworth, he said, "Hey, I know someone who could use a press agent–old Webbie."

"Who?" said Butterworth.

"Clifton Webb. He was in *Meet the Wife* with me, and used to be a dancer. I think he's going places as an actor, and all he needs is a little boost."

"If he can pay for it, I'm his man," Butterworth replied. "It's the money I'm most worried about."

"I tell you what," Nick said. "I'll pay you twenty-five bucks a week if you can guarantee we won't get in the papers."

"I can't *guarantee* anything," Butterworth replied.

"Then I'll pay you twenty-five bucks for every week we're not mentioned. If we appear in print, you lose the twenty-five for that week."

Butterworth thought about this. "All right," he said. "It's a deal."

MacDougall looked at his watch and said, "I'll leave you businessmen to yourselves. I have to work for a living." He finished his drink and thanked Bogart, then said to Butterworth, "I'll ask around," and left.

"One more thing," Butterworth said to Nick. "Suppose there's a legitimate news story about the club–what would you pay a reporter not to print it?"

"That would depend on the story," Nick replied. "The very least I could do would be buy him a few drinks."

"O.K. I've got to dangle some bait in front of these guys or they won't play."

"You know something?" Bogart said. "I think I'm watching the birth of a great publicity man."

Later that afternoon, Butterworth called Sarah. "Well, I have one job lined up," he told her. "It isn't much, but it's better than nothing. I've got a couple more possibilities, but I don't know anything for certain yet."

"Wonderful!" she said. "Does that mean you can come home for supper?"

"Actually, I ought–" Butterworth began, then realized he couldn't stand the wounded silence that would result if he backed out. "Yes, I guess I can make it," he said. "Tonight, anyway."

"When will you be out?"

"I'll just have to see. It'll depend on what else comes through."

"What would you like to eat? I'll go to the market right now."

"Please don't do anything special. I'll have whatever you were going to have."

"I *want* it to be special! Besides, I was going to have Cream of Wheat."

"Cream of Wheat for *supper?*"

"Oh, I have any old thing that pops into my head. When you're cooking for yourself, you don't really care. I want to know what you want."

"Well–maybe lamb chops?"

"Lamb chops it'll be. I'll even make paper frills to go on the bones."

"Please don't go to any trouble."

"I *want* to, ninny! This is a gala occasion!"

I wonder why I said lamb chops, he thought, as he hung up. I had lamb chops for lunch.

He went to the Circe on the way to the train, and found Bogart more or less where he'd been standing that noon. "I talked to Webbie," Bogart said, when Butterworth joined him. "He said he thought maybe he could work something out. Are you free this evening?"

"What time this evening?"

"Dinner time."

Butterworth closed his eyes. Dear God, he thought, why do you do this to me? Then he shook his head. "No," he said. "Any other time. I could come back around ten–" He stopped, as he thought of Sarah's reaction, and said, "No, I couldn't. Tomorrow–the next day –any time but tonight."

"O.K.," Bogart said. "I'll tell him."

"And ask him to forgive me. I've just made other arrangements."

"Sure. He'll understand."

Cream of Wheat for supper, Butterworth thought, as he watched the Bronx tenements flash past the train window. What kind of way is that to live? True, nobody put a gun at her temple and *made* her eat it—she herself said she ate anything that popped into her head—but still, what kind of life is that? And, more importantly, is it my fault? If I were home for supper every night you can be damned sure we wouldn't have Cream of Wheat, but does that make me responsible? No. No jury in the world would convict me. Gentlemen of the jury, I ask you to look at the defendant, a craven, hedonistic lout, who spends his time in speakeasies while his wife and babies eke out a bare existence in the country, living on roots and berries and Cream of Wheat! Is a man like that fit to walk in decent society? I say no! I say he should be confined for the rest of his natural life, deprived of all liquor and compelled to eat Cream of Wheat with a fork. By God, they might convict, at that.

The thought of liquor reminded him that Sarah would have none in the house, and he wished he'd remembered to bring a flask. Not that he really needed it, but he'd been accustomed to having a drink or two before eating. Well, it won't hurt me to go without just this one night, he thought. It isn't as though I hadn't had anything all day. Come to think of it, she'll probably smell it on my breath and that'll bitch up the evening before it even gets started. I should have bought some mints before I got on the train.

The pink afterglow of sunset showed through the trees, and the air rang with the cries of spring peepers, as he started the short walk to where he lived. He watched the dwindling red lights on the train as it headed up the line toward Scarsdale, and he wondered if he could ever become reconciled to being a commuter. The city and the country—or, more precisely, the suburbs—were so totally different that it seemed impossible a man could mix them and still retain a balanced outlook on life. A lot of people did, but for him they were two different worlds, each with its own advantages and its own drawbacks, and in his present state of employment it would be just one more shifting element in a wildly unstable situation. What he needed more than anything else was a feeling of solidity: a person, or a base, or an outlook that would remain unchanging, and that he could hold on to while the rest of the world skidded beneath his feet.

In this fretful state of mind he let himself into the house, and before he could close the door there was the sound of running feet, and Nancy came rocketing out of the kitchen and hurled herself at his knees. "Daddy! Daddy! Daddy!" she cried, and he picked her up and kissed her soft, jelly-covered cheeks. Then Sarah appeared in the kitchen door, wearing an apron over her evening dress, and Butterworth kissed her while still holding Nancy, thereby transferring some of Nancy's jelly onto Sarah's mouth. She laughed, and wiped it clean with her apron, and Butterworth said, "Where's Puddin?"

"In bed," Sarah replied. "I kept him up as long as I could, but then he began to get cranky, so I put him to bed. You'll see him later."

"I'm sorry I couldn't get out earlier," Butterworth said, "but I wanted to stay around and check about some more jobs. The more I get, the better off we'll be."

"Is it all right to ask what you're doing?"

"I guess you'd call me a free-lance publicist. I've got one–uh–industrial commission already, and I'm hoping to sign up with an actor to do his publicity. It's all still pretty vague." To himself he thought, why don't you come right out and *tell* her what you're doing? She's bound to know, sooner or later. You haven't exactly been lying, but you're being awfully damned circuitous about the truth. Out loud, he said, "We'll go into it all later. Right now, I want to clean up and make myself respectable." He put Nancy down, and patted the top of her head.

"I put out clean towels," Sarah said, as he started upstairs. "I hope you find everything you want."

On his way to the bathroom he stopped and looked in the room where Puddin slept and was surprised to see the child standing up, holding on to the bars of the crib, and staring at him with enormous blue eyes. "Hi, there," he said, and Puddin began to cry. Butterworth picked him up and made soothing noises, and Puddin's cries turned to screams, his face red and his fists clenched. Sarah came running upstairs, followed by Nancy.

"What's the matter?" Sarah asked, taking Puddin in her arms. "What happened?"

"Nothing," Butterworth replied. "I just said 'Hi,' and he started to yell."

"You must have wakened him, or frightened him in some way."

"I didn't! He was standing up, looking at me, and all I said was 'Hi, there.' "

"I guess it was just an unfamiliar face." Puddin had by now calmed down, and Sarah put him back in his crib. "There, now," she said. "It's only Daddy, and Daddy isn't going to bite you."

"I bit him once," Nancy announced, with satisfaction. "Right on the nose."

"Nancy, stop making up stories," Sarah said. "You never did such a thing, and you know it."

"I did," replied Nancy. "He bled like a stuck pig. All over the walls."

"Nancy! Go downstairs!"

"Have it your way," said Nancy, and left the room.

When Butterworth got in the bathroom, he closed the door and examined his face in the mirror. It occurred to him, as he looked at the gaunt features reflected back at him, that the last twenty-four hours had been as eventful, not to say momentous, as any he'd ever endured. It was just about this time yesterday that he and MacDougall had set out to have dinner at the Circe; in all, he'd probably had no more than five hours' sleep, and the bone-deep fatigue was beginning to set in. He felt that with a drink or two he might survive, but since that was clearly out of the question he'd have to slug it through on will power alone. He washed his face, thought about shaving, and remembered he'd left his razor in town. The hell with it, he thought. Maybe I'll grow a beard, and change my luck.

They had dinner by candlelight, and Sarah had made little frilled cuffs for the lamb chops. She was sprightly and gay, and kept up an animated conversation, only part of which Butterworth was able to follow. A lot of it involved the Thatchers, and other people he didn't know, and he felt his eyelids getting heavy as she talked. Finally, more to have something to say than for any other reason, he said, "I didn't leave Brady on my own, you know. I was fired."

"Oh, I know," she replied. "I guessed that the minute you told me."

"How?"

"You were too casual. You tried to make it sound like an everyday occurrence."

"I wasn't trying to deceive you, really. I wanted to break the news gently, and hope I'd have something equally good by the time I told you."

"And do you?"

"Not exactly." He filled her in on the situation so far, and concluded, "It just may take a little time, that's all."

"But you'll be able to live at home?"

"That all depends. If I'm going to be chasing around the theatres, I'll need a base in town."

"I see." She dabbed at the corners of her mouth with her napkin, then put it on the table. "Would you like some coffee?"

"I'd love some." He followed her into the kitchen, bringing his plate with him, and said, "That was a fine dinner. Just right."

"We try to please," said Sarah, turning on the heat under the coffee.

"By the way, since when has Nancy started telling these stories?"

"Like what?"

"Like biting Puddin on the nose. And that kind of flip approach—the 'Have it your way' exit line."

"I'm afraid that's a little girl named Daisy Peterson. Nancy met her through the Thatcher kids, and imitates everything she does. I've tried to discourage her, but she's always coming up with something new. I never know what she's going to say next."

"Does she see much of the Thatchers?"

"Heavens, yes. Mark and Violet often bring their kids when they come for three-handed bridge, and I take Nancy and Puddin when I go there. We practically live in each others' pockets."

"Sounds cozy."

"It's better than nothing. Cream and sugar?"

"No, thanks. Just black."

They had coffee in the living room, then Butterworth helped Sarah with the dishes. "I don't mean to be away all this much," he said, as he scrubbed the broiler pan. "It just seems to be the only way I can make a living."

"I know," she replied. "And I don't mean to complain. I simply get lonesome. Talking to children is fun for a while, but I find I need a change every now and then."

"Well, you always have the Thatchers."

"That's right," she said. "I always have the Thatchers."

They went upstairs quietly, and Sarah undressed in the bathroom. When, finally, they were in bed and had turned out the lights, they lay in the dark for a few moments, then Sarah put out a hand and touched him. "I remember you," she said.

"I remember you," Butterworth replied. He reached for the back of her neck and started to pull her toward him, and there came the sound of a baby whimpering. Sarah stiffened.

"Wait a minute," she whispered.

"He's only dreaming," Butterworth said. After a moment Sarah relaxed and rolled toward him, just as Nancy's voice shattered the stillness.

"Mummy!" she cried. "Mummy, come here! Puddin pooped his pants!"

Sarah sighed, and got up. She cleaned and changed the baby, kissed Nancy and told her to sleep well, then returned to her bedroom. Butterworth lay on his back, his arms spread wide and his mouth agape, and every breath made his palate rattle with a noise like a snarling lion. She lay down next to him, but it was like lying next to a donkey engine, and after a while she got into the other bed, pulled the covers over her head, and went to sleep.

When he left for the train next morning, she kissed him and said, "Will you be out again tonight?"

"I have no idea," he replied. He'd had to shave with her razor, which was like scraping his cheeks with a rusty hoe, and he wasn't looking forward to the ride in the crowded commuter train. "It'll all depend on what happens. I'll let you know as soon as I do."

When he got into the city he went to the apartment, where MacDougall was just getting up, and MacDougall could report no immediate progress in finding him a job. He said he'd had some thoughts, but it would take him a while to develop them, and in the meantime Butterworth had better keep looking. He went to the Circe around noon and there found Bogart at his usual place at the bar.

"What did Webb say?" Butterworth asked.

"No dice," Bogart replied. "His mother wouldn't let him."

"His *mother?*" Butterworth took the Scotch that Charlie had automatically made for him. "What's she got to do with it?"

"She calls the shots. She said he was too young to have a press agent—that he should wait until he's older, and a little better known."

"But that's the whole *point*—"

Bogart put up a hand. "Don't argue with me, pal," he said. "Argue with Mrs. Webb. And that, you might as well be warned, is like arguing with the First Division of the United States Marine Corps."

"Well," said Butterworth, after a moment, "thanks for trying, anyway."

22

In spite of, or possibly because of, the lack of publicity, the Circe's clientele continued to increase during the spring and early summer. Nick had to hire another busboy, named Felix, to help Raoul, and had to enlarge the door to the kitchen so there could be two doors, one in and one out. This happened after the third time the two busboys had hit the door from opposite directions at the same instant, causing an inordinate amount of breakage of dishes, crockery, and glassware. Metal kick-plates were added, to save wear and tear on the doors.

"What we really need is a larger kitchen," Marie said one day, when Nick was trying to replan the bar so as to accommodate more customers. He was off on a train of thought all his own, and seemed not to have heard her.

"I'm beginning to think Bogart was right," he said, as much to himself as to anyone else. "Close it down for a few days, then reopen under a new name."

"Why would you want to do that?" she asked.

"To use Bogart's words, get rid of the riffraff."

"Are you still paying Mr. Butterworth to keep us out of the papers?"

"No. After he got his first real job he thanked me and said he didn't need it anymore."

"It must be some job."

"He has several clients by now. A couple of actors, one producer —he's doing all right."

"Has he paid his tab?"

"Look—he's an old customer, and a good friend. I'm not going to ask him for money until we need it more than he does."

"That's not the way they do it in France," said Marie.

"And you're not in France, either. You worry about the kitchen, and I'll worry about the cash."

"I do worry about the kitchen. That's why I said we need a larger one."

"All right—we'll turn the whole place into a kitchen and let the customers wander around and peer into your pots. It would give it a nice homey atmosphere, don't you think?"

Marie hesitated, then said, "What's got into you, anyway? You're —you're *rancunier*—how do you say it? Rancid? Bitter?"

"I'm not bitter about anything. I'm just trying to think."

Marie started to reply, but the buzzer sounded as the first of the lunchtime customers arrived, and she went back into the kitchen.

The talk at the bar, usually consisting of reminiscences of the night before, centered this time on a particularly lurid murder that had been reported in the morning papers. Bobby Franks, the thirteen-year-old son of a Chicago millionaire, had disappeared two days previously, and yesterday his nude and battered body, the face stained with acid, had been discovered in a railway culvert just outside the city. His family had received two ransom requests, allegedly from one George Johnson (they were typed, not handwritten), and the boy's body had been found while his father was out trying to deliver the $10,000 demanded by the kidnapper. The only clue was a pair of thick-lensed eyeglasses found nearby; Bobby Franks did not wear glasses.

"If they catch the son of a bitch," said a man standing at the bar, "I hope they tie his legs to two brewery horses and let them split him apart."

"That'd be too quick," another man said. "Tie him bareass behind a car and drag him through the streets. That'd give him time to think."

"I mean, what kind of civilized person would do a thing like that?" the first man said. "Beating a little kid's head in, and then pouring acid on him. It's unnatural, is what it is."

McClain and Dorothy Peters came in and took their usual table in the corner. Dorothy was sniffling, and dabbing at her eyes with a handkerchief.

"The poor little son of a bitch," she said. "What good did it do him to be rich? What's all his inheritance going to do for him now?"

McClain signaled Charlie for two drinks, then said, "I don't see as how being rich had anything to do with it."

"It doesn't. It only shows that rich people can die, just like the rest of us."

"Did anyone say they couldn't?"

"No, but they seem to think that way. They think they've got some special kind of dispensation."

"I must ask a rich man, the next time I see one."

"You don't have to look far–just take the subway down to Wall Street. It's crawling with them." She blew her nose, then reached under the table and took McClain's hand. "Better yet, don't take the subway down to Wall Street. Stay here, where I can hold on to you."

"That sounds better," McClain replied.

Their drinks arrived, and they toasted each other and drank.

"Did I do anything terrible last night?" Dorothy asked.

"No," said McClain. "Why?"

"I didn't want to take a horse home, or put a street beggar through college?"

"You were fine," McClain insisted. "Why do you ask?"

"I don't know. I just hate it when I have blanks. I always suspect I've done the worst."

"As far as I'm concerned, you did the best."

"That's a pretty thing to hear; I wish I could remember it."

"I tell you what–we'll have another drink, and then maybe a sandwich, and then go back to my place. With only two drinks, you'll have crystal-clear recall. How does that sound?"

"That sounds absolutely first rate, except for one thing."

"What's that?"

"Who needs a sandwich?"

Roland Butterworth had lunched that day with a client, who insisted he wanted to go to the Algonquin. They sat in the so-called Rose Room, the main dining room, and Butterworth found that his client's eyes kept glancing around the room, as though he were waiting for someone to appear. He was an actor who had appeared in

Irving Berlin's *Third Music Box Revue* the year before and had received enough warm reviews to encourage him to continue in the theatre. He'd had no raves, but was convinced that all he needed was the proper break. "Actually, all I got in *Music Box* was sprayed with orange juice," he told Butterworth.

"How'd you do that?" Butterworth asked.

"Remember the 'Orange Grove in California' number?" the actor said. Butterworth nodded, although he'd never seen the show. "Well, they had a great idea," the actor went on. "All during that number they had stagehands squeezing oranges in front of the ventilation fans, so the audience got this nice orangy smell, and where I stood in the wings I got all the drip. In my hair, in my ears . . . I was a walking orange crush."

"We might be able to use that," Butterworth said. "Hang it on something timely, and–"

"Don't look now," the actor said, leaning forward, "but Marc Connelly just sat down over there. And here comes George S. Kaufman."

"To our table?" Butterworth asked.

"No–the Round Table. And there's Edna Ferber. Boy, they're all here today!"

Butterworth had heard of the Round Table, where a group of budding celebrities had lunch every day, but it had never occurred to him that it merited any such awe as this. "Anyway," he went on, "about your orange-juice experience, I'll see if I can . . ." The sentence dwindled off, as it was apparent his client wasn't listening, and after making desultory small talk he looked around for the headwaiter, and asked for the check. As they left the Rose Room he was able to get a quick look at the Round Table, and all he saw was a group of perhaps eight people, all of them young and most of them men, staring at their menus and occasionally crumbling bits of bread. Nobody spoke, other than to remark about something on the menu, and nobody so much as hinted at a smile. One man with dark, bushy hair, who was probably Kaufman, yawned so wide that his back molars were visible, and someone asked him how he'd slept. "Lousy," he replied.

"I had a strange dream last night," said a woman who might have been Edna Ferber, "but I can't remember it now."

"Probably just as well," said Kaufman.

Butterworth parted from his client on Forty-fourth Street and went down to the new offices of the *Herald Tribune*, on Nassau Street, to see Arthur Folwell in the drama department. On his way through the city room he spotted George MacDougall, who beckoned to him.

"Did you hear?" MacDougall said. "They got them!"

"Who got whom?"

"They got the guys who killed the Franks kid."

"Did it take *two?*"

MacDougall showed him a sheet of wire service copy, which announced that Richard ("Dickie") Loeb, eighteen, and Nathan ("Babe") Leopold, nineteen, two wealthy and brilliant University of Chicago graduate students, had been arrested for the murder of Bobby Franks. They were tracked down by Leopold's eyeglasses, which had been found at the scene, and conclusive proof was furnished by the type on Leopold's Underwood typewriter, which exactly matched that on the ransom notes. There was no known motive, except possibly the thrill of committing a perfect crime.

"I'll be goddamned," Butterworth said, handing back the piece of copy. "Do you think they'll get the chair?"

"They'll be lucky if they're not lynched," MacDougall replied. "The chair's too good for them." Then, as an afterthought, he added, "Are you doing anything tonight?"

"Not that I know of," Butterworth replied. "Why?"

"I may be having company after dinner. Do you think you could find something to amuse you until, say, about midnight?"

"Of course. I can go to a hotel, if you'd like."

"No, no. Midnight will be plenty of time."

"I mean it. There's no point having to keep your eye on the clock."

"It won't be on the clock, with any luck at all."

"Still. As a matter of fact, I've been thinking—I can afford to get a room at the Shelton, or the Allerton, or someplace like that, and you won't have to worry about this kind of thing."

"Nonsense! I wouldn't think of it." The tone of MacDougall's voice was just a shade too glib to be convincing.

"Well, think about it when you have a chance. I'll see you later."

Butterworth had dinner at the Circe and then, with the better part of the evening still ahead of him, decided to go over to Times Square and see a movie. Newsboys were shouting the headlines of the Leopold and Loeb arrests, making a sharp contrast with the generally festive Broadway atmosphere. He found that he had a wide choice of pictures: currently showing were James Cruze's *The Covered Wagon,* Douglas Fairbanks in *The Thief of Bagdad,* William S. Hart in *Singer Jim McKee,* and Rudolph Valentino in *Monsieur Beaucaire.* He felt he could skip both Hart and Valentino–Hart because he looked too much like a horse, and Valentino because his way of expressing desire was to bug his eyes wide open, which always reduced Butterworth to helpless laughter–and between the other two there was small choice. He'd seen Fairbanks in *Robin Hood* the year before and had been faintly depressed by the sight of a man his own age cavorting about like an ape, and he knew nothing about *The Covered Wagon* except that it concerned pioneer life, which had not as yet been dealt with in motion pictures. He was about to opt for *The Covered Wagon* on cultural grounds when he saw, down a side street, a theatre that was showing Buster Keaton in *The Navigator,* and that settled it. He forgot about culture and went to the Keaton picture, simply for the pleasure of watching a comic genius at work. Without really intending to, he found himself analyzing Keaton's deadpan technique, and thinking how he would portray the character in a similar situation. As always, he was awash with admiration, because the more he saw of Keaton the more he knew he was unique.

The picture was over comparatively early, and with still a lot of time to kill he drifted back to the Circe, which was noisy and crowded. As he went down the bar, looking for a place to stand, he heard a woman say, "He called me a flapper, so I went and looked it up, and you know what it is? It's a little bitty duck, so small it flaps instead of flying. The next time I see him, I say, 'Listen, Buster, you call me a duck just once more and we're pffft.' He says, 'Who called you a duck?' and I say, 'You did,' and he says—" Her voice was lost in the general babble, and Butterworth looked around and saw Dorothy Peters and McClain sitting at their usual table. Dorothy beckoned him to join them, and as he sat down she said, "I suppose you've seen the papers."

"I have," he said.

"That's the rich for you," she said. "Those two sons of bitches think just because their fathers have money they can do anything they want. That's the kind of people are running this country–rich bastards who'd split your skull just for the fun of it, and whom do they pick on? A poor little son of a bitch on his way home from school–"

"He was rich too, remember," McClain put in.

"Yes, but not as rich as they."

"How do you know?"

"How do I know? Whose side are you on, anyway? Are you trying to tell me you *condone* what those bastards did?"

"Of course not. I'm simply pointing out that this was not a case of the rich against the poor." McClain was trying to be patient, and only barely succeeding.

"And I suppose you'd say that Sacco and Vanzetti belong to the country club set," Dorothy said.

"What in God's name do Sacco and Vanzetti have to do with this?"

"Nothing. Nothing at all. They're only the perfect, shining example of what the rich will do to you when they get the chance. Here they rot in jail, a shoemaker and a fish peddler, while all the bankers and stockbrokers and their paid judges gloat at how they're going to string up a couple of Bolsheviks. They wouldn't know a Bolshevik from a Menshevik from a piece of mink shit, and they don't care just so long as they have someone they can string up in the name of making the world safe for democracy."

"You're out of your mind. Nobody's strung anyone up–Sacco and Vanzetti haven't even been sentenced. For all you know, they may get a new trial and get off scot free."

Dorothy gave a loud peal of laughter. "You're a comedian, aren't you?" she said. "You're the kind that makes jokes at a lynching. Too bad you missed Joan of Arc–you could have done a soft-shoe routine around the fire. 'Get off scot free' indeed! Would you like to lay a little bet on that?" As an afterthought, she added, "Or vice versa?"

"I think maybe we'd better be going," McClain said.

"Don't give me that 'we' stuff," she said, rising. "I can find my way alone."

McClain also rose. "Don't be silly," he said.

"And don't you be condescending. I am perfectly capable of functioning by myself." She picked up her purse and started for the door. McClain followed her and took her by the arm.

"Come on," he said. "I didn't mean to sound condescending. I'm sorry."

She shook her arm free. "Unless you want a punch right in that big mouth of yours," she said, "you'll go back to the table and mind your own business. Good night." She walked quickly through the entrance hall, and McClain heard the door close behind her. He returned to the table.

"You win a few, you lose a few," he said, as he sat down. "With her, she's so determined to find an underdog she sometimes gets confused. She'd root for the Kaiser, if she was sure enough people hated him."

"How many does she need?" Butterworth asked.

"I don't know, but when she heard he was chopping wood in Doorn, she remarked on how lonely he must be."

"Just because he's chopping wood?"

"Well, that doesn't normally gather a crowd."

"There's got to be something else bugging her."

"Have you talked to Mac?"

"Not about her."

"He should know, if anyone should."

"Why?"

"Well, when she wakes up in the middle of the night and calls me George, I get the picture her entire attention is not riveted on me."

"That's an ominous sign, certainly."

"On the other hand, when she's awake you'd think there was nobody in the whole damn world *except* me." McClain paused, then said, "I wonder if she thinks I'm an underdog."

Before Butterworth could reply, he saw MacDougall threading his way through the crowd of people at the bar. MacDougall joined them at the table, and said to Butterworth, "O.K. It's safe to come home now."

"You're early," Butterworth replied, glancing at his watch.

"One can't time these things to the split second. Incidentally, who did what to Dottie? I saw her going down the block under a full head of steam, weeping like a banshee."

"Weeping?" said McClain. "She was cursing when she left here."

"About what?"

"You name it. We thought you'd know better than we do."

"Oh. One of *those* nights." MacDougall picked up the drink that Charlie had placed in front of him and said, "Brought on, I would imagine, by Leopold and Loeb."

"How'd you know?"

MacDougall shook his head and smiled. "Experience," he said, and took a long swallow of his drink.

"What's bugging her, anyway?"

"I don't think she knows. I think she's looking for some kind of perfection and gets upset when she can't find it." Then, to Butterworth, he said, "How'd you like to do public relations for a mortuary?"

"What do you mean?" Butterworth asked cautiously.

"I ran across an undertakers' bulletin today, and this mortuary had an ad, saying they'd like to take on a public relations man. I've got the bulletin, if you want to apply."

"What kind of publication is this?" said Butterworth.

"Just what I said. They have news of interest in the embalming game, a column of jokes called 'From Grave to Gay,' a two-column cut of a stiff done up in evening clothes and propped in a corner with a cane, and the caption: 'In life they called him Jim'—you might say it's the morticians' *Vanity Fair*. I'll show it to you when we get home."

Butterworth thought for a moment, then said, "How much do they pay?"

"The mortuary? I don't know, but you could find out."

Butterworth took a sip of his drink and said, "I guess it doesn't matter what you publicize, just so long as you get paid for it."

"Kee-rect," said MacDougall, and they all raised their glasses and drank.

Later that night, when the last customer had been shooed out and the club swept clean and locked, Nick and Marie were walking home through the quiet streets when he said, "I've been thinking."

"What?" she said.

"I've been thinking it might be nice if you got out of the kitchen and lived like a lady. How would you like that?"

"What do you mean?"

"Well, we could get another cook to help Louis, and you could be a sort of hostess, like. That Guinan girl seems to have made a success of it, and it would give you a chance to meet some people."

"Is there anything the matter with my cooking?"

"Of course not! It's superior! I just—"

"Is it you're ashamed to be married to a cook?"

"Oh, cut it out. It's just that we can afford to hire another cook, and I thought you might like to meet some people for a change."

"There's nothing wrong with being a cook, you know. Look at Escoffier, look at Pellaprat, look at Brillat Savarin—"

"I didn't say there was! How many times do I have to tell you?"

She was quiet for a moment, then said, "Thank you, but I'm happy where I am."

"Fine. That's all I need to know." They walked on for a few moments, then Nick said, "Did you chain the back door?"

"I thought you did," she replied.

"I assumed you had, because you were cleaning up the kitchen."

"I assumed you had, because you always check the locks before we leave."

"Damn." Nick stopped. "I'd better go back."

"What difference does one little chain make? If someone wants to get in they're going to get in, no matter how the door is fastened."

"A chain makes it that much harder. You go on home, and I'll be with you shortly."

"Ah, mais il est idiot," Marie said, speaking more or less directly to God, and Nick turned back and headed for the Circe.

He was working the key to the gate when he heard a flurry of footsteps behind him, and turned around just as two men dived at him, pinning his arms to his sides. Nick struggled and kicked, but they managed to force him against the gate and tie him there, and then a third man, who walked with a limp, appeared out of the shadows and began to punch him about the head and body, breathing in short bursts with each blow. He must have had something in his hands, because his fists hit with the force of steam hammers. The last thing Nick remembered before he passed out was recognizing the man he'd shot in the leg, and he knew that the sooner he lost consciousness the better it was going to be. After a while there was only the sound of Nick's clotted breathing and, from inside the club, the noises of the three men breaking up the furniture.

23

Whether he wanted to or not, Nick was forced to accept Bogart's suggestion that he close the club for a while. The back-bar mirror had been broken, along with most of the crockery and glassware, and the chairs had been splintered and dismembered. The refrigerator had been opened and food thrown about the kitchen, and the stove had been smeared, inside and out, with congealed cooking grease. Luckily, the liquor stock had been locked away and was therefore intact, but almost everything else in the club needed either mending or replacing, and there was no point trying to serve customers until that was done.

Also, Nick was in no condition to be seen in public. His nose had been broken and both eyes were swollen shut; there was a hairline fracture along his jaw and three front teeth were missing; two ribs were cracked, and his left clavicle had been separated by about a half inch. He spent three days in the hospital and then insisted on going home, over Marie's loud protests that he would die before she could even get him to a taxi. It had been she who, worried about his absence, had come back to the club and found him hanging on the gate, and she had been sure then that he was dead. Even now, she couldn't shake the conviction that he was teetering on the rim of collapse and would shatter like a teacup in front of her eyes.

"You're not strong enough to come home," she protested. "Something will break."

"Honey, if it hasn't broken now it's never going to," he replied, through puffy lips. "Just give me a hand and help me out of here."

It was late summer before Nick and the club were ready for the reopening. There was no fanfare; the word was passed to a few of the regulars, and by Labor Day business was back to normal. In fact, the dinner business was such that Nick considered taking on a waiter, but Marie pointed out there wasn't room in the kitchen for Louis and herself, the busboys Raoul and Felix, *and* a waiter, so he added three dollars a week to Raoul's and Felix's wages and made them busboy-waiters, and eligible for tips. The only change in his, Nick's, routine was that he never left the club at night without carrying a gun, and he never let Marie go home alone.

"You thought that America was full of red Indians," he told her, "and that we had to lock the stockade at night to keep them out. Well, in a way that's how it is, except that these people make the Indians look like a bunch of pansies."

Marie laughed. "I never thought of Indians that way," she said. "I think I'll bake a cake, with an Indian *pédé* on top."

"How will you be able to tell what he is?"

"That's my secret," she said, and kissed him on the end of his nose.

On Wednesday afternoon, the second week in September, Butterworth made a round of the matinees of those shows in which he had clients appearing, then checked the box-office receipts in search of any startling material for news releases. The season so far had been slow, but it was still early enough so that he could hope to get newspaper coverage before some of the big names arrived and took over the feature space. Eugene O'Neill, whose *Anna Christie* had won the Pulitzer Prize in 1922, was due in with a play provocatively titled *Desire Under the Elms;* there was a Gershwin musical called *Lady, Be Good!* with the brother-and-sister dance team of Fred and Adele Astaire, and André Charlot was bringing a new revue over from London. Then Laurence Stallings and Maxwell Anderson had confected something called *None But the Brave, a Comedy with a Few Deaths,* which would undoubtedly be retitled before opening night, and there were the two perennials, still running since 1922: Jeanne Eagels in Somerset Maugham's *Rain,* and Anne Nichols' *Abie's Irish Rose,* the latter having survived a severe mauling by the critics and being apparently indestructible. All in all, Butterworth figured, he'd better come up with some good feature material, and come up with it quickly, or he'd have trouble justifying his fees. He had taken a room in the Hotel Seymour, on West Forty-fifth Street, and he needed every nickel he could lay his hands on.

He had also, at MacDougall's insistence, applied for the publicity job at the mortuary, which happened to be in Englewood, New Jersey, and whose director he had yet to meet. They had corresponded by mail and by telephone, but so far there had been no visual contact, and their exchanges of ideas had been vague and indefinite. The director had finally suggested that Butterworth make a list of ideas when he could find the time, and on that somewhat tentative note the matter had been left. He was paid a small retainer, as an indication of good faith.

After checking the matinees he went to the Circe, and was standing at the bar when MacDougall came in. "You're just the man I want to see," he said. "You got me into this jam, now you can get me out."

"Did you hear about Leopold and Loeb?" MacDougall countered. "They got off!"

"What do you *mean?*" Butterworth was incredulous.

"They didn't get the chair. Darrow persuaded the judge to give them each life plus ninety-nine years."

"That's not exactly getting off."

"No, but they're alive."

"How'd Darrow do it?"

"He talked for two days straight, and convinced the judge that Leopold is a manic paranoiac and Loeb a schizophrenic—whatever the hell that may mean. There was no jury, so the judge gave them life for the murder, and ninety-nine years for the kidnapping."

"Well, I'm damned," said Butterworth. "That Darrow must be some talker."

"Now, what's your problem? What jam did I get you in?"

"That mortuary job. I haven't had a single idea, and they're beginning to get impatient. The director wants to have a face-to-face meeting, and I don't know what to tell him."

"We ought to be able to think of something." MacDougall ordered a drink, sipped it, and said, "What makes news?"

"You mean man bites dog?" said Butterworth.

"No, names make news—I shouldn't have to tell you that. I think you should go after some big names, and if they're already dead see if you can't get them transferred to your place. It would make a hell of a story."

"Big names like whom? Lincoln?"

"I mean it. Start a—well, a Poets' Corner, and get Longfellow, Kilmer, Whitman—you know—names that'll draw. Try to sign up Frost. Sandburg. That kind of thing. Even if they turn you down, it'll be news."

Butterworth considered this, and was looking for some of the more obvious drawbacks when Bogart came in. "Well, now!" Butterworth said. "How's it coming?"

"Who knows?" Bogart replied, easing up to the bar and putting one foot on the rail. "We open in ten days, and they're still making changes."

"What's the show?" MacDougall asked.

"It's called *Nerves,*" Bogart replied. "It's young Bill Brady's production. I told you about it."

"You gave the cast. What's it about?"

Bogart's eyes glazed, and he sipped the drink Charlie had put in front of him. "I wish I knew," he said. "In the first act we're all at a Yale house party, and in the second act the men are in the officers' mess of a flying squadron in France. There's a lot of talk about cowardice and heroism, but I'm damned if I can get much more out of it than that."

"Somebody has a problem," MacDougall said. "When the actors can't tell you what it's about, look out."

"It's Benét and Farrar who have the problem," Bogart replied. "And I'm not sure they know what to do about it."

As it turned out, *Nerves* suffered from bad timing as well as script trouble. It opened the night after the Stallings-Anderson show, which had been retitled *What Price Glory?,* and the comparisons were invidious. Bogart was in the Circe after the second-night performance, when it was clear the play didn't have long to run, and he seemed unusually cheerful for an actor who was about to be out of work. Butterworth joined him at the bar and offered to buy him a condoling drink, but Bogart would have none of it.

"This round's on me," he said. "I'm celebrating."

"Celebrating what?" said Butterworth.

"The second good notice I've ever had in my life. Broun said I gave the most effective performance of the lot."

"I read that. And he said you were more real than any of the other 'Yale aviators.' Did you by any chance go to Yale?"

"I did not," Bogart replied, with some pride. "I was thrown out of Andover."

They touched glasses and drank, and Butterworth said, "Name me ten American poets."

Bogart stared at him. "Is this a game?"

"No. I just want the names of ten poets."

"Alive or dead?"

"Either. Preferably alive."

"Well, let's see–" Bogart stared at the back-bar, and began, "William Cullen Bryant, Ralph Waldo Emerson, Henry Wadsworth Longfellow, John Greenleaf Whittier, Edgar Allan Poe, Henry David Thoreau, Walt Whitman, Emily Dickinson, Edwin Arlington Robinson, George Santayana, Amy Lowell, Robert Frost– How many is that?"

"Twelve," replied Butterworth. "What else did you study at Andover?"

"I've forgotten. Now, if it's all right, will you tell me what this is about?"

"I seem to have taken a publicity job with a mortuary. Mac suggested we start a Poets' Corner, and I relayed the idea to the director, who thought it was the bee's knees. Now I'm stuck with trying to find some poets to bury there."

"Well, you'll do better to try for the living ones, like Frost, or Sandburg, or Edna St. Vincent Millay. Come to think of it, Amy Lowell is still alive–why don't you tap her?"

"I don't know how to phrase it. Everything I think of sounds wrong." He looked at the entrance, where McClain and Dorothy Peters had just come in, and said, "Here's someone who might have an idea." To Dorothy, he said, "How would you phrase an invitation to someone to be buried in your crypt?"

Dorothy stopped, then said, "How about 'Save the last dance for me'?"

"Did you ever notice how many poets have three names?" Bogart put in. "Ralph Waldo Emerson, Henry Wadsworth Longfellow–I just named about a half dozen."

"I have the feeling I'm losing my mind," Dorothy said. "What's going on here, anyway?" Butterworth explained his problem, and she said, "That's what you get for listening to MacDougall. Everything considered, you should count yourself lucky."

"It's a job," Butterworth replied.

"So is sheep stealing." To Bogart, she said, "My condolences on your play. When do you close?"

"Saturday, I guess," Bogart replied. "But I've got another one lined up. All I know about it is it's called *Hell's Bells.*"

"Well, it sounds cheery."

"As Roly said, it's a job. An old actor once told me that the only way to learn how to act is to keep acting. I'll take any job that comes along."

"I have an idea," Butterworth put in. "Who wrote 'Life is real! Life is earnest! / And the grave is not its goal'?"

"Longfellow," Bogart replied.

"I could use that as the lead-in to my pitch. Say that Longfellow was thinking of something more elaborate than a common grave, like for instance the Englewood Mortuary and its Poets' Corner, and what was good enough for Longfellow should be good enough for them. At least it would get their attention."

"I think you may have to do a little chumming first," Bogart said.

"What do you mean?"

"When you're fishing, you sometimes throw chopped bait in the water to attract the fish. That's called chumming, and I think you'll need a real poet in your crypt before you can draw any others."

"Do you know any sick poets?"

"Well, Amy Lowell is about fifty, and she smokes cigars. She shouldn't be good for too much longer."

"If it's all right with you gents I think I'll sit down," Dorothy said. "All this literary talk is making me a little dizzy." She and McClain took their drinks to the corner table, and Albert Hopkins, who had been listening to the conversation from a spot halfway down the bar, spoke up.

"I know a very sick poet who lives in Tenafly," he said.

Bogart and Butterworth turned and looked at him, and Butterworth said, "What's his name?"

"Lipworth," Hopkins replied. "Larry Lipworth."

"What's he written?"

"He's written a lot of poems for the newspapers, like an Ode to Winter, and Verses to Welcome Spring, and things like that. He also does his Christmas cards in rhyme. But he's certainly sick—I can guarantee you that. You can probably have him sometime next week, if you're quick about it."

Butterworth looked at Bogart. "Can you see the Larry Lipworth niche in the Poets' Corner?" he asked.

"Not as a come-on," Bogart replied.

"Thanks for the thought," Butterworth said to Hopkins. "We'll take it under advisement."

"You'd better be quick, is all I can say," said Hopkins, and sipped his drink.

The room was beginning to fill, individual conversations were lost, and at their corner table Dorothy and McClain were able to talk without fear of being overheard. She slipped one hand in his beneath the table and said, "How is he?"

"O.K.," he replied.

"I didn't mean to hurt."

"You didn't. I guess he's just—well, tender."

"I'm sorry."

"I'm not. Let's forget it."

"I can't forget it. I don't ever want to hurt you."

"You didn't hurt me! I told you, he's just tender!"

"All right, you don't need to shout. If you want to broadcast the message, you can give it to a skywriter."

"I wasn't shouting. I was simply rebutting."

"Ah, Fred, what are we arguing about? Why do we always seem to end by arguing?"

"I'm just trying to make a point."

"And you've made it. Maybe it's my fault—maybe I'm trying too hard to please you."

McClain started to say something, then stopped. "I'm not going to answer that one," he said. "No matter what I say, it'll be wrong."

"Maybe if we were married, this wouldn't all seem too important. As it is, I'm living in terror I'll do something to offend you and you'll walk out. If we were married, you'd have to think twice before you walked out. Well, one and a half times."

"That's just why we're not married. I don't want to settle down quite yet—I want to look around."

"So you've said. And what have you seen? The insides of speak-easies. If you don't mind my saying so, you could look around just as well from under the bed. Or maybe you have—I wouldn't necessarily be the one to know."

"This isn't going to be a lecture, is it?"

Her eyes filled, and she said, "Oh, God, there I go again. No, it isn't going to be a lecture. It's going to be a prelude to fun, fun, glorious fun; flaming youth making whoopee and dancing away the night. We'll drink champagne from my slipper, and watch the dawn come up like thunder out of Sheepshead Bay. We'll–"

"O.K., O.K.," he cut in. "We needn't run it into the ground."

She stopped, and nearby a man said, "I have fifty bucks that says Coolidge carries all forty-eight states."

"How can he get votes if he doesn't campaign?" another man said. "He hasn't even put his head out the window."

"He's got a theory that no candidate was ever hurt by not talking too much. I think he's right."

"I'm sure he'll beat Davis, but I'll bet you LaFollette carries Wisconsin."

"For fifty bucks?"

"For fifty bucks."

Dorothy turned to McClain. "Will you answer me one question?" she said.

"If I can," he replied, stirring his drink with his forefinger.

"How long does it take to look around?"

"What do you mean?"

"You said you want to 'look around' before you get married. Does that imply a month, a year, or a decade?"

"That's hard to say. When I got out of the Navy I told myself I was going to relax, and not let myself get pushed into anything. There'll be plenty of time for that later."

"Well, the war was over six years ago; do you think it's going to take another six years? Because I'm going to be getting long in the tooth pretty soon."

"I wouldn't say another six years, no. Just relax, and everything'll be all right."

"That's what they said to Marie Antoinette. 'Just relax, honey,' they said; 'put your head in this little slot here and count to three, and everything'll be all right.' Well, if she could do it I guess I can. In school they called me Spunky."

He laughed, and patted her hand. "That's more like it," he said. "I hate it when you're gloomy."

24

Christmas that year came on a Thursday, which effectively wiped out the latter part of the week as far as work was concerned. Most offices closed Wednesday noon, and while employees were required to show up for work on Friday, they went through the motions like sleepwalkers, waiting for the long and pointless day to end. Newspapermen were expected to be on the job at all times, on the indisputable theory that the earth continues to rotate regardless of religious calendars, and the minutiae of its rotation must be chronicled no matter what else may be going on. Of all the workers during the holiday week, press agents were the busiest, because with the decline of legitimate news more space became available for whatever people or projects it was their duty to publicize.

Business at the Circe was brisk the first part of the week, and then, come Wednesday afternoon, it was heavy. Marie had done her usual decorating, and Nick, in memory of their first Christmas, had persuaded the Salvation Army band to come in and play for the lunchtime customers. Butterworth, on his way to the train for Crestwood, dropped in for a stirrup cup and was greeted by the strains of "O Come, All Ye Faithful," rendered by fifty or sixty voices in assorted keys, accompanied by a trumpet, a trombone, and a French horn. Bogart, standing at the bar, saw him and laughed.

"How do you like my birthday party?" Bogart asked.

"What do you mean?" Butterworth replied. "Is this your birthday?"

"Tomorrow is. And for twenty-five years I've had to listen to someone else get all the applause. It's enough to turn a man into a Hindu."

"That calls for a drink. What'll you have?"

Bogart glanced at his cup and said, "I was having martinis, but now I guess I'd better switch to Scotch. I have to be home for dinner."

"Where's home?"

"A Hundred and Fourth Street, near Riverside Drive. Overshoot, and you land in the river."

"If I overshoot, I land in White Plains. I'll take the river any day." Butterworth ordered the drinks, then looked around and spotted MacDougall coming through the entrance. "Here's the quorum," he said. "Now we can get down to business."

"Why aren't you in Crestwood?" MacDougall asked, as he joined them at the bar. "I thought you'd be trimming a tree by now."

"I'm on my way," Butterworth replied. "There's plenty of time to trim a tree. Did you get the day off?"

"If they want me, they know where they can find me," MacDougall said. "You could fire a cannon through the city room and not even hit a copy boy."

"How did you make out on your Poets' Corner?" Bogart asked. "Did you manage to sign anyone up?"

"I got turned down by Amy Lowell, George Santayana, and Edwin Arlington Robinson," Butterworth replied. "Edna St. Vincent Millay said she liked the idea, but since she's only thirty-two she'd prefer to shop around a bit before making a final choice."

"Steve Benét is a poet," said Bogart. "So is his brother Bill. You might get one of them to play ball."

"He needs a name," said MacDougall. "Nobody's ever heard of the Benéts."

"By the time they're dead, they will," replied Bogart.

"This is immediate. The man's job hangs in the balance." To Butterworth, MacDougall said, "Maybe you'd better shoot for a dead one, like Longfellow. That at least will get some notice in the papers."

"I wouldn't know how to start," said Butterworth.

"Start with a letter to the Mayor of Boston. That'll get the ball rolling, and we can pursue it from there."

Bogart bought a round of drinks, and then MacDougall bought one, and when the cups were empty Butterworth looked at his watch. "I guess I have time for one more," he said.

"Of course you do," said Bogart. "It isn't even dark yet."

"How long does it take to trim a tree?" MacDougall asked. "It's so long since I've done it that I've forgotten."

"Depends on the size of the tree," said Butterworth. "A little one you can do in a jiffy. It also depends on how many ornaments you have. You have to put each one on separately."

"At our house we put 'em on with tweezers," Bogart said. "My father's a doctor."

"All I can remember is the smell of the tree," MacDougall said, closing his eyes. "It's the greatest smell in the world."

Butterworth looked at him for a moment, then said, "What are you doing tonight?"

"Me?" said MacDougall. "Nothing. I'll probably have dinner here, then stick around until they throw me out. If this gets dull I may go to Tony's, or someplace like that."

"How would you like to come to the country?"

"You mean for the night?"

"Sure. Have supper with us, trim the tree, then–whatever. Sing a few carols. You know."

"I'd love it, but what would your wife say? I mean, wouldn't I be crowding things?"

"Not in the least. You can sleep on the davenport in the living room, and nobody'll know you're there."

"Well, if you're sure–"

"Of course I'm sure. We'll finish this round, and head for the station."

"I ought to get your wife a present, or some flowers, or–"

"Oh, don't be silly. She'll be delighted to have you just as you are. You don't have to bring anything."

"Well, maybe I can find something in Grand Central. Candy, or some chewing gum. How's she fixed for Chiclets?"

Butterworth laughed. "I don't think she's ever had one in her mouth."

"They've started making a pink Chiclet that looks kind of festive. I don't know how it tastes."

"The kids would probably go for that. But I repeat—you don't have to worry about presents. Just relax, and we'll have an old-fashioned kind of Christmas."

Grand Central Station looked something like a monstrous Christmas package. Giant wreaths hung over the staircases, and the marble handrails were festooned with greenery, while the old DeWitt Clinton train, in the mezzanine, was bedecked with boughs of holly and balsam. Crowds of people, most of them carrying gaily wrapped packages, hurried through the concourse to the train gates, some helped by red-capped porters and others struggling to carry their burdens alone. These were the last-minute shoppers, and their lack of organization was evident in everything they did. Butterworth had done his shopping during the previous week, and his presents were contained in the overnight suitcase he'd bought for country visits, but MacDougall had nothing to carry, and it clearly made him uneasy.

"I really think I ought to bring something," he said. "Even if it's only a sprig of holly, or some mistletoe. Going out there with nothing, I feel like a bill collector."

"All right," said Butterworth. "If you insist, there's a florist around the corner. By the way, did you bring a flask?"

"No," said MacDougall. "Should I have?"

"Well, we'll see. She might have some medicinal whisky around, but I wouldn't bet on it."

"I'll just pop to the florist, and meet you at the train gate. O.K.?"

"O.K." MacDougall vanished, and Butterworth headed toward the lower level, wondering if this was as good an idea as it had at first seemed. It was too late to back out now, but he might be able to lessen the shock if he called Sarah to alert her. He went to a phone booth, gave the number to the operator, and put in twenty-five cents. There were three rings before Sarah answered.

"Hello?" she said, as though expecting bad news.

"Hi, there," Butterworth replied.

"Where are you?" Now she knew it was bad news.

"I'm in Grand Central."

"What train are you getting?"

"The 4:17. But what I called for—"

"It's almost that now. Shouldn't you be getting on?"

"I'm about to. I just thought I'd tell you I'm bringing Mac out with me."

There was a short silence, then she said, "Oh."

"He won't be any trouble, I promise. It's just that he had no place to go for Christmas, and God knows *I* wouldn't want to be alone on Christmas, so I asked him out. He can sleep on the davenport, and we can pretend he's not there."

"That'll be some pretending. The kids'll be down for their stockings about six."

"Well, we'll worry about that later. Maybe they can open their stockings quietly. My point is that nobody should be alone–"

"I know, I know. And it's very thoughtful of you."

"Do you have enough food? If you like, I can bring something out from–"

"We're fine, thank you. Just get here yourself, is all I ask."

"I will. Don't worry about that."

That went off better than I could have hoped, he thought, as he hung up. Maybe there's a lesson there: maybe if you announce things in advance you can save yourself a lot of grief, instead of waiting until it's a *fait accompli.*

He went to the train gate, noticing that the clock over the information booth showed 4:10, and he hoped MacDougall hadn't been caught in a last-minute crush at the florist's. He searched the crowd for a familiar face but saw nobody he recognized, and every time he looked back at the clock its minute hand had moved a notch or two forward. Finally, as two latecomers skittered across the floor and dashed through the gates, the trainman consulted his heavy gold watch, shouted "BoaRRD!" and closed the gates and switched off the overhead light. Then he cranked the list of stations out of sight and moved away, like an elephant looking for new grazing ground.

Butterworth went to the information booth, on the theory that MacDougall would go there when he realized the train had left, and he hadn't been there more than five minutes when MacDougall came down the marble staircase, part jumping and part toe-dancing, trying to make the best possible speed without falling down. He was clutching a red poinsettia plant in one hand and holding on to the stair rail with the other, and muttering apologies to those people he unavoidably bumped. Butterworth whistled to him and waved, and he came running to the booth.

"I'm sorry," he said, panting. "Am I too late?"

"There'll be another one in twenty minutes," Butterworth told him. "What happened–was the florist jammed?"

MacDougall breathed deeply several times, then said, "No, that wasn't too bad. But I figured I had time to pick up a bottle of Scotch from a tame druggist I know, and that was what took the time. He was doing a land-office business."

"Well, I'll call Sarah and tell her when to expect us," Butterworth said. "I won't be a minute." When he got Sarah, he said, "It looks as though it'll be the 4:45. Mac was delayed."

He could almost hear her jaw tighten, as she said, "All I need to know is one thing—will you be home for supper?"

"Of course we will! I just told you, we're getting the 4:45!"

"And a few minutes ago it was the 4:17."

"Well, Mac wasn't here then. He is now, and we'll get aboard as soon as they open the train."

"Where have you been—at the speakeasy?"

"I had lunch there, but that was a long time ago. Believe me, we're not going to miss this train."

"I'll believe you when I see you," she said, and hung up.

Well, so much for letting her know in advance, he thought, as he left the phone booth. I'd have been better off if we'd just showed up twenty minutes late and blamed it on a train breakdown.

Supper was, surprisingly, a cheerful meal. The children were full of the adrenaline of the season and were chattering on without saying much of anything, and Sarah was trying her best to make MacDougall feel at home. She radiated a charm that Butterworth had almost forgotten, and it occurred to him that life in the country was agreeing with her more than he'd imagined possible. When he compared her present mood with how she'd behaved in the city, he realized that it was worth any sacrifice to keep her where she was happy, and where she felt she was doing the best for the children. All other problems were secondary, and would have to remain that way.

After supper the children hung their stockings and then were put to bed, and when he'd heard their prayers Butterworth came down and joined MacDougall in the living room. MacDougall had poured himself a highball, and was contemplating the room as though deciding whether or not to buy it.

"I took the liberty," he said, indicating his drink. "Will you join me?"

"I don't mind if I do," Butterworth replied. "It's all in the spirit of the season." He took the bottle MacDougall had produced from his overcoat pocket and went into the kitchen and made himself a highball. Returning, he said, "Cheers and merry Christmas," and drank.

"Merry Christmas indeed," MacDougall replied. "And thank you for asking me. By the way, where's the tree? Weren't we going to decorate a tree?"

"I imagine she put it in the cellar," said Butterworth. "Let's look."

They found a five-foot tree in the cellar, and between them managed to wrestle it up through the kitchen and dining room into the living room. They knocked a coffee cup off a shelf in the kitchen and a candle off the dining room table, but MacDougall, who had his face in the boughs and was inhaling deeply, was unaware that anything had happened. "My God, that's a wonderful smell!" was all he said, over and over. They put the tree down in the living room just as Sarah appeared from upstairs. She was carrying a book in her hand, and she stopped when she saw the tree.

"Oh," she said. "Did you want to do the tree first?"

"What else?" Butterworth replied. "Where's the stand?"

"Would you join us in a drink?" said MacDougall. "I happen to have brought along some fine old Scotch, just off the boat."

"No, thank you," Sarah said.

"What was it you wanted to do before the tree?" Butterworth asked.

Sarah hesitated, then said, "Nothing, I guess," and tossed the book onto a table. "I'll get the stand and the ornaments." She left the room, and Butterworth recognized the book as *A Christmas Carol*. I hope she didn't think we were going to read that, he thought. He could imagine MacDougall twitching with boredom, his eyelids getting heavier, wanting a drink but not daring to interrupt the reading, and finally falling asleep in his chair. No—if she wanted a reading they could do it tomorrow, after MacDougall had left.

When, finally, the tree was trimmed, Sarah filled the children's stockings and then brought out a variety of colored packages and put them beneath the tree. Butterworth produced those presents he'd brought, and then Sarah got out the carpet sweeper and cleaned up the needles that had fallen from the tree in its progress from the cellar door. She retrieved the candle and threw the pieces of broken coffee cup in the garbage, while Butterworth and MacDougall freshened their highballs, after which Butterworth said to her, "I promised Mac we'd sing some Christmas carols. What should we sing?"

"That's up to you," she replied, putting the carpet sweeper away.

Butterworth turned to MacDougall and said, "What would *you* like to sing?"

"Let's sing 'O Little Town of Bethlehem,' " MacDougall replied. "That one always gets me."

They sang "O Little Town of Bethlehem" and "We Three Kings of Orient Are," and then Butterworth said, "Come on, honey, join in with us. What would you like to sing?" Before Sarah could say anything he went on, "I know. Let's sing 'Silent Night,' " so they sang "Silent Night" and Sarah joined them, in a muted contralto.

"Not too loud, or we'll wake the children," she said, when they'd finished.

"It'll do 'em good," Butterworth replied. "How many chances do they get to hear Christmas carols sung in the home?"

"Are you sure you won't join us in a drink?" MacDougall said to Sarah, and to Butterworth's astonishment she shrugged.

"Just a weak one," she said, and looked him straight in the eye as MacDougall went off to make the drink. When MacDougall brought it to her, she said, "Merry Christmas, all," and wet her lips, then set the glass down. "How about 'Good King Wenceslas'?" she said. "But remember—let's try not to wake the children."

Later, when MacDougall had been bedded down on the davenport and all the lights turned out, the Butterworths tiptoed up the stairs, checked the children, and made ready for bed. When at last they were settled down, Butterworth reached across and gently massaged the back of Sarah's neck.

"I can't tell you," he said, "how proud I am of you tonight."

"What for?" she replied, in a voice already half-clogged with sleep.

"For everything. For being so nice to Mac, for stringing along with everything—"

"I didn't do it for him," she said. "I did it mostly for you. I wanted you to know you still have a home you can come to. That is, if you want to."

"Of course I want to! It isn't that—"

"Mommy!" came Nancy's voice from the other room. "Has Santa Claus come yet?"

"Shhhh!" said Sarah. "Be quiet! No, he hasn't."

"When do you think he'll come?"

"I said be quiet! Go to sleep!"

"What time did he come last year?"

"Nancy, did you hear your mother?" Butterworth put in. "Go to sleep!"

There was silence, and then in a loud whisper Nancy said, "Mommy!"

"Shhhh!" said Sarah.

"Who's that with you?" Nancy hissed.

"It's Daddy! Who did you think it was?"

"I thought it might be Uncle Mark."

"Nancy, you've been dreaming! Now, go to sleep!"

There was a stuttering cough, and a yelp, and Puddin began to cry. Sarah flung herself out of bed, and for the next few minutes the only sounds were of her trying to quiet the children. When she returned, she pulled the covers over her ears and burrowed down among the pillows. Butterworth tapped her on the shoulder.

"One question," he said.

"Hmnf?" said Sarah.

"Who the hell is Uncle Mark?"

"I haven't the faintest idea. She must have been dreaming."

Butterworth turned the whole idea over in his mind, then decided there was nothing there to worry about, and went to sleep.

George MacDougall awoke with the sense that someone else was in the room. He heard gentle breathing, but the room was so dark that, except for the faint glow from a streetlamp outside, he could see nothing. At first he didn't know where he was, then his memory returned, but he still couldn't identify the extra presence. He craned his neck to look around and found himself staring into Nancy's wide-eyed face, no more than eight inches from his own. For a moment neither of them spoke, and then he said, "Hi," and Nancy vanished.

"Mommy, Mommy, Mommy!" she shrieked, as she pounded up the stairs. "Santa Claus is here! He finally made it! He's sleeping on the davenport! Come look!"

MacDougall heard the thump of feet on the floor above, and a barrage of harsh whispers, and finally there once again was quiet. He drifted back to sleep, and was awakened sometime later by what sounded like a rat in the Christmas wrappings. He thought of chasing it away, but the effort seemed too much and he knew it would eventually come back, so he put it down as a part of country living and went to sleep again. Shortly after six-thirty, when the first cold, gray light was beginning to show in the windows, Nancy's voice again cut into his consciousness, punctuated by loud shushing sounds from her parents, and then Puddin's name was mentioned, in increasingly shrill tones. Giving up any further attempt at sleep, MacDougall swung into a sitting position and saw Puddin, curled up like a chipmunk among the Christmas presents, surrounded by the paper he had torn trying to open them.

"I think I have your man down here," MacDougall called, reaching for his trousers. The rest of the family came down in various stages of undress, and only then did Puddin awake. He sat up and looked around him. Then he yawned.

"Is this all there is?" he asked.

MacDougall had to get a noon train back to town, and by the time he left, the living room had been cleaned up, the children were playing with their presents, and Sarah had started on Christmas dinner. "I'm sorry you have to leave," she said. "And I'm also sorry about all the confusion. You couldn't have had much sleep."

"It's the best Christmas Eve I ever had," he replied. "I can't thank you enough."

"I'll see you later on," Butterworth told him. "I'll probably get a late afternoon train."

Sarah looked at her husband. "We've been invited to the Thatchers' for supper," she said. "I more or less promised we'd be there."

Butterworth hesitated, then said, "O.K., then. I'll be in after supper."

"Wouldn't tomorrow morning do just as well?" Sarah asked. Her voice was neutral, and without emotion; she was simply asking a question, but Butterworth could sense a faint current beneath it, like a movement of water under ice.

"Well, we'll see," he said. "I've got a lot of work to catch up on."

Sarah didn't even pretend to believe him, and he decided to let the matter drop.

The children were put down for their naps after dinner, and Butterworth drifted about the kitchen in a vague attempt to help Sarah clean up. He picked things up and then, not knowing where they went, put them down again, and he seemed always to be standing in front of her when she was going somewhere. Finally he said, "Maybe I'd be better off out of your way," and started for the living room.

"Don't go," she replied. "I think it's time we had a talk."

He stopped. "About what?"

"About us."

"What about us?"

"Well–are we married, or aren't we?"

"Of course we're married! What a strange thing to say!"

"It's not so strange, considering the circumstances."

"I don't know what you're talking about."

"You live in New York and I live out here, and we get to see each other once a week, at the very most. What kind of marriage do you call that?"

"As I recall, it was your idea to move out here. You couldn't stand the city. I, on the other hand, can't make a living out here, so I have to live in the city. It's inconvenient, I grant you, but I don't see any other way to work it. Do you?"

"A lot of other men live out here and work in the city. It isn't as though there weren't trains, you know."

"How many of those other men have jobs that keep them until midnight or later? It'd be one thing if I got off at five o'clock, but you know as well as I do I can't. My life is all tied up in the theatre, and you simply cannot do that and commute."

"Now that you're your own boss, I should think you could set your own hours. It isn't as though you were still working for Brady."

"Now that I'm my own boss I have to work *more* than I did with Brady. Things are just beginning to get rolling for me, and I can't afford to let up for a minute."

"Is that why you spend so much time in the speakeasy?"

"Oh, for God's sake. In the first place I don't spend all that much time there, and in the second place a lot of the jobs I've got have come from my being there. I got the Brady job there, I got the mortuary job there; the first client I ever got came through a contact I'd made there–if I'd retired to the country after the *Trib* fired me, I'd now be digging ditches for the City of Yonkers. In this business, you have to go where things are happening."

Sarah scrubbed the corners of the roasting pan, then said, "So what do we do?"

"I don't see as we have any choice. Some day, if I make enough money, we may be able to work out a better way of living, but for now it's the money that counts, and I can't see any other way to do it."

"If I felt you wanted to come out it would be one thing, but I get the impression you feel put-upon every time you board the train. It feels as though you don't really want to see me."

"That's insanity! I love to see you! I love you! If I had my way I'd be with you all the time! It's just that it's impossible–can't you see that?"

"Yes, I can see it." She sighed, and added, "I guess, for the time being, that will have to do."

Supper at the Thatchers' was just about what Butterworth had expected. The Thatcher and Butterworth children ran in screaming orbits through the house; two vases and several toys were broken, and by the time the actual meal was on the table the children's exhaustion had deprived them of all appetite, and they pushed their food around their plates until it wound up either on the table, the floor, or their laps. Mark Thatcher lured Butterworth into the library, where they each had a short but satisfying shot of Scotch, and Violet Thatcher and Sarah spent most of their time in the kitchen, either preparing the food or clearing it away.

"The way I look at it," Thatcher said, as he and Butterworth refilled their glasses, "is, Christmas comes but once a year."

Butterworth waited for some corollary to follow this bit of wisdom, but none came, so he said, "How true," and wondered if he could catch the 8:47 back to town. His second Scotch relaxed him, and he decided he didn't want to give the impression he was hurrying.

He caught the 9:25.

25

The year 1925 started out deceptively slowly. New York City elected a new Mayor, one James J. Walker, a good-looking and affable man, who wore a top hat with grace and who seemed to bring the new spirit of the times to City Hall; Harold W. Ross, Walker's opposite in almost every respect, started a satirical magazine called *The New Yorker,* which almost died before it gained its feet; and, as the one big news story, Floyd Collins, a hitherto unheard-of spelunker, perished in a cave near Cave City, Kentucky, after frantic attempts to rescue him from beneath a fallen rock had been trumpeted throughout the world by the press and the infant radio industry. Calvin Coolidge, who, without opening his mouth in public, had defeated Democrat John W. Davis and Progressive Robert W. LaFollette the previous November, was inaugurated on March 4, in an aura of such total lassitude that the ceremony might as well have marked the opening of a Girl Scout cookie contest. Coolidge refined the philosophy of *laissez-faire* to its highest point: he took long naps every afternoon, got what exercise he felt necessary on a well-publicized electric horse, and, believing as he did that "the business of America is business," left everything to the businessmen to run as they saw fit.

The day before the inauguration, Dorothy Peters and McClain met at the Circe for lunch. She arrived first, and went to their usual table, and even as she sat down she felt uneasy: she felt as though she were seeing the room for the first time, or perhaps the last, and everything she saw took on a new dimension. She couldn't explain the feeling, because there was nothing visibly out of line, and he hadn't said anything unusual when he called her to make the lunch date. His voice had sounded preoccupied, but there was nothing new in that, and she finally put it down to nerves on her part. She was ten days overdue, and she could only hope to God she wasn't pregnant again. Getting rid of MacDougall's baby had been enough of a trauma; to have to go through it again would be almost more than she could stand.

She ordered a Scotch, and sipped it slowly while the room began to fill with people. She felt sure MacDougall would come in sooner or later, but she had no problem seeing him now; he was like a book she'd read long ago and had been fascinated with at the time, but now the pages were just so many blocks of type, unable to stir up any kind of emotion. But MacDougall didn't come in, and neither did Butterworth, and she wondered what could be going on that could keep those two from their spot at the bar. MacDougall, of course, might have an assignment, but for Butterworth the Circe was practically his office, and he must be either sick, or called to the country, or have had some similar disaster befall him, to keep him away.

Still McClain didn't come, and she ordered another Scotch and then began to worry. She saw him in the boudoir of some actress, trying to get dressed while she clung to him and begged him for just one more; then she saw him lying in a pool of blood in the street, run down and crushed by a fire engine, and a policeman going through his tattered wallet and finding a picture of her; and finally she saw him, one arm around Gloria Swanson's waist, slipping aboard the *Paris,* headed for Europe in the Honeymoon Suite, or *Suite de la Lune de Miel,* as the French would probably call it. She had worked herself into a fine jealous rage when at last she saw his face appearing through the crowd, and as he sat down she said, "Well, *you* certainly took your time."

"I'm sorry," he replied. "I had a customer–client–whatever you want to call it."

"I'll bet you did."

He looked at her. "What's that supposed to mean?"

"You should know better than I."

"Oh, cut it out."

"Cut what out? You said you had a customer, and I said I'll bet you did. What is there to cut out?"

"You're certainly feeling prickly today."

"That's a funny adjective, coming from you. Why'd you bother to put in the 'l'?"

McClain ordered a drink, and looked at her glass.

"Yes, please," she said. "If that look was intended to imply I've already had enough, you can forget it. To quote that gallant sea dog, John Paul Jones, I haven't yet begun to fight."

"That sounds ominous," McClain said. "What do you want to fight about?"

"*I'm* not the one who wants to fight. *You're* the one who was late."

McClain shook his head, as though to clear it. "Would you run through that again?"

"Forget it."

"I've already explained to you, I was late because I had a client. I can't walk out on a man with whom I'm doing business just because I have a luncheon date. I've got to work *some* time, you know."

"Are you implying that I'm interfering with your work?"

"Not implying, exactly."

"Then you're saying it."

"No, it's not that. It's just that there's nobody to whom I can delegate responsibility, so when I'm not in the office there's no business done. An engineer isn't like a broker, or a bank manager, who can let the underlings handle the work. I'm it. I'm the company."

"And when you're with me it's so much wasted time."

"I didn't say that. But it's sure as hell not getting any engineering done."

"Very well, then. I can take a hint." She started to rise, but he stopped her.

"Take it easy, for God's sake," he said. "Nobody asked you to go."

"I'd be the last one to want to get in the way of your success in business. I understand businessmen take their success very seriously."

"Sit down!" he said, and she did. "Now," he went on, "if I hadn't wanted to be with you, I wouldn't have come here. I enjoy—to put it mildly—being with you, but I don't enjoy fighting with you, and I didn't come here to fight. If that's what you want, then pick someone else; I want no part of it. Is that clear?"

"Perfectly," she said.

Their drinks arrived, and she sipped hers in silence.

"Now," said McClain, "would you like something to eat?"

"No, thank you. I'm not hungry."

"Do you mind if I have something?"

"By all means."

McClain ordered a steak sandwich and then, in an attempt to get the conversation going, said, "To think—by this time tomorrow, everything will have changed."

"What do you mean?" she said.

"Coolidge will have been inaugurated, and riots will sweep the nation. The Indian tribes will leave the reservations in mass buffalo hunts and, finding no buffalo except those on the nickels, will despoil the Treasury; bonus-crazed war veterans will rampage through the streets, and hordes of painted women from Schrafft's and Alice Foote MacDougall's will lay waste to every speakeasy in town. The carnage will be unbelievable."

Dorothy laughed. "What about the Visigoths?" she said.

"The Visigoths will be detailed to Westchester and Suffolk Counties. Special squads will rape and pillage in Oyster Bay, Great Neck, and the Hamptons, and the strewers of salt will cover Rye, Mamaroneck, and White Plains. There will, of course, be random raping and looting on the side."

"You paint a darling picture. I wish I could see it."

"Specially positioned motion-picture cameras will document the entire event. It will be history before your eyes, shown in a movie theatre—if, of course, there are any left."

"Are you sure you're not in the wrong business? I think DeMille could use you."

"My talents lie in many directions. It's just a matter of deciding which one to cultivate."

"That has a familiar ring to it."

"Everything is familiar. Everything's been done before." A busboy brought McClain's sandwich, and he ordered two more drinks and then said, "I hope you'll forgive me if I begin."

"Please," she said. "Stand not upon the order of your eating, but eat at once."

She finished her drink while McClain ate, and then she started on the new one. It was Tuesday, normally a slow day for the luncheon trade, but as she looked around the room it seemed to her that it was full of strangers. She recognized a few faces, none of which belonged to the regulars whom she knew, and she got the feeling that these people were here because it was the Place to Be. It irritated her, and it made her feel old, and she wanted to tell them all to go someplace else with their mindless chatter, and their smug looks of Having Made It just because they were at the Circe. Furthermore, she'd be willing to bet that no more than one in ten knew how to pronounce the name; most of them would say, "I was at the Circe for lunch," as though it rhymed with "purse." The hell with them. The hell with them all. She took a big swallow of her drink and looked at McClain, who was just finishing his sandwich.

"You know something?" she said. "You're funny."

"How's that?" he replied, dabbing at his mouth with a red-checked napkin.

"I can't make you out."

"Tell me what your problem is, and perhaps I can help you."

"First you say you don't want to settle down–you still want to look around a bit–and then you get all hot and bothered when it looks as though you might miss a few minutes of business. If that isn't being settled down I don't know what is, but if anyone were to *ask* you to settle down you'd say, 'Oh, I couldn't possibly–I still have to look at all the choices.' If you ask me, that's a load of total bullshit."

"It is two completely different things," McClain said, trying to control his voice. "What I do in business has nothing to do with my social life, and–"

"It seems to me it has everything to do with your social life, if it makes you forty minutes late for lunch."

"That's not the point! In business you have to be settled down to a *certain* extent, or you won't get any commissions. If I were to say maybe I'm an engineer and maybe I'm a dentist and maybe I'm a stockbroker, then nobody would know what I was and wouldn't come to me for anything, so I've got to say, God damn it, that I'm an engineer, and as such I'll do whatever jobs come my way. And if I'm going to do them I've got to *do* them, and not shove them aside for my spare time."

"Whereas you can shove me aside for any old time you happen to think of it."

"Oh, Jesus."

"That doesn't frighten me. You've got to call up bigger guns than that."

"I'll say one thing for you—you certainly know how to bitch up a luncheon engagement. If I'd known you were going to be like this, I'd have stayed at the office."

"Why didn't you? Another fifteen minutes would have made it a full hour, and you could say you forgot."

"There's no point going on with this conversation. Absolutely no point at all."

"I agree with you. And even if it were going to lead to something there'd be no point, because you know what? You're a lousy lay. You've got some idea that because you're good-looking that makes you a great lay, but I can tell you, Buster, I've been laid by toadstools that are better than you."

McClain rose without a word, put down his napkin, and left the room. As he threaded his way past the bar he thought he heard her call to him, but he neither looked around nor slowed down. He was out on the sidewalk before he remembered he hadn't signed the check, but by then it was too late to go back. I'll settle it up another day, he thought, and got in a cab and went to his office.

At the table, Dorothy sat absolutely still for about five minutes, and then quietly said, "I'm sorry. Oh, I'm sorry."

26

In the days following the raid, the Circe seemed, if anything, busier than ever. The fact that the Federals had been able to find no contraband gave the place an added aura, as though there were some divinity that protected it, and people felt safe just being there. A speakeasy in which one could feel safe was a rarity, and thus the Circe became doubly attractive to the public. The only person who was unhappy about this was Nick, who felt that the situation would lead to overcrowding, further notoriety, and, inevitably, another raid. Also, his recent beating had made him reluctant to be on the streets late at night, and he wished he could live in a place that was a little closer to his business. The obvious answer was to buy the whole building, but he didn't know if this was possible. He took the matter up with Frank DiMotto one day, when they were going over the accounts, and Frank agreed that it made sense.

"I'll get onto it," he said. "I'll let you know in a few days."

"Do those decorator people have a lease?" Nick asked.

"I assume so," said DiMotto.

"Then how do we get it?"

DiMotto gave him a long look. "You don't want to know," he said. "O.K.?"

"O.K.," said Nick, wishing he'd never brought the subject up.

"And for your information, those thugs who sandbagged you won't be giving you any more trouble."

"Oh," said Nick. "That's nice to know."

"For your information only."

"You bet." Nick had always known that DiMotto was part of a bootlegging group, but this sounded more like the Chicago gang wars than it did like simple bootlegging, and he wanted no part of it. One gangland killing always led to retaliation, and then to further killings until one side was wiped out, and that, to adapt the expression, was a hell of a way to run a restaurant. He tried to comfort himself with the thought that for everything you gain you also have to pay, but it didn't make him feel a great deal better. He told Marie about the new prospect later that night, omitting some of the more sordid implications.

"It looks as though you might get that new kitchen, after all," he said.

"Oh?" said Marie. "What's happened?"

"Frank thinks we should buy the whole building, and expand."

"I thought you said that would ruin the atmosphere."

"Well, it's either expand or have people crushed to death the way it is now. We just have more customers than we can handle."

She thought a minute, then said, "It does seem a shame. It's so homey now."

"I thought you were the one who wanted a bigger kitchen. You told me you and Louis were black and blue from bumping into each other."

"That was a joke. I was nervous."

"Of course, we can always expand around you, and keep the kitchen the size it is. Would you prefer it that way?"

"Of course not. I was just thinking of the *ambience.*"

"Well, I guess we'll have to think of the customers and let the *ambience* take care of itself."

He broached the subject to McClain the next day, when McClain came in for a drink around noon. Nick first asked how Dorothy Peters was, and when McClain said, "All right, I guess," Nick moved on to the subject of the enlargement of the premises.

"I'm not an architect," McClain replied, when Nick had outlined the plan. "I think you need an architect more than you do an engineer."

"Yes, but you forget one thing," said Nick. "If we have the bar down here, and the dining room on the second floor, we're going to need some fast way of dumping the liquor from the dining room in case of a raid. We need some sort of chute, or whatever, to throw it down. And we also ought to have a hidden service bar up there, so the guys aren't running from the basement to the second floor just for a glass of wine."

"I see your problem," McClain said. "I'll take it under advisement."

The front buzzer sounded, and in a minute Butterworth and MacDougall appeared. They were coatless, and seemed to bring a breath of spring through the door with them.

"What have you guys been doing?" McClain asked. "Running through the Park?"

"We've been deep in the drama," MacDougall replied. "How's Dottie?"

"You'd know better than I would," said McClain. "I haven't seen her since her dry dive."

"Oh," said MacDougall. "A rum Collins, please, Charlie."

"Make it two," said Butterworth. "Make mine a double."

"In other words," said McClain, "Mrs. Peters and I are no longer an item. All questions should be referred to the Information Desk. Now, what's this drama you've been delving into?"

"I finally got that play finished," MacDougall said. "Roly's read it and said he'll be in it. All I need now is a producer."

"I must be out of my mind," Butterworth said. "Hurry it up with that drink, Charlie. The sooner I fall unconscious the better."

"Have you showed it to a producer?" McClain asked.

"Lee Gottwald is reading it now. He said he'd let me know in a day or so."

"What part are you playing?" McClain asked Butterworth.

Butterworth was momentarily stricken mute, and MacDougall said, "It's sort of the lead, really. I wrote it with him in mind. What we want is a big-name leading lady, to play opposite him."

"Insanity," Butterworth muttered, taking the drink Charlie put in front of him. "Total, wild-eyed insanity."

"What are you going to do about your clients?" McClain asked.

Butterworth shrugged. "Until we go into rehearsal–if we do–I'll keep with them. After that, we'll just have to see."

"And your Poets' Corner?"

Butterworth glanced at MacDougall and said, "I seem to have blown that one. It was doing all right until we tried to get the Mayor of Cambridge to ship Longfellow down to us. He wasn't amused."

"That was my fault," MacDougall put in. "Although I must say it seemed like a good idea at the time."

"So what happened?"

"So I got fired," Butterworth said. "But then, what the hell." He took another pull on his Collins and appeared to relax slightly.

"Is it all right to ask what this play's about?" McClain said.

Butterworth closed his eyes, and MacDougall said, "Well, it's a sort of murder story, but with a few laughs." He touched his knuckles to the bar and said, "A lot of laughs, I hope. This guy gets involved in a murder plot, and rumrunners and gangsters and you name it."

"Sounds like a nice trick, if you can pull it off."

"Well, that'll be up to Roly. He's the one that gets the laughs." Another gentle knock on the bar.

"I wish you'd stop saying that," Butterworth said. "Can't you tell people I'm just a butler, or something?"

"Stop worrying–you'll be great. I told you, all you have to do is be yourself."

"So long as they don't mind me as myself strangled with stage fright."

"Everybody has stage fright. Some of the biggest stars throw up opening night." The buzzer sounded, and in a couple of moments Bogart entered the room. "Here's the man who can tell you," MacDougall said. "Humph, what do you do to get over stage fright?"

"Shoot yourself," Bogart replied.

"Thanks," said Butterworth. "That's just what I wanted to hear."

"Who's got stage fright?" Bogart asked. MacDougall explained, and Bogart bared his teeth in a wide smile. "Well, what do you know?" he said. "Our boy is going to be a thespian!"

"This one time only," said Butterworth.

Bogart laughed. "We'll see," he said.

Gottwald called MacDougall two days later and said he'd like to produce the play. "I figure I can bring it in for five thousand," he said. "A lot depends on who we get to play the dame."

"Who were you thinking of?" MacDougall replied, not yet sure he wasn't hallucinating.

"The way I look at it, you should always start at the top," Gottwald replied. "Then you got plenty of room to maneuver, and by opening night you won't find yourself hiring Chinese."

"Who would you say is the top?" MacDougall asked.

"There's several up there. Ethel Barrymore, Laurette Taylor, Minnie Maddern Fiske–I've sent it to Barrymore already, and then we'll see. There's always Gladys Cooper, but I think she's doing something in London. Jeanne Eagels ought to be through with *Rain* any year now, and if Ina Claire isn't doing anything she'd be a good bet. Like I said, there's a lot of choice. As for the man, the country bumpkin–"

"I've already got someone for that," MacDougall cut in. "I wrote the part for him."

"Oh? Who?"

"His name is Roland Butterworth. He–"

"There's a press agent named Butterworth. Used to work for Brady."

"That's the one. He's–"

"Has he ever done any acting?"

"That's not the point. The point is, I wrote the part with him in mind."

"Look, George, you could have wrote the part with Cal Coolidge in mind, but that don't mean he's gonna act in it."

"I know. But I've seen Roly act–in an informal sort of way–and I know he'll be good. I'm sure of it."

"Well, I'm not sure I want to lay out five thou–"

"Do me just one favor. Hear him read, and then if you don't agree you can get whomever you want. O.K.?"

Gottwald sighed. "O.K.," he said. "As a last resort, I suppose he can be an understudy."

MacDougall ran into Butterworth that night at the Circe and said, "What are you doing tomorrow afternoon?"

"What time?" Butterworth replied.

"Oh, say around three o'clock."

"Nothing special. Why?"

"Gottwald would like to have a look at you."

"Why?"

"He's never met you. He'd like to see what you look like. I guess he'd also like to hear you talk."

"You mean this is a reading? A tryout?"

"It's nothing of the kind. If he has to cast a woman to play opposite you, he's got to know what you're like."

Butterworth considered this, then said, "You know, I've been thinking. It's all very well to—"

"Just stop thinking and do as you're told," MacDougall cut in. "Actors aren't supposed to think."

"That's just it. I'm not an actor."

"Let Gottwald be the judge of that."

Butterworth began to crack his knuckles, pulling each finger until it made an audible click. "I thought this was supposed to be a free country," he said.

"Shut up and have a drink," said MacDougall. "But don't have any before you see Gottwald, and for God's sake stop doing that to your hands."

Butterworth had one drink before going to Gottwald's office, and as he mounted the dusty, creaking stairs it suddenly came to him that he had nothing to worry about: if he didn't qualify for the part the whole silly idea would be over, and he could go back to being a press agent. He'd never wanted to be an actor in the first place; it had all been MacDougall's idea, and this was his chance to show how wrong it was. Feeling ten years younger, he all but ran up the remaining stairs, and entered Gottwald's office without knocking. Gottwald and MacDougall were sitting with scripts in front of them, and in a corner a mouse-colored woman was going through a filing cabinet. Gottwald was short and stocky, and was hunched down as though expecting the ceiling to fall. His nose and cheeks were cobwebbed with red and blue veins. MacDougall made the introductions, and Gottwald stared at Butterworth for a while without speaking. Butterworth returned the stare, almost but not quite smiling. If he thinks he's going to make me nervous he's got another think coming, he said to himself. Just let him try, and see what happens.

"All right," Gottwald said, at last. "I assume you've read the script."

"That's right," Butterworth replied.

"Would you mind going through a couple of sides, just so's I can hear you?"

"Not in the least." Butterworth took the script Gottwald handed him, and MacDougall read the cue lines from his script. As he read, Butterworth remembered that the lines had been written with him in mind, and it fascinated him to see another person's impression of how he talked. To give MacDougall credit, the lines came easily, and there were no false notes or awkward phrases. They read through to the end of the scene, and then Butterworth smiled and handed the script back. Gottwald's fingers opened and closed, but the rest of him remained immobile and silent.

"I'll be a son of a bitch," he said finally. "He's a natural."

"I told you," said MacDougall.

"I'd like to see him do it from a stage." Then, to Butterworth, "Can you project your voice?"

"I don't know," said Butterworth. "I never tried."

Gottwald gave a wintry smile. "We can take care of that," he said. "If it doesn't carry, we can get a voice coach."

All at once, Butterworth's insecurity began to return. "Wouldn't you rather have a regular actor?" he said.

Gottwald laughed. "Regular actors are a dime a dozen," he said. "But to get one who doesn't know he *is* one—that's something that happens once in a lifetime."

Butterworth's next problem was breaking the news to Sarah. He thought of waiting until Sunday, when he was in Crestwood, but he had the feeling that his visits to Crestwood tended to wind up in some form of argument, or tension, and he'd like if possible to make the day a cheerful one. The Sunday after the raid, when they'd gone to the Thatchers' to see the children's play, had been an unmitigated disaster: Puddin had thrown up during the performance; Nancy and one of the Thatcher children had taken to fighting over a tennis racquet; Sarah, in trying to clean up after Puddin, had upset an end table and broken a lamp; and when Mark Thatcher and Butterworth retired to the library for a quick shot of whisky, they were accused by their spouses of being louts and cowards. The Butterworths' return home was made in almost total silence, broken only by Nancy's sobs and Puddin's spasmodic whining.

So, rather than risk spoiling the upcoming Sunday with what was sure to be an unpopular announcement, he decided to make it over the telephone, where a broken connection could always be simulated if things got too rancorous. He went to the Circe and stood at the bar, trying to figure out the best method of approach. He had to tell the truth, and at the same time skirt as best he could the dangerous areas, such as what they were going to live on once he started rehearsals. MacDougall entered the room, and slid alongside him at the bar.

"What did I tell you?" MacDougall said.

Butterworth shook his head. "It beats the hell out of me," he replied. "How would you like to break the news to Sarah?"

"No, thanks. I'm going to have enough trouble with the paper."

"How are you going to work it?"

"I'm going to do both things as long as I can, and then I guess I'll ask for a leave of absence. If they won't give it to me, I'll quit."

"It occurs to me," Butterworth said slowly, "that we're both putting ourselves fairly far out on a limb. If this thing flops, we're in deep trouble."

"Never even think it may flop," MacDougall replied. "Always assume it'll be a success."

"I heard there are going to be between forty and fifty musicals on Broadway this season. Do you mean to tell me they're all going to be successes?"

"No, but their producers think they are."

Butterworth ordered another drink, and one for MacDougall. "The least I can do is pay for your drink," he said, when MacDougall started to protest. "For better or for worse, you've probably changed my life."

He thought of calling Sarah from the pay phone in back, then realized he'd probably run well over the allotted three minutes and couldn't be punctuating his conversation by dropping change into the box. He signed the check, told MacDougall to wish him luck, and went back to his room at the Seymour.

Sarah answered on the first ring, and knew immediately that something unusual was afoot. He generally called only once a day, in the morning, and to hear from him at four-thirty in the afternoon was an ominous sign. "What's happened?" she asked.

"What do you mean?" Butterworth replied. He'd hoped to start the call in a casual manner, but that was no longer possible. "You sound as though I were calling with bad news."

"Aren't you?"

"Why must it be bad? Isn't it possible I might call with some good news as well?"

"I suppose it's possible, yes."

"Well, this is good news. At least *I* think it is. I'm going to be in Mac's play."

There was a silence, and then Sarah said, "Why?"

"Well, Mac wanted me to, and I talked with the producer and he thinks I'd be good in it, and–well–you never can tell. It might be a lot more money than I'm making now."

"How much?"

"We haven't discussed salary yet, but I wouldn't be surprised if I got two or three hundred a week. Of course some actors get a lot more than that, but I'm not really an actor."

"Oh, I don't know."

"Anyway, we don't go into rehearsal for several weeks, so there's plenty of time to make plans. I just thought you should be the first to hear."

"That's very sweet of you. Would this mean you'd be traveling around the country?"

"Not that I know of. We might go to New Haven first, or Boston, but certainly no farther than that."

"It all sounds quite exciting."

Butterworth, having braced himself for an argument, now found he had nothing more to say. "Well, there it is," he said. "I just thought you'd like to know."

"Who else is going to be in it?"

"I don't know yet. I don't even know who the director is. Gottwald–that's the producer–has sent the script to Ethel Barrymore, but so far hasn't had any reaction."

Sarah laughed. "Oh, my," she said.

"What?" said Butterworth.

"To think of you in greasepaint. I'll hardly know you."

"I take it off when I leave the theatre. You won't have to worry about the pillowcases."

"That, my love, was the least of my worries."

There was a short pause, then Butterworth said, "I'll talk to you tomorrow," and hung up, feeling, for reasons he couldn't explain, faintly uneasy. He did clients' work the rest of the afternoon, then went to the Circe for dinner, and was back in his room in bed by ten-thirty. He didn't get to sleep until around two.

27

As Gottwald had suspected, the first six actresses on his list were unavailable: Ethel Barrymore returned the script with a charming note saying she'd just signed a contract with another producer, Laurette Taylor was contemplating doing a play in England, and Mrs. Fiske had been told by her doctor to rest her voice for at least six months; Gladys Cooper was in fact in London, Jeanne Eagels was still playing in *Rain,* and Ina Claire said that, although she loved the script, she was anxious to try her hand at a musical rather than a straight comedy. It was a season when the plays very nearly outnumbered the actors, and the actors could afford to be choosy. One of the biggest hits was a musical called *Garrick Gaieties,* in which all the performers were unknowns and the music and lyrics were done by a couple of youths named Richard Rodgers and Lorenz Hart, who had scored a Columbia University Varsity Show but had never had their work produced professionally before. The play opened in May of 1925, a risky time in view of the lack of adequate cooling facilities; it survived a June heat wave and went on to play for a total twenty-six weeks. Among the unknowns in the cast were Sterling Holloway (who sang "Manhattan"), Libby Holman, and Lee Strasberg. One reviewer called it "the most civilized show in town."

MacDougall's play had hitherto been untitled, and at Gottwald's insistence he set out to find a name that would be euphonious, descriptive, and, if possible, provocative. Gottwald's point was a valid one, which was that an untitled play carries with it a tentative air, suggesting impermanence and indecision, which tends to make an actor wary. Too many actors have taken parts that, during the inevitable rewriting, have been dropped from the play, and the experienced ones develop a nose for the soft spots, the lack of a title being a particularly ominous one.

MacDougall handed the problem to Butterworth at the bar at the Circe, adding that the sooner they came up with something the better. "He doesn't want to send it out again until we've got a title," he said. "And people are already being signed up for next fall."

Butterworth thought a moment, then said, "What about *Out of the Frying Pan?*"

"Too long," replied MacDougall. "He wants to keep it crisp."

"Oh. Then try *Murder, My Dear.*"

"Not bad. Let's make a list." He took a piece of folded copy paper from his pocket and wrote down the title. "It's not quite right," he said, looking at what he'd written. "What about *Fast Company?*"

"Write it down," said Butterworth.

They had listed six titles when Albert Hopkins appeared beside them at the bar. "Playing word games?" he asked.

"In a way." MacDougall explained the problem, and Hopkins sipped the drink he'd been carrying with him. "You say this woman plants a bomb in her husband's office?" he said.

"She causes it to be planted," MacDougall replied.

"What about *Pop! Goes the Husband?*"

"My God!" said MacDougall. "I think he's got it!"

"You're wasting your time on Wall Street," Butterworth said. "You should be in the writing game."

"I'd thought of it," Hopkins replied, "but it always seemed like too much work. In my business, you just sit back and let the money roll in."

"I'd always thought it was more complicated than that," said Butterworth.

"A well-trained chimpanzee can do what I do. It's just a matter of not rocking the boat."

Butterworth looked at MacDougall. "Maybe we should remember that," he said, "just in case—"

"Don't say it!" MacDougall cut in. "There is no 'just in case' here!

With a title like this, we can't lose." He rapped his knuckles on the bar.

"People on the Street are superstitious too," Hopkins observed. "I never in all my born days saw such a list of do's and don'ts. Don't sell if the quoted figure is divisible by five–don't buy if you can't see the Palisades–don't buy if the cleaning woman appears wearing a derby hat–you can't imagine all the mumbo-jumbo that goes on."

"I thought you just sat back and let the money roll in," Butterworth remarked.

"I do," said Hopkins. "I don't pay any attention to all that nonsense."

Gottwald sent the newly titled script to Lillian Marchbanks, an ingenue of a few seasons back who was trying to make a graceful transition into the more mature, or character, parts, and she accepted immediately. She was in a sense preferable to the others, in that her name was still recognized but she was not going to hold out for an unreasonable sum of money, and he figured he could pay her $500 a week and Butterworth $300, and still hold to his $5,000 budget. He reasoned that if *Garrick Gaieties,* with an unknown cast and an eleven-piece orchestra, could come in for $5,000, then he, with only one name player and no music, should have no trouble doing the same. His director, a onetime actor named Croswell Garnett, could be relied on to get the best possible performance out of Butterworth with the least possible strain. Garnett remembered the various insecurities that bedeviled actors and always tried to be as encouraging as he could. In Butterworth's case, the only problem would be in making sure that everyone in the house could hear him.

The first reading took place on Monday, August 17, under an unshaded work light on a bare stage. The company, looking about as theatrical as so many druggists, sat on folding chairs in a semicircle facing Garnett, while Gottwald sat off in a corner with his hat over his eyes, and the assistant stage manager scurried about with Dixie cups full of coffee.

"All right," Garnett said, when everyone had been introduced. "We'll go through it once, just for the words. Don't try to do any acting."

That's a good one, Butterworth thought, as he opened his script and folded the cover back. Don't try to do any acting–I couldn't act if I had a loaded shotgun pointed at me. What am I going to do when he says, "Now begin to act"? Maybe a dead faint would be the simplest way out of the whole thing.

The reading went on for what seemed like a long time, and at the end Garnett said, "Are there any questions?"

Lillian Marchbanks held up her hand. "Just one thing," she said. "It seems to me that when I tell Rodney to go downtown I ought to be a bit more devious. As it stands, even the dullest lout would know I'm up to something."

"I assume it would be in how you played it," Garnett replied.

"But the words are wrong. I can't say those words without giving the whole thing away."

"Well, we'll ask the author about it later."

"Where is the author, anyway? Does he assume his words are chiseled in marble and can never be changed?"

"The author is currently employed by the New York *Herald Tribune*. At this stage in the game, he isn't too necessary here."

"It's only the play I'm thinking of, mind you. I don't give a damn what the author does with his time."

"I think you'll see enough of him before we open," Garnett said quietly.

They went through the play again, this time putting some feeling into the lines, and after Butterworth's first speech Garnett said, "Excuse me—could you read that the way you did the first time?"

"I guess so," said Butterworth, and gave it a flat, disinterested reading.

"That's it," said Garnett. "Keep it that way. All right, let's go on."

I'm damned, Butterworth thought. Is that all there is to acting?

It turned out there was a good deal more, which he found out as rehearsals progressed. There was also the interplay of personalities, which in some cases produced tension that crackled in the air like summer lightning. Rodney Lupin, an actor who played one of the rumrunners, had at first seemed simply to be a quiet, introspective young man, but it turned out he was seething with rage a good deal of the time. At what, no one was quite sure, but it burst through the surface at one rehearsal, when Arthur Chiswick, who played another rumrunner, nudged Lupin in the ribs. Lupin stamped his foot, and his face turned red.

"Will you *stop* that?" he said. "It drives me *crazy!*"

"It's just a piece of business," Chiswick replied. "Nothing personal."

"Is it in the script?" said Lupin. "Show it to me in the script, or else keep your elbows to yourself!"

"Would you prefer I pinched you?"

"All right, let's get back to work," Garnett put in, before Lupin could reply. "Arthur, instead of nudging him, try just snapping your fingers."

"Under his nose?" said Chiswick hopefully.

"No, just snap them. All you're trying to do is get his attention."

"In which I have succeeded beyond my wildest dreams," said Chiswick, and they started the scene again.

The play didn't begin to take form until the actors had memorized their lines and were working without scripts, and then it became apparent that there was a sag in Act II. The action stopped, and the actors just stood around and talked, and the momentum that had been building since the opening curtain was lost. At the end of rehearsal Garnett took MacDougall aside, and outlined the problem. "You've got to have some Rome burning," he concluded. "You've got to plant a firecracker under a chair, to give suspense. Do you know what I mean?"

"I think so," MacDougall replied. "I'll give it a whirl."

For the next three days the actors rehearsed the first and third acts while MacDougall rewrote the second, and by the end of the week the new pages were Mimeographed and handed out. MacDougall had asked the paper for a leave of absence, which had been denied, so he quit his job and was able to devote all his time to the play. As it turned out, all his time was just barely enough: with the improved second act there appeared to be a bad letdown in Act III, and when Act III had been strengthened it made Act I look weak and uninteresting. There developed an apparently endless round of strengthening, shoring up, and general rewriting, until the actors were blurry from learning new lines and forgetting old ones, and whatever cohesion the play had once had began to come unraveled.

In the circumstances, with things changing from day to day, everybody began to have ideas for new lines. In one scene Lillian Marchbanks was supposed to say to Butterworth, "When you left the farm did you ever dream that New York would be like this?" a line which she changed to read, "What was on your mind when you left the farm?"

"Hold it," Garnett said. "Let's read it the way it was written."

"It's stupid the way it was written," Lillian replied. "This way, the line has much more depth."

"Would you let us in on your secret?" MacDougall said, from the seats. "In what way is this line deeper than the original?"

"It's open to more interpretations," Lillian said. "It's a sure laugh line."

"Are you looking for laughs in every line?"

"Well, somebody's got to get them. God knows they're not in the script."

"The audience will be the judge of what's funny and what isn't," Garnett put in. "For the moment, let's stick with what's on paper."

The assistant stage manager, who always wore sneakers on the job, appeared onstage and held up his hand. "May I make a suggestion?" he said.

"What?" said Garnett.

"What if the whole scene were played in bed? That would cut down on all the moving around, and the audience could concentrate on the lines."

"An interesting thought," Garnett replied. "I'll bear it in mind."

The assistant stage manager vanished as silently as he had come, and Sergei Vassilov, the set designer, who was sitting next to MacDougall in the fourth row, leaned over and whispered, "You've got to say one thing for that man—this is no surface stupidity. This goes bone deep."

A further complication was caused by Justin Hadley, who played the part of Lillian Marchbanks's husband. Since he was killed at the end of the first act he had only one solid scene, and he was of several minds as to how to play it. "I'm not sure of my motivation," he said, discussing the scene with MacDougall and Garnett. "I don't know why I do what I do, so I don't know how to play it."

"You do it because it's there in the script," said MacDougall, who had spent most of the night doing rewrite, and whose patience was becoming jagged around the edges. "What more do you want to know?"

Hadley looked at him with an expression that mingled pity and contempt. "If there is no 'why,' there's no point in my playing it," he said. "Just as one instance, the place where I ask her to bring me some nuts from the pantry. Why do I ask her? Do I want to get rid of her? What's my motivation?"

"Your motivation is you want some nuts," MacDougall replied.

"You mean I'm *hungry?*" Hadley's voice expressed total disbelief.

"You've got a drink, and you want some nuts to go with it. What's so strange about that?"

Hadley rolled his eyes heavenward. "I mean, really," he said.

"I have an idea," said Lillian Marchbanks. "Suppose when he asks me for the nuts, I give him a look and say—"

"No," MacDougall cut in. "I know what you're going to say, and the answer is no."

"I'm only thinking of the play," Lillian said, and turned away.

Finally, a week before they were to open in New Haven, the script was, so to speak, locked in; there were to be no more changes. This allowed the actors to concentrate on their performances, but there was also a feeling of incompleteness, a sense that something that should have been done had been left undone, although by this time nobody had the perspective to analyze what it was. Everything now depended on timing, prayer, and the hope that the critics would be in a good mood.

The New Haven opening started well; there were early laughs, and the audience seemed to be enjoying themselves, but somewhere about halfway through the second act the laughs began to taper off, and the third act was played to almost total silence. There was perfunctory applause at the end, but nobody could disguise the fact that the play had laid an egg. The reviews confirmed this, and the following day Lillian Marchbanks handed in her notice, to take effect in two weeks. Gottwald, Garnett, and MacDougall met in Gottwald's suite in the Taft Hotel to decide whether to fold the play immediately or try to make emergency repairs and hope for a miracle in New York. Gottwald was all for closing it, but Garnett demurred.

"I still think we have a chance," he said.

"Give me one reason," said Gottwald.

"Get rid of the coroner scene," Garnett replied. "The coroner's description of what the bomb did to Justin kills every laugh thereafter."

"That's a good scene," MacDougall protested. "They'll eat it up in New York."

"They didn't eat it up last night. They spat it out, and quit laughing."

"This is New Haven. People in New York are used to that sort of thing—it's part of their life."

Garnett shrugged. "It's your play," he said. "But I counted the laughs after the coroner scene, and it was like going over Niagara Falls in a barrel. Vroom!" He made a nose-dive motion with his hand.

"I think we ought to close it now," Gottwald said. "Take our bath, and forget the whole thing ever happened."

MacDougall thought a moment. "I tell you what," he said. "Play it the way it is tonight, and if the same thing happens we'll cut the scene. O.K.?"

Garnett looked at Gottwald. "O.K. with me," he said.

Gottwald spread his hands. "What the hell," he said. "Five thousand here, five thousand there—all right. See what happens."

At the same time, Butterworth was on the phone to Sarah, telling her of the disaster. "We may fold tonight, or we may play out the week," he concluded. "In either case it doesn't make much difference. We're as good as dead."

"Oh, love, I'm sorry," she said.

"I'm not. I should have known better than to get involved in the first place. I should have known better than to come to New York."

There was a pause, then she said, "What do you mean?"

"Just that. I've bitched up everything I've tried to do. I never should have left Massachusetts."

"Isn't it a little late to think about that?" Her voice took on a cautious note of hope.

"It's never too late. If I had my way, we'd go back tomorrow. But I guess that's neither here nor there. I'll call you when we get to New York."

"Might you even be able to come out to the country?"

"Not if we're still playing. We'll just have to see."

"I guess that's always the answer. We'll just have to see."

"I guess it is. But I'm not kidding—find me a job on a farm, and I'll jump at it."

"I'll see what I can do."

The house that night was only about half full, and the laughs were sparse to begin with, but following the coroner scene the reaction was almost hostile. About a dozen people left at the next intermission, and more walked out during the third act, until by the final curtain there were less than a hundred people in the house. Garnett assembled the company onstage when the work lights came on.

"All right," he said. "This will be our last night in New Haven.

We're going to make one more change—a relatively simple one—and I've the feeling we may have a different story in New York. We'll have a run-through in New York on Thursday, by which time the change will be ready. This is not, believe me, the end of the world; I wouldn't be surprised if it was just the beginning." He then took aside the actor who played the coroner, and as gently as possible told him he needn't bother to come to the run-through in New York. The actor looked stunned, but also faintly relieved.

For Butterworth, opening night in New York was like a fever dream, with bright lights and gong-like echoes and the surging sounds of laughter, which washed over him like surf. He was unaware that he was acting; he was picked up and carried along by the audience reaction, and when, at the end, it was time for the curtain calls, he was astonished to hear cheers when he stepped forward. This is insane, he kept telling himself. This kind of thing just doesn't happen. At last the curtain fell for the final time, and Lillian Marchbanks was kissing him and Garnett was kissing him, and he tottered back to his dressing room in a state of numbed disbelief. Sarah had come to the show with the Thatchers; Mark Thatcher congratulated him and said, "Next thing we know you'll be playing Hamlet," and Sarah kissed him, crying uncontrollably. Then the Thatchers went back to Crestwood, and Sarah joined him at a cast party to wait for the reviews. She had managed to stop crying, but she couldn't think of much to say; she held his hand tightly, as though she might fall through the floor if she let go.

"A new comedy star lit up the Broadway sky last night," was the way the *Herald Tribune* review opened, and the reviewer then went on to compare Butterworth with Keaton, Chaplin, and Harold Lloyd. The *Times* was equally complimentary although less euphoric, and commented that the team of MacDougall as writer and Butterworth as actor was one of those natural phenomena that occur, like spontaneous combustion, for no visible reason but with incendiary effect. The *News* called the play "a wow"; the *American* thought it "one of the funniest plays to come down the pike in a long time," and the *Mirror* commented that Lillian Marchbanks was "a dish for whom any man would gladly sin." Even *Variety,* which had slaughtered the play in New Haven, remarked that "some alchemy has been worked, which turned a turkey into a b.o. smash."

Sarah had arranged for a woman to stay overnight with the children, and after the cast party she returned with Butterworth to his room at the Seymour. He was wide awake, full of adrenaline and a certain amount of Scotch, but she suddenly felt as though a plug had been pulled somewhere, and all her strength had drained away. She was barely able to get into bed before she fell asleep, and Butterworth sat up and had a final nightcap by himself.

He slept until about eleven o'clock next morning, and when he awoke the first thing he saw was a note on the dresser. He picked it up and read:

Dearest–

I figured the sleep would do you good, so I didn't wake you when I left. I promised Mrs. T. I'd be out before noon. Do you still feel like leaving N.Y.? Call me when you wake up.

x
S.

He made some coffee, then put through a call to Crestwood. There was no answer, so he got dressed, and headed for the Circe for lunch. I'll call her later on, he thought. She's probably got the kids out at the market with her now. He remembered her description of her trips to the market, with Puddin riding in the express wagon while Nancy pulled, and it suddenly occurred to him that, if the play lasted as long as seemed likely, he'd be able to buy Sarah an automobile. My God, he said to himself, I never thought I'd know what it's like to be rich; there could be some very pleasant times in store here. He started to whistle, and he was still whistling as he went into the Circe and was greeted by cheers from the people at the bar.

28

The next two years passed in a sort of euphoric haze. Butterworth felt that he was stepping from one cloud to another, and everywhere he went he was recognized. The play ran for a full year, and by the time it closed MacDougall had written another one, in which Butterworth received star billing. Scripts were sent to him in such numbers that he couldn't read them all, and he asked Albert Hopkins, his Wall Street friend from the Circe, if he'd like to help out by looking them over in his spare time. "After all," Butterworth told him, "you were the one who named the first play, so you have a certain stake in all this."

"It's funny you should mention it," Hopkins replied. "I was thinking of pulling out of Wall Street completely, and this would give me something to do."

"Why pull out?" Butterworth asked. "Why not sit around and rake in the money as well?"

"I have a feeling that time has about passed," Hopkins said. "I think it's being run by nothing but greed, and that can lead to trouble."

They were standing at the bar in the newly enlarged Circe, which to Butterworth had lost a good deal of the charm of the earlier place. What had been makeshift decor was now a conscious attempt to be cozy, and there was a gloss to everything that fairly shouted success.

A speakeasy should never look successful, Butterworth thought. It should always look as though it was about to be raided, because the furtive atmosphere was part of its appeal. For the rest of the public, however, merely being allowed in was a sign of their own success, and they came in such numbers that the place was just as crowded as it had been in one room. McClain's mechanism for dumping liquor was so successful that, short of blasting, the Federals would have had no way of finding the stock, and they contented themselves with raiding establishments that would produce a little more in the line of publicity.

And publicity—that is, selective newspaper reporting—was a burgeoning phenomenon, in that it could set its sights on a certain person or event and blow it up out of all proportion to its actual worth. Rudolph Valentino's death, in August of 1926, set off a period of distaff hysteria that was nurtured and magnified by the newspaper reports, and when, on April 10 of that year, a fifty-one-year-old character known only as "Daddy" Browning married fifteen-year-old Frances Bell Heenan, otherwise known as "Peaches," the more lurid of the tabloids outdid themselves in salacious and speculative reporting, to the point where the marriage, a flimsy arrangement at best, was a total shambles by October. Single-handed, the *Daily Mirror* got the Hall-Mills case reopened and Willie Stevens brought to trial, but there was no more evidence than before, and the DeRussey's Lane murders went unsolved. The Ruth Snyder–Judd Gray case was something else again: they were convicted, first in the papers and then in court, of the murder of Ruth's husband, Albert, and a news photographer with a camera strapped to his ankle managed to get a shot of Ruth in the electric chair just as the current hit her. It occupied the entire Page 1 of the *Daily News,* under the headline: "DEAD!"

There were, of course, more legitimate news stories, such as Lindbergh's flight to Paris in May of 1927, but his subsequent return, along with such lesser events as Gertrude Ederle's swimming of the English Channel and the Prince of Wales's visit to the United States, were trumpeted by the publicity people until whole forests of newsprint were consumed in their reporting. Writing in *Vanity Fair,* Walter Lippmann remarked that "The [publicity] machine itself is without morals or taste of any kind, without prejudice or purpose, without conviction or ulterior motive . . . It is guided by newspaper men. They are the watchers who scan the horizon constantly looking for the event which may become the next nine days' wonder . . . The go-getters of the publishing world set the pace."

The story that had been seven years in the making finally reached its climax in 1927 when, on April 9, Nicola Sacco and Bartolomeo Vanzetti were sentenced to death. (The fact that in November of 1925 one Celestino Madeiros had confessed to the crime did nothing to get Sacco and Vanzetti off the hook.) Public outcry reached such a pitch that Massachusetts Governor Alvan T. Fuller appointed Abbott Lawrence Lowell, president of Harvard, to head a commission to look into the trial proceedings; to nobody's surprise Lowell's group found that the trial had been legal in all respects; on August 4 the Governor ordered the execution to proceed, and on the twenty-second they were electrocuted. Protest marchers surged around the Charlestown jail and clogged the narrow streets of Boston, and there were demonstrations and American-flag burnings throughout the world. One British periodical said that "for the first time in 150 years, the flag of the United States has been treated in every land as the symbol of a great wrong." A good picture of the inflexibility of the Lowell commission was given by the press critic in *The New Yorker,* who wrote: "One of the saddest sights in the world is a reporter trying to get a word out of Abbott Lawrence Lowell of Harvard. He walks straight ahead, without even looking at the questioner, and shakes his head grimly in impregnable refusal to talk. The reporter is placed in the position of a sporting gentleman trying to pick up Julia Ward Howe, and is equally successful."

The day after the Governor's order for the execution, Butterworth was at the Circe following the first reading of a play in which he was to open in September. Most of the people at the bar were strangers to him, and he was looking around for a familiar face when a voice behind his elbow said, "What's the matter—are you so successful you don't talk to your old friends anymore?"

He turned and saw Dorothy Peters standing there. Her eyes were larger than he'd remembered, and there were shadows beneath them that were not caused by makeup. "Well, look who's here!" he said. "Where've you been keeping yourself?"

"Here and there," she replied. "I didn't want to run into you-know-who. Or perhaps I should say you-know-whom."

"But that was two years ago! What've you been doing?"

"Mostly I've been thinking. And learning."

"I wish I could say the same. Will you have a drink?"

"Thanks, I've given it up."

"Oh? That seems like a curious thing to do."

"I have no clear memory of anything since the opening of the League of Nations, in 1920. All I have are flashes, and pretty ugly ones at that. I must have been tight for the better part of seven years."

"Then what brings you here?"

"If you must know, I was hoping to find you."

"Why me?"

"I seem to remember you had some interest in Sacco and Vanzetti."

"I suppose you could call it that. That's what got me fired from the *Tribune.*"

"And now you're just going to let them die?"

"I don't know what you mean. How can *I* stop it?"

"You can join in the protests. A group of us are going up to Boston and block the entrance to the jail."

"And that will save them?"

"It'll be an expression of public outrage. It'll tell those fascist bastards in Boston how the common people feel. They'll have to trample us under their horses to get into the jail."

"But aren't the men already *in* the jail?"

"God damn it, you're trying to hide behind logic, and this issue goes far beyond logic. The issue here is humanity, and the savagery of the fascist capitalistic repression. If a few of us are trampled under the Cossacks' horses, it could very well be the beginning of the Revolution."

"What is this word 'fascist' you keep using? I don't know what it means."

Dorothy took a deep breath, and in a voice crisp with sarcasm said, "I suppose you've heard of Little Red Riding Hood?"

"Yes."

"Good. Then you might also have heard of Mussolini?"

"What do they have in common?"

"Nothing! You just seem to have been out of things, so I thought I'd start at the beginning!"

"All right, go ahead. Remember, it was the word 'fascist' I asked about."

"What do you know about Mussolini?"

"Nothing, except he's made the trains run on time."

"Well, he is fascism. He invented it. It's a system where the individual counts for nothing; the corporations and the government run the country, and the government is one man–Mussolini. It is dedicated to blind obedience, with war as its ultimate goal. As Mussolini himself so sweetly put it: '*Credere, obbedire, combattere,*' which means, 'Have faith, obey, fight.' "

"You have been doing some learning, haven't you?"

"I had a lot to catch up on."

"And you think the people of Boston want to go to war?"

"I didn't say that! I said they're fascists because they don't give a shit for the little man, and the government is in league with the corporations."

"Oh."

"I can tell from here I've lost your interest."

"Not in the least. I just never looked at it quite that way before."

"Then you'll come up to Boston with us?"

"I'd like to, but I can't. We started rehearsals today."

"And you can't miss one day's rehearsal? Or maybe even two?"

"Of course I can't."

"Even a big star like you? Don't tell me you don't have an understudy."

"That's not the point. The point is that if I *am* the star, then I have to be on hand."

"Aren't we getting a little noblesse fucking oblige here?"

"We're getting nothing of the sort. And since when have you started talking like a stevedore?"

"I beg your pardon, milord. I'm sorry if the language of the common man offends your sensitive ears."

"You know something, Dorothy? You're becoming a bore."

"*I'm* becoming a bore? *I* am?"

"I heard somewhere that people tend to turn into what they despise the most, and I must say you're headed down that road. You used to be bright, and witty, and–"

"Listen to me, you pompous fascist bastard! When we meet at the barricades, you're going to be the first one–" She was interrupted by Nick, who, hearing the tone of her voice, had suddenly materialized from across the room.

"Take it easy, Mrs. Peters," he said, coming between her and Butterworth. "If you want to have an argument, do it somewhere else."

"I'm not the one who's arguing–he is! Just because the son of a bitch is rich, he thinks he can–"

Before she could say anything more, Charlie had put one hand on the bar and vaulted over it, his apron flapping, and between them he and Nick got her out into the entrance hall. She was shouting incoherently, and her voice lingered until the front door cut it off. Butterworth found he was trembling, and people on both sides were staring at him.

"I'm sorry about that," he said, to nobody in particular. Charlie returned, and this time went through the hinged opening at the end of the bar. "I admired your leap," Butterworth told him. "That must take quite a bit of practice."

"It's sort of like pole vaulting," Charlie replied. "Once you learn it, you never forget."

Nick joined Butterworth and said, "She is becoming a royal pain in the ass. That's the second time I've had to put her out."

"When was the first?" Butterworth asked.

"A couple of days ago. She was handing MacDougall the same line she was handing you."

Butterworth thought of the theory that people tend to become what they despise, and said, "She certainly has changed in the last little while. I wonder what brought it on."

Nick shrugged. "Who knows? Maybe she baked her brain with all those sleeping pills."

He moved away, and Butterworth sipped his drink and considered his own condition. Leaving aside the fact that he no longer thought of liquor as the root of all evil, he didn't feel he'd changed too much. Granted, he was not the homebody he had once been, but that was dictated by financial necessity rather than any real inclination of his own. Given the chance, he'd stay in the country all the–well, to be honest, not *all* the time–say at least a part of the time. Just because he'd found things he liked to do in the city, it didn't mean he was a roué, or a rakehell, or a degenerate of some sort. So he took a drink now and then–so what? He was still a conscientious, hard-working, sober, faithful–unless you want to count one slip–person. And that one slip shouldn't really count: he'd been seduced by an actress who was looking for a part in his play, and he'd acquiesced simply because it seemed like the gentlemanly thing to do. It wasn't as though he'd seduced *her,* or they'd had an affair, or anything like that; it had been just that one time–actually two–and that was that. As far as his inclinations and intentions went, he was as faithful as Rin Tin Tin. He finished his drink, and stared for a long time at the back-bar. All right, he thought, let's boil it down to one question: what would the you of seven years ago think of the you of today? The answer was inescapable. He looked down and saw that Charlie had slid another drink in front of him, and he fought down the urge to pick it up and drink it in one long gulp. I won't touch it for five minutes, he told himself as he looked at his watch. I may have slipped here and there, but I still have my self-control.

29

On October 6, 1927, Warner Brothers released a picture that would, almost overnight, set the film industry on its ear. It was called *The Jazz Singer,* adapted from a mawkish play of the same name, and it featured the veteran May McAvoy and a popular musical star named Al Jolson. What made it different was that, while a good deal of it was silent, the musical numbers had been recorded on wax and synchronized with the action of the film. This was not the first use of sound—Warners had recorded the score of the John Barrymore picture *Don Juan* the year before, and Fox had already put sound in their Movietone Newsreel—but it was the most successful: the picture made two million dollars, and started a stampede among the other companies to convert their equipment. There was a ripple effect that spread in all directions: singers, hitherto ignored by the movies, came into demand; actors and actresses whose voices recorded poorly, or whose method of showing emotion had been simply to bug out their eyes, were replaced by stage-trained performers who needed only to learn the subtleties of acting before a camera; and the old subtitle writers, whose contributions had been limited to scraps of dialogue and transitional directions such as "Came the Dawn," and "Meanwhile, Back at the Ranch," gave way to dramatists who could write believable dialogue as it was needed. In comparatively short order, movie-theatre marquees across the country carried the legend: "All Talking, All Singing, All Dancing."

There was action on another front during this period, and that was in the world of crime. In 1920 a young hoodlum named Alfonso Capone, born in Naples and educated in the Five Points Gang in Brooklyn, moved to Chicago to act as strong-arm for his friend Johnny Torrio, also a graduate of Five Points, who had come out to the Heartland to corner the bootleg market. Capone and his men used the simple tactics of killing anyone who got in their way, and thus started what became known as the Chicago beer–or gang–wars. In 1924 they killed their prime rival, Dion O'Banion, in his flower shop; in 1925 Torrio was shot but not killed, and Capone took over full leadership; in 1926 he escaped a machine-gun attack on his headquarters by members of O'Banion's old gang; and in 1927 he supported William Hale Thompson, otherwise known as "Big Bill," the Republican candidate for Mayor of Chicago. Thompson won, in an election known as "the pineapple primary" (pineapple being the term for a hand grenade), which was monitored by four thousand police at the polling places and uncounted machine-gun cars cruising the streets. Capone paid heavily in bribes to civic and police officials, and the administration looked on his activities with a benign if not totally blind eye. He consolidated his position two years later when, in what was known as the St. Valentine's Day Massacre, his torpedoes lined up seven members of the Bugs Moran gang in a garage and machine-gunned them to death, leaving Capone in charge of all bootlegging, gambling, prostitution, and dance halls in and around Chicago. Thompson added to his own stature with the locals by announcing that if King George V were to come to Chicago, he would "bust him one in the nose."

The Chicago gangsters received more publicity than any of the others, and the name Chicago became synonymous with crime, corruption, and killings, but that didn't mean there were no gangsters in other cities. Wherever there was illicit liquor traffic there were people trying to muscle in on the action, with obvious emphasis on the coastal or border places where the liquor was brought in. In New York there were several lesser gangsters, each with his own territory, and no concerted action was made to take over the whole city, as had been done in Chicago. But each bootlegger was part of a larger organization, and a speakeasy owner who got his liquor from one bootlegger also got his ice from a certain dealer, his limes from a particular fruit importer, and had his tablecloths, napkins, and towels laundered by a designated establishment. It was a system that was all set up and running smoothly, ready for subsequent takeover by the Mafia.

One night in spring, when Nick and Marie had retired to their apartment on the top floor of the building, Marie turned out the light over her bed and lay in the dark for a while before speaking. Twice she started to say something and then stopped, and finally Nick said, "All right. What's on your mind?"

She hesitated. "I was followed today," she said.

"What do you mean?" Nick propped himself on one elbow, and stared at her shadowy form. "By whom?"

"I don't know. I went over to Central Park to get some air after lunch, and after a while I realized there were these two guys walking behind me along the bridle path. I think they were mobsters."

"What makes you think so?"

"They wore light gray fedora hats. Only mobsters wear that kind of hat."

"You were imagining things."

"Maybe. But then I went up to the edge of the reservoir and they followed me there, and when I saw a mounted policeman on the bridle path I headed for him, and they vanished. They were pretty damn interested in me until they saw that policeman."

Nick lay back and stared at the ceiling. "I'll ask Frank tomorrow," he said. "Did you get a look at their faces?"

"No. They had their hat brims turned down."

"Well . . ." He couldn't think of anything else to say.

"It wasn't the danger I minded, so much as the fact that it spoiled my walk. I see little enough fresh air as it is, and to have these two *salauds* come creeping along just made me furious. It made the whole day lousy."

"You ought to get out more," Nick said.

"How can I? With all I have to do around here, it's lucky I get out at all."

"Get someone to take over for you. You don't have to be in the kitchen *all* the time."

"Nobody could take over for me. Who could make sure the food is done properly? Who could keep Louis away from his radio? Who could–"

"What is this radio program he's hooked on?"

"It's about a couple of *nègres*—Andy and Amos, they call them—and it comes on every night at seven. From seven until quarter past, I have to watch him like a hawk or he'll slip off in a corner and turn on his radio. All they do is mispronounce words, from the little I've heard."

"Can't he listen to them and work too?"

"I won't let him. It's bad for morale. Pretty soon we'll have Raoul and Felix and the waiters saying, 'Ah's regusted,' and 'Awah,' and all that stuff. It would be like a zoo."

"I think what you really need is a vacation."

"And close down the place? Don't be silly."

"I remember you saying you'd like to see some red Indians. Wouldn't you like to do that?"

"There is nothing I would like better than to go to the far West and see cowboys and red Indians and grizzly bears and covered wagons and the Pony Express and all that, but I just can't do it and have a decent kitchen too."

"Well, we might close down, just for August. Don't they do that in France?"

"In France, everything closes in August. You can't even get arrested in August. Here, it would be different. People would forget you after a month."

"They haven't in the past. I think I'll talk to Frank tomorrow."

"Do you have to ask Frank's permission for everything you do?"

"Of course not. Well, no. Not everything."

The next afternoon Nick went to DiMotto's office, which had moved from the furniture warehouse and was now in a brownstone house off Gramercy Park. He had to go past three different bodyguards, all of whom nodded to him but said nothing, and by the time he reached the inner office he had the sensation that guns were pointing at him from every direction. DiMotto was sitting behind a mahogany desk, on which were silver-framed pictures of his wife and children. In front of him was a thick ledger, and a note pad.

"Hiya, kid," he said, as the door closed behind Nick. "Take the load off your feet. What's on your mind?"

Nick sat in a red leather armchair, and told of Marie's having been followed. "It may all be her imagination," he concluded, "but she says they really took off when the cop appeared."

"Maybe she shouldn't go to places like Central Park," DiMotto said. "Maybe she should stick a little closer to home."

"Well, that brings up the next question," Nick said. "I think she's getting a little cabin fever. I think she needs a vacation."

"No problem there. Send her to the Catskills."

Nick shook his head. "It's not as easy as that. So long as the store is open, she won't leave it. I'd like to close down for, say, August, and let everyone take a breather."

This time it was DiMotto who shook his head. "Impossible," he said. "That place is a gold mine. Shut down for a month, and you're losing fifty grand, maybe a hundred. That kind of mazuma don't grow on trees. Speaking of which"—he leaned forward and flicked back a few pages in the ledger—"I notice you been carrying several people on the cuff for some little time now. I thought we agreed that was bad business."

"Not several people," Nick replied. "Just two or three. I've got an agreement with McClain, whereby he does our engineering work in exchange for food and drink, and I think you'll agree he's been worth every nickel. If it weren't for—"

"What about Butterworth?" DiMotto cut in. "And what about MacDougall? What've they done to make themselves useful?"

"They're different. They're a couple of the oldest customers we've got. When Butterworth lost his job I told him not to worry about the tab, but that didn't mean I was giving it to him for free. That just meant he should pay me when he could. He's the only one who's been on the cuff for any length of time."

"And you know what he owes us?"

"Not to the penny, no."

"He owes us eleven grand, and change. To be exact, it's eleven thousand, one hundred and three dollars, and forty-seven cents."

Nick whistled. "I didn't realize," he said.

"Yeah. And now he's in the chips, I think we better start seeing some of that dough. And the same goes for MacDougall; he owes us about fourteen grand."

"What am I supposed to do? I can't very well go up to them and ask them for that kind of money."

"No, but you can tell 'em to get started paying. And cut off their credit until their accounts are square."

"That's impossible. I'd never see them again."

DiMotto shrugged. "The way I look at it, it don't do us much good when we do see them; it just runs up another bunch of figures."

Nick got up and went to the window. He could see the trees of Gramercy Park, bright green in their spring foliage, and he could see a nursemaid with a perambulator, walking on the sunny side of the street. Two boys who were playing stickball stopped until the nurse had passed, and then continued their game. Finally Nick turned back to DiMotto.

"What'll you give me for my share of the business?" he said.

"What do you mean?" replied DiMotto.

"Just that. I'd like to sell out."

"And do what, for chrissakes?"

"Nothing, for a while. Just relax. Then I might start up a small joint, like what we were when we started. This has gotten too damn big."

"You're crazy, kid. Where'll you get your hooch?"

"I assume I could use the same bootlegger."

"You assume wrong. In this business you're either with us, or you're against us. You'd have to tie in with someone else."

"So what?"

"So I know most of the others. You wouldn't be happy. You think this is tough, try it with the Jersey mob, or some of the waterfront boys. I tell you, kid, if you stick with us you'll be a millionaire—if you try to switch over, you won't be worth cold snail shit."

"I hadn't thought of switching. I just thought I'd try it on my own."

DiMotto laughed. "You ought to know better than that."

Nick thought for a while, then said, "Yes, I suppose I ought. It was just an idea, really. For a moment, it seemed to make sense."

The next time he saw Butterworth at the Circe was on a Wednesday, between the matinee and the evening performance. Butterworth had dropped in for a sandwich and a beer, and Nick, who had been rehearsing his speech ever since he'd seen DiMotto, tried to sound as casual as he could.

"How's the play coming?" he asked.

"O.K.," Butterworth replied. "We're doing near capacity, which this season isn't bad at all."

"What's so special about this season?"

"Well, last year was the biggest one ever, and this year looks to be just about as good, so the competition we've got is something fierce.

We're playing against *Street Scene, Journey's End, The Front Page, Funny Face, Show Boat*—you name it. If you can do near capacity in that league, you're in good shape."

"I should think a big season would make more people come to the theatre."

"You could look at it that way, but I like to be cautious. I feel lucky just being where I am. The whole thing is still a dream, as far as I'm concerned."

Nick cleared his throat. "I was talking with Frank the other day," he said.

"You mean your partner?"

"That's right."

"He should be feeling pretty happy too."

"He is, but"—Nick cleared his throat again—"he's kind of upset that I've let some people's tabs run on so long."

"You mean for instance mine?"

"You were one of those he mentioned."

"Well, tell him I'll start paying it back. How much do I owe?"

Nick hesitated. "A little over eleven thousand dollars."

There was dead silence for almost half a minute, then Butterworth said, "Jesus, Mary, and Joseph. Why didn't you tell me?"

"I didn't know it had got that big."

"When does he want it?"

"Oh, he's in no particular rush. He'd just like it if you'd start paying it off."

"Well—sure. I'll do it as I can. I've had a lot of expenses recently—I bought Sarah a car, and Nancy's got to have a lot of dental work done—but I'll do what I can. Will that be all right?"

"Oh, sure. I'd never have brought it up, only Frank likes to keep things up to date."

"Sure, sure. I know what he means."

Nick put a hand on Butterworth's shoulder. "Just to show there's no hard feelings, this round is on the house."

Butterworth laughed and said, "Thanks. I guess I'll need every bit I can get."

He came back after the evening performance, and found MacDougall standing at the bar. "A picture of the playwright at work," Butterworth said. "Have you found a second-act curtain?"

"I never find second-act curtains," MacDougall replied. "I make them come to me. That's why I'm so successful."

"I had a swell curtain line come to me this afternoon, in the form of a dun from Nick. It seems I owe the joint eleven thousand dollars."

"I owe them fourteen," said MacDougall, sipping his drink.

"It doesn't seem to worry you much."

"Why should it? Warners just bought *Pop!* for two hundred and fifty."

Butterworth stared at him. "You lucky bastard," he said.

"You mean you haven't talked to your agent?"

"I am my agent. Why?"

"You ought to get a real one. You're going to have some dickering to do."

"What the hell are you talking about?"

"One of the conditions of sale was that you play the part you had in the show. They must have had it in mind all along, because they didn't kick up any fuss."

"Are you trying to tell me—"

"That's right. Now, stop gaping there like a fish on the dock, and have a drink."

"But I've got a run-of-the-play contract with—"

"That's one of the things you'll have to dicker about. There are ways of getting out of everything."

Butterworth took the drink that Charlie had put in front of him and raised it to his lips. "I'm not sure I like the idea of living in Hollywood," he said. "From what I've heard, that's a pretty frothy bunch of people out there."

"You don't have to *live* there, nitwit. You just stay there while you're making the picture. Besides, where else can you pick up that kind of money?"

"I don't know what kind you're talking about."

"That's why you need an agent."

"Yes, I suppose I do. I never thought the day would come."

"It isn't as though I were going to be *living* there," he said to Sarah that Sunday, after they'd finished a picnic lunch on the porch. "I'll just be there while we're making the picture, and then I'll come right back."

"When do you leave?" she asked.

"Not for a while yet. Mac has to do the screenplay, and they have to have everything ready first. It may be midsummer before they need me."

"Won't it be awfully hot?"

He shrugged. "That's something over which I have no control."

"Well, don't forget to take your bathing suit. It might come in handy."

"Daddy, are you going to see Tom Mix?" Nancy put in.

"It's entirely possible," said Butterworth. "I guess anything is possible."

"Tom Mix sucks eggs," said Puddin.

"Puddin!" Sarah exclaimed. "Where did you ever hear that expression?"

"Benny says it," Puddin replied. "What's wrong with it?"

"It's indelicate. I don't want to hear you say it again."

"Can I say it when we're at the Thatchers'?"

"No."

"Suppose Benny says it?"

"Puddin, stop arguing with your mother," Butterworth said. "When she tells you to do something, you do it."

Puddin subsided, glowering, and Sarah said to Butterworth, "Another thing you ought to take is a Panama hat, with a wide brim. The sun in California is supposed to be very dangerous."

"I've been in the sun before," Butterworth replied.

"Yes, and you had a mild sunstroke. If you have to do any acting outdoors, you should insist on wearing a hat."

"All right."

"This isn't foolishness, you know. It's for your own good."

"I know."

"You sound as though you're agreeing just to humor me."

"Not in the least. It's a very sensible suggestion."

"Daddy," Nancy said, "is Tom Mix's horse real?"

"I assume so," Butterworth replied. "What else might it be?"

"Well, if President Coolidge rides an electric horse, wouldn't it be a good idea if Tom Mix did too?"

"That's one of those imponderables," said Butterworth. "If I find out the answer, I'll let you know."

"Do you have dark glasses?" Sarah asked.

"No, but I can get some."

"You'd better put it on a list, so you won't forget."

"I'll do that." Butterworth yawned, stretched, and looked at his watch. "My God," he said, getting to his feet. "I almost forgot."

"What?" said Sarah.

"We have a rehearsal this afternoon."

"On a *Sunday?*"

"We've got a cast replacement, and we have to run him through a couple of times. He starts tomorrow."

"Can't someone stand in for you?"

"No. Most of his scenes are with me. If we hurry, I can make the 3:47."

"I'll drive you to the station," Sarah said. "Come on, children, let's get in the car."

"I have to pee," said Puddin.

"Then you stay here. We don't have time to wait."

"I'll hang on," said Puddin. "I'll put a rubber band around it till we get to the station."

"I'll have a talk with you later," his mother said. "And then I'll talk with Uncle Mark about his children."

It was the first week in September before Butterworth left for California. The oven-like heat of August, which softened the tar in the streets and drove tenement dwellers to take their bedding to the fire escapes, had abated enough so that heat prostration was no longer a problem, but the Fire Department still opened hydrants so that children could play in the gushing water, and people walked whenever possible on the shady side of the street. The Circe had installed several large ceiling fans, which did little more than circulate the warm air, but Nick had put McClain to work on an air-cooling device that he hoped would, by next summer, make things a good deal more comfortable.

Butterworth had sent his steamer trunk on ahead by Railway Express, so he had only one suitcase to take with him to the train. He checked it in Grand Central an hour or so before train time, then went over to the Circe for a farewell drink. It was still too early for the after-business trade, and the only customers were a couple sitting at a corner table, and a solitary man deep in thought at the bar. Nick was at a table near the entrance, having a cup of coffee while he went over the accounts. He invited Butterworth to join him, and Butterworth sat down.

"I thought you'd gone already," Nick said.

"I'm on my way," Butterworth replied. "I'm taking the *Century* tonight."

"The place won't seem the same without you. Let me buy you a drink."

"Isn't it about time I started paying cash?"

"There's plenty of time for that. What would you like?"

"The usual, I guess. Oh, and"–Butterworth produced a flask from an inside pocket–"can Charlie fill this? It's going to be a long train ride."

"You bet. Charlie, a Scotch for Mr. Butterworth, and fill this up with the same."

"Coming right up," said Charlie.

"This is very decent of you," Butterworth said.

"What the hell. I don't like losing old friends."

"You're not *losing* me. I'm going to be back in six weeks."

"I know. But it's the end of something."

"Like hell it is. I'm going to make this one picture, and then I'm going to pay off my bills and live like a civilized human being. I'm going to turn over a whole new leaf."

Nick smiled and shook his head. "You can't," he said. "You can't go back any more than I can."

"What would you go back to?"

"I'd like to have a small, family-type joint, like what we were when we started. But things just don't work out that way, so"–he shrugged–"here I am."

"Getting richer by the minute."

"And hating it."

Butterworth took the Scotch that Charlie gave him and raised it in salute. "Here's to it," he said. "And thank you. For everything."

"My pleasure."

Butterworth drank, then glanced at his watch. "I've got time to make a quick call home," he said. "Excuse me a minute." He rose, went to the newly installed telephone booth, and put through a call to Crestwood. There were two rings, and then a man's voice said, "Mrs. Butterworth's residence."

"May I speak to her, please?" Butterworth said, trying to recognize the voice.

"May I ask who's calling?" said the voice.

"This is her husband," Butterworth said coldly. "Who's this?"

"Roly, you old son of a gun, I didn't recognize you–I thought you were on your way to California! This is Mark Thatcher."

"Oh, hi, Mark," Butterworth said. "I didn't recognize you, either. May I speak to Sarah?"

"Sure thing. Just a minute."

Sarah came on the line and said, "Yes?" in the voice she used when she anticipated bad news.

"I just thought I'd call before I get on the train," Butterworth said. "Just to tell you that I love you and am going to miss you, and things like that."

"That's very dear of you. Thank you."

"And kiss the children for me, will you?"

"Do you want to talk to them?"

"I don't have time. I've got to run. Just kiss them for me."

"All right, I'll do that."

"And–well, I guess that's all. I just thought–" He left the sentence dangling.

"Thank you for calling, dear, and have a good trip."

"I will, thank you. 'Bye."

" 'Bye."

She hung up, and Butterworth stared at the holes in the mouthpiece for a few moments, then put the receiver on the hook.

He gave his bag to a redcap, then checked in at the gate to the *Twentieth Century Limited,* feeling the muted excitement that comes with the departure of a special train. He walked down the red carpet, past the observation car with its lighted sign on the rear platform, and down the long line of cars with steam rising quietly between them, until he came to his car, which was named "Wappinger Falls." Overcome by the atmosphere of luxury, he tipped the redcap fifty cents, then was shown to his compartment by a white-jacketed Pullman porter. The dark-paneled compartment, with its soft lights and womb-like sense of privacy, brought on a feeling of nostalgia, although he couldn't say for what, and he wished he were traveling with someone to share the surroundings. He washed in the stainless steel basin, combed his hair, and then left the compartment and walked back to the observation car, where a spray of red and white carnations decorated the serving table. He ordered a cup of coffee from the steward who had appeared, like a genie, from nowhere, then sat and watched through the window as shadowy figures hurried along the platform.

Slowly, almost imperceptibly, the platform began to move, and then the train picked up speed as it clattered through the maze of switches that led to the tunnel. Bright daylight and the tenements of Harlem appeared, and the train continued to gather speed until it came to 125th Street, where it made a short stop and then proceeded across the river. So far, it's just like going to Crestwood, Butterworth thought. The train is somewhat better, but the route is the same. Then at the Mott Haven yards the train bore left, headed for the water-level route along the Hudson River, and the tracks for Crestwood vanished in the distance. Butterworth watched as the last traces of New York dwindled away, then he took out his flask and poured a splash of Scotch into his by now cold coffee.

Well, God bless her, he thought, as he lifted the cup to his lips. I hope she's happy.